THE END OF DREAMS

THE END OF DREAMS

MARCUS LEE

BOOK 3
THE GIFTED AND THE CURSED

Copyright © 2021 by Marcus Lee

All rights reserved. The rights of Marcus Lee to be identified as the author of this work has been asserted by him in accordance with sections 77 and 78 of the Copyright, Design and Patents Act 1988.

This is a work of fiction. Names, characters, places, and incidents either are the product of the author's imagination or are used fictitiously. Any resemblance to actual persons, living or dead, events, or locales is entirely coincidental.

No part of this publication may be reproduced, stored in retrieval systems, copied in any form or by any means, electronic, mechanical, photocopying, recording or otherwise transmitted without written permission from the publisher except for the use of quotations in a book review.

ASIN: B08TRKGS9N
Paperback ISBN: 9798598984192
Hardback ISBN: 9798333915290

For more information visit: www.marcusleebooks.com

First print edition January 2021
First eBook edition January 2021

M&M
♥

BY THE SAME AUTHOR

THE CHOSEN
Dark Fantasy - Epic Fantasy - Action & Adventure - Sword & Sorcery

Book 1 - THE MOUNTAIN OF SOULS

Book 2 - THE LAST HOPE

Book 3 - THE RIVER OF TEARS

Book 4 – THE OLDEST FOE

***

THE GIFTED & THE CURSED
Dark Fantasy - Epic Fantasy - Fantasy Romance – Fairytale-esq

Book 1 - KINGS & DAEMONS

Book 2 - TRISTAN'S FOLLY

Book 3 - THE END OF DREAMS

Book 4 - THE CIRCLE OF FATE

***

THE BLOOD OF KINGS & QUEENS
Dark Fantasy - Arc of Redemption – Fairytale-esq

***

POEMS INSPIRED BY TRUE LOVE
Free Verse - Rhyming - Acrostic - Bard's Tales

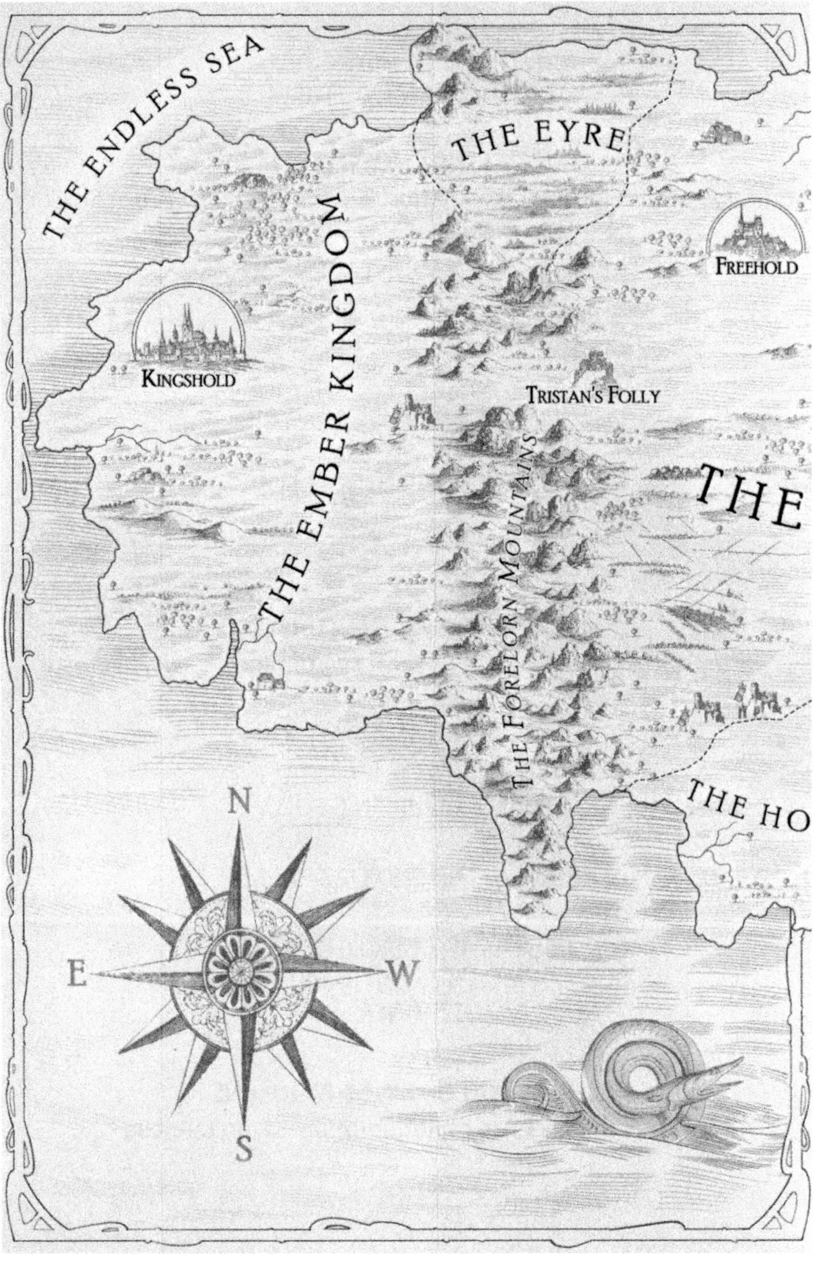
THE ENDLESS SEA
THE EYRE
THE EMBER KINGDOM
FREEHOLD
KINGSHOLD
TRISTAN'S FOLLY
THE FORELORN MOUNTAINS
THE
THE HO
N
E
W
S

FREEMANTLE

FREESTATES   FREEGUARD

FREEMARCH

RSELORDS

THE
DESERT
TRIBES

THE SOUTHERN SEA

Chapter I

Taran, Rakan, and Yana rode east, frequently looking over their shoulders, fearful of what might be following.

They'd just witnessed the fall of Tristan's Folly. It was hard to grasp that the mighty fortress that was once their haven was now in the hands of Daleth and his army. So many had died valiantly defending those walls, but it hadn't been enough to stop the horde. Now they were fleeing once again, but this time without Maya.

They'd been riding hard all day, changing horses intermittently to keep them fresh. Now, as the sun dropped toward the horizon, Taran spotted the forty-odd men from the garrison who'd fled before them as the final wall was lost.

The soldiers were gathering firewood, preparing a camp for the night as Taran, Rakan, and Yana rode in. Smiles of recognition mixed with relief greeted the new arrivals.as the soldiers stopped what they were doing.

Rakan raised his voice.

'We might have left the fortress behind us, lads, but that doesn't mean the danger was left behind too. Do you want to take the risk of lighting fires when Daleth's lancers might be scouring the countryside as we speak?'

Taran saw realisation hit home in the soldiers' eyes as they looked around fearfully at the shadows encroaching on the makeshift camp.

'Mount up,' he commanded. 'We'll ride further south away from the trade road and into those heavy woods yonder. Whilst speed is our ally, so is concealment. Quickly now, sunset is almost upon us.'

The soldiers responded, running to their tethered horses and shortly thereafter cantered across the plains toward the dense woodland Taran had indicated.

As they reached the trees, they dismounted and led the horses into the dark, tangled undergrowth. It wasn't long before the plains were lost from view, and all they could see were the trunks around them. Still, they pushed deeper until the trees thinned and they found themselves in a small, grassy clearing.

'Make camp here,' Rakan ordered, looking around with a discerning eye.

Taran wasn't about to disagree, ceding to Rakan's experience.

'Blankets only. No fires and no talking,' he called, catching everyone's attention.

He turned to Rakan and leaned in close.

'Choose men for sentry duty,' he said softly. 'I know you don't trust anyone else, but you need rest as much as any. I'll take my turn whenever it comes around, so make sure you include me. Also, Kalas' armour is too bright, I think you should remove it. You can be seen from leagues away.'

Rakan nodded and stomped off into the gloom.

Shortly after, several men grumbled good naturedly as they headed off to take the first watch.

'Let me inspect your wounds whilst there's still a little light,' Yana said, moving alongside. She sat, patting the ground next to her.

Taran stood for a moment, ensuring he hadn't overlooked anything, then did as requested.

'Tomorrow you'll help the other men,' he muttered gruffly before extending his tightly bound forearm.

Yana met Taran's gaze.

'I intend to. I'm also going to teach them how to treat their own wounds and each other's. I can wield a sword, so a man can treat a wound.'

Taran snorted, but said nothing.

Yana carefully unwound the bandage and leaned forward, sniffing to see if there was any hint of corruption, while also allowing her hair to fall gently across Taran's arm. She let her breath play along his skin while she inspected the wound, then drew back, smiling.

The End of Dreams

'It seems to be doing fine, but I still need to apply salve.'

She withdrew a small, stoppered jar from her satchel and gently rubbed the cream along the jagged cut.

Holding his arm, attending to him, being close, quietly thrilled her. She hoped in her heart that her care would somehow reach him in a way her looks failed to. However, while the amulet had dulled Taran's pain, her hope that it would amplify his base desire for her was ill-founded. It seemed only two desires had increased, to kill without mercy and seek revenge.

At some stage, she'd need to remove the amulet so he could love once again. When though, would be the hardest decision. Too early and memories of Maya could overwhelm him, making him do something foolish.

She needed to be patient, but when he was so close, and his bare skin was beneath her hands, she could barely control herself.

'All done,' she said softly, packing the jar away.

Taran nodded in gratitude and lay down on the forest floor to sleep.

Alongside him, Yana did likewise.

Closing her eyes, she recalled the time that she lay pressed close to Taran's sleeping body in the keep, and flushed at the memory. Now, here she was, once again within touching distance, and not being able to touch was proving a painfully exquisite experience.

Careful footsteps approached, and she rolled over to see the Rakan's dark figure silhouetted against the sky through the trees.

'We did the right thing camping here,' Rakan whispered. 'I estimate around four hundred lancers crossed the plain but a few moments ago. Fortunately, it's too dark, and they were moving fast, so didn't notice our trail. We need to be ready to move at first light in case they, or another group, come across it in the morning.'

'Double the sentries,' Taran replied softly.

'Already done it,' Rakan chuckled. 'I'll join the first watch and come wake you at midnight. Now, get some rest.'

Yana lay gazing at the stars as Rakan's footsteps moved away.

She used to do this a lot when she was a child. Her grandfather, Laska, had always doted on her. She'd been his favourite and could do nothing wrong in his eyes. She remembered him telling her once, that wishing on a falling star would see the wish come true.

She'd spent weeks waiting for one, and then when she'd almost given up, one had flashed across the sky. Beyond excited, her wish made, she waited for her father to return from the halls of the dead. Days later, despondent, she realised he wouldn't be coming home. Her grandfather had lied to her.

Yet here she was looking up at the sky, hoping to see a falling star, to make her wish come true.

Taran's breathing deepened, slowed, and she knew he'd fallen asleep. She resisted the temptation to roll next to him, to feel his warmth.

Not yet.

Then an idea came to her. I'll have you Taran heart-stealer, she thought. A star would certainly have to fall to make it happen, she was sure of that, and the star was Maya. Once Maya was gone for good, all of Yana's dreams could come true.

The other problem was Tristan. Now Astren was out of the way, Tristan was the only one who knew of her involvement in coercing Maya into marrying him.

Wouldn't it be just perfect if they both went at once?

She smiled into the darkness, enjoying the direction her thoughts took her. For if both Tristan and Maya were to depart from this world, then who could be better placed to take power over the Freestates than the commander of its armies?

The hero who'd won the war.

Her smile disappeared. Won the war. However much she let herself dream, this was where it could all unravel. Winning or even surviving this war would be nigh on impossible.

Yet Taran had said he had an idea to turn the tables, and if so, she'd do everything possible to support him and help any plan come to fruition.

She'd be the shoulder he came to lean on and the arms he turned to for support. Patience, she told herself, patience, and with that she fell asleep, dreaming of falling stars.

***

The End of Dreams

Daleth strained to keep an impassive face as the royal healer attended to his wounds.

He'd refused sleep weed and the other potions he'd been offered to ease him into slumber or dull the pain. As his body shook under the physician's hands, he questioned this decision for the hundredth time.

The physician paused, aware of his discomfort, but Daleth nodded for him to continue.

He'd been carried from the wall on a stretcher into the keep, and the humiliation of the memory was almost as painful as his wounds. His army needed to know he was still the chosen of the gods, and the story of him shunning any form of pain relief would circulate and restore his dented reputation. He was stronger than any mortal man, was above pain, and yet in his head, he screamed in agony and couldn't wait for this to be over.

Over one hundred years of life stretched behind him.

During that time, he'd fought dozens of conquests, faced thousands of enemies, steel against steel, skill against skill, and many times received injuries.

But none like this.

His martial skills, acquired over nearly a century of combat, had been brushed aside by the mortally wounded Kalas with such indifference that he'd felt like a child. He'd been brought to his knees, utterly powerless.

He'd not felt frightened since he was a sickly youth. But Kalas had put a fear inside of him that had haunted his dreams for far too long. Even now, all he could see were the daemon's red eyes and flashing blades.

Only Alano's intervention had saved him from certain death, and now even Alano was gone. But so, at last, was Kalas, whereas he, the Witch-King, was alive. Once recovered, he'd go on to be the most feared king the world had ever known, for surely the gods were testing him.

Yes, Kalas had been a test, and one he'd overcome. A saying from his long-dead father came to mind. *Judge a man not by the strength of his friends, but by the strength of the enemies he leaves dead upon the battlefield behind him.*

In which case, he should be judged fearsome indeed.

The thought cheered him, and the healer stood back, having finally finished his work. The pain was sickening.

'Tell me,' Daleth asked, forcing strength into his voice. 'How many days before I can walk again? How long before I can lead my men into battle?'

The healer seemed startled at the question and looked around as if for support. The only other men in the chamber were some of Daleth's bodyguard. They stood witness to their king's fortitude in dealing with pain that would have made any other man scream for mercy.

'Spit it out, man. How many days?' Daleth growled.

'But, but, my king,' the healer stuttered. 'You're lucky to be alive. Your injuries were so severe. The stomach wound just missed your gut, and your legs … the thigh muscles need time to heal. They were almost severed.'

'So how long?' Daleth roared, impatience and pain adding an edge to his voice.

'Considering the multitude and depth of your wounds, it will be next summer before you're well enough,' the healer whispered, shaking like a leaf. 'That's assuming no infection brings you low, or the fever, or a winter's cold.'

The man gulped and waited in trepidation, expecting his life to be forfeited for delivering such dire news.

Daleth looked at the healer, his anger dissipating.

'Fear not, you've done your duty, and I'll punish no one who serves to the best of his ability. Be warned though. Should I die in your care, my bodyguards will ensure you take a week to perish in screaming agony. But I doubt that will ever come to pass, for you'll care for me as if your life depended on it, which, of course, it now does.'

'Now tell me. Can I be moved from this damned fortress before winter's arrival? The army can't stay here over winter. We need to get to the lowlands, for without shelter, many will succumb to the elements.'

The healer kept his eyes lowered.

'My king. You'll suffer from tremendous pain if we attempt to move you, so I wouldn't recommend it. But if we wait until autumn's end, the risk of you dying will lessen.'

The End of Dreams

'You mean the risk of us dying,' Daleth smiled mirthlessly. 'Now leave. I need to speak to my men.'

Once the healer had left, Daleth turned to Baidan, the latest man to head his bodyguard since Krixen had died to Kalas' swords on the wall. Baidan stepped forward and knelt at the side of his king's bed.

'Report,' Daleth ordered.

'Our lancers have scoured the countryside around the fortress but have encountered no form of armed resistance. They came across villages and farmsteads, although some were empty of the peasantry who lived there. Those remaining spoke the same tale of the young and firm journeying eastward to Freeguard to attend a betrothal ceremony for their king. The remaining peasants had no idea they were even in danger, at least until they were put to the sword.'

Daleth couldn't help but laugh despite his stitches and grimaced with pain.

'Are you serious? Tristan is planning to marry?'

'Yes, my king.'

Daleth thought for but a few moments before snapping his fingers.

'Of course! He's pulling every able-bodied man to him, so he can field them in the coming battle, even if they don't know it yet. He's tricking them rather than telling them the truth in case they desert his cause before they've even joined him.'

Baidan nodded, eyes wide in appreciation of his king's deduction.

'I assume the lancers didn't apprehend any of the soldiers who fled the fortress?' Daleth asked without much hope.

Baidan confirmed with a simple shake of his head.

'Right. Give the lancers free rein to roam, kill, and cause general mayhem, yet order them to leave some alive wherever they go.'

'Forgive me, my king. I seek only to learn. Why leave any alive?' Baidan asked.

Daleth smiled graciously.

'The pursuit of knowledge needs no forgiveness, Baidan. You've a lot to learn. A peasant levy is of little threat, yet even less so if it has fear in its heart. Those survivors will bring it to them. They'll likely run from any fight if they hear stories of the terror that awaits them if they turn against us.'

Baidan scratched his chin, embarrassed.

'But why don't we just kill them all? They'll not be sufficiently proficient in combat, and we'll suffer few losses whilst we enjoy slaughtering them.'

'Baidan, while I know that you're fearsome with a sword, you are far less adept with a plough,' Daleth explained patiently. 'We need some of these peasants alive, for how else will we be fed in years to come? We might be slayers of men, but we still need to eat. Now, enough questions. There are other matters I need you to attend to.'

Daleth stifled a moan and managed to keep his face impassive.

'Firstly, make sure our lancers understand not to journey beyond the southern border posts that the Freestates forces will likely have abandoned, otherwise, they'll enter the lands of the Horselords. We'll deal with them soon enough, but not yet.'

Baidan nodded.

'As you order, so shall it be.'

'Secondly,' Daleth continued, 'I assume several of the Freestates wounded are still alive?'

'Yes, my king.'

'In which case, see what information can be extracted from them that might help our cause. Offer them freedom and gold to loosen their lips. After that, whether they've talked or not, let our soldiers entertain themselves with their torture. Advise them to be careful and not to kill them swiftly. A reward will go to those who keep their victims alive for the longest in the most exquisite agony.'

As the door shut behind Baidan and the other bodyguards, Daleth closed his eyes, fighting the agony that wracked his body. He just had to endure the pain over the next few hours, and then the sweet misery of the wounded would give him some much needed respite.

Even now he could feel the trickle of strength the lands to the east were giving him. He'd recover a lot sooner than the healer realised, although not in time to lead the campaign this side of winter.

Damn it. He'd be unable to fight for months, thanks to one man.

No, not an ordinary man, a daemon who was dead.

Daleth breathed deeply, ordering his thoughts. He was alive and after all, what was a few months recovery when he'd already lived more than a century? Nothing would change in that short time, least of all the outcome of this war.

With that calming thought, he reached for the goblet of sleep weed infused water he'd declined earlier, quaffed half of it, and relaxed as drowsiness washed over him.

As he slipped into slumber, the last thing he saw were those red eyes staring malevolently at him from beyond the grave.

**

With her horse moving at a brisk trot, Maya enjoyed the breeze in her hair as she looked at the surrounding landscape.

She'd taken to riding away from the slower moving column of men that surrounded Tristan, and he'd not tried to stop her from doing so. Still, that didn't mean he left his asset entirely unprotected.

Five guardsmen shadowed her at a respectful distance.

One called Ferris, whom she'd tended on the wagons, had recovered enough to ride with the king once more. He seemed to be nominally in charge and respected her unspoken desire to be left alone, for which she was grudgingly grateful.

After being brought up in the domain of the Witch-King, this kingdom seemed rich and verdant beyond belief. Everywhere the land flourished where people allowed it to do so.

Of course, some areas were deforested, the land given over to crops or orchards, but these simply added depth to the stunning patchwork of colours all around.

She sighed at its beauty and wondered what Taran would have said were he next to her. Likely, whatever he said would have been punctuated with kisses to enhance an already beautiful vista. She sighed again, but this time in longing.

Travelling through such countryside did a lot to lift her mood, and she hoped it would help return her gift to full force. Frustratingly, it still continued to fade, possibly because the land didn't call out for her help. Yet deep in her core, she wondered whether it was to do with Taran's absence.

It was Taran who'd managed to release her gift when it had been blocked by Brandon back at Laska's encampment. Was he now the only catalyst powerful enough to free it once more?

She laughed sadly. Maybe once Tristan knew that his most valuable asset could barely bring a rose to bloom anymore, he might decide she wasn't worth marrying after all.

The more she thought about it, the more she liked the idea. She'd gladly trade her gift, never to come forth again, to escape this situation and return to Taran's side where she belonged. For a while, daydreams about Taran filled her thoughts. When he was in her arms again, she'd never let him go while her body still held breath.

She was distracted from her reverie by her horse snorting and focussed once more on her surroundings.

Without noticing, she'd approached some farm buildings.

In front of a farmhouse, a skinny little girl played with a rag doll in the dust. The girl smiled, and her white teeth shone brightly within a grubby face half-hidden by a mop of dirty, blond hair.

Maya reined in her horse, dismounted, and led it through the gate into the front yard. A couple of chickens squawked indignantly, and a small dog came running, yapping at her horse. She whispered soothingly in her mount's ear, and it remained placid, seemingly unbothered by the tiny assailant.

However, the noise had roused the girl's mother, for the next moment, the door to the farmhouse banged open. A red-faced woman came out, angry words about to spill from her lips until she saw Maya.

Her eyes widened as she took in the horse with its expensive saddle and trappings and then, in the distance, the mounted bodyguard observing her movements.

She dropped to her knees.

'My lady. How might I serve you?'

Maya stepped forward, motioning the woman to rise and looked around the farmstead.

'This is good land,' Maya observed. 'How is it that you and your daughter look so thin? Are you both unwell?'

The woman's eyes dropped.

'No, my lady. We're just a little hungry, is all.'

The little girl skipped around them both, her laughter bright.

Maya was confused.

'But you must have food aplenty. These fields surely yield enough crops to feed you all handsomely?'

The End of Dreams

'Pardon me, my lady,' the woman replied, 'but it's the taxes. We pay so much in food to the crown, there's not enough left after the collectors come around.'

Maya shook her head in disbelief, thoughts of her own village coming back to her. The constant struggle to keep everyone fed whilst wagons left to go to the capital full of the tithe that Daleth demanded.

Was it that the common folk were mistreated everywhere? The wealthy never going hungry whilst the poor suffered to feed them? What was it about power that so corrupted people?

Maya gazed over the fields.

'Do you have no one to help tend them?' she asked, wondering why the two seemed alone.

The women nodded, smiling, displaying a yellowed row of gapped teeth.

'I do, my lady. My husband and two sons are normally here, but they're heading east to the betrothal ceremony. It's said the king is to marry a beautiful princess and everyone who attends the celebrations will be given coin. So my lads have gone off, as that way we can eat well when they return with the money.'

Maya couldn't believe her ears. Her forced betrothal to Tristan was being used to get the men of this land to go to Freeguard. It took only moments to realise why, and this deceit also meant that many women of this land would be left to fend for themselves.

'Are you unaware that the Witch-King's legions will be riding across these lands a week or so from now? You and your neighbours will be put to the sword or worse if you stay. The betrothal is just a ruse to get the men of this land to join the king's army!'

The woman scoffed.

'Pardon my disbelief, my lady, but that just simply isn't true. Our King Tristan would be as bad as the Witch-King himself if that were the case. I don't believe it, I just don't believe it.'

As bad as the Witch-King, from the mouth of a stranger. This served to reinforce Maya's belief that all kings were serpents. The only difference was that some were bigger than others.

'Listen to me,' Maya said, lowering her voice as if they were being overheard. 'It's true. Daleth is coming. His soldiers will sow death and chaos across the lands. Your husband and your sons will be conscripted into Tristan's army, and if you stay here, you'll also be a casualty of this war. You must flee eastwards as fast as you can. I'm the Lady Maya, and I beg you to leave.'

Maya knelt, reaching for her gift, to show them the truth of who she was, to give a sign that the woman couldn't ignore, nor her neighbours. But her gift was beyond reach, however hard she tried, and the woman and little girl looked at her, confused.

Maya rose and reached into her satchel, giving the women the neatly packaged food she always kept for the ride.

'Eat well today and tell everyone you know to head east.' She returned to her horse, mounted and rode away, eyes misting.

'Is it true, mother?' the little girl asked. 'Was she the Lady Maya? Was she telling the truth about bad soldiers coming?'

The woman shook her head, smiling sadly.

'For a moment, girl, I really thought she might be. But it's been told that the Lady Maya works miracles wherever she passes, and that grasses grow under her feet. I couldn't see anything beneath her feet but dirt. So no, she wasn't the Lady Maya, just some crazy noble most likely. Still, we now have food, so she's not all bad, whosoever she is.'

'So, we're not leaving home then, mother?' the girl asked again.

'No, my little love. We'll stay right here and wait for your father and brothers.'

Holding hands, they watched as the woman rode away, then walked back to the farmhouse, stepped inside and closed the door.

***

Chapter II

King Ostrom of the desert people stood in his stirrups, looking back at his army stretching into the distance to where they disappeared in the desert haze. His robes billowed, keeping him relatively cool despite the growing heat of the morning sun. Similarly garbed, his men looked like the sea on a windy day as their clothing rippled in angry waves.

Twenty-five thousand of his finest troops amassed to avenge the death of his firstborn. Except for his personal guard, all the men were on foot. Almost all carried body-length shields, and their long ironwood spears swayed above them like masts.

The Council of Elders had tried convincing him of the folly at bringing so many men to fight for the Lords of Greed, as they called the people of the Freestates. Still, as Ostrom had said, it wasn't to fight for them, it was to avenge the death of his son, the heir to the throne, killed by an agent of Daleth.

However, there was another reason as well.

He was bored.

Peace was good for his people, good for trade, and good for growth. But, for him and his army that had fought endlessly for eight of the last ten years to secure his borders, peace also brought soul-destroying boredom. It was said that Daleth's army was enormous, so what better way to banish the current monotony than facing such odds?

Of course, he'd had to leave behind enough soldiers to keep the people of his cities in check, as well as keeping the forts manned on the south and east borders. Whilst the last two years had seen a cessation of hostilities with his kingdom's neighbours, no prudent king would put temptation in front of an enemy by leaving the backdoor to the realm wide open.

So, he'd left eight thousand spearmen under the command of his second-born son, acting as regent in his absence. This son, Santar, had none of his erstwhile elder brother's humility, rather, he was full of pride and fire, impatient and quick to temper. Ostrom hoped the weight of responsibility would shape Santar into a man who could inherit and wear the mantle of kingship with success and honour.

He looked around and wondered when he'd start to see the beginnings of trees and grassland as the desert finally gave up its hold on the land.

What it was he and his ilk disliked about the green land to the north, he didn't know, but he knew what he liked … the desert. It was clean, so pure, an eternity of sand. No matter how deep you dug, it was all the same, full of order. Even after a battle, no trace would be left of the broken bodies, weapons, or blood within a few days. The desert would cleanse itself as if nothing had ever happened.

The same could be said of the sea, and those were the two places his people felt happiest.

In some ways, the dislike his people held for where they were heading had been one reason they'd never sought to conquer some of it for themselves. Better to use them for trading partners, and war over the endless dunes and mighty sandstone mountains to the south.

The sun was slowly rising above the horizon. They marched only at night, for it was the sole way to cross the desert and survive the heat. It would soon be time to make camp for the final daytime because, despite the need for haste, keeping his army strong for battle was also important.

As they'd journeyed further north, the temperature had become cooler, so tomorrow, they'd change their routine of travel and march under the blessing of the sun.

He turned the head of his horse toward that of his seer, Ultric. Ultric had the gifts of spirit talk and travelling the spirit paths. Ever since the age of ten, when Ultric's gift came to light, he and his twin brother, Altric, had been in service to the crown.

Since that time, they'd proved invaluable.

The End of Dreams

Plots to overthrow him were discovered by their arts, and they also served to coordinate battles and skirmishes. They'd been pivotal in maintaining his reign's longevity and helped his spearmen move from one victory to the next, giving them the reputation as some of the best fighting men to have ever walked.

This was the first time Ultric had left the land of his birth, and Ostrom knew this experience would be invaluable in years to come. Once visited, Ultric could spirit travel to these lands anytime he desired.

'How is Ultric today, and does he have any wisdom to share?' Ostrom asked, and the dead white eyes of his seer turned toward him. It never failed to amaze Ostrom that one so blind could see so much.

'My king,' Ultric replied, bowing his head in the direction of Ostrom's voice. 'I've again been unable to contact King Tristan's seer, Astren. It's been many nights since our last contact, so it's likely he perished in the fortress in which he served. I also spoke to Altric, who assured me that your son has had scant opportunity to make mischief or upset any of the nobles.'

Ostrom laughed good-naturedly.

'Getting up to mischief is part of Santar's nature. I only hope there's a kingdom left when we're done with the Witch-King.'

Ultric nodded solemnly.

'You're right, my king, yet I know you'd be quite happy to find a new war upon our return to keep you entertained. Surely that's exactly why you put Santar in charge instead of someone more reliable?'

Ostrom slapped his thigh.

'Surely you've the sharpest eyes of anyone I've ever known. Who knows whether we'll ever see home again, or breathe our last on foreign soil? But if we return, why not have something fun awaiting us?'

Ultric smiled happily at the thought, then tilted his head to one side.

'Another seven days will see us at Freeguard. That's where we'll find the Lord of Greed himself, ready to welcome us.'

Ostrom wiped sweat from his brow, a sure sign it was time to make camp. He called a halt, and his signallers flagged the order. Shortly, as far as he could see, his men began erecting their bright, white, silken tents to shield them from the rays of the rising sun. They'd eat, drink and then sleep for the majority of the day, except for those who stood guard.

His personal guard finished putting up his tent, and he dismounted, his back aching horribly. Everyone knew what was to be done, there was hardly any need to give orders as they'd campaigned together for so long.

He stepped inside, looking forward to a good sleep. He was getting too old to rule and fight, and the final reason he'd come on this expedition was that it was his time to die.

Had he stayed at home, keeping the peace, Santar would have tried to usurp him this year or the next. The last thing he wanted to do was kill and bury his remaining son, who was too inept to succeed despite his vigour and youth. The lad just wasn't sharp enough.

This way, he'd solve the problem of succession, for surely to face nearly a hundred thousand men would be to greet death itself. He'd soon join his forefathers and drink the waters of the oasis, look down, and no doubt despair at his remaining son's constant failures.

But before then, he'd kill as many enemy warriors as possible to serve him in the afterlife, and with luck, Daleth would be amongst them. If not, well, Santar might be keeping his father company sooner than expected.

***

'We're almost there,' Rakan shouted. 'Push hard!'

Rakan risked a glance over his shoulder, cursing at how close a hundred of Daleth's lancers were, the tips of their long weapons glinting evilly.

They'd been caught on rolling, open countryside, and were heading frantically for a large farmstead that stood atop a hill. There was no woodland they could reach in time before they were cut down, so the farmstead was the only place to make a stand. Dismounted, they had a chance, whereas on horseback, not only were they outnumbered but outclassed.

'We're not going to make it,' Yana cried desperately.

Taran looked back, the hard smiles on the faces of their pursuers plainly visible. Yana was right.

The End of Dreams

'Release the spare horses,' he ordered, shouting at the top of his lungs to be heard above the pounding hooves and howling wind, letting go of the lead ropes that kept them in tow.

Everyone followed suit, and suddenly forty riderless horses slowed and turned aside, obstructing the chasing lancers. It disrupted their charge long enough so that the group made it to the farmstead.

They rode in amongst the wooden fences, walls, barns, and sheds. As they clattered into the empty yard before the main building, they leapt off their mounts. Men frantically closed gates, turned abandoned wagons over to cause further obstructions, and then drew swords and unslung shields.

The lancers approached, but rather than trying to force their way past the obstacles, stayed at a distance, circling the farmstead. The man, who was likely the troop captain, conversed with another, who rode off back the way they'd come.

'Dammit, that doesn't look good,' Rakan muttered. 'I hoped they'd be foolish enough to attack, for on foot, they aren't half as evil as on horseback. I thought, despite the numbers, we'd have a good chance, but they think the same from the looks of it. As sure as the sun rises in the east, that one's gone off for reinforcements.'

Taran looked to the sky, hoping that somehow it was later than he knew it would be, but it was still early morning.

Yana followed his glance, understanding what he didn't say.

'He'll be back with reinforcements before it gets dark?' she half questioned.

Taran nodded grimly as he stared after the departing rider.

'If we ride out, we die. If we wait, we die.'

He looked around at the men, many of whom were glancing at him for orders. He nodded to some, his face hard, not showing any signs of emotion, for in truth, he felt little. The amulet took everything away, leaving things so matter-of-fact. Yet the one surging emotion it encouraged at this moment was anger. Anger that this might stop him from getting his revenge on Daleth and Tristan should he die here in this foul-smelling, deserted farmstead.

Taran turned to Rakan.

'Have the men check the buildings. We might be lucky, and find a dozen bows with several hundred arrows hidden under some straw.'

Rakan laughed at the joke with grim humour.

'Yes. Better to keep the men busy than thinking about how soon they might die.' He stomped off, talking to some of the men in a low voice.

Taran strode toward the barn, and Yana followed.

Having inspected the crossbeams at the entrance, certain they'd hold his weight, he started to climb. It wasn't easy, and he came close to losing his grip a few times before he stood upright on the roof and looked around, shading his eyes, bracing against the wind.

It was a good vantage point, for the farmstead was on the brow of the hill. Earlier, as they'd fled, there hadn't been the chance to look at their surroundings. Now he could take stock.

To the south, at the bottom of the hill, was a large lake, its distant shore hazy in the distance. There'd be no escape that way. The land between the farmstead and the lake was open pasture for grazing, and the dry grass waving furiously in the blustery wind was not quite tall enough to conceal a man.

To the north, in the distance, he could see dense woodland, and that was where they needed to get to. Once amongst the trees, they'd have a far better chance of escaping. Again, in between, it was just grassland, nothing to use as concealment, and they'd never make it. The lancers were far superior warriors when in the saddle, and their horses were faster, with more stamina than their own, which weren't warhorses.

He counted the lancers astride their mounts and found there to be one hundred and twenty against their forty. One thing to be grateful for was they didn't have any bows either, or this would be over even quicker.

How to escape?

This would end when the lancers decided it would.

When reinforcements arrived, the lancers would attack on foot. It didn't matter that his men were more skilled, they'd be overwhelmed by the sheer weight of numbers.

Taran climbed down, dropping the last bit, and Yana came forward to steady him.

The End of Dreams

Her eyes were bright with hope, Taran noticed indifferently. Somewhere, deep down, he wondered whether he should try to keep her spirits up, but the thought disappeared even as it formed.

'I think we'll be dead by sunset,' he said, shrugging his shoulders at her unspoken enquiry, and left her open-mouthed behind him as he went to find Rakan. The smell of cooking drew him, and sure enough, he found Rakan next to a fire.

Rakan stood and moved slightly to the side with Taran, away from the men.

'What did you see?'

Taran told him of the woodland way to the north, beyond the open ground as well as everything else of note.

Rakan shook his head, his face glum.

'Even were Kalas with us, I'm not sure I'd fancy our chances. Without him, I don't know what we can do. But I'm damn sure I won't just wait here to be slaughtered. Once the lads have had something to eat, what do you say to setting the time of our demise? We can go out to meet those vermin at the moment of our choosing.'

Rakan waited for an answer as Taran, deep in thought, stood staring at the men.

Yana came to stand by Taran's side.

'Will you save us? Will you save me?' she asked quietly.

Taran turned, his smile was grim.

'I might, with luck, be able to save our lives, but I fear our souls were lost a long time ago.'

He beckoned for Yana to follow him and walked back to the barn, Yana close behind.

***

Captain Huskan looked to the sky, wondering which of the gods he must have pleased, for surely today's gift was unlike any he'd received before.

The wind was ferocious on the top of the small hill, and the clouds sped across the sky as if racing to escape the slaughter that would soon happen below them. He laughed in giddy expectation.

Earlier that morning, as he and his lancers had decamped from a good night's sleep in some woods, there on the plains below had been around forty Freestates soldiers on horseback, making their way eastward at a gentle canter.

Huskan's eyes were sharp, and he'd whistled through his teeth when he saw the embellished armour of the damned enemy commander, shining like a beacon amongst the riders. Here was a prize beyond measure, the man who'd shown such skill in defending the fortress, and by killing two Rangers in single combat.

He had one hundred and twenty of the finest lancers, and they had the height advantage as he led his men down the hill to intercept the enemy cavalry.

Not that they were really cavalry, it was plain to see these were just mounted soldiers. Whilst they no doubt had fine skills with a sword on foot, when on horseback, they'd be no match for his lancers with their years of experience of fighting from the saddle.

Without cover, the lancers' pursuit was spotted almost immediately, and the race had started. Huskan was an experienced leader and didn't push hard at first, knowing that his men's riding skills and their mounts' stamina would make up the ground irrespective. The more the enemy soldiers fruitlessly tired their horses trying to escape, the easier the slaughter would become when they were caught.

The distance had closed as he knew it would, and then a farmstead had come into sight. His order to charge had come just moments too late. The enemy managed to evade certain death on the point of a lance with the canny move of fouling the charge by releasing their spare mounts into the lancers' path.

Yet now, as he sat astride his horse, looking at the farmstead, he knew it was just a matter of time, and their blood would still stain the ground.

His men had been impatient to attack immediately, not understanding why they should share the glory and reward with another troop. However, once the blood rush subsided, and they'd thought through the prospect of fighting on foot against a skilled enemy, the grumbling had given way to a chorus of agreement.

The End of Dreams

So they'd spread out, circling the farmstead at a distance, just in case they had an archer or two, but that didn't seem to be the case so far.

He chuckled to himself. The small band of Freestates soldiers had really only delayed the inevitable, for no help was coming. They couldn't attack on foot, which was their strength, nor could they hope to outfight the lancers on horseback. They were outnumbered, and the only fight where they might inflict any casualties was the defensive one they'd chosen. His lancers would have to fight on foot amongst the buildings when the time came.

Yet he'd soon have over two hundred and forty men against forty. It wouldn't matter then how good the enemy might be, they'd be overwhelmed, for there was nothing to stop his men attacking from all sides at once.

He looked at the sky again. It was midday, and he expected the other lancers to be with him by mid-afternoon, so just a little more patience and the show would begin.

Like the others in the troop, his horse had been trained from an early age and showed a discipline only matched by its rider. Yet suddenly, it shifted under him, whinnying in distress.

The panicked sound of more horses calling out quickened his pulse, and he brought his attention quickly back to the farm.

His eyes opened in surprise, for the soldiers in the farmstead were throwing burning torches over the wooden railed fences into the long grass beyond. Then he smelled the smoke that the horses' finer senses had picked up moments before.

What were the enemy doing?

Suddenly, the buffeting wind, which had been bullying the clouds across the sky, fanned the growing flames into hungrily consuming the long, dried grasses. The next moment, he was doing all he could to control his horse as it screamed in terror as smoke billowed across the landscape.

All around, his men struggled to a lesser or greater degree.

The smoke was black and thick, and his eyes were watering when suddenly, screams of pain matched the horses' cries. Dark shapes started appearing from the smoke, pulling men from their saddles, butchering them swiftly.

'No!' he cried, as he let the horse have its head, and it turned, bolting away from the swirling flames and smoke. Yet even as he did so, he found himself falling backwards, his hands and legs no longer having the strength to hold on.

This is strange. Why am I lying on my back? he thought.

The smoke and clouds seemed to be moving slower and becoming fainter. He had to give it to the enemy commander, he'd have bet a month's pay that they'd never get out of that bind.

A figure in embellished armour moved above him, and Huskan laughed, although it was more of a rattle.

'That was a plan of genius,' he tried to say, but the words never left his lips, for the clouds suddenly smothered him, and he gasped his last breath.

***

Daleth sat, ordering his thoughts.

In his injured state, he was unable to personally lead his army further east, so any further conquest of the Freestates would need to be under the leadership of one of his many captains. This would have been his favoured choice, yet several tortured Freestates soldiers had all confirmed that a further army waited to face him.

It seemed Tristan had been busy, successfully forging a formal alliance with the Eyre and desert tribes.

Without further intelligence confirming the enemy numbers ranged against him, he'd be sending in his army blind, and only a fool would do that.

So now before him stood two Rangers with the most unbelievably subtle gift, and it was their time to serve. Usually, Rangers worked in teams of five, but these two were so special that they were usually kept apart from their brethren.

He hadn't thought he'd need them yet, but then he hadn't foreseen being relegated to bed with stitches holding his guts inside, both legs unable to support him, let alone an unknown force rallied to oppose him. Yet, in some ways, the turn of events would make this a different and more interesting war than simply slaughtering the enemy head-on.

The End of Dreams

That the Rangers shared the same gift was almost as remarkable as the fact that they were brothers, twins. Identical whenever they wanted to be, yet completely different at other times.

The fact was, Daleth never truly knew what they actually looked like, and he wondered if even they did anymore. Yet somehow, he always knew who was who. This earned him their respect over and above the crazed devotion they'd been indoctrinated with from the earliest of ages.

'Sit, my friends,' he said, gesturing to the chairs his bodyguard had set out before they'd departed a short while ago.

As the twins relaxed, concern shone from their eyes.

Daleth shrugged dismissively.

'Fear not. I'll be ready for battle before winter is over. Then I can look forward to sparring with you both once you've helped bring this immediate part of our conquest to a timely end.'

He nodded to Jared.

'You'll head east on the morrow to Freeguard. According to some recently departed garrison men, it seems that an alliance of enemy forces are rallying there. Your objective is to infiltrate the Freestates ranks and work your way to Tristan's side, where he'll be at your mercy.'

Jared's face split into a knowing smile, showing his appreciation.

Gregor didn't look so happy.

'Have I displeased you, my king?' he asked, dropping his head low. 'Can I not accompany my brother in this most important of quests to double the chance of success?'

Daleth reached over despite the pain it caused to shoot through his body, grasping Gregor's shoulder until the Ranger raised his eyes.

'No, Gregor. I've an equally important task for you. I must be seen to be nigh on impervious to harm, a figure of divine strength and constitution, not as I currently am. Go amongst the men as my ambassador, so that they fall to their knees in homage to my strength, as if I were touched by the gods themselves.'

Gregor's eyes shone, as much as his brother's, and he bowed low, touching his forehead to Daleth's hand.

'You honour me this day like no other in my life,' he said, voice filled with fervent devotion. 'When would you wish me to take up this mantle?'

Daleth smiled, the skin around his eyes creasing.

'Now is as good a time as any, Gregor, then you can report to me after.'

Gregor reached out, grasping Daleth's forearm. This time, when his eyes met those of his king, he stared as if he were imprinting every line of Daleth's face in his mind.

As Daleth watched, Gregor started to grow in stature. His tunic split away as his shoulders broadened, he became taller, and a moan of terrible pain escaped his lips at the torment his body suffered at this sudden growth. Sweat and tears ran in furrows down his face as his hair lengthened, darkened, and his face began to change.

Daleth gripped Gregor's forearm hard in support until the transformation was complete.

Now when Gregor lifted his head once more, Daleth found himself looking at his own mirror image.

Daleth turned to Jared.

'When you finally dispose of Tristan and assume his guise, you'll be King of the Freestates. You must attempt to turn all the allied forces to our cause, but if that's unachievable, then either disband them or simply leave them leaderless to be crushed, as was the initial plan. Reach out to me when you arrive at Freeguard, and keep me informed of your progress whenever possible.'

The gift of the shapeshifter was almost unparalleled; the enemy would literally never see them coming.

***

Seven more days of relative freedom, just seven more days.

Whilst she was riding in nature's embrace, Maya could almost pretend that she was free. Free of constraint, free of duty, free of Tristan. Almost.

Yet now the journey was nearing its end, she found it harder to see nature's surrounding beauty. Her thoughts often turned inward and backward toward the happiest moments of her life with Taran, avoiding thoughts of whatever bleak future was ahead.

They'd passed through many small towns and villages, and whilst the countryside looked healthy and bountiful, the general population looked only a little better than the folk she'd grown up with. It seemed that everyone was forced to work hard to survive in a land whose bounty should have let people live their lives in happiness with full stomachs and healthy children.

Their entourage slowly grew as they travelled, for the riders constantly enticed people to attend the betrothal celebration.

Maya was sickened by the duplicity.

She'd confronted Tristan about it, demanding that the people be told the truth now, not when they arrived at Freeguard. His scathing laughter and that of his accompanying cronies had left her cheeks blushing even as she scolded him.

His words were still loud in her mind.

The people of this land are sworn to serve me. Yet if I asked them to join my army to fight the Witch-King's horde, few would. People would be frightened. They'd refuse or run away at the first opportunity. I'd need to make an example of those who refused or disobeyed. That would mean nailing half of them to posts throughout the countryside to encourage others to abide by their oath of allegiance.

As Maya thought about his words, her mood dipped even further, for she'd had no response that wouldn't have been ridiculed. It was impossible to teach him the folly of his ways. It seemed lies and deceit were acceptable in the Freestates if they gave you power, however much it corrupted everyone.

Yet even as these thoughts passed through her mind, she laughed at herself. Sadly, kingdoms would always be full of those who sought power over their neighbours, whose greed would enrich them at the cost of their fellow man.

She had to wake up to the reality of these lands, even if they were so bleak. Her time with Taran and the intimacy they'd shared had given her hope that love could conquer all. Sadly, it seemed few shared her optimism, not in this world, not in this life.

As ever, she was shadowed by her guards, and when she dismounted, they kept a respectful distance. They seemed happy with their role, for they avoided the drudgery of staying with the slow-moving column, instead following her as she roamed the countryside.

She sat in lush grass, looking up at the clouds, wondering if Taran was also gazing at the same sky. Whichever way her thoughts turned, they always ended with him. They were her safe haven when her spirit was low, the light in the dark. She missed him keenly.

From a pouch at her side, she took a small, withered flower she'd picked from the side of the road earlier, and concentrated, calling on her gift. She did this every few hours, and as ever, it came, but so slowly and with very little strength. Her gift felt blocked as it had been when Brandon, the Ranger, first confronted her at Laska's settlement.

Yet nonetheless, the flower rejuvenated ever so slowly at the cost of a terrible headache.

She was under no illusions now, her gift was fading, and she knew it was linked to her inner happiness. She'd been relatively happy before she'd met Taran. Her life as a hunter for the settlement had allowed her to roam free, while transforming her secret garden had filled her with joy. The problem was, having experienced love, being without it took away the colours, the tastes, the scents from all around. Now, it was as if she lived in a world of grey.

In the distance was a slow-moving line of horses, wagons and a large number of countryfolk, mostly men. They'd been lured from the fields, small towns, and villages, on the back of lies and the promise of a few coins they'd likely never see.

Maya was angry. Angry for the people like her, who'd always been used and lied to. Yet for the first time in her life, she was in a position to do something about it.

Here these people were, leaving behind husbands and wives, young sons and daughters, to fight for a king who despised them. Even if they won, who would they go home to? The very people they loved would probably be dead, slaughtered for the fun of it. As she'd discovered, life was not worth living without the ones you loved to share it with.

Tristan was gaining an army by lying to them, but she knew in her heart they'd train and fight twice as hard if they realised they fought to keep the ones they loved alive.

She might not have her gift anymore, thanks to Tristan, but she now had power because of him.

The End of Dreams

She mounted her horse, her heart still sad, but now filled with resolve. Even if she couldn't have the love of her life next to her, she'd make damn sure those who had the chance could be with theirs, and had them by their side till their last breath.

She turned in her saddle and beckoned to Ferris, the leader of her guard. She'd need help to make this happen, and someone she could trust. She hoped Ferris was the one.

Yes, this was the right thing to do.

Then she smiled, because even if it didn't work, she couldn't wait to see the look on Tristan's face after she'd tried.

***

Chapter III

There were thirty of them left now, and they were all injured to a lesser or greater degree, but at least they were alive.

The desperate plan to start the wildfire had been a dangerous one, but at least it gave some of them the chance to live, whereas staying at the farmstead would have meant certain death.

Taran looked around and found everyone in the same state, slumped over the back of their horses, covered in soot, with blistered skin on their hands or heads. The flames had been indiscriminate and unforgiving in who it burned.

Of the twelve men they'd lost, only four had been to the lances of the enemy. The others had fallen to the very inferno they'd started.

The amulet Taran wore did little to ease the pain as he held the reins of his horse, which, like the man it bore, was also burned with patches of raw, blistered skin showing through its coat.

Taran turned to Rakan beside him, and despite the pain, his father smiled.

'I've seen you looking better, son,' Rakan noted, 'but also in worse shape too. You should've seen yourself before Maya brought you back from the brink ...' He stopped, knowing mentioning Maya's name was not going to help Taran's mood.

Yet Taran laughed humorously nonetheless.

'Indeed, we could all do with her healing skills right now, although whether she'd want to pay the price anymore is anyone's guess.'

Taran rose in his saddle and nodded in satisfaction, for there below them was the city of Freemantle.

The End of Dreams

They'd pushed themselves and their horses to the limit, knowing that they had to reach Freemantle ahead of any pursuing lancers. Here, they could rest and find provisions to help them recover from their wounds, or at least keep them alive a little while longer.

They rode down the hill, staying on the road as speed was more important than stealth at this stage. They were in no fit state to fight, not any of them.

As they got closer, they could see around a hundred figures gathering in the main street, and for a moment, Taran worried that the lancers had got there before them. However, as he approached, it became apparent they were splendidly dressed city folk. The civilians stood looking warily back at the filthy and bedraggled Taran and the following troops.

The soldiers looked to Taran for orders, so he raised his hand to signal for patience. His attention was on the city folk, for none knew the city better than them.

He tried to use his gift but heard nothing but whispers in his mind when he focused, so gave up, feeling frustrated.

What was the point?

It hardly came to him anymore. Not since Kalas' last stand had his gift responded.

He rode up to a well-dressed man holding a golden staff, standing at the head of the small crowd, and nodded in greeting. The man responded in kind, although he and the others behind him looked like they might turn and run away at any moment.

Taran dismounted slowly, every part of him hurting as scabs broke open. He knew just how horrific he must look to these people. Likely they'd no idea whose army they were from, for even Taran's embellished armour was blackened beyond recognition.

He'd initially considered ordering or threatening them to give help, yet as he considered this, he realised they'd likely disobeyed orders, and stayed here in the city instead of fleeing east. Instead, he took a different approach.

'People of Freemantle,' he said, voice croaking. He licked his lips and tried again. 'Good people of Freemantle. We seek your help, for as you can see, we're in sore need. Don't be concerned that we seek it for free. We'll pay you handsomely for your assistance, for we carry coin and would expect nothing without giving something in return. For that is the Freestates way, is it not?'

The people nodded, and some of the hostility disappeared as they realised they were dealing with Freestates' troops.

Taran turned to Yana.

'Gather whatever coin the men have and bring it to me.'

Yana dismounted and hurried off to do as Taran ordered.

Taran looked again at the man before him.

'I'm Taran, Lord Commander of King Tristan's forces. We need, as you'll note, mostly medical assistance as well as food and water. We'll stay for one, maybe two days at the absolute most. We also need our horses cared for, as they're in as much need as us.'

Yana came up beside him as he finished and passed over a sack.

Taran hefted it, and the jingling caused the man's eyes to widen.

'This is yours if I have your word that you'll help as requested. We'll ask for no more, but we expect no less.'

The man reached out and took the throat of the sack, but Taran didn't let go.

'Understand me,' he said quietly, pulling the man into what looked like a friendly embrace but was anything but. 'If you don't give my men the help they deserve ... If you try to hold back on the care ... If you try to disappear into the city with the coin without fulfilling your end of the bargain ... know this. My men and I will hunt you down, every single one of you, and we'll cut out your eyes and tongues to leave you wandering, bleeding, and blind until you starve to death.'

He released the man, smiling broadly, and the man stumbled back, white-faced, holding the sack as firmly as Taran held his gaze.

'What's your name?' Taran asked.

'My, my name is Humphrey,' stuttered the man.

'Well, Humphrey. Lead the way,' Taran ordered.

They didn't go far. The houses alongside the main thoroughfare were the most palatial, and it seemed that these people had all taken up residence nearby, and suddenly it made sense. These people were the greediest of all. They'd seen the departure of the many as a perfect opportunity for the few to seize the wealth of the city for themselves.

Humphrey led them through gilded gates and up marble steps into a home of such opulence that the soldiers looked around in wonder.

Swiftly they were ushered through and out to the back, where another low building for bathing stood.

Rakan sidled over to Taran.

'Don't they realise that they won't live long enough to truly enjoy what they've taken?' he asked, then continued without waiting for an answer. 'Still, without their greed, we might have found ourselves wasting time scavenging through an empty city, and time is something we've precious little of. If we get a day of rest, it'll be a godsend.'

Yana, who was listening nearby, came over.

'We all need more than just a day. If we weaken any more or allow wounds to get infected, we'll be lucky if any of us see Freeguard. Assuming we aren't cut down on route!'

The men were removing their armour when Humphrey returned.

'Food and drink will arrive shortly,' he said, not meeting Taran's eyes, 'and I don't think it's appropriate for a lady, however dirty she might be, to bathe with the men.'

Yana's laugh was full of good humour.

'I am indeed of noble birth, and I might add, King Tristan himself bestowed upon me the title of Lady of the Royal Court. So, whilst I have no problems sharing a bath with so many men, I fear the water might be somewhat soiled by their filthy bodies. So lead away.'

Rakan watched Yana follow Humphrey, then groaned as he tried to unstrap his armour.

Taran turned to him.

'Keep that on,' he said softly.

'Have you read something?' Rakan asked quietly, forgetting his pain.

Taran shook his head, frowning.

'It isn't my gift. Rather, as I look around, I have to ask … Did our small sack of coins have so much value compared to the riches these people have surrounded themselves with. Surely now food is more valuable than gold, for where will they get more from? No, something is wrong. I'm sure of it. If it means we wait for our bath a little longer, then so be it. Let's have half our men stay ready whilst the other half bathes. Warn them to be ready to fight should the need arise. If they hear me praise our good king in conversation, you'll all know something is awry!'

Rakan grimaced then walked swiftly amongst the soldiers, talking softly.

Taran moved to the rear end of the building and carefully tried the door handles. The doors were held closed from the outside.

As he wandered back, the main entrance to the room opened.

Humphrey entered, leading two dozen men carrying food, wineskins and fresh clothing. His face betrayed his surprise at finding Taran, Rakan, and half the men still armoured.

'Wash the dust from your throats, my friends,' he said, sweeping his arms to encompass them all. His men stepped forward and leaned down to give the soldiers in the bathing pool the skins before passing the rest around the room.

Humphrey stood, waiting expectantly for them to all quench their thirst, but the soldiers simply held their wineskins and looked to Taran.

'Forgive them,' Taran said, stepping forward, 'but they're full of tradition despite being men of the sword. When we stand as guests in the house of a Freestates noble, surely tradition dictates that the host drinks not only first, but the most, to honour the gods of greed.'

When Taran offered his skin back to Humphrey, even without his gift, he could read Humphrey's body language with ease. His dilated pupils conveyed the fear within him. So when Humphrey started to graciously decline, Taran raised his hand and interrupted before he got a word out.

'No!' Taran said. 'We'll follow tradition, and you and your men will raise a toast to our good King Tristan.' He chose these last words carefully, and as he said them, the garrison soldiers quickly drew weapons and herded the panicked serving men to the back of the room at the point of their swords.

The soldiers in the pool got out and began readying themselves as Rakan stepped forward, his wickedly sharp dagger in hand, and pushed Humphrey up against a pillar.

'Tell me ... what's in the wine and food?' he asked menacingly, the dagger tip drawing blood from Humphrey's neck.

'N-n-nothing in the food, just a little sleep weed in the wine to help you rest and recover from the injuries you suffered is all,' he stammered, and carefully reached out to a plate near his fingertips and brought some dried meat to his lips.

Rakan lowered his dagger a little.

Humphrey popped the food into his mouth and chewed.

'You see,' he said, 'it's safe.'

Taran thought quickly, then called to the soldiers on the other side of the pool.

'Search them,' he commanded, and they roughly frisked the serving men. Every one of them bore a concealed dagger and cord.

Taran stepped forward as Humphrey started crying.

'Let me guess,' Taran growled. 'The plan was that once we'd fallen unconscious, you'd bind us and use us in exchange for your lives and continued life of privilege under your new benevolent monarch, Daleth!'

'What shall we do?' called one of the soldiers.

Taran looked across briefly, then turned back to Humphrey.

'You're lucky. I should carry out my promise to take both your eyes and your tongue, but you can avoid that fate by telling me where Yana is being kept, and where our horses are.'

Humphrey stammered his response before Taran nodded.

Rakan drew his dagger across the man's throat. As he did so, screams sounded briefly from the far side of the room as the soldiers butchered the men, following his lead.

'We need to secure our horses and retrieve Yana. Then we need to do what we came here to do,' Taran commanded the assembling soldiers. 'These men had decided to ally themselves with the enemy, so anyone who hinders us can meet the same fate. However, spill no blood unless you must, for some might still genuinely help once they know of the fate that befell these.'

Taran picked five of the men.

'You stay here and get these bodies cleared out. Some of us still need that bath. Follow me,' he commanded and strode back toward the mansion.

Swords drawn, his soldiers followed, eyes grim. Some were still covered in grime and soot, but all were splashed with fresh blood.

***

Daleth was pleased with the progress of his recovery, even if he wouldn't be able to move around without pain for another month or two.

The wounded's' misery and the new life he felt from the land to the east had kept infection away, and he was healing faster than any normal mortal man.

Now the pain was manageable, his thoughts were positive. Only a fool dwelled on the past, allowing it to hold him back, but a strong man focussed on shaping the present and future.

As Daleth sat in what had once been Tristan's bedchamber in the fortress, he considered his next move.

Jared was still about a month away from reaching Freeguard, assuming he made good and unhindered progress. It would likely take the winter for the Ranger to carefully infiltrate the palace. It wasn't just a case of Jared slaying Tristan and assuming his guise. He had to learn to talk, move, and act like Tristan, not just appear to be him. Thus, Jared would need to work his way into a position whereby he could observe and learn for months before he struck the final blow.

Gregor, because he'd known Daleth his whole life, had no such problems in assuming the mantle straight away. Frustratingly, Gregor had done such a good job that it was now presenting its own problems.

The Ranger had reported that, when he walked amongst the army, they'd looked upon him as a god. Even the fact that Kalas had injured him so terribly now only added to the awe in which they held their king. Recovering from heinous injuries in such a short space of time was nothing short of divine.

This now led to Daleth's quandary.

There was now no valid reason for the army to remain here if he was supposedly full of rude health. Now the soldiers were grumbling that their conquest of the Freestates seemed to be on hold for no good reason. Where was the slaughter, the revenge, and the wealth they'd been promised?

Fights had broken out. The army was now camped throughout the pass and surrounding area. Many had rooms within the keep, whereas others were jealous at being left out in the elements. The amulets that suppressed love, pain, compassion, and all the other things had the benefit of also increasing anger and jealousy. Now, without an enemy to release it upon, his soldiers were starting to take it out on each other.

Daleth mused a little while longer. He hated being unable to lead the fight himself, and whilst Gregor was as skilled a killer as any Ranger, none of them had the truly strategic mind that Alano once had.

He couldn't entrust the conquest of the Freestates to anyone but himself, but there was always the destruction of the Eyre and the Horselords. He'd intended to deal with them last, for they were but a nuisance, yet perhaps this would prove a distraction for many of his men while battle-hardening them.

'Forty men killed today, and as many injured due to squabbles,' Daleth spoke softly to himself, thumb and forefinger stroking his chin. He shook his head, looking at Gregor. 'Normally I'd have a hundred men nailed to a cross to set an example over this lack of discipline, but this time the fault is not theirs. They're acting as I'd want them to, full of fight and wanting blood, so blood they shall have.'

Daleth steeled himself as a wave of pain washed over him, but he was in control, and it subsided.

'Whilst you still hold my form, you'll command Julius to lead the Nightstalkers and thirty thousand infantry north. Their objective is to take the city-state of Freehold and use that as a base to push into the lands of the Eyre. The majority of the fighters in both will have already joined Tristan's new alliance, but Julius can slaughter those who remain. The women, older men and any children are to be left alive, although Julius' men can have whatever fun they please with them. We'll need some survivors to rule over once this part of the conquest is finished. After he's dealt with the Eyre, have him winter in Freehold and meet with us at Freemantle before the spring thaw.

Gregor nodded, hanging on every word.

'As for you,' Daleth continued, 'to reward your loyal service, you'll personally lead thirty thousand spearmen, two thousand lancers, and the same number of archers to take Freemarch as your base. You'll then push into the grasslands of the Horselords, but not in my guise.'

Daleth smiled as Gregor's face shone with pride and honour.

'You'll slaughter any and all armed resistance you encounter, and believe me, the Horselords will fall upon you relentlessly like rain from the clouds when you encounter them. Their lands are sacrosanct to any but their own, and their goddess will demand they fight you the moment they see you. But they lack cohesion, and our spears will make short work of them, especially as they'll come at you piecemeal.'

Daleth rubbed his hands together as he briefly visualised the slaughter, but then focussed on more pressing matters.

'All those soldiers not engaged in yours or Julius' campaign will march in two days to shelter at Freemantle. Once you've secured our southern flank, I expect you to join us there before the end of winter, ready for our thrust eastward in the spring.'

'I will winter in Freemantle and will be ready to lead our assault as soon as the snows have thawed. In the interim, I'll keep the men in Freemantle busy, training and drinking. At least there, no one will argue over whether they've a roof over their heads. Freemantle is supposed to be a city of such wealth that we'll all be sleeping in a palace. The only thing I need to do is make it to Freemantle without the men seeing how weak I've become after my supposed full recovery.'

Gregor cleared his throat, and Daleth nodded encouragingly.

'Might I suggest you stay here whilst the army marches ahead, and follow on shortly thereafter? You'll have time to heal by then, but more importantly, you can travel at a slower pace with just your bodyguard.'

Daleth smiled broadly as he tapped the side of his nose.

'Gregor, your mind is as sharp as you are loyal. It's an excellent idea. Just know I'll want a report every night once you cross the border.'

Gregor bowed.

'Of course, my king. I'll not fail you. On that, you have my word.'

Daleth smiled.

'I know you won't, Gregor. I have the utmost faith in you and your brother. Now, send in Baidan. There's much to organise, and you have an army to prepare.'

***

Maya leant back and half-smiled.

The stars were mostly hidden by clouds, and the camp was settling down for the night. Food had been eaten, washed down with wine, and the men nearby were succumbing to fatigue.

The End of Dreams

Tristan was convening with Galain and some other minor lords who were travelling with them, and it wouldn't be long before people started turning in for sleep.

There were nigh on a thousand peasants, as Tristan referred to them, whose camp was forced to set up some distance away. Whilst the peasants were allowed to breathe the same air, they weren't tolerated anywhere near the wealthier classes at night in case of theft or simply bumping into them.

Maya stretched, stood, then ambled away from the fire and nodded to Ferris. He and the other guards followed, as if escorting her back to her bedroll.

Tristan had given up on trying to have her sleep in a tent next to his and Galain was happy enough not to bother erecting another. So, this wandering was nothing out of the ordinary and yet tonight would be different.

Instead of stopping at her bedroll, they hurried west toward the glow of the disappearing sun and the twinkling campfire of the peasant camp.

It wasn't far to walk, yet Maya's pace was brisk. Her stomach knotted with apprehension at what she was about to do and the ramifications of her actions.

The countryfolk, as Maya preferred to call them, had a camp centred around a large communal fire so that people could come and eat together. As they drew closer, Maya could hear the hum of conversation interspersed with laughter.

Ferris and the other four men-at-arms remained close, because not every soul here would be a gentle one. This far from the main camp, no one else would come to assist if she got into trouble.

Blankets and bedrolls were strewn around, although no one had yet turned in for the night. Maya was relieved, for she wanted to address them all, to be heard by everyone.

She stepped out from the cover of the trees into the firelight. Almost immediately, the buzz of conversation died as people turned toward the new arrival and the soldiers flanking her.

A tall, thin man stood and walked toward them, and from the way people followed him with their eyes, he was the unofficial leader of these gathered people.

'My name is Silonas. What do you want here? I think you're lost. This is no place for those of the genteel class nor those who serve them.' Yet his voice lacked conviction, for he was confused by the leather garb she wore and the sword belted at her waist.

His tone was not friendly and nor were the eyes that met hers as she looked around. Yet she didn't feel trepidation or fear as she moved forward confidently, and the man backed away before her purposeful stride.

She stood with her back to the fire, its light making her white hair shine as if gold. Ferris and the other soldiers fanned out to either side, a few steps behind.

'Do you know who I am?' she called. 'I doubt it. Although you may have heard of me. It's my name that's being used to bring you east, away from your farms, your homes in search of coin. People call me the Lady Maya, but I'm no more of the noble class than any of you, nor do I have any wish to be.'

Mocking laughter echoed from the crowd, but Maya didn't let it distract her.

'You think I lie? What if I told you I wasn't born of this land, that in fact, I was but a peasant girl who came from lands far away to the west, from the realm of the Witch-King.'

Murmurs swept through the crowd, and the man who'd first confronted her spoke again.

'It's said the Lady Maya has hair of the purest white, and certainly, you bear the look, and you have soldiers here that would back up your claim. But it's also said that you carry the gift of healing, so if you're who you say you are, show us.'

'Yes, show us!' the crowd cried.

Maya raised her hands, and silence descended.

'It's true, I used to have that gift, but sadly it's deserted me of late, along with any happiness that I once had. That is why I stand before you now.' Her head lowered as she spoke, hair falling over her face, but she straightened once again, sweeping it back, her gaze strong.

'I've not come here to lecture you, nor to thank you for coming to see a betrothal ceremony that in truth I've no wish to go to myself. I'm here to tell you the truth and give you a choice. I'm here to give you the chance to save whatever happiness you have.'

As she spoke, her hands moved, emphasising her words and the watching crowd stared as if spellbound.

'Ask yourself. Why are the wealthy merchants, the nobility, heading east with not just their retinues but their possessions? Ask yourself. Why, in a land of the selfish, ruled by the King of Greed himself, is he willing to offer you coin for nothing but attending his betrothal ceremony?'

Maya paused briefly, letting those watching digest her words.

'So when you ask yourself those questions and realise that something isn't quite what it seems, then consider my answer.'

She raised her voice, holding the crowd with her intensity.

'I've come from the land of the Witch-King. I not only fled him, but I fled his soldiers. He has no choice but to come and conquer the Freestates, for his every breath stole the life from his kingdom which died beneath his very feet. For him and his army, to stay there is to die.'

'You know of his reputation, that he has eternal youth, and that is no myth. Daleth's longevity is sustained because he stole the life from the very land he ruled, and the people therein.'

'For the last four weeks, his army has attacked Tristan's Folly, the fortress that kept these lands safe. A fortress that has, in all likelihood, been overrun as I speak.'

Surprised murmurs and muttering started to rise, but Maya raised her hands, and everyone fell back to silence.

'So, why is our king offering you coin to come east? It's because he intends to put swords in your hands to face the threat of Daleth and his hordes who sweep across these lands.'

'I lost the one I love to this war, and I stand before you with the truth, for I wish none of you to share my fate. There's still time for some of you to return to where you came from, to fetch your wives or lovers, sons or daughters, and then flee to Freeguard with them, not without them!'

A shocked silence greeted her words before shouting erupting as everyone starting calling out questions. It was some time before the crowd settled enough for Maya to continue.

'I hear you,' she said. 'You feel betrayed, and any other time I would say a king who lies to you does not deserve your allegiance. Yet I also find myself asking you to return to fight by his side, but this time truly understanding why. The reason is simple, and it's the very reason that I chose to turn and fight, and why the love of my life turned and fought against Daleth, a man who was once his king.'

'You could run, you could let Daleth win these lands, and likely some of you might live through the slaughter and return one day to your homes. But let me tell you this. Those lands would rot and decay beneath your feet. However much time and effort you put in, the land will wither and die.'

'You think you're taxed unfairly now, and I would agree. But trust me when I say you would wither and die along with the land, slowly and surely. Your young men would be taken to serve in Daleth's army as he continues his conquest across every kingdom from here to the unknown. Your young women would be taken to serve the army's pleasures.'

'Everywhere he will leave a wasteland.

'He is endless darkness beyond which there's no light, and one day, if he wins this war, there'll be no one left to oppose him, and this world will die. Eventually, he'll be the last man alive, until finally, he consumes himself.'

'My gift, my own power may be lost to me, but whilst I have breath, I will fight for you because I am one of you. I will help provide for you because I care for you. I might one day be the queen of these lands if we live through this war, but I'll be one who is honest, who cares, who loves and who will always share. I know that might not be the Freestates way, but that is my way!'

'So what are we to do?' several people called.

'Those of you who have left family behind should leave tonight,' Maya answered without hesitation. 'Go get them with as much haste as possible and any others you come across.'

'Return to Freeguard in full knowledge of why, not under a veil of deceit. Bring food, bring supplies, but leave everything else for speed is of the essence. The enemy will soon own these lands, and make no mistake, if you're discovered, you'll be cut down as Daleth's men will offer no clemency.'

'At Freeguard, the armies of the east will gather. From the Freestates, from the Eyre, from the Desert, and there you'll join them,

The End of Dreams

stand by them, stand by me. This war isn't just for our lives, but for the lives of our children, and our children's children. Together, we must win this war.'

As she spoke, her eyes glowed, and her gift, which had been dormant, showed itself, albeit briefly. The grass around her feet grew, and flowers appeared. Everyone fell to their knees in awe as they gazed at the light emanating from her body.

Yet it disappeared almost as quickly as it had come and again Maya found it like a distant whisper in her mind, and however hard she tried to hear it again, it wasn't loud enough.

People started approaching her, mostly men, but some were women who'd already travelled with their husbands, and they asked for her blessing.

'I am no priestess,' Maya protested, but until she laid her hand upon them, they wouldn't let her be. So she did as they asked.

'Is it true?' one old woman asked loudly. 'You're truly from the lands of the Witch-King?'

Others echoed the question.

'It's a long story,' Maya laughed, but people started sitting in a circle demanding she tell it.

The old woman came forward and put her hand on Maya's shoulder.

'Tell the story, start from the beginning and do not lie,' she said, smiling, showing her broken teeth.

Before she knew it, Maya found herself sitting upon a large tree trunk. She told those listening of her early years, of concealing her gift, and how its discovery led to her incarceration. She told of her rescue by a soldier who'd betrayed the Witch-King, the soldier who'd become her prince, the love of her life. Finally, she recounted how later to save his life, she'd been forced to agree to marry King Tristan and had left Taran to his fate, their hearts broken asunder.

She hadn't meant to be so honest, to tell the whole story to so many strangers, but it was as if there hadn't been a choice and she'd been compelled to do so. When she finished, the old lady waved at her before disappearing into the darkness.

There was a hushed silence followed by cries of dismay as people registered how the story had ended, and this time when they gathered around her, they gazed upon her with compassion and love.

'Don't worry, he'll come for you one day. There is more of this story still to be written by the fates!' Many told her similar things in various ways.

Maya's eyes filled with tears as many said their goodbyes, and she wished them the speed of the gods on their journey. Many took up their belongings and used the light of the stars to return west again, to find the loved ones they'd left behind.

Ferris leant in, his own eyes moist.

'Excuse me, my lady. We need to return. It's unlikely we'll be missed, but we tempt fate the longer we're here.'

Following Maya's nod, the soldiers gently and reverently separated her from the adoring throng, and they moved back toward the royal camp.

'Where did you learn to capture people's hearts and minds like that, or do I already know?' Ferris asked quietly as they walked.

Maya smiled in the darkness.

'You do know the answer to that, Ferris, for his stories captivated my soul from the moment I met him. I learned from my beloved Taran.'

She was glad it was dark then, for tears streamed down her face as she remembered him.

Was he alive, or was he dead or dying? Did he still think of her, or had his love gone as cold as a winter's morning?

'I'll try to find you, my love,' she whispered, but she knew she could no more spirit travel than grow wings and fly.

The tears flowed harder now, and whereas once upon a time they had healed the land upon which they fell, they now simply moistened the earth like rain.

***

Chapter IV

Taran sat astride his horse, looking back at Freemantle.

The city shone like a jewel on the plain, yet that dazzling brightness hid a pestilence he was glad to leave behind.

After putting Humphrey and his men to the sword, they'd gone in search of Yana. By the time they found her, she'd already cut a man's throat who'd tried to force himself upon her, and together they'd secured the enormous household. Once the entrances were barricaded, they'd felt safe enough to eat, sleep, and tend to their wounds and those of their mounts, which they'd recovered and moved into the vast gardens.

Yana had worked tirelessly, having obtained healing salves handed over by the remainder of the inhabitants, terror shining brightly in their eyes.

Now, as Taran cast his gaze over the soldiers moving past, his lips pursed grimly in satisfaction.

True, they were all wounded, bound tightly in bandages, but they were clean once again, as were their dressings. Even the horses seemed brighter for the two short days of rest they'd enjoyed.

Taran reached up to idly scratch the bandage covering half his face. He'd never look quite so handsome again, that was for sure. It covered a large burn on his cheek that had badly blistered the skin, and it would be scarred and twisted when healed.

'Are you all right, son?' Rakan asked, sitting astride a horse alongside.

Taran turned his attention away from the city.

'I'll be able to pass for one of Daleth's soldiers again soon with my new scars. Just like the old days!'

Rakan's laugh was half-hearted, and his eyes were sorrowful.

As the soldiers rode past, Taran spoke a few words to each, encouraging them, jibing a little to keep them sharp. As much as they needed him, they all needed one another to survive.

'What were you looking for?' Rakan probed. 'The sooner we're off the brow of this hill, the better, for we're too easily seen.'

Taran nodded.

'You're right. I was curious to see if any of the city folk would come to their senses and follow us.'

Rakan's laugh barked out.

'They'll die clutching their silver and gold and hold on to it with their last gasping breath. You warned them enough of what fate will befall them. My main concern is whether they'll point the lancers in our direction before they're put to the sword, ensuring they're swiftly on our trail.'

Taran's frown deepened.

'That's a good point. Let's get some distance between us and those vermin.' He dug his heels into the horse's flanks and cantered past his men, who picked up the pace to follow.

They rode hard the whole day, alternately pushing the horses and then letting them walk and recover. Shadows had stretched long on the ground as the sun dipped slowly toward the horizon, when they spotted a large farmstead. Around twenty people were scattered over the fields finishing their day's labour, and everywhere was a hive of activity.

'I can't see any weapons,' Rakan observed. 'I think they're actually the farmers who own this place.'

Taran nodded, and they rode down the hill.

As they approached, three men walked out toward them.

Taran raised his hand, and the troops behind stopped. He signalled to Rakan and then to Yana.

'They'll trust us more with a female face amongst us,' he explained.

The smile that had started to lighten Yana's face disappeared.

Having dismounted, the three of them strode forward. The farmers extended their hands in wary greeting, and everyone clasped wrists, the atmosphere relaxing.

The older man, white-bearded but still strong-looking, introduced himself.

'My name's Zachard. These are my two sons, and this is my farm,' he said, sweeping his arm behind him.

He looked closely at Taran and Rakan, then peered past at the soldiers behind.

'What in the name of the earth goddess happened? You look like you've been in a terrible fight. Was it a band of brigands?'

Rakan's laughter rolled out.

Zachard frowned.

'Did I say something funny?' he asked, looking a little affronted at what he perceived to be mockery.

Rakan shook his head and smiled in apology.

'I'm not laughing at you, just at the biggest understatement I've ever heard in my life. In some ways, you're right. We did have a terrible fight, only there were over one hundred thousand brigands, so I'm not sure *band* quite does the number justice.'

Both Taran and Yana laughed along, with Zachard and his sons joining in too.

Zachard's questioning gaze suddenly saw through the laughter, and he put his hands on his sons' arms, quietening them.

'You're not joking? he asked in disbelief.

'No,' Taran said flatly. 'Far from it. We're all that's left of the western garrison that fought against Daleth and his army. They're not far behind us, so why on earth are you still here bringing in crops when a thousand enemy lancers could ride over yonder hill any day now?'

The three men looked shocked.

'There's trickery here,' the eldest son said. 'Only two weeks ago, we were told by a royal emissary of the king's betrothal and promised coin to attend. We held a vote, but all decided to stay for harvest, otherwise the year's crop would've been lost. How could the king hold such a ceremony at a time of war? It makes no sense, and one of the stories is a lie!'

Taran stepped closer, anger bright in his eyes, and Zachard and his sons stepped back, suddenly afraid of the battle-scarred soldier's glare.

'Look at me!' Taran commanded. 'If you don't believe what you hear, believe what you see. Look at my men. They're all that's left of fifteen hundred soldiers who stood and fought against Daleth while the king turned and fled.'

'Excuse me for a moment,' Zachard murmured, warily eyeing Taran, and stepped away to discuss with his sons.

'Relax,' Rakan said quietly, placing his hand on Taran's shoulder. 'He meant no offence in questioning what's just been revealed to them.'

Taran nodded despite the amulet keeping his anger roused at being distrusted. He had to fight to stop himself from drawing his sword to answer this small insult. At times the amulet just deadened his emotions, and at times like this, all he wanted to do was spill blood.

Zachard turned back to Taran.

'Forgive my son's earlier words. He meant no harm or disrespect. It's just a shock to learn that if we stay here, we die, and yet everything we have is here.'

Yana had been following the conversation. She couldn't believe they were wasting time here with meaningless peasants, but saw an opportunity to be the person Taran might want her to be.

'No,' she said. 'Your lives are everything, the lives of your sons and the workers in those fields. This land will go nowhere if you leave it now. Yes, your crops will go unharvested, but the land will not be stained with your blood. Should we win this war, it will be yours to reclaim, but to reclaim it, you'll need to help fight for it. The lies you were told, enticing you to come to Freeguard for a betrothal ceremony, were, in fact, a means to conscript you into military service.'

Taran's face betrayed his surprise at her words as his eyes searched her face, seeing nothing but sincerity.

'That might explain why it was just the men who were promised coin if we attended,' the youngest son muttered.

Zachard looked at the darkening sky and then to the men sitting patiently behind Taran in their saddles.

'If we're in as much danger as you say, then you're all welcome to stay the night. I'd ask that you tell us everything over this evening's meal, so we can all make an informed decision on what to do on the morrow.'

Taran nodded.

'We accept, and my men and I will respect your wishes on where to sleep.'

Rakan turned toward the soldiers behind and beckoned them forward. As he did so, he leant in close to Taran.

'After what happened at Freemantle, we let them drink the wine first,' he said softly.

Taran's cold eyes met his father's.

'Indeed we do. We trust no one who isn't one of us, and if there's any sign of duplicity, we kill them all. Now let's go get some food.'

***

Tristan was in a rage. He couldn't remember the last time he'd been so angry.

On the best of days, there was nothing to be happy about, and he felt like a blind man stumbling along, being pushed from all sides by an ungrateful and unforgiving crowd.

Every year of his life, bar this last one, had been privileged. He was from a noble family, educated to the highest levels, trained to accrue wealth from an early age and, most of all, he'd learned how to enjoy it to an exquisite degree.

He hadn't expected his kingship to be an entirely smooth passage, for, in the land of the greedy, everyone sought what others had, envy was rife, and anyone of breeding desired to be king.

The nobles and merchants of the other Freestates cities often connived against him, but it was all part of the bigger game. It was a game he played well with a pair of loaded dice. Who had more wealth than the king to bribe, obtain intelligence on his rivals, thwart their plans, and revel in their fall from grace?

He'd played the game of greed so well, for so long, that he'd felt nigh on untouchable.

But this was a different game.

This was a game of war.

Here there were few subtleties that he could understand, and he was lost, relying on others with equally little knowledge. He was unprepared and desperate. Worst of all, he'd been fooled.

This is what hurt the most. He'd been fooled by Daleth, fooled by Anthain and now by Maya.

He'd known she was a woman of will and had no experience of the subtleties of the royal court, or her place within it. But this, her latest action, was inexcusable. As he sat there awaiting her arrival with Galain standing at his shoulder and a few minor nobles from Freemantle, he pondered on what to do, what example to set.

She was still valuable in many ways despite her gift diminishing, which he'd come to accept as true. Her own belief, and he was sure it was well placed, was that her power was linked to her feeling of wellbeing.

Once she saw the comfort and privilege of being his queen, her happiness and value would increase exponentially.

Still, that was a long way away, and her actions had jeopardised his plans, so she'd feel his anger now and had better show unbridled contrition.

The flap to his tent was pulled back, and Maya swept in.

Immediately Tristan felt his self-control about to slip, for there was no remorse in her features whatsoever, yet before he could explode, she spoke.

'My king. I'm glad to have this audience, for we've a lot to talk about,' Maya said, taking the initiative. Ferris had told her of Tristan's boiling anger, and she'd planned her address already.

'As you know, I spoke to the countryfolk last night,' she continued, unable to refer to them as peasants. 'To further your goal of raising a civilian levy, I spoke to them of the importance of fighting against Daleth. Furthermore, to ensure they did this with an iron resolve, I advised them to seek their families' support, whom they'd mistakenly left behind.'

Maya raised her hand as Tristan was about to speak, and he was so shocked he didn't utter a word.

'The army at your disposal,' Maya continued, 'will eventually number in the region of forty thousand men should you raise enough of a civilian levy. I know there's so much on your mind that you might, just might have overlooked the logistical need for all of them to be fed. That's one hundred and twenty thousand meals a day, and they'll need to be cared for when injured. Now, where would the cost of labour for all of this come from? I've simply ensured it's not from you or the noble classes, but predominantly from the civilians themselves.'

'So, that's why last night, I sent the majority of them on their way. They'll now return in all haste with their families to assist in this great undertaking of fighting Daleth and keeping you on your throne.'

As she finished, she bowed her head subtly.

Tristan sat there, open-mouthed. He was still angry, but damn if what she said didn't make sense as well. He'd completely overlooked everything she'd pointed out, as had all the advisors he'd surrounded himself with.

Needing a vent for his anger, he looked around the tent.

'So why in the nine hells did no one else think of this?' he shouted. 'From now on, we bring everyone we come across.'

'We also need to take their food and livestock with us too. Not only do we need to feed our army, but we also don't want to be feeding Daleth's horde,' Maya added.

'As she says!' Tristan shouted. 'Send more riders out. I want the whole damned countryside coming to Freeguard immediately.'

'Your riders need to tell them the truth, the whole truth about Daleth, his armies, and the plague on the land he'll bring with him. You will still promise them coin when they come, the same coin you pay to your soldiers.'

Tristan spluttered in rage.

'You push too far,' he snarled.

Maya held his gaze.

'All right, dammit. Have the riders tell them the truth, but tell them they'll receive half the pay of a regular soldier,' Tristan growled, then looked at Galain. 'Well?'

'Well, what?' Galain asked, his eyes wide.

'Well, what are you waiting for,' Tristan shouted. 'Why are you still standing here? Get out of this tent, all of you! Get out and make this happen, and you …' He scowled at Maya. 'From hereon you attend my meetings and don't go behind my back. Do you hear me?'

Maya smiled, utterly indifferent to his rage, and turned, leaving the tent as Tristan started throwing things around in anger.

***

Taran woke early before the sunrise to the smell of hay. Yana lay next to him, a little closer than usual, and annoyed he went to push her away, but stopped himself.

The knowledge of what the amulet did to his senses sometimes allowed him to fight its influence, but not always. He'd come close to drawing blood last night simply because Zachard's son had cast doubt on his word.

'Let's walk,' Rakan whispered, interrupting his thoughts, pointing outside in the semi-darkness.

Taran followed carefully, for most of the men remained asleep, exhausted by recent events. However, lookouts had still been rotated throughout the night and woe betide any who Rakan found neglecting their post.

The air was cool but heavy with the smell of manure as they walked from the barn. Everything was quiet, as though by some unspoken accord nature held its breath. Soon though, everyone would be rising, with Zachard and all those at the farmstead intending to depart shortly after first light.

'What's on your mind?' Rakan asked, as they moved to sit on a fence, facing the brightening horizon.

'We need to get word to Tristan,' Taran almost spat the name, 'of the fall of the fortress. More important is to let him know of the injuries that Daleth suffered. It's unlikely he'll recover from those wounds until the New Year. If so, I've a feeling he'll not seek a full-on battle till then.'

Rakan scratched his head and nodded.

'I agree. But the way you say it makes me think there's something else on your mind.'

Taran met Rakan's gaze.

'There's so much hatred in my heart for Tristan. I know if I see him, I'll drive my sword through his belly, whatever the consequences. I need more time before I can set foot in the same city as him, let alone the same room. Last night, it became apparent that it's not just Zachard

The End of Dreams

and his family out here. There must be hundreds of others who haven't heard the call because they didn't know the truth and because this land is their life. They'll die on the very soil they've nurtured unless we take the time to warn them of the peril they face.'

Rakan smiled broadly, looking relieved.

'I'm glad your compassion is returning, I really am ...'

Taran's blank stare stopped him, as did his reply.

'This isn't about compassion. This is about having men strong enough to wield a sword or a spear in our army, to give us a chance to face Daleth and not get swept aside. If they die piecemeal out here, their deaths will mean nothing. If we have months to train them, whilst they won't be so skilled, they'll be more likely to cut pieces off of the enemy than each other.'

'I see,' Rakan muttered, concerned. 'So tell me, why do I get the feeling it will be me returning to Freeguard with this news whilst you wander the wilderness? Have you considered Maya in all of this? You could see her again and find out what was behind her leaving. You must feel the need to see her, son. I saw what you had. It was like nothing I could have ever believed possible.'

'Return with me,' he continued, grasping Taran's shoulder. 'I'll keep you apart from Tristan and stop you from doing anything rash. Let's reunite you with Maya and find a way to pry her apart from Tristan. Surely that's what your heart truly desires under the torment you're suffering?'

Taran's look was blank as he replied.

'If I hold anger toward Tristan, then my feelings toward Maya are abject indifference. She chose her path. A king over a prince!' He snorted at the last word. 'Power and wealth over poverty and love. She made the choice that almost everyone in this world would make. I don't blame her. I simply don't care for her anymore.'

Rakan was shocked.

'How have you changed so much?' he asked, looking into Taran's eyes as if he could find the truth there. 'The more I listen to you, and how quick to anger you've become, the more I see in you, the person I used to be.'

As he said this, his eyes opened wide.

'Nooo,' he said. 'Tell me you haven't?'

He reached out slowly, tugging at Taran's breastplate whilst Taran watched impassively. The dull glint of an amulet's chain confirmed Rakan's fears.

'Oh, Taran, my son. Why did you do this?'

'You know why!' Taran growled. 'I was losing my mind, and now, now nothing bothers me. I can think of Maya without wanting to break down in tears. I could even see her and not feel a thing. Things are much clearer now, I know what I have to do to achieve what needs to be done.'

'To kill Daleth and then kill Tristan,' Rakan sighed. 'I'd hoped maybe as time passed, you'd reconsider this goal. Now I see why it will never change. But beware, you might have lost your grief, but wearing that will make you lose your soul.'

Taran shrugged, utterly indifferent.

'It's an exchange I'm happy to make. Now enough of that. Today, you take half the soldiers and make haste to Tristan at Freeguard. Order all who you pass along the way to pack lightly and follow you. As an officer who served at the fortress, whom he personally knows, Tristan will listen to and believe your report.'

'I'll send some of the men due north to try and rally any families who've remained in their towns and villages and have them head to Freeguard. I'll sweep south for two weeks and do the same.'

'The fact we haven't seen more lancers makes me wonder if they've been cautioned on how far east they can ride. So, whilst we'll mostly travel at night just in case, I feel confident that we won't run into any large groups of the enemy.'

'But what if you do?' Rakan prompted.

'Then likely we'll fight, and we'll die.'

Taran shrugged as if it didn't matter.

'Then I better say my goodbyes now, just in case,' Rakan said, pulling Taran into an embrace. 'I love you, son. Take this extra time to heal, and try to take that damn thing off, for whilst your heart might be beating, you aren't living as long as it's around your neck.'

Taran chuckled, and for a moment, a genuine smile appeared.

'Just look after yourself, old man. I've a feeling Freeguard will be as dangerous a place as here with Daleth's men on the loose. Tristan will have been quite happy for us to have died at the fortress. I intend to continue to disappoint him.'

'Now, let's rouse the men,' he continued. 'There's work to be done before we leave.'

Together, they walked back to the barn, long shadows like the spirits of the dead, long on the ground behind them.

***

In the last two weeks since Maya and Tristan had arrived in Freeguard, they'd established residence within the city palace, a grandiose structure, almost as opulent as the one in Freemantle.

On arrival, Tristan had gleefully displaced the previous owner, the governing noble, Lord Duggan, who, despite his fury, had been forced to reside in one of his other properties across the central square.

He seemed as unhappy with Tristan's presence as Maya was, and she wondered if this common dislike could lead to an alliance. However, she didn't entertain the thought for long as the two men were cut from the same cloth and were as bad as each other.

Tristan now held court from an enormous audience chamber on the palace ground floor, and Maya could see from his satisfied look that he was enjoying himself immensely.

It took a while to understand where that happiness came from, as ultimately this would be a war they were unlikely to win. However, Tristan was living in the moment and enjoyed lording it over all the other nobles who normally kept well away from Freemantle and his direct rule. Now, due to circumstance, they were all in one city and Tristan revelled in his role as king.

What empowered him even further, and currently subdued any resistance to his rule, were the five thousand Eyre archers and twenty-five thousand desert warriors who'd made camp outside the city. With the leaders having pledged allegiance to the three nations' alliance, with Tristan at its head, he was an all-powerful monarch … for now.

Freeguard was a huge fortified city surrounded by worryingly low walls, which were not very thick, and had fallen into disrepair over the years. Soldiers were at work repairing them, but after witnessing what had happened at Tristan's Folly, they didn't make Maya confident that they'd keep Daleth's army at bay.

Maya had initially been invited to the daily meetings of nobles and merchants, which now included the king of the desert tribes, a man called Ostrom, and the Eyre captain, a formidable woman called Dafne.

The entire alliance now fell directly under Tristan's command, and he'd yet to decide who to pick as the overall military commander.

In total, including Freestates garrison soldiers from other towns and cities, there were thirty-five thousand trained fighting men, and whilst it seemed a vast number, it was insignificant compared to the Witch-King's army.

Tristan, Duggan, and most of the Freestates nobles all shared the same opinion. With the odds so heavily in favour of Daleth, they felt that fighting from behind the walls was the best way to balance the numbers.

Only Ostrom and Dafne raised their voices in favour of going to meet the enemy. Dafne suggested guerrilla warfare utilising her archers' best skills, whilst Ostrom wanted to battle shield-to-shield, for that was the way his men always fought. Their weapons and skills weren't for fighting from walls, rather they were for fighting in formation on the battlefield.

Today's disagreements were so vociferous that Maya had excused herself from the meeting as soon as she was able and now tried to find something that would make her incarceration somewhat more bearable.

As with Freemantle, the city populous was mostly nobility and wealthy merchants. Except for the numerous servants, the people of Freeguard were as unpleasant a bunch as Maya had ever had the displeasure of meeting. Even at this time of war, she could see vendors putting up food prices to take advantage of the new coin the soldiers brought with them when they came to the market.

It sickened her that they were determined to make a profit from those who'd protect them when Daleth arrived, in what, a few weeks to a month?

How they could possibly enjoy their ill-gotten gains in this short period was beyond her.

The End of Dreams

While the city itself held buildings of interesting design, and truly no expense had been spared in its grandeur, the city was too large to simply ride out of and enjoy the countryside and then return in time for dusk. Also, the surrounding countryside was now filled with the tents of the desert tribesman, the Eyre and countryfolk.

As of this moment, the population of Freeguard had not seen fit to offer any of them accommodation within the city limits. It would seem they would only be allowed to stay inside once they were required to defend the walls, and in all likelihood would be expected to sleep on them as well.

Fortunately, the palace had vast gardens to the rear.

They were surprisingly unkempt and overgrown, for it seemed Lord Duggan had been loath to spend money on a gardener throughout the whole year. Thus, with autumn imminent, they'd become wild and overgrown, which she much preferred to some of the manicured gardens she'd seen throughout the city.

So today she wandered slowly along its paths, ducking and swaying to avoid the reaching tendrils of the vines and the snagging thorns of the many rose bushes that grew with wild abandon.

She frequently stopped to smell the blooms, and the fragrance of some filled her with mixed emotions, for whilst they were heavenly, she wished to share them with Taran.

Where was he? How was he? Was he dead?

She couldn't bring herself to believe this was the case, so surely he must be hastening to Freeguard at this very moment.

Her spirits lifted, then crashed down again.

Would he be happy to see her? Was he planning to rescue her? What would happen when he encountered Tristan? The same tortured questions tumbled through her mind so fast that she sat down on a bench in the shade of a tree.

She breathed slowly, trying to clear her mind, when she heard footsteps. They were hesitant, and for a moment they seemed stealthy, but then she relaxed, for it was more that they were simply cautious. She stood and walked around the paths until she came across a man swathed in robes, and recognised him as King Ostrom's advisor.

'Hello,' Maya said, welcome for the distraction.

'Greetings, Lady Maya,' Ultric bowed to her. 'Have I disturbed you?'

'No, not at all,' she replied. 'I've found some tranquillity here. This garden is so beautiful, even more so, for it's unkempt and wild.'

She paused, suddenly self-conscious, for Ultric was blind, and here she was extolling its virtues that he'd never see.

Ultric smiled broadly.

'Indeed it is, and some of these roses are desert blooms which you can find around an oasis, and thus they remind me of home. They have such a heady perfume. Here, try this one.'

He reached and gently bent a stem downward.

Maya leant forward to try its scent.

'That's incredible,' she breathed. 'It's so strong I can almost taste it.'

Ultric laughed. It was genuine, and full of good humour.

'You could if you wish. The petals are edible, and we often use it in our food as a spice.'

Maya was a little puzzled.

'Forgive me ...' she started to ask.

'You want to know,' Ultric interrupted, 'how a blind man could reach out to grasp a rose, knowing what and where it is. I know, it surprises most people, but just like you, Maya, I have the gift of spirit travel. So I've flown these gardens, and my memory is such that I can see them in my mind even as we speak, which when the world is so dark for me, is very easy to do.'

'That's incredible,' Maya whispered, but Ultric wasn't finished.

'Would you believe,' he continued, 'that blindness has other benefits? My gift extends to my other senses being finely attuned. My skin is so sensitive that I can feel the beating of a butterfly's wings near that rose. I can taste on the wind the scent of every bloom in this garden. Last and perhaps my most finely tuned sense is my hearing. I can hear the rustle of that insect running past our feet.'

He nodded downward to indicate a small beetle scurrying along.

'What might surprise you the most, is that I can hear in your voice the undertone of utter sadness that you do so well to hide, but which threatens to bring you to tears at the strangest of times.'

Maya gasped.

'I think you presume too much, Master Ultric. There's no sadness in my voice.'

Ultric shook his head.

'I may not be your friend, Maya, although maybe one day if we live long enough we might become such, but I can assure you I'm no enemy. Nor do I seek to gain an advantage over you. You just lied in your denial. I heard the sadness in your voice when you smelt the rose and told me how incredible you found it, because for whatever reason, at that moment, you felt both wonder and incredible sadness. Now, tell me I am wrong.'

'You're wrong,' Maya responded hesitantly.

Ultric laughed.

'This could go on for a while.'

Maya laughed with him.

'It's amazing,' Ultric observed. 'Even in happiness, when you laugh, there's pain. You may not realise it, although I'm sure you do most of the time, but it's there. Not in every word you speak, but strangely in those where I'd least expect to hear it. Who laughs and is also sad? You're very intriguing.'

Maya sighed and smiled half-heartedly.

'One day, I might share with you the story of how my pain came to be, but not until I know you better. When I do tell you, it will be nothing but the whole truth.'

'So what lifts your heart?' Ultric rubbed his jaw, pondering. 'Gardens obviously ... which would lead me to assume all nature does. Your gift of spirit travel and healing naturally. But what else?'

Maya paused, wondering whether to share what was on her mind, but saw no reason not to.

'My gift has deserted me of late. I can no longer spirit travel, and as for my gift of healing ... that's also lost to me,' she said honestly. 'But before any of that mattered, it was helping my family and people. I've always helped provide. I was a hunter in my settlement, and yes, I came to love the forests and all of nature.'

Ultric stood silent for a moment in contemplation.

'I've never heard of a gift that was lost and not found again. Be patient, for I'm sure it's but a matter of time. As for you helping people, why am I not surprised? You have a pure soul, and in this city, yours might be one of the very few to be seen as such.'

'Now, knowing what makes you happy and embracing it, is perhaps the first step toward reclaiming your gift. Why not try helping those you care about? Try and help the people, the countryfolk, or as the high browed like to call them, the peasants. They need help, and I'm sure you're in a position to help provide it.'

Maya's face lit up.

'Yes, it would be good to have something useful to do, although I could walk around gardens such as these all day and be happy.'

Ultric laughed softly.

'No, you couldn't,' he said. 'Not yet, but maybe one day you could.'

Maya laughed along with him.

'I fear my hunger is demanding an end to our conversation,' she said, as her stomach rumbled. 'Will you be alright here?'

Ultric raised his hands, turning around.

'I can assure you I see these paths almost as well as you. Now, after you've eaten, find a way to do that which calls to you.'

As Maya's soft steps grew fainter, Ultric stood amongst the roses, contemplating.

Their meeting hadn't been a coincidence. No one took much notice of a blind man, and he'd been walking the city the last few days. A blind man was always disregarded, but he always learned so much more by listening than seeing.

Much of what he'd learned simply confirmed what he and Ostrom already knew, that Tristan and the Freestates folk were only interested in wealth, self-preservation and were selfish and greedy.

Importantly though, he'd discerned there was no deceit in the tale of Sancen's death, which was the main reason Ostrom and his army were here, nor about Daleth's power and intentions. So, even if Tristan himself was unworthy, the cause of trying to avenge the death of the king's son was a noble one, and worth dying for. There was nothing the desert people loved more than to die against impossible odds for a noble cause.

Yet the most interesting thing he'd heard was not from the lips of the nobles, the king, or any of the Eyre, it was from the countryfolk he'd not even intended to visit. Had it not been for a tiny child taking his hand he'd never have gone to their camp, but she was so engaging with her chirruping voice as she clumsily repeated a story her parents had told her, that he accompanied her the entire way.

Her story had piqued his interest, and he'd spent a whole day listening intently to others, and throughout, further whispers and detail had reached his ears, and he'd been enthralled.

Maya had said she'd tell him her story once she got to know him better, but it was a story he, in truth, already knew the most of.

The camp's talk was how a gifted old woman with the power to invoke the truth had coerced Maya into revealing her true self, expecting to find a web of deceit as often practised by the nobles of the Freestates. Instead, Maya had told them a story that had kindled the imagination of all those who'd heard it.

Ultric smiled to himself as he walked slowly down the path back toward the palace, his feet carefully placed on the uneven path.

What he'd enjoyed the most about the story was how it evolved even as he listened. Likely now it had changed even more, but the reaction of Tristan, if it ever reached his ears, would be interesting to observe.

The countryfolk spoke of Maya, and how her one true love would one day come for her, and how no one, not the Witch-King or their own king, would be able to stand in his way.

In a world that was constantly dark, it was the stories of those around him that brought it to life, filled it with shades of grey, and yet this story had the potential to show him the colours of the rainbow.

***

Chapter V

Taran held his finger to his lips.

'Quiet,' he mouthed, and the soldier who'd cursed while tripping over a root held up his hand in mute apology, looking suitably abashed.

Horses snickered softly on their picket line, and Taran wished he could warn them to be quiet as well.

Noise travelled easily in the early hours as night gave up its hold on the land. Today however, the darkness appeared more reluctant than usual to let go.

A thick fog hung heavy on the air with not a breeze to shift it, and as Taran looked around, a cold sense of foreboding seeped into his bones.

The pre-dawn light barely permeated the woodland in which they'd camped, and the men sat or moved amongst the trees like wraiths. Some ate, whilst others relieved themselves amongst the bushes, and conversation was minimal. The men on guard duty returned to their gear to get it ready. It would soon be time to move on.

Taran winced a little as Yana tended his wounds. The salve on his burnt face stung briefly as she bandaged it again.

'It's been five days since we split from Rakan and the others,' she said in a hushed voice, as she tied the bandage off. 'When are we going to head east to Freeguard?'

Taran nodded his thanks before answering.

'Soon. Today or tomorrow maybe. We'll check out the local villages those farmers pointed us to, then it'll be time to turn east.'

Yana was about to say something when a horse whinnied, then the call was taken up by others, but this time with a hint of alarm.

The End of Dreams

Taran's head whipped up to see dozens of figures swirling through the mist.

'To arms!' he shouted, dragging his swords free from their scabbards. 'Form on me. On me!'

Screams of mortal pain echoed as groups of enemy lancers on foot suddenly appeared, as if from another plane of existence.

Soldiers hurried to Taran's side. Some had shields, others only had their swords. There were just fourteen of them, the others lying dead on the cold ground.

They formed a circle, facing outwards, protecting each other's backs. Yana stood behind them, sword drawn, ready to fight. Yet quiet descended, the lancers disappearing back into the fog as quietly as they came.

Heartbeats slowed, shields lowered, and hopes began to rise until a thrown lance suddenly cut through the mist and buried itself in a swordsman's chest. While his screams split the air, as if by this painful command, dozens of lancers materialised from the fog, mere strides away. They carried curved sabres and shields, their eyes bright with bloodlust.

Another of Taran's men fell in the first moments, leaving but a dozen to stand against the attackers. As the lancers closed in from all sides, Taran's men fought ferociously, Yana sheltering behind them.

As survivors of Tristan's Folly, they were all extremely skilled soldiers, but they were outnumbered, exhausted, and carrying wounds. After a minute's intense combat, a command rang out from the fog, and the lancers withdrew, leaving three of their number dead upon the ground.

Silence descended once more, but only briefly, and again the enemy closed in before shortly withdrawing. This time the bodies of a further five lancers were joined by two more of Taran's men.

Taran knew the longer the battle lasted, the less chance they'd have to survive. The lancers' tactic was working well, but maybe he could turn it against them while the fog remained.

He turned to Yana and his men as the enemy pulled back after another probing attack.

'Hold together,' he ordered. 'I'll be back.'

Quickly he stooped and grabbed a plumed helm from a dead lancer to replace his own and darted into the fog before the next wave of enemies appeared.

The amulet roused his bloodlust. He wanted to charge, screaming his battle cry as he ended lives, delivering retribution. But he pushed back against its influence, needing to act without the rashness of anger.

He crouched, then amongst the darkness, the jingle of armour and a crackle of twigs gave away some approaching lancers. He saw a group of shapes to his right and darted amongst them, slashing and hacking before spinning away in the next instant, leaving men screaming in his wake.

He trod softly, circling, and six more lancers began to appear.

'Behind you!' he shouted, and the men spun at his warning, seeing his plumed helm, believing him to be one of them. He fell upon them as they turned their backs, an easy slaughter.

He continued this tactic until he heard Yana desperately shouting his name. Other groups of lancers were attacking them once more. He sprinted back toward the sound of battle, shouting orders to imaginary men, forcing some of the attackers to turn, believing a larger force had come upon them.

His swordsmen and Yana fought desperately, but instead of joining their thinning ranks, Taran darted out from the fog, striking swiftly, before withdrawing. His myriad of attacks from different directions wreaked havoc on the lancers' morale, and they broke off the assault, retreating swiftly through the fog.

He moved like a vengeful spirit after them, and soon the retreat turned into a rout. He didn't stop chasing until they all lay dead, except for one.

As Taran ran into the lancers' empty camp, there on the other side, he could see a captain frantically saddling his horse. Had he just carried on running, or leapt on bareback, he would likely have got away.

Taran didn't say a word. Instead, he stalked over, and the captain froze, suddenly aware of his presence. The lancer's shoulders sagged, and he turned, drawing his sabre, hatred mixed with fear in his eyes.

Four times their weapons crossed, and each time Taran's swift blade left a deep cut on the captain's arms. Knowing how outmatched

The End of Dreams

he was, the captain backed away, but tripped, falling heavily onto his back, and the sabre skidded away from his weakened grasp.

Taran moved to stand over him.

The captain looked up, blood running into his eyes, making him squint through a red haze. Above him, through the swirling fog, he saw death, dripping in blood like a daemon from the depths of hell, and he blanched in horror.

'Kill me quickly,' he begged, blinking furiously, trying to clear his vision.

Taran paused. The desire to torture this man and have him scream in agony coursed through him. As he tried to fight against it, an idea formed in his mind. He smiled, teeth bright against the blackened skin of his face beneath the helm.

'You can live on one condition,' Taran offered.

The captain nodded frantically, saying nothing.

'You just have to give Daleth a message for me.'

'If you let me live, then I swear I will,' the captain promised, hope blossoming in his eyes.

Taran smiled maliciously.

'Let me spell it out for you!' He twisted the injured captain roughly around, then cut away the man's cuirass and shirt.

'You'd better stay still, as you wouldn't want me to have to start this again!' With a dark laugh, Taran started carving his bloody message into the screaming captain's back with his dagger.

When he'd finished, the captain was still alive but had passed out from the pain. Taran left him and followed the trail of corpses back to his camp.

Yana and five men were still alive, but two of the five soldiers had terrible wounds and moaned in pain as Taran knelt next to them. He looked to Yana for direction, and she shook her head slowly.

'I cannot save you,' he told them as the others looked down. 'We can leave you food and water, but it'll only extend the pain you suffer. Or, I can take your pain away?'

First one man and then the other nodded, their eyes fearful.

'Then sleep, my brothers,' Taran said softly, plunging his dagger into the heart of first one, then the other so quickly that they didn't even register the blow.

'What now?' Yana asked fearfully, and the three remaining soldiers waited anxiously for Taran's response.

'We'll head east, toward Freeguard,' Taran assured them. 'Not everyone I want to kill wears an enemy uniform.'

Yana smiled to herself, for she knew exactly who he meant, and if Taran killed Tristan, then she'd only need to take care of Maya.

***

Rakan and fifteen survivors from Tristan's Folly reined in, looking at the spectacle before them. There in the distance lay the great city of Freeguard, and as they beheld it from atop a small rise, all around it was a bustle of activity.

One of the men turned to Rakan.

'We've ridden this far and not once been challenged. You'd think they'd have watchers out to forewarn them of enemy scouts.'

Rakan's face was grim.

'The fact you've pointed that out shows me that you've a better understanding of the requirements of war than anyone down there,' Rakan growled. 'Maybe we should get you a promotion.'

The man laughed.

'I've learned it from you, Captain. There's not been a night when you haven't had us up watching, and I remember the first night that the enemy lancers rode by. We'd all have been dead by now, if not for you.'

The other men all nodded and voiced their agreement.

Rakan's smile was genuinely warm as he looked around at them.

'We've come a long way together and learned a lot on this journey. We're all sword brothers now, for we've lived through the darkest of times, and found in each other someone we can rely on. We've bled for one another, we've killed for one another, and in days to come we'll be called upon to do the same, and I know I can count on every one of you.'

'When will Commander Taran re-join us?' voiced another.

Rakan's smile slipped a little.

'He promised he'd be a week at most. I know you want him back, and you know I do too.'

The End of Dreams

'Aye,' all the soldiers agreed.

'It might look like a lot of men down there,' Rakan observed, 'yet we know Daleth still has a horde numbering ninety-odd thousand trained troops. We'll need every arm that can wield a sword, even if it's only been used to swing a scythe. That's the reason Taran stayed behind, to round up more of the people to help defend our noble king and his realm.'

Many of the men laughed at the last, and Rakan laughed along with them.

'Let's not forget what we truly fight for,' he continued. 'I remember Maya's speech as we stood on the walls of Tristan's Folly about us being gifted with wives or lovers, children or mothers, fathers and friends. We fight for those that we love, not for a king or a nation.'

The men all nodded, remembering that day, before Rakan interrupted their reverie.

'It's time for us to join those who'll be our new brothers in arms and prepare them for what's to come, for none know more than we.'

He urged his horse forward, and the soldiers followed. They cantered down the main road toward Freeguard, passing through an encampment of desert soldiers, their armour covered by billowing robes.

Finally, they approached the open city gates where sentries stood overlooking the flow of people in an out of the western entrance.

The crowd parted as Rakan and his mounted soldiers approached. They rode under the gatehouse and dismounted in a courtyard off to the side, where some low barracks buildings stood back from the road. Rakan laughed as he and his men stood there. They all looked in a terrible state, bandaged, battered, and singed. Whilst they wore Freestates armour, they could have been anyone.

He looked about and strode over to a bored-looking sergeant.

'Soldier. Do you know who I am?' Rakan asked in a growl.

The man turned, looking Rakan up and down, noticing he wore plain Freestates armour. But recognising a voice used to giving orders he was unsure how to address him.

'No, I don't ...?'

'Captain,' Rakan filled in the blank. 'Now tell me, do you know any of my men?' and he nodded to where they stood.

'No, I don't,' repeated the sergeant, somewhat confused at the line of questioning, his eyes flickering across the filthy soldiers behind.

'What if I told you we're not Freestates soldiers, but spies for Daleth sent here to assassinate the king?' Rakan asked.

The sergeant gulped, the colour draining from his face.

'But you're not. Are you, Captain?' he asked, a pleading look appearing on his face.

Rakan smiled cruelly.

'Best you hope not, man. Best you hope not! But maybe if a group of soldiers just rides in through your gate in future, you might consider challenging them!'

'But we have many new soldiers passing through here every day,' complained the sergeant. 'I've no idea who might be one of Daleth's troops!'

Rakan sighed.

'You see the desert men?' he asked, pointing out one. 'Do you notice anything different? What about that man from the Eyre, does he stand out in any way?'

The sergeant looked confused, and Rakan was about to vent his anger on him until he realised it wasn't this man's fault at all.

'The Eyre are green-skinned, and the desert tribesmen are black-skinned. Therefore, you don't need to worry about any of them being Daleth's men. So, don't look to challenge all who pass through, just those who have scars on their faces and a dead look in their eyes.'

The sergeant saluted in acknowledgement.

'Now, where are the city stables and the other barracks?' Rakan asked and listened as the sergeant gave directions in response.

'My final question is, where's the king staying?' Rakan asked, and again the soldier told him. 'Now,' frowned Rakan. 'If I really was here to kill the king, that's the type of question you should listen out for, don't you think?'

The sergeant looked as if he would faint as Rakan's men laughed behind him and they turned away, leading their horses into Freeguard.

It wasn't too unlike Freemantle. It was a city built for trade, and thus along its main streets leading toward the palace, the wealthiest had their palatial homes. Intermittently, along each route, markets sold expensive trade goods as well as food.

The End of Dreams

Rakan stopped at a stall which sold fresh fruit. He picked up a bunch of blood berries.

'How much?' he asked.

'One silver piece,' the trader responded, holding out his hand.

Rakan recoiled in shock at the outrageous price.

'Let me ask you again,' he said, lowering his voice. 'How much for these blood berries ... and if you ask a price, that is, shall we say, *exploitive*, your blood will be adding to the taste.'

One look at Rakan's hard face made the trader swallow hard.

'For one of our finest soldiers, that will be a copper,' he said, voice quavering.

Rakan nodded approvingly.

'Better. That's an honest price. Now, if I hear that you're overcharging any of my men who come by, you and I will have a little chat, won't we?'

'You're not the judge around here!' the man exclaimed in indignation.

Rakan smiled wickedly.

'You're right,' he said. 'I'm not the judge, but be sure of one thing. I am the executioner!' He turned away, leaving the man shaking behind him.

He followed the directions given to him by the sergeant, and shortly he and the other soldiers came to the central city stables. Like every other structure, the facade was white-clad stone and ridiculously opulent for such a functional building.

Rakan and his men led their horses in and were met by the elegant stable master, a tall man in white robes who arched his eyebrows in indignation at their appearance.

'We want to stable our horses,' Rakan explained the obvious. 'They're in real need of assistance, many are injured, but they're good mounts, and I'd like them looked after properly.'

'I think you're in entirely the wrong place,' the stable master replied haughtily. 'This stable is for the horses of the upper class, not the class you wish to put yourself in. Nor could you come close to affording my rates!' He started to turn away, waving his hand dismissively.

As he did so, he found his hand trapped in a vice-like grip and cried out in a high-pitched voice. One of the stable boys fled the entrance, and the stable master pulled a wicked smile.

'You'd best let go of my hand, you filth, before it's too late!'

He yelped even harder as Rakan squeezed some more and the man fell to his knees, tears in his eyes.

'What is it with this plague of a city?' Rakan snarled. 'All I want is to stable our horses. I ask you politely, and you answer with an insult when these horses require help. This is a stable, those are horses. We are soldiers of the king's army, and soon we'll be killing, bleeding, and likely dying to keep your skin intact. I think you should reconsider your position and offer to stable these horses for free, damn you. Have you any idea of the storm that'll hit when Daleth arrives?'

'Never mind Daleth,' laughed the man weakly, 'I think you should be worrying about meeting a friend of mine.'

He nodded toward the stable entrance, where a man in jewelled armour stood with a dozen men at his back.

Rakan put his hands on his hips, laughing.

'Are you serious? So, who might you be?'

The man looked disdainfully at Rakan.

'I'm Captain Tolgarth of the city watch, and you're definitely in the wrong place, my man. I think a night or two in the cells for laying a hand on a highly regarded citizen of Freeguard will show you the error of your ways.'

Rakan shook his head.

'If you try to arrest me, Captain, I'll show you the error of your ways, be sure of that! This fool,' he said, gesturing to the stable master behind him, 'refused to look after our mounts, which, as you can see, are in dire need of help. In the days to come, we'll need these horses to fight in the war. So, I suggest you tell this man to look after our horses, and then we'll be on our way.'

Tolgarth shook his head, sneering.

'I don't know who you are or where you're from, but from the look of you, I'd say you live in a dung heap. I'm not even sure that armour you wear even belongs to you, for you look like a peasant. Now hand over your weapons before it's too late!'

Rakan shook his head slowly and laughed.

The End of Dreams

'I thought I'd hate this place,' he said, 'but I'm already starting to like it. I've not even been here a morning, and already I'm going to have myself a good fight.'

Rakan stepped away from his men.

'As it happens, Captain, I'm equal to you in rank, so I challenge you to a friendly fight to settle this impasse. Just you and me. We can leave our men out of it because I don't want to see the blood of so many unsettle the horses here. What do you say, fists or a duel with swords if you have the stomach for it? Of course, you could apologise, tell this man to stable our horses, and we can forget it altogether. What do you say?'

Tolgarth's smile was condescending. He eyed Rakan like a cat would a mouse.

'You've no idea who I am, do you?' he sneered. 'I'll cut you into pieces and feed your carcass to the dogs! Weapons it is.'

Rakan stretched his arms. His burns weren't healed, his muscles were sore and stiff from so many days in the saddle, and yet he suddenly felt alive.

'What rules do you want to fight by?' Tolgarth asked, stepping confidently forward.

Rakan butted him hard in the face, breaking Tolgarth's nose, spilling him to the floor.

'My rules,' Rakan snarled as he knelt across the fallen man's shoulders and punched him hard several times in the face.

Rakan stood and drew his sword, placing the tip against Tolgarth's neck.

'You told me you'd cut me to pieces and feed me to the dogs. So what should I do to you?' he asked, looking into the petrified eyes of the bloodied captain at his feet.

'I have a suggestion,' Rakan offered before the man could answer. 'We call this a draw, and you tell your friend to stable our horses. Is that a yes?' and he pushed slightly with his sword, drawing blood.

Tolgarth nodded weakly.

Rakan turned to the ashen faced stable master.

'I'll return here tomorrow and every day thereafter to check on our mounts. If one dies, or I find any of your friends waiting for me, I'll slit your stomach open and strangle you with your guts!'

Rakan turned back to Tolgarth who had his hands pressed to his face, trying to stem the flow of blood from his nose and eyebrows as his soldiers helped him to stand.

'Your captain tripped and had a bad fall. We all saw that. It was a good thing we were here to help,' he lied suggestively.

Tolgarth nodded weakly.

'Let's go,' Rakan said to his men, and they left the stables behind. 'Now let's find you a place to sleep. Then I'll have myself an audience with our lord and master, King Tristan. I have a feeling today will get even more interesting.' He chuckled, rubbing his knuckles. 'Let's see how many more skulls I need to split.'

His men laughed as they followed him.

Life around Rakan was never dull.

***

'You're going ahead with it?' Galain asked in surprise.

'Of course, I'm going ahead with it,' Tristan responded, annoyed. 'The value of that woman is beyond compare, and she's not too hard on the eye either.'

They sat in the audience chamber at the start of the day, having just broken fast. Soon, King Ostrom would arrive with Dafne, Lord Duggan, along with some of the other city nobles and merchants, with their myriad complaints.

'Forgive me, my king,' Galain pressed, 'but you've asked me to always be honest with you. Her gift was truly beyond value, and for that alone, I'd say everyone would understand you marrying a low born, but her gift has not manifested itself once of late. The flowers you asked to be left in her room are dying, and the gardens where she spends much of her time haven't shown any signs of renewed growth. By all accounts, her gift was so strong and uncontrollable during her escape that she left a trail through the wilderness a blind man could see. I really don't think she's faking its loss.'

Tristan said nothing, so Galain pressed on.

'True, she's beautiful despite her ageing, but many more beautiful young women would happily take your hand formally, many of whom are from families of wealth and influence. Why not choose one of those instead? Then, if you wish Maya's counsel, have her attend court at your whim, not have her close by causing trouble.'

Tristan pondered for a while.

'Everything you say is correct, and I appreciate your candour in this regard, but from her very lips, she's said her failing gift is linked to her happiness.'

Tristan smiled shrewdly.

'Money can buy us anything, Galain. Once she's married and has power and wealth, she'll be happier than ever before. What's love compared to that? No, the betrothal ceremony goes ahead. We must show the people, and our troops, that we believe this war can be won. If the marriage is planned, then that will reinforce everyone's belief.'

'But, my king, what if we don't win?' Galain asked hesitantly. 'Surely we should be making contingency plans for your safe departure. If Daleth's forces lay siege, how will you ever escape with your life or wealth?'

Tristan looked at Galain sharply.

'I chose well in keeping you by my side. I'd not considered the possibility of being trapped here, and dying was never part of my plan. Yes, we'll need to use the alliance forces to hold back Daleth's assault, and with the time that gives us, we can escape across the desert. Wealth can buy a man position anywhere in this world, and gold is gold wherever you travel. Start making quiet arrangements, and …'

Tristan paused as loud shouting came from the corridor outside.

Suddenly, the doors to the audience chamber burst open, and Rakan surged in. Filthy, armoured, and covered in stained bandages, he shook off the efforts of several guards to restrain him. As he pushed through, they all leapt on him, and under the weight of six men, Rakan was borne to the floor, cursing loudly.

'Apologies, my king,' called a sergeant, as a dozen more guards came running in to help restrain Rakan. 'I don't know where this ruffian came from, but we'll have him flogged and thrown in a cell immediately.'

Tristan waited a moment as Rakan was dragged to his feet and, for a moment, entertained the idea of having the punishment carried out. Rakan had no respect when it came to dealing with him as a king and perhaps now was the time to remind him.

'Captain Rakan,' he said, none too warmly. 'Whilst your arrival is welcome, albeit surprising, your manner of presenting yourself is most definitely not. I assume my men tried to advise you that it was not yet time for me to receive an audience and you decided perhaps that those orders did not apply to you? Let me assure you, Captain, that my orders apply to everyone from King Ostrom, whilst he's our guest, all the way down, and it's a long way down, to a captain such as yourself.'

Rakan's face reddened at this and Tristan smiled inside, for he knew his words had struck home. Rakan was proud, and it was easy to hurt a proud man.

As he spoke, King Ostrom arrived. The heavyset desert king raised an eyebrow as he moved past Rakan and the guards, and then Dafne, the commander of the Eyre, swept in too. Duggan and the other nobles followed in order of seniority and all the while, Rakan was held like a criminal in the guards' grasp.

'You may release, Captain Rakan. There'll be no need for further punishment, Sergeant. However, I'd be very interested to know where the captain in charge of palace security is. Surely he should've been overseeing the external security of this residence?'

'What is your captain's name, Duggan?' Tristan asked. 'He should be held to task for being so lax as to let this intrusion happen.'

'Tolgarth,' Lord Duggan replied. 'Captain Tolgarth. He's in the care of our healers. A dozen men were said to have set upon him in a dark alley, and he's lucky to be alive, but it will be several days before he returns to duty. I think in this instance, the fault is not his, my king.'

Rakan chuckled, and Tristan raised his eyebrow.

'Do you think a Freestates captain being assaulted is a laughing matter, Rakan?' Tristan snapped. 'Just because you survived the fall of my border fortress doesn't give you the right to be so damned disrespectful.'

King Ostrom leaned forward from where he sat, suddenly interested.

'You were at the fortress, Captain?' he asked, cutting over Tristan.

Rakan nodded.

'That I was,' he replied. 'Right till the end. I came directly here to advise of such and report on developments.'

'Good man,' Ostrom applauded, and Dafne nodded in agreement.

'A good man?' Tristan shouted, annoyed at both being interrupted, and seeing Rakan praised. 'If he survived the fall of the fortress, it's because he ran when he was supposed to stay and fight. So, tell me how good a man can he be?'

Rakan answered before anyone else could.

'You're right, my king. I ran, that's true. But not before you, and not as fast as you!'

A shocked silence fell over the chamber, and everyone waited for Tristan to explode for they could see his anger building.

Then suddenly, Dafne's laughter rang out into the silence. She was a big woman, but her laughter was high and light, and it was full of good humour.

'I wonder if he's as good at fighting with his sword as he is with his words,' she gasped, wiping her eyes. 'He got you there, Tristan. He really got you there!'

Tristan didn't know how to respond to this. First the insult and then being laughed at.

Then Ostrom joined in. His deep resonating laugh contrasted Dafne's, and then the merchants and nobles joined in.

'Quiet!' Tristan called, with a wide grin firmly fixed in place.

The laughter was at his expense, but the only way to diffuse it was to go along with it. 'He does fight as well with his sword, it's true. But he needs to be wary of how freely he strikes with his tongue just in case I order it removed. He needs to realise a good joke can have bad consequences!'

Everyone laughed again, but as he said this, Tristan fixed Rakan with a warning look.

'So, Captain Rakan. What have you come to tell us?' Tristan enquired. 'I believed the lord commander was under orders to hold to the last man, so I'd have expected to receive him in person to explain his disobedience, and to throw himself upon my mercy.'

Rakan's face darkened, but not in anger this time, rather more in sorrow as he reflected for a moment before beginning his story from when Tristan had left the fortress to arriving at Freeguard.

When he finished, there was a brief pause before Ostrom and Dafne began asking questions.

For most of the morning, Rakan answered all that was asked of him, until finally the questions stopped and silence once again fell as people digested all he'd said.

'So,' Ostrom summarised, 'you feel it likely we'll have until spring before Daleth launches his attack, but even then we'll be unable to withstand his forces. I suppose the good and unexpected news is the additional time. I already knew the bad news before we came, but to hear it from the mouth of an experienced warrior is different to hearing it from the mouth of Tristan's emissary.'

'Yes. Where is Astren?' Tristan demanded. 'Did he not flee with you? You didn't speak of him once in the recounting of your tale.'

Rakan shook his head and shrugged.

'I don't know. He disappeared some days before the fall, and I know not where to. Perhaps he slipped away late one night, or took his own life as did others.'

Dafne looked Rakan in the eye.

'You speak with authority and knowledge about Daleth and his forces. Where did you come by such information, for surely all you've recounted couldn't have been seen by your eye alone from the fortress walls?'

Rakan smiled.

'I'm impressed by your astuteness,' he said, returning her gaze. 'I was until recently in Daleth's army. That was before I escaped and joined the Freestates forces along with my new friends.'

'Your friends being?' Dafne pressed.

'Kalas, who was lord commander, the Lady Yana, Taran, who became the lord commander on Kalas' death, and of course ...'

'Me,' said a voice, and everyone turned.

There stood Maya. She wore a dress made of spun silk, and it clung to her like a second skin, shining in the morning light glinting through the windows. There were murmurs behind hands, for despite her beautiful garb, from her belted waist hung a sword and long dagger.

'You can take a peasant hunter from the fields and dress her as a lady,' Duggan said quietly to a noble next to him, 'but she is, and always will remain, a peasant.'

Dafne shot Duggan a cold look, and he smiled back, unconcerned by her harsh gaze.

The End of Dreams

'Can you believe someone took my hunting leathers?' Maya complained loudly.

Laughter echoed around the room as she ran past the surprised guards to enfold Rakan in a long hug.

'You look awful,' she observed, smiling, tears in her eyes. 'How's my Taran?' she whispered. 'Tell me he lives.'

'He lives,' Rakan responded briefly before letting go and standing back.

Dafne coughed, bringing the attention back to her.

'So, with all your experience having fought first with, and now against Daleth, how are we to best him? How can we win this fight and save not just our lives, but the lives of our children to come and the very land they'll live on?'

Rakan lowered his head, kicking his boots against the polished floor for a moment before raising his eyes.

'We can't win,' he said. 'I just can't see how.'

Loud gasps and shouts of denial and anger filled the room from many of the nobles.

'If fifteen hundred of you killed nearly ten thousand, then surely our combined forces of thirty-five thousand men will be more than enough,' Duggan called over the noise. 'You exaggerate the threat for your own purpose, whatever it may be.'

Rakan face darkened as he shook his head.

'We had walls three times the height and twice the depth of those which surround this city. We also had but one wall to defend at a time across a narrow pass that funnelled his troops, and we had the greatest warrior that ever walked this land amongst us. He's now dead, and I've no idea how we can defeat Daleth. The Witch-King could take this city in a myriad of ways and to meet him on the open field would also invite certain defeat.'

'King Tristan and many others here believe we should fight from behind the city walls,' Dafne offered, 'and yet you say we'll lose. Ostrom and I favour meeting them in the field in different ways, and again, you say we'll lose. So, can anyone tell me how we can win?'

'I know someone who might be able to,' Rakan advised, looking at Tristan. 'After all, who better to ask than the surviving lord commander of your forces in the west? He told me he had an idea to help balance the fight, so I think we should hear what he has to say. Taran will be here within a week, and he'll be very happy to advise you, my king, and I'm sure you two will have a lot to discuss.'

'That title was only bestowed upon him by Kalas, as was his previous rank of commander,' Tristan retorted. 'I'm not sure he's truly earned either rank over loyal, longer serving, and far older soldiers in my service. It might be I choose to replace him on his return.'

Rakan shook his head.

'You might be right when you refer to his youth, and yet it wasn't Kalas who held the men of the fortress together. It wasn't Kalas who helped ease the pain of the wounded and dying. It wasn't Kalas who brought the giants to fight for our cause, and it wasn't Kalas who discovered the ambush that would have taken our lives when we arrived.'

Rakan paused, letting the weight of his words settle, then continued.

'I tell you this, my king. Taran is a born leader, and all the men followed and worshipped him at the end. His gift has made him a warrior beyond peer, and now, with Kalas' death, he may well be the eminent warrior in our ranks. Yet, even if this isn't enough to sway you, ask yourself this question. If you take away too much from a man, and he has nothing left to lose ... what path might he then follow?'

Mystified looks met this announcement, as everyone in the chamber bar Tristan, Maya, and Galain, tried to understand the hidden meaning of the words that Rakan spoke.

Ostrom was listening intently to something his advisor, Ultric, was whispering in his ear, and he smiled at Rakan.

'I'd like to meet this Taran you speak so highly of, for if you hold him in high esteem, I'm sure he's worthy of respect. I suggest, King Tristan, we now discuss in detail how this changes our preparations for war. Let's have Captain Rakan join you, Dafne, and I, in a closed meeting. Even if his words are somewhat blunt and disrespectful at times, this is a time of war, and as such, we cannot always afford to stand on ceremony.'

Tristan nodded and ordered everyone else to leave the chamber.

Maya gave Rakan a parting hug.

'Come find me soonest,' she said softly, before striding out.

There were few dissenting voices, for many of the nobles had far more interesting things to do with their precious time.

Tristan gestured to Galain, who stood at his shoulder, and they stepped to a corner of the room to speak quietly.

'Rakan's news changes everything. We likely have the autumn and the winter before we see any serious sign of Daleth's forces and much can happen in this time. We'll meticulously plan for an eventual departure, but other things can now take precedence.'

Galain nodded and Tristan lowered his voice even further.

'Firstly, I want you to prioritise the betrothal ceremony for this week before our loyal Lord Commander Taran returns. I want there to be no doubt in Maya and Taran's mind that the agreement Maya and I have was binding and remains so.'

Tristan leant in even closer to ensure he wasn't overheard.

'When Taran returns and finds out, he'll possibly react in a way that will leave us in a position to deal with him without fear of judgement. He's too young to understand the subtleties of this game, and he'll play into my hands for sure. We just need to make sure we have enough guards on hand in case things get unpleasant.'

'But how will the Lady Maya act in such a situation?' Galain asked.

'Maya will then see my compassion when I spare him for his transgressions,' Tristan chuckled. 'However, with the war coming, I think it quite likely our lord commander might find himself in the thick of the fighting and some wicked heathen can deal with the situation for me.'

Galain smiled.

'A good plan, my king, and a devious one.'

Tristan turned back to Ostrom, Dafne, and Rakan.

'Right, we have a lot to talk about. Let's get started, shall we?'

He nodded to Galain, who shut the door on his way out.

***

Chapter VI

Taran didn't know who was more exhausted, him or his horse. Then again, as he looked either side of him, Yana looked worse than he felt and the three soldiers even more so.

They'd been travelling carefully toward Freeguard, several times having to lie low as they spotted distant cavalry, knowing they were Daleth's lancers. Having only been on the move for an hour since dawn, they'd recently spotted another troop and had taken shelter in some woods until it was safe to pass.

The horses were grazing, pulling at the grass amongst the trees, happy for the early respite.

'How many people do you think we've sent east?' Taran mused, looking toward Alexan, one of the remaining soldiers.

'Well, the last village alone had nearly two hundred dwellers. Add that to the others, and I reckon nearly a thousand. Hopefully, they'll gather more to them as they go.' Alexan counted on his fingers, checking his numbers.

Taran nodded, thoughtful.

'The question now is whether they'll survive the journey to Freeguard or be cut down along the way. Right, we've waited long enough. Let's move,' he ordered, remounting, and the small group left the dark embrace of the woods behind.

They rode cautiously until midday, staying near cover wherever possible, knowing how vulnerable they were. Taran cursed himself, for they could have taken some enemy uniforms and lances to deceive the enemy from a distance. He committed the idea to memory. He wouldn't make the same mistake again.

The End of Dreams

A deserted looking farmstead appeared, and Taran decided to risk seeing if they could scavenge some rations. They rode down slowly, eyes scanning the horizon, and as their horses moved onto the flattened ground before the farmhouse, they found it empty.

After a final look around, Taran turned to Alexan.

'Go see if that farmhouse holds anything we can use,' he ordered. 'We'll keep watch.'

'I'll go check the well, and see if we can replenish our water,' Yana offered.

It wasn't long before Alexan returned, shaking his head.

'This place has been looted clean, and from the number of boot prints inside, I'd say by soldiers.'

Taran nodded in acknowledgement as he turned toward Yana, who was ashen-faced, coming back from the well, shaking her head.

'Is it dry?' he asked.

'It's been fouled,' she muttered, mounting her horse.

They flicked the reins of their mounts and rode on. As they did so, Taran leaned over the edge of the well. The sun was high in the sky, and as Taran looked down, he could make out the bodies of a woman and child, floating, dead white eyes staring up as if in accusation.

Taran urged his horse forward.

'It's obvious Daleth's lancers are ranging far and wide. They haven't had to be cautious, for there's no one to stop them.'

They continued riding in silence until Alexan called his attention to a large plume of smoke rising above the brow of a hill. They rode to just shy of the crest and dismounted.

Taran and the men crawled slowly to the brow and looked over through the long grass, leaving Yana holding the reins as a lookout. Below them was a village and several of its huts, with their straw roofs, burned fiercely.

Malicious laughter was interspersed with screams and pleas for mercy, as the villagers, who'd been rounded up and bound, were slowly and systematically killed in all manner of ways.

Taran looked at the men either side of him.

'There's nothing we can do, damn them,' he cursed. 'There are around fifty lancers.

'Damn them all,' Alexan agreed, as the screams continued, and with it, the laughter.

Taran lay there watching for a moment. Thanks to the amulet, there was something about the screams that sounded harmonious. He shook the unwelcome thoughts from his mind.

'We'd best return to our horses and give this village a wide berth,' he ordered. 'If we don't get ahead of these scum whilst they're entertaining themselves, it'll be us getting butchered before long.'

They began to edge backwards.

Suddenly, their attention was drawn back to the village as loud shouts erupted. As they watched, a girl of no more than seven summers slipped from between a group of laughing soldiers and started running away as fast as her little legs would carry her.

A woman, undoubtedly the girl's mother, started screaming for the girl to run, to not look back, and a lancer with barely a glance punched her in the face, silencing her.

Even from a distance, Taran could see the girl's face was filled with sheer terror, and he knew every moment they watched, the danger of being caught increased. They should mount and ride off. What did he care if the girl died? What was another death when hundreds had already died, and thousands more would soon join them?

The girl ran erratically, and for the moment, that was keeping her alive. The lancers were taking it in turns to cast their long weapons at her. Miraculously, every one missed her by barely a hand span as she stumbled toward the crest where Taran and his men lay.

Please die, he thought. Please die before you get here.

But her little life seemed charmed.

'We need to go, now!' Alexan hissed in his ear.

Taran barely heard him, transfixed as he was by the spectacle, by the inevitability of the girl's fate.

Then, as she drew closer, he began to see her in more detail. There were clean streaks where tears ran down her cheeks, and she had wild, frizzy, black hair, and large brown eyes. There was something strangely familiar about her look, something …

'Maya,' he whispered, as another face, surrounded by light, appeared in his thoughts.

The End of Dreams

The next moment, he was sprinting over the brow of the hill, running to the girl. He swept her into his arms, pulling her from the path of a thrown lance that would have claimed her life a heartbeat later.

'Live,' he said to her softly, putting her back down. 'Run and live!'

He pushed her toward the crest where Alexan and the others lay, still hidden in the grass. With a last look from those huge, frightened eyes, she turned and ran.

There was no option to follow the girl, for the lancers were almost born in the saddle, and with their superb horses, would overtake and slaughter Taran and the others in short shrift. So he turned back toward the village and started to run, drawing his swords, roaring a battle cry.

The lancers' laughter quietened as they drew sabres and came to meet him, foolishly not forming ranks or mounting their horses. They just sprinted toward this lone fool in blackened, filthy armour, who, with half his face covered in bandages, sought to attack them all.

'I'll die to protect you, Maya,' he heard himself say, as he met the first lancer, cutting through him, leaving the man crumpled in his wake.

Face after face flashed before his eyes, the clash of steel loud in his ears before they fell away screaming or sometimes frozen-faced, already with death's grip firmly upon them. Then gradually, he felt the world start to slow, and his breath came in gasps. The surviving lancers no longer came toward him. Instead, they now stood back warily, sabres held defensively.

He looked down to see a dagger protruding from his shoulder, and blood flowing heavily from a wound to his thigh. His swords seemed to weigh more with every passing breath.

The lancers slowly moved around him, and the last of his strength began fading away as blood trickled into his boot. He tried to raise his blades, to take more with him in his final moments.

He never heard the lancer come up behind him. All he knew was suddenly he was falling, and the grass felt pleasantly cool against his face as darkness closed in.

***

Jared sat in a dirty wagon looking at the peasants travelling around him, nauseated by the smell and the filthiness of the clothes they all wore.

He'd been heading east for just over three weeks and had passed Freemantle to the north a couple of days before. Daleth's lancers were under strict orders not to foray along his specific route, and after initially travelling alone, he'd stumbled across some refugees heading to Freeguard. He'd joined them after spinning a tale of how he'd been forced to flee his village, which had been attacked several days' travel to the west.

He hadn't said too much, feigning to be a little simple, for his knowledge of the Freestates was limited. He needed the time to learn their ways, accents, and customs so he could fit in perfectly.

The people didn't trust him yet, not because they suspected him of being anything other than what he said he was, but because he was not from their village.

He'd volunteered to drive a wagon and, whilst doing so, listened intently to the chatter going on around him. There was a sense of disbelief amongst these peasants, that their lives, which were already pitiful, would soon get worse. The Witch-King was coming to kill them all, yet there was also a parallel sense of hope that he found laughable.

The hope was based on a tale the village elder had told everyone to get them to follow him. It was a story of how a young huntress and her lover had fled the Witch-King's clutches after defeating his evil soldiers time and again. She was supposedly the immortal daughter of the goddess of life and had come in disguise to fight beside them, leading them to victory. Afterwards, she'd heal the land, become its queen, and everyone would live happily ever after.

He'd almost spat out his stew when he'd heard the whole tale around the first night's campfire, but at the same time, there were elements of truth in the story. Even now, he couldn't help wonder how so many fellow Rangers had fallen once the hunt for the girl and her companions had got underway.

He wondered if he'd get an opportunity in days to come to finish that story once and for all. Daleth would be ecstatic if he managed to succeed where so many of his brothers had failed, and he'd do anything to earn his king's praise.

His biggest worry was that when they reached Freeguard, security might be tight, and his story might unravel under scrutiny when no one recognised him or exposed a poorly told lie. He had to make sure he fitted in perfectly.

To that end, for the last two days, he'd been studying one of the younger men, Charel, who kept a little to himself and seemed somewhat insecure.

Hour after hour, he silently practised Charel's voice, studied his mannerisms, the way he'd lower his gaze when one of the girls who obviously liked him flirted as she walked by. It was interesting to note how another man looked upon Charel with hatred whenever she did so.

The caravan had five wagons in total, pulled by some stinking old oxen and around forty men, women, and children, heading east. Their pitiful belongings were piled high, threatening to fall off the back of the wagons on the uneven route they chose.

They stayed away from the roads for safety and applauded themselves that they'd travelled so far without sight of the enemy, never knowing one was amongst them the whole time.

Every day was long, and Jared kept his head down, apparently focused on the track ahead. Yet the look was deceiving, because from the corner of his eye, he followed Charel's movements. Jared memorised who Charel spoke to, who he avoided, who he looked in the eye, and even how he ate when they stopped for a quick lunch.

Now evening approached, the elder called a halt at the edge of some woodland, and everyone started to get a camp ready.

Jared wanted to tell them how stupid they were to light a fire that could be seen for leagues, but he kept quiet, helping to unharness the oxen as others gathered firewood and cleared ground to sleep on.

As ever, he stayed away from the campfire where everyone sat talking and eating. New stories were hard to come by in a small village community, and they'd want to know all about him if he sat with them. Instead, he sat eating cold food from his pack, waiting for the moment he knew would eventually come, and come it did.

Charel stood, mostly ignored by all, and walked toward the woods to relieve himself.

Jared, from beyond the firelight, followed him.

It wasn't completely dark yet, and he flitted from shadow to shadow completely unseen until he was mere steps away.

Suddenly, Charel turned, apprehension in his eyes, which eased a little as he saw Jared.

'Go find your own bush,' he murmured, but Jared stumbled, head down, reaching out as if he were about to fall, and Charel instinctively grasped his hands.

'Are you alright?' Charel asked.

Jared held on, not looking up, pushing himself through the change as quickly as he could, needing the physical touch to perfect the transformation. Then it was done.

He withdrew his hands, reaching behind as if to rub his back. Instead, he reached into the waistband of his trousers for a dagger. As he finally stood upright, he stared into Charel's face, studying the final look of horrified surprise. Yes, he'd remember just how that looked, he thought, as he drove his knife through the peasant's eye and into the brain. He left it there as he caught the falling body, lowering it behind a bush.

He stripped quickly, changing into Charel's clothes, rubbing them hard against his face, so he had more of their scent, then stepped out from behind the tree, adjusting his leggings as if he'd just relieved himself.

'That's where you've been hiding!'

Jared looked up to see the girl who'd been flirting earlier walk over, tossing her hair in the dim light.

'You're always so shy,' she teased, biting her lower lip.

She came right up to him, and Jared knew that if she glanced behind, she'd likely see the naked body and her screams would rouse the camp. He raised his hands up to her face, intending to snap her neck, but stopped.

Instead, he grabbed her shoulders, pushing her back toward a tree until she was pinned against it, her breath coming rapidly.

'I'm not always so shy,' he said, kissing her hard on the mouth before they fell to the forest floor, hands grasping for the other.

A while later he said his goodbyes but remained and quickly concealed Charel's body as the girl walked off. Smoothing his clothes, he returned to sit at the fireside amongst the peasants. No one took a second glance his way as he reached for a platter of food and started nibbling as Charel had always done.

The girl sat opposite, long hair concealing her face, yet he felt her eyes upon him for the rest of the night.

Later, as he lay down on his bedroll, he smiled. Perhaps this journey wouldn't be so tedious after all.

***

'That filthy pig's waking up.'

Taran heard the voice through a fog of pain and gradually opened his eyes to discover a dozen lancers observing him, silhouetted against a roaring fire and a darkening sky. Behind them were fifty or so village folk, trussed and still alive in an animal pen, although for how much longer, who knew.

One of the lancers spat before turning away, and Taran idly watched the spittle run from one of his boots to the grass beneath.

He sat against a wooden post and struggled to move. His hands were tied firmly behind him, and his left arm felt weak. His shoulder and thigh were heavily bandaged, yet this didn't stop the pain that came in waves. That his captors had treated and bound his wounds meant either they wanted him to stay alive long enough to be tortured or had other things in store.

His armour and weapons were gone, but he still wore his shirt. Beneath the remaining sleeve, he could still feel the tightness of the leather arm guard that Drizt had given him, and he wondered if his captors had found the small, poisoned blade within.

Several men gathered closer, and a sergeant with hideous scars of rank on his face knelt.

'We know who you are. You're the commander who was at the fortress. Last time I saw you, you were on a handcart, almost dead, about to be exchanged for our king's pet daemon.'

He paused, waiting for Taran to say something, then continued into the silence.

'Even with half your face burned up, I'd know it was you even if you weren't wearing that fancy armour, which we'll take as payment for our brothers that you slaughtered earlier today. I'd heard you were good, but what you did today was just wrong. Then again, it's not all bad. We'll get a good reward for capturing you, and we won't have to split it so many ways now. So, what on earth were you thinking, wasting your life to save one stupid little girl? She'll die out there tonight or tomorrow, and you'll be taken to Daleth. You should have simply passed us by and left us to our fun.'

Taran thought quickly. It seemed they either hadn't bothered looking for, or at least hadn't found, the girl, and that meant Yana, Alexan, and the two other soldiers were still free.

'What can I say,' Taran said. 'I was a bit bored, and I'd heard you lancers couldn't swing a sword for pig's dung, so I thought maybe I'd teach you a lesson.'

The sergeant laughed, and then smashed his fist into the bandaged side of Taran's face. The pain brought tears to Taran's eyes, and his anger rose. To kill this man, to maim him, to cut out his eyes would be so pleasurable.

'I expect you were a fairly good looking lad once, but not anymore,' mocked the sergeant. 'We can still mess up the other side of your face if you keep making smart-assed comments like that. Now, even though you've just woken up, you may as well get yourself some sleep. We'll leave at first light, once we've torched this place and had a bit more fun with our friends here.' He nodded at the villagers, all bound and huddled together.

One of the lancers checked the bindings on Taran's feet and wrists before they sauntered to the fire where they sat eating and drinking. Eventually, one by one, most of them went off to find rest in some of the undamaged huts.

Taran watched from between half-closed eyes the whole time. He counted eight guards, which meant there were likely the same number around that he couldn't see. While these lancers were wolves amongst sheep, they remained in enemy territory and took their security seriously.

Yet they'd made mistakes.

They seemed to have set around half of their remaining number on watch. That meant they'd have to stay up half the night before they roused the next shift. By that time, it was likely no man would be fully awake and sharp.

The End of Dreams

The final mistakes, he noted, and he'd learned all of this from Rakan in one of his many lectures, was that they hadn't paired up, and stood too far apart with little sight of one another as they stared out into the darkness.

Occasionally, a guard would look his way, and he kept his head down, pretending to be asleep. Soon they stopped checking, but he waited a little longer for there'd be but once chance of escape. Slowly, he started twisting his hands in their bindings.

They'd bound his wrists behind him, but only so tight as to ensure he couldn't free them, not so tight that the blood would be cut off, and thus they'd also bound his upper arms too. His ankles and upper legs were also tied, and he acknowledged the thoroughness of their handiwork.

After many failed attempts, he wriggled his fingertips under the sleeve against the leather arm guard. He closed his eyes, silently thanking whatever gods might be listening, for the metal hilt of Drizt's small blade was still there.

Ever so carefully, he wriggled it loose, knowing that if he cut himself in the slightest as it came out, he'd die from the salamander poison that permanently marked its blade. As it came free, it dropped from his grasp to the ground. He was about to reach for it with his fingertips when he stopped, for if he grasped the blade, he'd stay slumped against the post for good.

He slowly straightened his legs, pushing his torso and chest up and away from the post, allowing his arms to angle toward the floor. It was incredibly painful on his neck, but he forced himself to run his fingers slowly through the grass until he'd located and held the dagger.

Carefully, but firmly, he pushed the dagger's needle-sharp point into the post and then lowered himself down so that his bindings rested on the blade and started with the smallest movements to cut the ropes.

Five times the blade came free, for he'd no leverage to push it deep enough, but eventually, the ropes binding his wrists parted. His upper arms were still bound, so he repeated the manoeuvre, again and again, this time with the dagger as high up the post as he could manage before lowering himself down and moving his arms to cut the bindings.

The cramps he suffered whilst trying to do this were excruciating, but he persisted through the pain. What drove him more, the need for revenge or the need to escape, he couldn't be sure, but eventually his upper arms were free. He relaxed, momentarily enjoying the relief from being in such an uncomfortable position.

It was now short work to cut the bindings of his legs and feet, all the time peering into the darkness. With the fire reduced to embers, it was hard to see the guards, but that also made it hard for anyone to see him.

It wasn't the middle of the night yet, so he had plenty of time to make his escape before the change of guard. He'd be long gone before daybreak and would find some woodland to hide in before the lancers came searching. They'd be foolish to enter that to hunt him as he intended to kill a guard and help himself to some weapons before he left.

Lying face down, he slowly crawled through the grass toward the boundary fence, passing the pen where the villagers were bound. As he did, he froze for a moment as his eyes met those of the mother of the girl he'd freed. Even in the darkness, he knew it was her, perhaps a residual part of his gift helping to make the connection, and he willed her to remain quiet.

He slithered silently, the sky faintly light to the west, and he moved toward the perimeter until finally, he saw the still figure of a guard silhouetted against the sky.

Grasping his dagger, he crept forward, aware the man foolishly wore his helm, muffling his hearing. He yanked back on the helm's crest, so the chinstrap pulled the man's neck taught and plunged the dagger in deep before ripping it free. The splatter of blood seemed loud as the man's legs spasmed for a few moments before they stilled.

Taran lowered the body to the floor and mostly through touch in the darkness, divested the lancer of his weapon belt and a pouch of coins. Now properly armed, Taran returned Drizt's dagger to its sheath.

Frustratingly, the man had no food or water.

Taran knew without either, he didn't have the equipment to survive in the wild unless he came across a farm or other people, but he'd have to take the risk. Carefully, he stepped through the wooden fencing and headed west for a while, intending to turn north and then east to skirt the village.

As he walked, he thought of the mother who'd looked at him in the darkness, then the girl, and he stopped. Keep moving, he said to himself. What do you care … lambs are always slaughtered by the wolves. Yet he soon retraced his footsteps.

It wouldn't be long now before the change of watch, and as soon as they found one body, the alarm would be raised, so he moved swifter than he'd have liked. He crossed the fence where the guard's cooling body lay, and worked his way around the perimeter, delivering death to the tired and unsuspecting guards.

He'd killed six more when he stumbled on a fallen fence post just as he was approaching his eighth victim. His leg, weakened from his earlier injury, gave way, and he fell with a thump. The man turned and called out an alarm just as Taran recovered and lunged at him with the sabre. It wasn't a clean blow, and the man's scream echoed into the night as he succumbed to the wound.

Shouts grew throughout the village as the lancers responded, and Taran knew he should leave. But it was dark, and in the dark, he was but one of many shadows. Perhaps some more souls could still be reaped. He stumbled and looked down, seeing his leg bleeding through the dressing, the loss of blood making him light-headed.

Torches flickered to life as the gathering soldiers grouped together and the fire began to grow as kindling was thrown upon it, bringing light to the village.

I could still leave, he thought to himself, but smiled ruefully as realism hit. He could hardly run away now, for he could barely walk.

Taran limped slowly into the growing circle of light.

'I don't suppose you'd consider fighting me one at a time,' he laughed bitterly. 'It seems I'm feeling a little tired from my late-night revelry' He swayed as if a little drunk.

He could see the whites of the bound villagers' eyes staring as they twisted on the ground to witness his death, and stepped forward unsteadily. The lancers moved as a group toward him when the sound of hoofbeats filled the air.

'Are you really going to fight me from horseback?' he jibed tiredly. 'Learn to stand on your own two feet.'

Then, from beyond the light, three horses charged into view, and as the lancers turned, expecting their brothers to deal the death blows, they instead found Alexan and the other two soldiers leading a dozen horses straight into their packed ranks.

The lancers were literally flung from their feet, broken by the weight of the charging horses, and whilst a few still remained standing at the fringes, the damage done to their comrades was horrific. Men screamed, twisting and writhing upon the floor as the mounted soldiers turned and charged back at the men, swords slashing down, cleaving, and chopping. The few remaining lancers broke, fleeing into the darkness, dropping their weapons, not looking back.

Yana rode into view and before her on the saddle sat the little girl Taran had saved. Yana rode over to Taran and jumped down, supporting him as his legs began to give way. The little girl jumped off the horse too and ran to the pen imprisoning her mother.

'It looks like you can't do without me,' Yana smiled as Taran wrapped his arm around her shoulders and she half-carried him to the fire. 'Let's have a look at you and see if we can patch you up some more.'

Alexan and the other soldiers approached, dismounting swiftly.

'You're late,' Taran said sternly, then laughed at Alexan's outraged face. 'Thank you, my friends,' he said, reaching out to grip first Alexan's wrist, then those of the other two. 'Now, release the villagers, and as for the wounded lancers, let the villagers deal with them as they wish.'

As he slumped to the ground with Yana attending to him, the moans and cries from the wounded men began to rise then turned to screams as the vengeful villagers started meting out their own brand of justice.

How sweet that sounds, Taran thought, then fell unconscious.

***

Daleth had entered Freemantle under cover of darkness several days after his main forces had arrived. They'd carried out their orders with relish, sweeping the city for residents and putting them to the sword after gleaning any usable information.

He'd left a thousand men behind at Tristan's Folly to clear the corpses, taking the amulets, armour, and weapons from his fallen warriors. They'd catch up as soon as they were able, bringing everything with them, including any useable items or supplies looted from the fortress.

No good commander discarded anything useful whilst on a campaign, and his attention to detail had been polished over a lifetime of conquest and planning. The bodies of the slain were to be burned. Disease was an evil spirit that could carry on the wind, or so the healers always said, and he wouldn't risk that blight, and hard work kept the men from fighting one another.

The journey by wagon had been incredibly painful and exhausting. With every jolt, he swore to himself that he'd handsomely reward any engineer who crafted a wagon that didn't break even the unharmed parts of a man's body during such a journey.

Upon arrival, he'd taken up residence in the royal palace within the chambers that were, no doubt, once Tristan's. Busts of the Freestates king were everywhere, such had been his vanity, although there was no denying the artistry that had gone into them. In fact, every room, every building, the city itself, was something to behold. This was a kingdom built on wealth accrued over centuries of trade, and the merchants and noble class had spent this whole time competing with one another in finding ways to show this.

To live in the Freestates cities, you had to be wealthy or a slave, for there was no room for peasants. In some ways, Daleth could admire a ruthlessness of oppression that almost matched his own.

Yet how colossal their failure in spending nowhere near enough to defend this vast wealth, simply hoping that peaceful relations would protect them. Now they'd been forced to leave so much of it behind in their hasty departure.

Daleth couldn't yet walk unaided, but as the only soldiers in the royal palace were his bodyguard, or occasionally Rangers, he'd no need to hide his injuries. Those closest to him were so devoted that most would slit their own throats if he asked.

Each day, to distract himself from the pain of recovery, he was assisted throughout the palace to examine the different rooms. It mattered not whether they were used for residency, official matters, or even administration, he took an interest in them all.

There were occasional empty plinths and faded marks on the walls where a piece of artwork or sculpture had been removed, but the wealth left behind was breath-taking.

Likewise, the reports from around the city were the same.

Whilst most of the population had left, they'd not had the time to take the majority of their possessions with them. Not that his soldiers appreciated the art or architecture, they preferred simpler things like gold that could be spent on drink and women.

Still, in some ways, he'd have been happier had this place been a burnt-out shell. Living in such accommodation might allow his men to get soft over the winter while he healed, so he'd have to keep them sharp and occupied.

To that end, Baidan, the captain of his bodyguards, had sat with him, discussing how the men would best spend their time over the coming months.

The city had an enormous theatre that seated thousands, so this would now be transformed into an arena for the men to continue honing their weapon skills. Others would be tasked to hunt and gather, maintaining their stamina and strength while ensuring stores and woodpiles were kept full for the coming winter.

Lastly, the surrounding countryside would be scoured, and any surviving peasants rounded up. Some would be put to work while others would be entertainment for his men, so the relentless slaughter his lancers had enjoyed till now would be curtailed, just a little.

He wasn't interested in winning the population's acceptance, not when his conquest went beyond these lands. But he'd feed on them in time as much as he did from the land, so keeping enough alive was important.

The list went on and on until Daleth was satisfied that not a day would go by without his men getting harder and stronger. When they were eventually unleashed in the spring, they'd all be better warriors than they now were.

What felt even more satisfying was receiving new life from the surrounding vibrant realm. Freemantle was at the centre of the Freestates, and the tendrils of his gift reached out like the trade roads, gorging on the heartlands. This aided his recovery, and by winter he'd be back to full strength even if it was too late to lead an assault on Freeguard.

He'd even stopped taking sleep weed to help him deal with the terrible pain. Not that it had dissipated. Every time there was a spasm, he'd see those red eyes of Kalas and curse him, but with the new life enthusing him, he felt strong enough to deal with it. After all, he was chosen by the gods themselves, and surely they'd look down upon his strength in dealing with adversity and know they had chosen their champion wisely.

The thought warmed him, and he leaned back, closing his eyes.

Time to sleep. Time to reach out with his gift. Time to feed.

***

Taran groaned, wondering if his whole body was broken.

Of late, he awoke every morning feeling far older than his years and often discovered something new hurt, having been injured the previous day.

He eased upright in a small bed upon a straw mattress that, despite the blankets, was as uncomfortable a bed as he could possibly imagine. If he hadn't been unconscious when he'd been placed upon it, he'd have never been able to fall asleep.

As he examined his surroundings, he saw Yana slumped in a chair, a blanket across her, fast asleep. Furtive movement in the back of the hut caught his eye, and he stiffened, reaching for a weapon until the darting shadow turned into the little girl he'd saved.

Her face lit up in a white smile that contrasted against her filthy face as she saw he was awake, then she turned and ran into the shadows again. Moments later, she reappeared from behind a curtain alongside her mother, who bore a food tray.

The little girl skipped forward, holding her finger to her lips, warning Taran to be quiet, motioning to Yana as she jumped onto the bed at Taran's feet and lay down, hugging his legs.

Taran stifled a moan, for she rested her head against his thigh where he'd been wounded. Yet she became aware of his discomfort, mouthed a silent apology, and sat up again.

The mother moved quietly to the bed, and Taran's stomach rumbled so loudly when he looked at the food that the little girl laughed.

Yana awoke to the sound of the girl's merriment and smiled.

'That little girl stayed by your bedside the whole night while I tended to you, even when we had to clean your wounds. She's a tough little one, and I think you're her hero.'

The mother smiled sadly, placing the tray gently on Taran's lap.

'We all think that,' she said, lowering her head. 'We all saw what you did, coming down that hill alone against all those soldiers. None of us will forget what you did, and none of us will forget what they did either.'

She wiped a quick tear away.

'We hadn't heard about the war until they rode in yesterday, and we didn't know who they were. At first, they didn't hurt anyone, just ordered us all together. Then they started to ask questions, and when we didn't know the answers, then ...' and she couldn't carry on for more tears ran down her face, and her shoulders shook.

Taran ignored her distress and looked past at Yana.

'We need to get moving as quickly as we can.'

Yana shook her head emphatically.

'We can't risk you riding today, not in your state. Your leg wound is deep, and you'll limp for a long time to come. The shoulder wound wasn't pretty either. You won't wield a sword in that hand for a while, I'm sure.'

Taran hissed through his teeth.

'But if we're caught here, that's the end of it. We need to move out today. Those lancers who ran into the night might come across another troop and return.'

The woman looked up, her eyes bloodshot.

'Where will you go?'

Taran looked at her, worn, broken, aged beyond her years.

'To Freeguard, and it must be today. The king is there, and we'll join his forces. We've spent the last week telling farmers and villagers alike to head there for safety and to join the army. We didn't get to you soon enough it seems.'

'But you did get to us,' the woman said, 'and that's all that matters. If Freeguard is where you're going, then we'll help you get there, and the men that are left will join you to fight this evil. Whilst living under Tristan's rule has been harsh, at least we lived without fear. I hold no love for Tristan, his tax collectors are ruthless, and we often go hungry, but these soldiers of the Witch-King, they just killed us for sport.'

Taran turned to Yana.

'However bad my wounds, we need to move. Those lancers all had horses and weapons, so there are likely enough horses for everyone left in the village. Even if many here haven't ridden before, it will be quicker than on foot. Have every adult armed and carrying lances too. That way, from a distance, it's possible we might be mistaken for lancers if spied by other troops of Daleth.'

'Good idea,' Yana said. 'I'll get on it. But you'll have to ride in a wagon thanks to that leg injury.'

Taran grimaced and sighed.

'I hate wagons, but if keeping my leg means breaking my back, I'll do it!'

Memories swam through his mind of the last time he'd ridden a wagon with Maya as a prisoner, and he was momentarily struck by a terrible feeling of loss. What was wrong with the damn amulet? First, the little girl reminding him of Maya, and now this.

Yet even as he worried, the angst faded, and his emotions flattened.

He broke fast as Yana and the woman disappeared from the hut to make arrangements for everyone to leave. Only the girl stayed behind. She just sat staring at him with those huge brown eyes from under her unkempt hair, tilting her head from side to side occasionally. After a while, she came over and sat right next to him.

'What's this?' she asked, pointing at his amulet. 'I've seen that all the bad men wear them.'

Taran thought to ignore her, his mind full of the journey to Freeguard, and how quickly he could recover and be able to fight again.

The girl had other ideas, as she leaned right across till her face was right in front of his.

'Well?' she demanded, in her high voice, eyes bright and mischievous. 'I won't go away even if you ignore me!'

She poked her tongue out.

Taran felt anger well inside of him, but he pushed it aside. Save it for the enemy, he thought, and this girl definitely wasn't one of them.

'You're right,' he said. 'It's worn by bad men, by all the bad men. They wear it so that they feel anger, feel the need to inflict pain, and so that they feel no remorse when they do bad things.'

'So why do you wear it?' the girl asked. 'It isn't pretty. In fact, it's heavy and ugly.'

Taran looked coldly at her.

'It's because I'm bad too!' He scowled, wanting her to leave him alone.

The girl screamed, but only for it to turn to laughter, which rippled through the room, but then her eyes took on a faraway look.

'You're not bad, Taran broken-heart. You saved my life for the memory of the one you love, and in time, you'll die for that love as well. You're not bad, you're just lost!'

With that, her eyes seemed to focus again, and looking a little shocked, she jumped off the bed, leaving Taran silent in disbelief.

The door opened, and in walked Yana, as the girl ran out.

'It sounds like you two were having fun,' she smiled, 'but it's time for us to go. We found your armour and weapons that they took. Lucky for us they didn't find that nasty dagger Drizt gave you.'

She helped Taran from the bed and into a new shirt, trousers, and boots that the villagers had provided.

Shortly after, they stepped outside, blinking in the light to find the remaining villagers assembled before the hut. Behind them, the dead lancers' horses they'd attempt to ride were held by his soldiers.

The girl's mother stepped forward first and knelt, taking his hand, and kissed his palm.

'With this hand, you gave us life,' she said.

'There's no need,' Taran complained, trying to pull away, but she held on with surprising strength.

'There is a need,' she said, looking up, holding his gaze firmly. 'We need to do this, and my daughter tells me you need to know this.'

One after another, all the other villagers did the same, many with tears in their eyes. Only after expressing their gratitude did they clumsily mount the horses. They were fortunate for the horses were trained to accept an injured rider and remained still, despite the unfamiliarity of the villagers.

Yana led Taran to a wagon already hitched to a horse.

'They worship you, or maybe I should say, we worship you.'

She blushed.

Taran went to step up into the seat, but Yana stepped forward.

'No! You're riding in the back,' she scolded, as he looked to mount and take the reins. 'There are plenty of blankets back there to make your ride comfortable and who knows, maybe there's room for two and an even more comfortable ride if you care to ask.'

Taran sighed, shaking his head as he gingerly climbed in, and the smile dropped from Yana's face.

'One day, Taran heartbreaker,' she said, under her breath, 'one day you'll be the one doing the asking.'

With a twisted smile, she took the driver's position, cracked the whip, and aimed the wagon toward every rock she could see.

***

Chapter VII

Maya awoke after a mostly sleepless night with fresh determination to make the best of her situation.

Galain, who Maya had initially thought was decent enough, had turned out to be Tristan's mealy-mouthed advisor. He'd somewhat joyfully informed her before she'd retired the previous night, that the betrothal ceremony would be at the week's end and she'd shortly be fitted with a dress suitable for the occasion.

She'd surprised herself with the indifference with which she'd received the news. Taran, without doubt, would save her and stop this from happening. The wedding was a full year away, and it was easy to believe it would never occur. Of course, if Daleth was victorious, then there'd be no happy ending whatsoever for anyone. Irrespective, after a night of thinking, she'd decided to use her position to make changes within this pretentious city and surrounding areas.

It had been frustrating to see Rakan, and yet not have time to exchange any words of importance regarding Taran, and she'd been unable to find him later in the day however hard she'd searched.

The talk of the palace was that Daleth had been severely injured during the fall of Tristan's Folly. It seemed that an attack was now unlikely before spring and yet this good news also brought more challenges, hence Maya's early rise.

She'd heard many laughingly call her the peasant princess behind her back, but she'd now have the last laugh. Following the betrothal ceremony, she'd have royal privilege, for even betrothal gave her the right of rule.

The End of Dreams

It seemed the Freestates had a long-standing tradition that a royal marriage was always a full year after betrothal. This allowed the king of the Freestates to see how frugal his future wife was with the royal wealth. Should she fall out of favour, or spend more than she accrued, then the marriage plans could be happily voided with all haste and validity.

So she intended to wield her new power in a way that no Freestates ruler had before. She would use it to give things away, and again, maybe this was a way she could get Tristan to reconsider their agreement.

She'd indeed be the peasant princess, for she'd be the princess of the peasants.

Her hunting leathers had supposedly been taken for cleaning, yet it was more likely Tristan's attempt at having her look more like a lady of the court. So, having swiftly washed and dressed and foregone any breakfast, she walked from the palace in a green dress cinched around her slim waist with a sword belt. Beneath its hem, she still wore leather boots despite the ridiculous number of silken shoes that had been put in her room.

'Keep up,' she gently mocked Ferris as her long stride had him and the other guards struggling to stay abreast.

'Why aren't we riding, my lady?' Ferris huffed.

'Whilst I like riding,' Maya admitted, 'I'm going to be a princess of all the people. The common folk don't ride thoroughbred horses, and thus at least for today, neither shall I.'

The city was huge and densely populated, but this early in the day, few were about, and with empty streets, Maya set a relentless pace.

She loved the walk. The air was fresh, the sky clear, and there was hardly a sound. It reminded her of when she used to hunt for her settlement before the populace had begun to stir. Now, just like then, she'd left early so that those who would want to know her whereabouts would still be asleep and unlikely to hear of her journey until too late.

Her steps took her along the north thoroughfare, lined with large merchant and noble houses. It seemed each Freestates city followed a similar plan. The wealthiest families bought properties that gave them a view over all trade coming in and out and the quickest route to the palace.

Unlike Freemantle, this was a walled city, and whilst many of the walls were in disrepair, there were but four main gates allowing access, with barracks for the city garrison at each one.

Maya paused as they approached the gate, studying the long, low buildings housing the city soldiers, barely less opulent than those of the merchants. Nothing looked out of place in this city, and the barracks had statues in the courtyard of heroic figures in martial poses.

A couple of tired-looking sentries stood on guard, leaning on spears, but apart from that, there was no activity yet.

'Let's take a look here before we go any further,' Maya declared, turning sharply left toward the barrack gates, Ferris and his men hurrying to keep up.

The sound of the approaching group roused the two sentries, who looked up sleepily, their eyes widening as they saw Maya and the soldiers accompanying her. They came forward, crossing their spears in front of them.

The younger of the two smiled nervously, unsure of what to say or do, but the older one looked at them with disdain.

'You've got the wrong place,' he said. 'This is for the city garrison, not you lot from Freemantle or wherever you're from!' He challenged them with his stare.

Maya turned to Ferris.

'If these men haven't lowered their spears by the time I count to five, you are to cut their right hands off at the wrist.'

She fixed the older guard with a cold stare as Ferris and his men put hands to the hilt of their swords.

'One,' Maya began, and the guards suddenly looked uncertain. 'Two.' She heard Ferris' sword start to scrape from its scabbard. 'Three.'

'Wait, wait.' The older soldier smiled awkwardly. 'I'm sure this is a simple misunderstanding.'

'I'm sure it must be.' Maya frowned. 'You're barring access to the future queen of the Freestates. I expect you've heard of the ceremony at this week's end and now recognise your mistake in raising a weapon against me.'

The two soldiers almost dropped their spears as they brought them to their sides.

Maya swept past without saying another word, Ferris with his four soldiers following, grinning from ear to ear.

They first went to the low buildings that would have bunks for the soldiers who garrisoned the city.

'Ferris. How many soldiers does the Freeguard garrison have?'

'A thousand, I believe,' he said, 'or at least that's how many I learned Duggan draws coin for. Yet I'd be surprised if there are anywhere near that many. It's a good way to make coin when there are likely less than half that amount.'

Maya nodded in acknowledgement, pushing open the door to the first low building.

Ferris whistled softly.

'Will you look at that,' he murmured.

They walked through the long building amongst barrels of wine stacked high to the ceilings, bales of silks and other luxuries.

'Am I right in thinking that if there were a thousand garrison soldiers, then this room should be full of them sleeping?' Maya asked.

Ferris' shocked look was all the answer she needed.

They discovered the same in the second and third buildings, and as they stepped out into the morning light, there before them stood a tall man in gilded armour, his face swollen and with a broken nose.

'Who the hell are you?' he demanded, his eyes sweeping across them. 'What are you doing in my damned barracks?' As he spoke, his voice rose to a shout.

Maya stood unbowed before his fury, looking levelly into his eyes.

'Who do you report to?' she asked, but continued before he could answer. 'I'll tell you. You report to Lord Duggan. Lord Duggan now reports to the king, and now it will not just be the king, but the queen too. So you now report to me. You know who I am and you did so before you addressed me, for I know your guards went to tell you. You now have only one way to stop your rank being stripped away.'

'I've done nothing wrong,' Tolgarth blustered, 'and Lord Duggan will not allow any mistreatment of me, a loyal soldier to him and the realm.'

Maya's face, which till now had remained calm, darkened.

'Forget what I said earlier, I won't strip your rank,' and for a brief moment, a smile began to form out on Tolgarth's broken features.

'Instead, I'll have you executed for theft,' she continued. 'I believe you've been drawing pay for a thousand soldiers, whereas you have maybe a quarter of that at most. You see, the men I sent to spy on the other barracks gave me the same disturbing news that I've witnessed here myself,' she bluffed. 'Barracks empty of men but full of luxuries.'

Maya saw Tolgarth's pupils widen and knew she was on the mark.

'Of course, you might have nearly eight hundred men sleeping in that building that would typically house nearer fifty,' and she nodded toward the final building they'd yet to visit, 'but I doubt it. Now, what do you think your patron, Lord Duggan, will do when he finds out you've been siphoning his gold? I also think he'll be rather displeased to find out you've used his money to accrue luxuries and trade them under his nose. Likely without paying any taxes as well.'

She saw every one of her words hit home. Tolgarth's face was as white as a sheet.

'I think Lord Duggan will even ask to be the one who hacks off your head with a blunt sword. Come,' she said to Ferris, 'Captain Tolgarth cannot see the executioner's axe for the hood that's already over his head.'

She turned toward the gates.

'No wait, please wait!' Tolgarth cried dropping to his knees, his hands held beseechingly in front of him. 'What can I do to make amends? If you said there was something I could do, I could do it and more. You're my queen … you just need to ask, and I'll obey!'

Maya turned her gaze upon Tolgarth, feeling nothing but loathing for this man, but instead, she hid this from her face.

'Look at me!' she commanded, and his eyes, full of tears, rose to meet hers. 'My betrothed, King Tristan, has promised that every man levied who fights for him will receive half the pay of a regular soldier and would be armed, armoured and trained upon their arrival here.'

'I'd heard something about this,' Tolgarth whispered.

'You'll implement and honour that promise, and you'll make your queen and king proud of you so that we forget your unfortunate mistake. The mistake you made was not trying to accrue wealth, for that is the Freestates way and laudable, it was getting caught doing it at your lord's expense!'

'So, when the countryfolk arrive throughout the day, you'll house them in the barracks, feed them in your mess halls and pay them with the coin you've accrued over these years. Finally, you'll have them trained as if your very life depends upon it, which as I'm sure you realise, it actually does!'

Tears ran down Tolgarth's face, but unmoved, Maya continued.

'Men loyal to me will be watching you and your garrison soldiers in every barracks at all times. You won't know who they are even if you look for them, for they'll be hidden amongst the country folk. This way, any abuse, any failure to pay their wage, feed them or train them, and I'll know. If this happens, our deal will be cancelled, and your head will be taken from your shoulders.'

Maya looked down at Tolgarth's snivelling face.

Tolgarth clutched at her ankles, a desperate man.

'Thank you, my queen. I won't fail you!' he cried.

Maya shook herself free and walked with Ferris and his men from the barracks to the main thoroughfare and out through the city gates.

Ferris exchanged looks with his fellow soldiers behind her back as they followed, and their faces were all the same.

They looked awestruck.

Till this morning, they'd only seen the compassionate Lady Maya, the bringer of life. Now, here was a ruthless side that would bring death upon any who stood against her will.

It was a long walk up the hill to the northwest of the city, but Maya's long stride quickly covered the ground. Sunlight poured through gaps in the clouds, causing her green dress to shine like an emerald, while her long, pure, white hair was like freshly fallen snow.

It was fortunate that the weather was still mild, she thought, although autumn was arriving. Even if Daleth didn't attack till spring, a harsh winter without proper shelter might see many of the countryfolk, her folk, perish. Thus, she'd gone to give them the good news about the start of training in the barracks and the coin they'd earn.

By the time she'd reached the small tents of animal skins and the crude shelters, hundreds had already gathered to greet her, coming forward to reverently touch her arm. Children surrounded her in a ring, joining hands, singing, and her eyes widened in shock as she realised they sang of her.

Someone had turned the story she'd told them into a song, and suddenly men and women joined in too, almost like a prayer. Her cheeks blushed, and she laughed in embarrassment, while at the same time, was humbled by their love.

A man raised his hand in greeting from amongst the throng, and she recognised Silonas from her journey to Freeguard. Whereas before he'd met her with distrust, this time he walked up to her and knelt.

She reached out, placing her hand gently on his head, and he rose with a broad smile as if he'd just met a long-lost daughter.

'Lady Maya,' he said 'you've not forgotten us, and nor have we forgotten you.' He gestured to the children who'd started singing the song once again. 'More people join us each day, some believing in Tristan's lies, but thanks to you, they quickly learn the truth. It's hard for us, being so far from home, but you're further still, so what you can bear, so can we.' As he spoke, he led her to a fire, and she sat on a stump with him before her.

Many people gathered to watch and listen, but they kept a respectful distance. Ferris and his soldiers did the same.

Silonas suddenly looked aghast.

'We've no food prepared to offer you,' he said in a panic, looking around frantically for some cooked meat. The only thing to catch his eye were some dead rabbits brought in earlier by a hunter.

Maya laughed kindly, her smile reassuring.

'There's plenty of food here, we just need to cook it.'

She quickly scooped up the rabbits, drew her dagger and started expertly flaying and gut the animals, to the delight of all watching.

Soon, the smell of cooking meat filled everyone's nostrils as she spitted the carcasses and put them over the glowing coals of the fire.

She stood, raising her voice.

'Autumn and then winter are coming, and whilst I know you're strong and good people of the land, you've no homes and no food stores ready for the coming harsh months. You've probably heard that Daleth won't attack until next spring due to injuries he received in the taking of Tristan's Folly and I can confirm that, as far as I know, this is true.'

Murmurs met her announcement, and there was a general nodding of heads.

'So, for now,' she continued, 'your closest enemy is hunger and the elements. You must prepare warmer shelters until such time as I can organise your housing within the city.'

'We'll be fine!' someone shouted, and others took up the call.

Maya shook her head, raising her hands for silence.

'You humble me, for you're far nobler than almost all of those who claim that title living there.'

She raised her hand, pointing to the glowing city below them.

'Now, I'm here to deliver on a promise I made to myself and that I received from the king following our last meeting on the road. You came here to fight for the land and the people you love. However, you're also here to protect everyone who lives there.' Once again, she indicated Freeguard.

'We fight for you,' someone cried, and other similar words were shouted.

Maya raised her hands until, once again, quiet descended.

'I know you care not for them, but from now on, they will start caring for you. As of today, those menfolk who accompany me on my return will be paid to train as Freestates soldiers. This means they'll be able to start providing for you and be able to protect you when the need arises.'

For a moment, silence met her announcement, and then everyone started dancing and laughing. Singing broke out, and Maya suddenly found herself lifted aloft above the crowd that swelled as the news spread like wildfire through the encampment.

Briefly, the people's happiness lifted her own malaise, and she shone with an inner light, as her gift found the briefest release. But then, as she wished Taran were present to share the moment, it disappeared again as if locked behind a door. Unreachable.

The sun was way past its zenith when she returned to the city. The peasant army, as they proudly called themselves, at her back.

***

King Ostrom sat in his private chamber, deep in thought. As the early afternoon sunlight warmed him through the window, he had to admit he enjoyed the comfort of the palace, but that didn't stop him staying with his men outside the walls every other night.

After years of rule, he knew that when men saw you share their pain, when you shed your blood alongside theirs, then you could walk into the nine hells and they'd walk with you, asking for nothing but the honour of dying by your side.

The Freestates people had no honour, worshipping a god of greed, where loyalty was bought and was as fickle as a game of luck.

He could tolerate the folk of the Eyre. No, in fact, upon reflection, it was more than that. Dafne was a woman he respected, and her archers, who'd initially seemed undisciplined, were beyond skilful with the bow.

They'd effectively been at war with the Witch-King for decades. Daleth had used their lands as a proving ground for his warriors, sending them in to fight, to hone their survival skills, and thus the Eyre were no strangers to war.

It seemed King Tristan, whom they'd sworn to follow, was the weakest link in this army, and so were the Freestates soldiers, or at least most, for there were always exceptions.

Captain Rakan was one, as were the handful of men who'd fought for weeks and survived the fall of Tristan's Folly. However, they were but a few, and Rakan wasn't even a Freestates man of birth, he'd been a product of Daleth's army. If he was anything to go by, then this was a war they'd be unlikely to win.

Likewise, it seemed the absent lord commander, who was somehow Rakan's son, was also once in the Witch-King's army. Maybe the best way to win this war would be to get all of Daleth's soldiers to defect, and he chuckled at the thought.

He was between a handful of sand vipers and a fire lizard. There was no way he could turn that didn't seem to lead to death, either slow or fast.

Turning his army around and marching back across the desert was not a choice. Honour forbade it, the quest for glory forbade it, and death against impossible odds meant his soul would be pulled to the bosom of the sun goddess herself when he fell. Throughout his long life, he'd won every battle, every war, yet it seemed he'd lose this one.

A cough interrupted his thoughts, and he opened his eyes to look at Ultric, who was seated across the table.

'I'm sorry, Ultric,' Ostrom said grimacing, 'my mind is full and no doubt you're about to fill it even more.'

Ultric smiled.

'I hate the feel of this place. I cannot stand the people, but at least the food is incredible.' Juice ran down his chin as he bit into a ripe fruit.

Ostrom laughed.

'True, it's not bad, but your sense of taste is also enhanced to help compensate for your lack of sight. Now, enough about the food. Tell me what you've heard and learned.'

Ultric finished the fruit before wiping his chin clean, while Ostrom waited patiently for him to order his thoughts.

'Firstly, you'll not be surprised to hear that our men are impatient to fight, the more so because of the odds they face. They're helping repair the walls, but they grumble for they've no wish to hide behind them, yet their discipline remains as firm as your own.'

Ultric steepled his fingers his blank gaze fixed on Ostrom.

'Next, the Eyre. Dafne is a strong woman, and the men under her command are all experts with the bow, although I worry about their resolve. They ask who is guarding their lands while they guard the Freestates. They're volunteers more than regular soldiers, so some may well disappear in the middle of the night.'

'Go on,' Ostrom murmured when Ultric paused.

'The Freestates soldiers,' Ultric continued, 'are of varying calibre depending on which town or city they've been drawn from. Most are more suited to collecting taxes and arresting drunken merchants than doing any real fighting. However, there are, of course, exceptions. This Lord Commander Taran might be a fascinating piece in the game. By all accounts he's incredibly young, and once carried a gift of mind-reading and influence, although rumours are that it's currently denied him.'

Ostrom leaned forward, his interest piqued.

'We heard of him in our meeting. He was pivotal in defending Tristan's Folly and after its fall stayed behind to rally countryfolk to the cause. Tristan moved the conversation on quite quickly and tried to diminish his achievements when Rakan brought his name into the conversation.'

Ultric nodded sagely.

'Tristan is fearful of Taran's return, and I now know why. The countryfolk camp is awash with a story of the Lady Maya and how she's unwillingly betrothed to Tristan. She also suffers from losing her gift. The story goes on to say how her one true love will return to rescue her, restore her gift, and take his revenge on the one who stole her from him. Taran and Maya were lovers, and King Tristan used his power to separate them.'

Ostrom's eyes widened at the news.

'That explains Tristan's odd behaviour and could well lead to trouble.'

'Indeed,' Ultric agreed, 'Finally, I've just discovered that Lord Duggan is seeking support to overthrow Tristan, claiming he's about to waste the crown's wealth on arming, training, and paying peasants. This is a sin in the eyes of the Freestates, and Duggan will quickly gain support.'

Ostrom rubbed his temples with the palm of his hands, considering the information presented to him.

'So, in summary. We're in a fractious coalition that could fall apart at any moment, from desertion to civil war, or even a vengeful commander removing the head of his king. So, in the end, we might be the only ones fighting if the Eyre go back to their homeland and the Freestates forces kill themselves in the interim.'

Ostrom laughed long and hard.

Ultric raised an eyebrow, unsure as to the source of his king's amusement.

Ostrom slowly controlled himself.

'I was worried,' he explained, as his laughter dissipated, 'that if we didn't fight Daleth's army before the winter, I'd be bored to death. Yet, my friend, it seems we'll have a lot of things to keep us entertained.'

Ultric, now understanding the joke, laughed as well.

'These are entertaining times, my king. Entertaining times indeed.'

***

The End of Dreams

Maya waited to see Tristan, but the door to the audience chamber remained closed. Muffled, raised voices sounded through the thick wood, putting her slightly on edge. She'd been wandering the palace gardens enjoying the afternoon sun, when a retainer had found her, breathlessly advising that the king demanded her presence.

The doors finally opened to the audience chamber, interrupting her thoughts, and the guards bowed as she passed through. As she entered, she saw some of the Freestates nobles, including Lord Duggan, leave through the side doors along with King Ostrom and Dafne.

Only Tristan remained. His face was serious, angry even.

She hadn't been looking forward to seeing him anyway, so she waited patiently for Tristan to start.

'So what has my betrothed got to say for herself?' Tristan demanded sarcastically.

'I'm not your betrothed yet,' Maya responded snappily, irritated by his tone, and she crossed her arms over her chest, staring at him.

'You'd like that, wouldn't you?' Tristan snarled. 'To renege on our agreement, or for me to release you from it. Yet earlier today and behind my back, you were, oh so very happy to wield the power betrothal grants you. Have you any idea of the trouble you've caused me with your deed? You even come here with your dress covered in mud as if to show contempt for your position.'

'I care not for clothing, position, or wealth,' Maya said defiantly.

'You forget yourself!' Tristan roared. 'It was YOU who offered anything to me in exchange for Taran's life, and it was YOU who accepted the terms. Have you forgotten or does your memory fail you, or do you consider your oath no longer binding?'

Maya smiled without warmth.

'Oh, I remember the choice you gave me, my king. One, a life without my love, and oh yes, the other a life without my love. Such wonderful choices. But, I remember my oath, and I'm grateful that Taran still lives. If only you'd thought it through though, because my gratitude would've been a hundredfold had you given me Taran's life without condition.'

Tristan went to say something, but Maya continued regardless.

'Now you're angry because I no longer have worth, I no longer have my gift, and you're to be betrothed to a worthless, peasant princess. That's how the nobles view me, for they don't believe the tales that are told. Rather, they think them fantasies and believe your choice is driven by love or lust. What could possibly be worse for the king to be found guilty of such a heinous crime when choosing a wife?'

'It's that and more,' Tristan growled, 'and you damn well know it. Lord Duggan has been telling everyone how my future queen is bringing peasants into the city and not only arming and armouring them, but paying them too.'

'You already agreed to do it!' Maya interrupted, grimacing in disgust. 'How could you go back on your word so quickly? Are their lives worth nothing to you? Is your crown not worth the coins you'd pay them?'

'It wasn't the time, nor your place to do it,' Tristan raged, 'and it's up to me what promises I keep, not you! I'm a laughing stock, and Duggan has the support of nearly half the nobility now. This could bring me down!'

Maya shrugged indifferently, and Tristan's face turned a deeper shade of red.

'Now, let me make this crystal clear. Should my kingship be removed, I can assure you, neither you nor Taran will survive my downfall, even if it costs my last coin. My last order will be to have your heads removed! So tell me, how are we to get out of this mess, for we're both in serious danger!'

Maya's face was impassive, even though Tristan's words shook her. She knew it was no idle threat, but she composed herself.

'Fear not. What Lord Duggan has omitted to tell the other nobles or yourself, for he was unaware, was that I brokered the deal so that not one single copper for this will come from the Freestates treasury. In fact, it's being paid for by Lord Duggan himself. His Captain Tolgarth has been siphoning coin from him for years, and I used that knowledge as leverage to impose my will.'

Maya lifted a hand, forestalling any interruption.

'So, I'm training your peasant army for nothing, arming them for nothing, armouring them for nothing. On the other hand, Lord Duggan is the one paying for everything. The very words he's using to try and usurp you for being inadequate in the protection of wealth will be the very words that'll see him cast down when you reveal this fact.'

Tristan sat there open-mouthed as he assimilated everything Maya said to him, and slowly a smile spread across his face. He sat back in his chair and started laughing so loudly that, for a moment, Maya thought he'd gone slightly mad.

'You may not have your gift,' he said, once he gathered himself, 'but you show cunning and ruthlessness worthy of my hand, even if you don't want it. I know why you played this game, and I applaud you for your effort in trying to make me reconsider our agreement. But you've now caught yourself in a web of your own making. Our betrothal ceremony still goes ahead the day after the morrow. Now leave me be, I need to plan how to break this amazing news in such a way that will see Duggan brought to his knees, and when he begs for mercy, he'll find none.'

Maya stalked from the chamber. Her earlier happiness at what she'd done for the countryfolk quickly faded, leaving just sadness that made her stagger under its weight. She'd indeed been too clever for her own good, and now she'd have to go through with this damned betrothal ceremony, not that she'd really thought she could avoid it.

The only way for this wedding to be stopped was for the war to be lost or Tristan to die, and she now found herself wondering if that was a price worth paying. Yet how could she wish that if it meant this city, its people, the very folk she'd tried to help, being destroyed just to save her heart. She couldn't be that selfish.

She sighed. There had to be another way, there had to be, and Taran would find it if so. But, as she walked back to her chamber, her heart found it harder to believe.

She was no longer gifted, she was just cursed.

***

Rakan sat astride his horse, looking back over the trail behind them, Freeguard two days distant. He wore regular Freestates armour, having reluctantly left Kalas' set behind.

He was under no illusions that his promotion to major, a rank he hadn't encountered before, had been a way of removing him from the city. Yet, if he put all his personal misgivings aside, at least the mission he was on had been the right strategic move to make. It had been on his recommendation, even if he hadn't anticipated being put in charge of it.

He'd wanted to wait at Freeguard a few more days to see if Taran arrived, but instead, now hoped to run into him as he headed back west to gather intelligence on the whereabouts of Daleth's army and lancers.

Everyone hoped Daleth would now wait till spring to launch his final assault and yet that couldn't be entirely counted upon until it was proved to be so. There was also nothing to stop his men scouring the countryside and slaughtering the population that still refused to leave their lands.

So now Rakan was in charge of over two thousand men that would soon be split into twenty separate centuries positioned ever outward from the city like spokes on a wheel. With orders not to engage the enemy, unless assured of victory, they were to build small redoubts, preferably hidden on the edge of woodland, and light signal fires should any sizeable enemy force approach Freeguard. Should that happen, they'd withdraw backwards along the route, joining with the next force, so that their numbers swelled during any withdrawal.

Each century had seventy-five desert spearmen, a further twenty archers, and finally five mounted troops that could be used to communicate swiftly with other nearby groups if the need arose. They also carried supplies for two weeks that would be regularly replenished by the last few mounted soldiers Rakan had seconded to his mission.

The lack of mounted troops was a huge disadvantage when Daleth had so many lancers to call upon, and Rakan knew they could ill afford to lose any mounts in this exercise.

As they travelled west, they'd occasionally come across families or individuals with their meagre belongings in backpacks, on small handcarts, or wagons heading east. Rakan always took time to question them all, asking why they travelled, if they'd had sight of Taran, or encountered enemy forces.

The answers he received were varied.

Some fortunate few travelled, still unaware of hostilities, coming for the betrothal ceremony. Others had been influenced by Maya and some even by Taran. Sadly, most had seen their villages attacked and had been left alive when all of their family and friends were dead. Their faces were gaunt, bloodied, often blackened with soot, and they looked lost of the will to live.

Daleth was making this a war of minds. By ensuring there were some survivors, he knew tales of terror would weaken resolve. A broken soul would be a liability, taking many more to care for them. By allowing some to live, he was ensuring that any common levy Tristan tried to raise would be weakened by their experiences.

Rakan sighed, turning his attention ahead, he indicated to a copse of woodland. The next century in line started peeling off from the main column, saying farewells to their brothers in arms, and onward the rest of them pressed.

Yestereve had been Maya's betrothal celebration, he suddenly realised, and his heart sank. He'd not had more than that briefest moment in the audience chamber with her, and yet her first thought had been for Taran, her face full of hope as she asked. There was more to this than met the eye, and he knew his appointment had been to ensure he'd not have the time to find out what.

Poor Maya and Taran.

Things had been far simpler when they'd been running for their lives, and he now regretted the decision that had seen them turn and fight. He looked at his hands, the skin slowly healing from the burns, although his arms were blistered and still weeping.

He remembered when Maya had first laid her hand upon him, healing his skin where she touched him. At that moment, everything he knew, everything he believed in, had started to unravel. Then shortly thereafter, he'd seen the world clearly for the first time since donning the amulet.

Those damned amulets, and now Taran was wearing one, stolen from the dead to deal with the pain of Maya's betrayal. Yet having seen that light in her eyes, he knew no love had been lost, but maybe, just maybe, she'd been stolen like the amulet.

Rakan seized upon this idea, knowing his train of thought was the right one. There was nothing a Freestates king wouldn't do to acquire a prize like Maya's gift in a land where possessing wealth and flaunting it was the highest sign of success.

Damn Tristan, but that had to be it. He'd probably used Taran's capture as leverage, first refusing the exchange, but following his private meeting with her, he'd changed his mind and the next day Maya had disappeared.

If this was true, and he felt sure it was, it was the only explanation that made sense, then this story would have only one end. Taran was already seeking revenge on Tristan, and this was just further justification.

Yet Tristan was no fool, and he'd be ready in case Taran tried something. With Taran's gift denied him, he worried Taran would fall foul of his emotions and whatever Tristan might have planned.

Damn. If all this makes me feel sad, how must Maya be feeling right now, he thought. A tear formed in his eye. He considered wiping it away, but let it fall instead, for some thoughts were too sad to pretend they weren't there.

**

Chapter VIII

Maya looked at herself in the long, silvered mirror in her chamber. It was made with exquisite craftsmanship, and yet she couldn't appreciate its beauty, nor did she really see herself as she stared at her reflection.

She still wore the dress from the night before, having returned to her chamber after midnight, and fallen asleep in tears moments later.

Who was this person in the mirror?

As a young girl, her parents had never been able to afford such a luxury, so she'd only ever seen her face in the reflection of a still pool, or a bowl of water, yet now she didn't recognise herself. The face of a young, old woman looked back, aged by using her gift to save the one she loved. It had been worth it, for Taran always looked at her with eyes that saw beauty in everything she was, whether it be the white hair, the crow's feet, or the smile lines around her mouth.

She still had the body of a much younger woman, and yet there was no longer youth or happiness in her eyes.

The night before had, thankfully, passed in a blur. Festivities took place across the city, and everyone had joined in, from servants to nobility. What better way to forget the threat of war than a night drinking, eating, dancing, and laughing, and yet Maya had done none of these.

Thankfully, Tristan had hardly been near her, yet she'd heard him boasting of her gift in the audience chamber. Not of her lost ability to heal the land, but in her ability to save wealth and have Lord Duggan removed from his position in one simple, deadly move.

The nobility no longer looked upon her with scorn. Instead, they lauded her sharp mind and her evident grasp of the importance of wealth. Unable to bear these compliments for they'd hurt more than their insults, she'd left the palace celebrations. With the ever-watchful Ferris in tow, she'd escaped into the city to lose herself in the crowds.

Except, of course, she was known wherever she went, for her looks made her stand out. She'd heard herself described in many ways; a creature of beauty and grace, old yet young, full of laughter yet doused in sadness.

Yet at least she didn't feel quite so trapped once out amongst the people of the city. The gates were open and the countryfolk, including those now training in the city garrisons, sought her out. Publicly they congratulated her, and then behind their hands offered condolences. They knew of her story.

'Don't fret,' many said. 'He'll still come.'

Maya knew Taran would, and it was her only consolation. Yet Tristan, now more than ever, would never willingly release her from his servitude. She couldn't help but fear for Taran's safety from a king who would stop at nothing to keep his possessions safe.

A knock on the door of her chamber startled her, and she called for the visitor to enter.

Ferris gingerly poked his head around the door, and she beckoned him in.

'Look what I have for you,' he said, stepping forward to lay upon the bed her hunting leathers that she thought never to see again. They'd been cleaned, waxed and buffed to a lustre, as had her boots.

Maya clapped her hands.

'Thank you, Ferris. I cannot tell you how much something simple like this means. All this finery is not me and never will be. I couldn't care less about all of this,' she said, waving her hands around the room.

'I know, my lady,' he said bowing, 'and the people know. That's what gives them hope, that a queen like you can make such a positive difference to them.'

Maya's face dropped, sadness evident at the mention of her future title.

Ferris looked horrified.

'I'm so sorry. That was a thoughtless thing to say.'

The End of Dreams

Maya forced her sadness away. She wanted to share her hopes with Ferris about Taran coming to save her, but kept them to herself.

'Don't worry, Ferris. A year is a long time, and we've to win a war against an ageless Witch-King and a merciless horde before my fate is sealed. The likelihood of my wedding currently seems remote, so worry not about your choice of words.'

Suppressing a big sigh, she smiled instead.

'Leave me,' she ordered gently. 'I need to get rid of this horrible thing,' and she plucked at her dress. 'I'll be ready to face the day shortly in something more fitting for a peasant princess.'

Ferris closed the door behind him, and Maya made haste in removing her dress, then washed before donning her old clothes.

This time, when she looked in the mirror, she saw more of her old self, and she smiled sincerely this time. She was a hunter, a fighter, and needed to keep ahead of the wolves that would bring her down.

She opened the wardrobes, pulling out her sword and dagger and belted them to her waist. Then she unwrapped the bow that Drizt had given her from its waxed leather covering.

She turned it over in her hands, enjoying the smooth feel of its polished wood, and then reached in pulling out a quiver of arrows.

Today, she was going to be what she'd always been. If the immediate future held no light for her, she would turn to her past.

She opened the door to find Ferris and his four companions waiting.

'Time to go hunting,' she ordered, and strode down the corridor with them following behind.

***

Taran stood before the western gates of Freeguard, favouring his right leg with Yana next to him. The city walls were a hive of activity, with soldiers making repairs. Encampments dotted the landscape, desert spearmen, Eyre, and Freestates soldiers everywhere. The number seemed vast, but Taran knew they weren't enough.

Alexan and the two soldiers had gone ahead and were talking to the gate guard. The villagers who'd kept them company on their journey were dismounting around Taran. They'd divested themselves of the lancers' armour some days ago after Taran deemed they were close enough to Freeguard to be safe.

One by one, they came to Taran, taking his hand, kissing his palm, gratitude shining in their eyes. They'd all taken turns caring for him on the journey, for every one of them saw him as their personal saviour.

Last to come to him was the child he'd saved, alongside her mother.

The older woman kissed his palm, saying what was now almost a prayer.

'With this hand, you gave us life.' She stood away as her daughter skipped forward, laughter in her eyes. But the moment the girl's hand grasped Taran's, it faded, and tears ran down her face.

'You will only know the briefest happiness again before you die,' she said, then stumbled back, and turned, crying to her mother.

'I am so, so sorry,' the mother said, looking horrified, as both Taran and Yana stared at the child, who was crying inconsolably.

'It's no cause for concern,' Taran said dismissively. 'Happiness is not something I care about anymore.'

He stood watching and waiting as the horses were taken inside the city, while the villagers were directed northwest to the hills. *It's incredible*, he thought. *They have space for horses, but not for these people.*

'What are we waiting for?' Yana probed, gently squeezing his shoulder. 'How about we forget this war, forget this place, and just ride off east across the desert? We could well find happiness there.'

Taran didn't respond, for he was trying to control the sudden rage he felt inside. The insatiable desire to ride to the palace, to find Tristan and drive his blade through the king's greedy heart.

After a few deep breaths, the rage subsided, and the nothingness that was the amulet's default feeling washed over him again. At times like these, he understood what Rakan had gone through when he wanted his revenge on Snark. A desire that had stayed with Rakan for years until it had been satiated by Taran's hands.

'Come,' Taran instructed, ignoring her question, as he limped toward the gates leading his horse. He wore his armour, polished to a sheen by the villagers as their way of thanking him for his deeds, and the gate guards stood to attention as he passed.

Taran was tired, so tired.

The End of Dreams

As he and Yana followed Alexan's directions to the palace, he noted with interest as they passed some barracks, that many of those training were not regular soldiers, but people like the villagers he'd saved.

At least Tristan had done something right.

The moment the man's name entered his mind, he again forced himself to quell the rising anger.

It was a long walk, and they could have ridden, but Taran wanted to take his time, for whilst he couldn't use his gift anymore, he wanted to gauge the feeling of the local citizens they passed.

For the most part, he heard grumbling about how peasants and foreign soldiers were befouling the city. The other complaints were around how the war would affect profits and how dare the king's men requisition wagons and horses.

Taran despaired.

How could anyone be worried about money when their blood would soon spill across the streets on which they walked? This war was so nearly upon them, would be nigh on impossible to win, and yet all they could focus on was wealth and keeping the city free of anyone but the privileged.

However, was his narrow-minded goal of killing Daleth and Tristan thereafter any better? The rush he felt as he considered the question assured him it was. He picked up his pace, trying through sheer force of will to keep his gait steady and unaffected by the still healing wound to his leg, or the various burns that still wracked his body.

People stopped and looked wonderingly at them as they passed, for Taran's armour marked him as a soldier of the highest rank, and Yana's looks were captivating.

'See how all the men look at me?' she teased Taran, enjoying the attention. 'Yet, in this world of ours, I only want one.' She tossed her head as she walked, flashing her smile flirtatiously.

As the palace came into sight, Yana checked Taran's dressings, shaking her head.

'The stitches are pulling,' she sighed. 'You used to be so young, fit, and handsome. Now look at you, all broken. Yet there's still something about you. Perhaps it's those broad shoulders or your strong arms, or maybe something else entirely,' she added winking.

Taran couldn't help but laugh.

Yana beamed as they approached the palace together. The gates and the palace entrance beyond were heavily guarded by spearmen and archers, an unbreakable ring of security.

In front was a vast central square, where under the disapproving glares of local merchants, groups of armed men and women from the Eyre, desert tribes, and Freestates garrisons mingled during their free time.

Yana turned to Taran.

'Now that our allies have arrived, all they need is a leader. Now all they need is you.'

As they neared the iron gates to the palace grounds, their way was barred by the crossed spears of two desert soldiers who looked at them, frowning.

'I don't recognise you,' one said, 'and you're too young to be wearing the armour of a Freestates Commander, so you must have stolen it.' His knuckles whitened slightly on his spear shaft.

Taran smiled wryly, the burn on his face stretching.

'I am indeed very young to be wearing this armour,' he replied, 'but it was a gift from my beloved King Tristan, who I believe, as head of the alliance, is now your lord and master too. As for who I am, I'm Taran, Lord Commander of his army of which you're part, meaning you report to me. I'm here to see the king, so stand aside before I take your spear and beat you over the head with it!'

The guard stepped back with a disarming smile, whereas his spear butt flashed up to hit Taran across the side of the face.

Instead, the guard found himself on his back, head spinning.

He managed to focus long enough to see Taran, a dark look on his face, holding a dagger to the throat of the other guard whose spear lay on the ground.

The Eyre archers on guard duty had bows drawn, and other soldiers ran swiftly toward the sound of the commotion, weapons ready, uncertain as to what was happening.

Taran raised his voice, taking the initiative.

'I had a close friend once from the Eyre, a man called Drizt. He fought with me on the walls of Tristan's Folly and died there by my side. He was the finest archer I've ever seen, a true god when a bow was in his hand. If all of you are anything like him, then we're lucky indeed to have you with us.'

He lowered his dagger and leant down to reach out his hand to the fallen spearman, and pulled him unsteadily to his feet.

'I also fought alongside five hundred of your desert brothers,' he continued, 'who'd once been captained by Sancen, the son of your king. They were fearless, and the last forty of them chose to a man to die with honour rather than escape. Alone, they faced down over ninety-thousand men so that I could come here to carry on the fight. Their courage and story will forever remain an inspiration to us all.'

He looked around, spotting Alexan and some other Freestates soldiers who'd ridden with Rakan, beckoning them over.

'Lastly, I had the honour of fighting with some of the finest swordsmen this land has seen in these men standing see beside me. I saw their brothers cut down, yet they never faltered, and bled the enemy in their thousands. Their skill is to be admired and feared.'

He turned slowly, aware that everyone in the square was silent, listening intently to his words.

'I honour the fallen for what they gave, and they gave everything to keep the Freestates, and every other kingdom for as far as eagles fly, free of Daleth's rule. But first, before their ultimate sacrifice, they gave me their friendship, and I would in time hope to find that same friendship, that same bond, with you and your comrades, and would offer mine in return.'

'I came back to carry the memory of their sacrifice with me so that they're never forgotten. To do that, I'm going to ensure that we win this war, but first I need you to know who I am, to trust who I am.'

'I am Taran, Lord Commander of King Tristan's army, and thus the alliance army. I'm your brother, whether my skin is the same colour as yours or not. I'm your friend, whether you know me or not. But first and foremost I'm your commander, and I'll lead you, bleed with you, and fight alongside you. But, from this moment forth, you *will* follow my orders without question and without hesitation!'

Suddenly the Freestates troops lifted Taran onto their shoulders, passing him around while a roar erupted from the throats of every soldier in the square. The desert soldiers thumped their spears against shields, the Freestates men did the same with their swords, and the Eyre archers rattled their arrows against bows.

The ground shook as those present stamped their boots on the flagstones with the noise of a thunderstorm.

Yana looked on in rapture as Taran was carried through the gates on a tide of men, Lord Commander of the king's armies. If this war was won, surely one day he'd be king, and she'd find a way to be his queen.

The sun shone upon the square, and it was as if the gods themselves had anointed their champion.

***

Tristan's head pounded, and all this bickering was just making it worse. The meeting had been going on for most of the morning, with no consensus found.

He wanted to continue fortifying and defend, Ostrom was keen to make a pre-emptive attack, while Dafne encouraged raiding and harassing wherever possible. Each faction wanted something different, and thus only themselves to command the combined armies.

There had to be a way out of this impasse, for whilst they were all being civil to one another, cracks were starting to show as tempers frayed.

His thoughts were interrupted by rumbling, not unlike the noise made by Daleth's horde when it had attacked the fortress.

Tristan looked up in consternation.

'What's that sound?' he asked worriedly, as it grew louder, filling the audience chamber where he sat with Ostrom, Dafne, and several other nobles.

Ostrom looked at Ultric who, as ever, sat close behind his shoulder.

'What can you hear?' he asked, his hand going to the sword hilt at his hip.

Ultric shook his head, perplexed.

'It isn't clear,' he murmured, 'but I don't think it's fighting although I can hear the crash of spear upon shield.'

Ostrom was taking no chances.

The End of Dreams

'Weapons,' he shouted, and some of the nobles in the room nervously drew daggers whilst Dafne stood beside him, shortsword in hand.

Tristan motioned for the guards to open the chamber door. As they did so, the noise rolled over them like waves upon a beach.

'By the gods, are we undone?' Dafne asked, staring down the long hallway past the guards, all of whom gripped swords or spears nervously.

The huge doors at the far end swung inward, and everyone readied themselves, yet the huge mass of armed men beyond were all alliance soldiers, and instead of pushing in, they stopped. Then the front ranks parted, and a man was carried forward on the shoulders of two men of the desert and two women of the Eyre.

He wore the embellished armour of a Freestates commander and was wrapped in several bloodied dressings, yet as he was lowered to the ground, his bearing was strong. He strode toward the audience chamber, a woman of striking beauty by his side.

The Freestates guards relaxed and several stepped forward, embracing him, and he spoke briefly to each in turn as he made his way along the corridor.

Ostrom turned toward Tristan, who was motioning frantically to Galain. Tristan's aide disappeared through the side doors, only to reappear moments later with a dozen guards following. Whilst everyone else in the room had already sheathed their weapons, these guards kept their hands on their sword hilts.

'This is interesting,' Ostrom whispered to Ultric. 'I do believe we're about to meet the man we've heard so much about.'

Tristan waited impatiently as Taran took his time, talking to a final soldier before entering the audience chamber with Yana at his side.

The doors closed behind him.

Taran had changed so much since Tristan had last seen him. His face on one side was terribly burned, and Tristan couldn't help but feel happy that his boyish good looks had been stolen away. Likewise, his arms were covered in wounds old and new, and the dressings around one thigh had signs of fresh blood on them.

Yet the happiness evaporated when Taran's eyes met his, for Tristan glimpsed a frightening darkness there that chilled him to the bone.

Then suddenly it disappeared, as if hidden behind a hastily drawn curtain. Now, instead, Taran's eyes looked upon him with indifference, as if he were nothing but a roach on the floor.

Tristan felt his blood boil even further when Taran briefly glanced at the guards Galain had summoned, then smiled mockingly, knowing exactly why they were there.

'My king,' Taran said, bowing ever so slightly, Yana following suit at his side.

Looking across to Ostrom and Dafne, Taran bowed even lower, adding to the subtle insult.

Tristan had taken enough.

'Where have you been?' he demanded. 'We've already been debriefed by Major Rakan as to the fall of the fortress. Did you not feel it appropriate as the surviving senior officer to make that report yourself? I'd begun to think you'd deserted and run away,' he continued, trying to goad Taran into anger and a rash move.

'No, my king,' Taran said, with a smile that didn't extend to his eyes. 'I was never good at running. I find myself better at fighting and killing those who would do me and mine wrong.'

He stared into Tristan's eyes, holding the moment.

'Yet you're right,' Taran continued, 'I am late for which I apologise. I was scouring the countryside for your loyal subjects to encourage them to fight for our noble cause. Like me, those who were willing to fight and kill for the ones they loved came here.'

Tristan's face turned redder and redder at Taran's veiled threats, and yet Taran had said nothing so overt as to allow Tristan to make any move on him.

Before Tristan could gather his thoughts to respond and gain the upper hand, Ostrom rose and walked toward Taran.

'We've heard so much about you,' the desert king said. 'Rakan told us of your prowess in resisting Daleth's horde and in holding the men together till the end. Now I see with my own eyes that my men, loyal to me, the men and women of the Eyre, and your Freestates brothers, have carried you to the very doors of this palace, accepting you as their leader. What did you do to earn my men's loyalty in such a short space of time?'

Taran paused, then shrugged, deciding to tell the truth.

The End of Dreams

'Well, it all started with me knocking one of your guards on his ass,' he admitted.

Ostrom's eyes opened wide in shock, and then he started to laugh. The Desert King held his sides as tears ran down his face.

'You did what?'

He laughed, putting his arm around Taran's shoulders and carried on without pause.

'Tristan, I'll be honest. I didn't want you to lead my army even though you led the alliance, and I know Dafne felt the same, but I'll tell you this. If my men are willing to follow this man of yours, then I'm happy to put them at his command as long as he's willing to consider my advice.'

Dafne rose.

'Aye,' she said. 'I wouldn't have believed it had I not seen it with my own eyes. He can lead my archers on the same condition.'

All faces turned to Tristan.

Inside, Tristan was furious. He'd intended to demote Taran, to provoke him into a stupid action, to remove him as a threat. Instead, he was now being forced to make a decision that made him sick inside, but he had no choice.

He smiled broadly, swallowing with difficulty the bile that rose from his stomach.

'Of course, Lord Commander Taran leads the army. He was automatically promoted to that responsibility on the death of Kalas.'

Suddenly Tristan had a thought and smiled at his own deviousness.

'Now, Lord Commander Taran. We have twenty-five thousand of the finest spearmen, five thousand elite archers, around five thousand Freestates swordsmen, with roughly five thousand peasants in training. Tell us all and tell us simply ... how you intend to win this war with this powerful army?'

Taran looked at them all, letting the silence draw out.

'If we face Daleth with what we have, we can't win. We'll all die,' Taran said with certainty. 'But at least it will be a glorious death!'

A shocked silence greeted this declaration, and Tristan smiled inside with satisfaction.

'By all the gods,' Ostrom roared. 'A glorious death!' and he started laughing again. 'King Tristan, where did you find this gem of a man?'

Dafne's laughter matched that of the desert king, and to Tristan's horror, everyone in the room joined in, not wanting to be seen afraid.

Taran was back, and everyone loved him!

'Lord Commander,' Tristan said, feigning graciousness, but feeling sick as he did so. 'You're sorely injured. Whilst we'd all enjoy hearing of your exploits, I think it prudent that you take two days to rest and recover a little. Following that, we'll press you further and seek your advice on how we might avoid this glorious death if at all possible.'

He chuckled, keeping up the pretence of levity.

'You and Yana will be shown to quarters befitting your rank and station, and I'll have Galain call upon you two mornings hence, when your mind and body are sharp and focussed. In the interim, Galain will have details of the preparations that are currently underway brought to you for your consideration.'

Tristan looked to Ostrom and Dafne, who nodded politely, although it was obvious Ostrom was impatient to question Taran further.

As Galain led Taran and Yana from the audience chamber, Tristan smiled to himself.

He still had his best card to play, and the greatest thing was that it would play itself in time. Then he'd have Taran right where he wanted him.

***

Jared sat looking down at his bowl of food, and true to his guise, nibbled away slowly, always keeping up the persona he'd stolen.

After a while, it wasn't just the look of himself he found familiar, but the actions themselves, for they became second nature to him. Even a father or mother would be hard-pressed to notice the difference, had he studied his target thoroughly before shifting.

Of course, no matter what guise he took, inside he was still a Ranger, a killer of men. He couldn't wait to discard this pathetic form, and at this very moment was considering whether the gods had smiled on him, for an unbelievable opportunity had presented itself.

He was less than a week from Freeguard having travelled unaccosted across the width of the kingdom. He had to admit that these folk had moved with a purpose worthy of a small degree of admiration.

The End of Dreams

It seemed years of toiling in the fields, rising before dawn and working till after sunset, had given them a discipline he'd been surprised to find.

Then, this very evening, they'd been intercepted by a formation of around five hundred men, and there at the head of them was the fugitive Rakan.

Rakan had questioned Jared's group of travellers thoroughly, asking whether they'd seen any enemy. He'd talked to every adult in the group by which time darkness was falling, and had subsequently offered them the security of camping with his force for the night.

Now, across the very fire at which Jared himself sat, Rakan and several of his soldiers sat eating and talking. They were oblivious that death was potentially mere heartbeats away should Jared choose to deal it.

It wasn't that Rakan seemed relaxed, far from it, and again Jared felt some admiration for the man. He had the experience to post double sentries all around the camp, and each soldier carried two stakes. These had been planted in the soil to provide a hedgehog of sharp points that would foul any cavalry charge upon them.

He'd heard Rakan organising his men into shifts for the night, ensuring they'd receive hot food to help keep them awake. All of the soldiers slept in their armour, however uncomfortable it might be.

'Better to be sore than dead.'

He'd heard the men groan at Rakan's saying, but more out of familiarity than complaint, believing Rakan would help keep them alive if they but followed his orders.

Jared had long hair, and with his head bowed could look through it and observe unnoticed whilst appearing to stare at his food. Instead, he memorised every move, every nuance, every facial expression Rakan pulled. Surely taking his guise would not only see one of Daleth's most wanted dealt with, but would also give him direct access to the other fugitives as well as the king himself.

It was almost too good to be true, and yet Jared was unsure.

Firstly, a figure as important as Rakan would need to be studied for weeks if not longer to ensure any shift by Jared would go unnoticed by those who knew the deserter. He was just too public a figure for people not to realise something was strange or different if Jared put a foot wrong.

Secondly, Rakan and his men were travelling toward Freemantle under orders. So, to turn around and ride back without knowing what mission parameters he was operating under could lead to questions and perhaps even complications for disobedience.

Lastly, were the terrible burns all over Rakan's forearms and neck.

Jared could take any shape and any size, yet shifting required physical contact with a live subject. How long it would take his body to replicate the peeling skin and open sores he didn't know, but the thought repulsed him.

Jared scooped some more broth into his mouth, wondering if tonight he should seek Daleth's counsel, because the risk might be worth taking. Perhaps simply killing Rakan during the night would be the best option. Who would suspect a thin village boy who couldn't look someone in the eye?

As he mulled this over, a pair of heavy boots came into view, stopping before him, and he looked up to see Rakan staring down, a frown etched upon the fugitive's face.

'You've been looking at me all night,' Rakan stated. 'Yes, you might be hiding behind that greasy shock of hair, but you've been trying to catch what I've been saying and studying me since I sat down. Now, I know it's not my good looks that captivate you. So, I'm asking myself, what is it that makes you take such an interest in me, boy?'

As Rakan said this, he spun a wicked-looking dagger in the palm of his hand.

The conversation stopped around the fire, and Jared felt his blood run cold. He looked down, shaking, trying to act as if he were scared witless.

'I don't buy it,' Rakan challenged, crouching down. 'Who knows this man?' he asked loudly, and murmurs of acknowledgement came from all around. Jared smiled a little inside as people talked on his behalf, saying they'd known him all their lives and that he was a simple, peaceful soul.

'Look at me!' Rakan commanded.

Jared lifted his head, trying to look everywhere but directly into Rakan's eyes, suddenly afraid that Rakan could see inside his soul. How could this be? No one could tell what he was, especially someone who didn't even know him.

The End of Dreams

Rakan shook his head in frustration.

'You might be who they say you are, and there are plenty talking for you, but keep your distance, boy. I'll have my eyes on you the whole night. There's something about you. You're a wolf in sheep's clothing, of that I'm sure!'

Rakan stood, snarling, then turned away.

All of Jared's thoughts of taking Rakan's life or shifting to his form faded away. He'd not be able to report this to Daleth. The Witch-King would be furious and doubt Jared's ability to continue with the mission. Better to keep his head down, continue with his journey to Freeguard, and find an easier target.

By all the gods, he'd love to snuff Rakan's life out. But even now, Rakan was watching him, and Jared knew he'd never get the chance before the morning sun.

Next time, he thought to himself, next time, Rakan, I'll show you just who I am, and you'll die on the tip of my blade. You'll die confused, wondering at the point of death how you were killed by your own hand.

The thought consoled him a little as he headed for his bedroll. From the corner of his eye, he noticed that most everyone looked at him slightly differently now, as if Rakan had sowed a seed of doubt in their minds.

The sooner he got rid of these people, the better.

Less than a week to Freeguard and then he'd have a whole city to choose from and hide in. Then, he'd reach out to Daleth and revel in the king's praise.

He wrapped himself in a blanket, but it took him a long time to fall asleep, for he felt Rakan's eyes upon him the whole time.

***

Daleth felt stronger, and with the aid of a polished, wooden staff, was now making his way slowly around the palace. He pushed himself further each day, much to the healer's annoyance, but also astonishment.

Torches burned, for it was late in the night, yet he was having so much rest that his hours of sleep and wakefulness were all mixed up.

Not that it mattered, especially as he was unable to step outside and show the troops in the city the real him, whatever the time.

He knew his soldiers wondered why they were not pushing forward with the conquest of Freeguard when many of their comrades would soon be sacking the city-states of Freehold and Freemarch before moving on to slaughter the Eyre and the Horselords. Still, he kept them busy enough, so they didn't have much time to grumble.

Yet Daleth sympathised with them.

He thirsted for combat, and this enforced rest was testing his patience. Julius and Gregor would soon enjoy the thrill of command and battle, and here he was, the king, a prisoner in this palace. The only glory he'd find would be in their nightly communications. Gregor had the power of spirit talking and would be able to share his thoughts vividly enough for Daleth to appreciate in their entirety what his Ranger had experienced.

On the other hand, Julius would communicate through an overseer, and those snivelling wretches were unlikely to have been anywhere near the combat itself. Still, he'd enjoy hearing of the Nightstalkers' conquests, for they were an evil, bloodthirsty bunch.

He didn't expect either of them to meet much armed opposition from the city-states of Freehold and Freemarch, for these were open cities with no walls, and likely all their fighting men had journeyed east to join Tristan's main army.

The swamps of the Eyre and the grasslands of the Horselords would be where the main fighting would happen.

While facing the smaller foe, Julius' forces would likely have the more difficult time, for the Eyre were the ultimate guerrilla fighters. The Nightstalkers were like a hammer, but there was no anvil to pin his enemy against. The Eyre never stood and fought, but instead faded away before any advance, using poisonous darts and arrows that even the youngest Eyre seemed to fire with deadly accuracy.

On the other hand, Gregor's enemy would come to him, steel upon steel. The reputation of the Horselords was fierce. They didn't tolerate anyone not of their kind, which was a shame for they'd have made interesting allies had he thought he could have their allegiance.

He sat in a sumptuous leather chair.

The End of Dreams

Without asking, watered wine, bowls of fruit, and meats were placed near at hand by his ever-present bodyguard. He mulled over in his thoughts the morning reports he'd received.

The lancers continued to run amok, relishing in the slaughter as they wreaked havoc across lands. His Rangers also gathered information using their skills, adding to the terror the population suffered, and so far there'd been next to no resistance.

Suddenly a distant whisper rustled in his mind, and he immediately recognised the voice of Jared. He closed his eyes, opening his mind, and welcomed him like a son.

'My king,' Jared reported, 'I've arrived at Freeguard and am outside the walls in a camp overlooking the city. Tomorrow I'll enter, and it seems my job will be made easier, for as you surmised, every able-bodied peasant is being trained for war. I'll use this route to gain access to Tristan.'

'You are my favoured son,' Daleth assured him, saying the words he knew Jared wanted to hear. 'I knew I could rely on you, and I've no doubt you'll succeed in your mission and earn my deepest thanks. Reach out to me when there are developments, and know I'm already proud of what you've achieved thus far.'

Daleth felt Jared's pleasure resonate through his thoughts, but ended their connection.

He opened his eyes, wincing a little at the headache even this brief communication brought him. His body was still weak, and it had affected his mind too, for the two were intrinsically linked. Being incapacitated, he missed the ability to fly above the lands almost as much as he missed riding his horse and swinging a sword. One day soon, he'd be able to do all of them again.

Baidan appeared from the next room, and Daleth looked at his captain with a raised eyebrow, inviting him to speak.

'My king,' Baidan said uncertainly, 'I know you're not receiving reports directly, and I'm loathe to bring this one to your attention, but a captain of lancers has just returned and presented himself. He's the sole survivor of his century, and I think you should hear his tale directly.'

Daleth took note of Baidan's trepidation. Baidan's behaviour was unusual, for he knew Daleth wasn't seeing anyone except for bodyguards, Rangers or his physician. So, for Baidan to bring this to him meant it was indeed worthy of his attention.

He already sat behind a heavy table, his injuries and poor state of health well concealed. Nonetheless, he requested a heavy cloak to ensure nothing was left to chance before nodding to Baidan that he was ready.

A few minutes later, the lancer was shown in.

His face was white from pain, and he walked slightly bent forward, his upper body bereft of armour, with only a cloak around his shoulders. Every step was tentative and unsteady, but Daleth also picked up on the man's fear. Most captains would be nervous about meeting their king, but this man's demeanour was intriguing, to say the least.

Daleth gulped some wine from his goblet before refilling it, and then he offered it to the captain.

'Drink,' he said, his voice deep and full of authority.

The captain hobbled forward to take the goblet, gaining some strength from the alcohol within as he quaffed the contents.

'Now sit.' Daleth gestured to a chair opposite. 'You're obviously injured and in pain. Tell me quickly so we can get your injuries seen to. Why does the head of my bodyguard believe you're special enough to meet me in the middle of the night?'

Whilst his words were meant to calm the man, beads of sweat ran down the captain's brow. Daleth wondered how much pain or fear the captain had experienced for the amulet's influence to be so overcome.

'My King,' the man murmured, bowing his head, unable to raise his eyes now the time to report was upon him. 'I led a century of your lancers east and returned this night the sole survivor.'

Daleth nodded.

'You must be a ferocious fighter to have survived. Now, tell me of the battle and the force that defeated you.'

The man shook his head as if in denial, then spoke so softly that Daleth could barely hear the man's words as he explained in detail of ambushing a small enemy unit. Then he hesitated.

'Dammit,' Daleth roared, 'speak up and continue! Tell me without fear of reprisal. What force came along and defeated you and your men at the point of your victory?'

The End of Dreams

The captain finally looked Daleth in the eye.

'It was but one man, my king, one man only. But he was a creature of darkness, a thing of the mist. He let me live after he'd slaughtered all of my men on the condition I delivered a message to you.'

'What message?' Daleth demanded.

'I don't know,' admitted the captain, tears in his eyes as he levered himself to his feet. He turned his back on Daleth before unclasping the cloak, letting it fall to the floor.

Daleth's eyes widened at the horrific wounds on the man's back and then realised that a message was carved into the skin amongst the blood. He pushed himself unsteadily to his feet, lifting the flagon of wine.

'Be still,' he commanded, and poured the contents onto the captain's back, washing away the dried blood to read the message.

Kalas is coming!

The room spun, and Daleth's heart pounded in his chest.

He pulled a dagger from his belt and desperately plunged it again and again into the unsuspecting captain's back. Even as the dying man fell to the floor, Daleth knelt over him, hacking at the words.

'My king,' Baidan shouted, running forward as Daleth fell back, moaning in pain as his stitches pulled. Blood began to soak through his dressings.

'Leave me be!' Daleth shouted. 'Leave me be!'

But as Baidan stumbled backwards, Daleth grabbed his wrist.

'No, don't leave, double the guard. I want torches lit in every room, and I want a thousand men patrolling the grounds outside this palace day and night. Do you hear me? Day and night! The gods help anyone who lets a torch go out without another to take its place.'

As Baidan ran off shouting orders, Daleth poured himself more and more wine, drinking each goblet without pause.

Kalas was coming ... yet Kalas was dead. He'd seen the man's body burn on a pyre, damnit. Yet Kalas was coming. Kalas was coming!

He didn't stop drinking until finally, the goblet fell from his hand, but even as sleep claimed him, red eyes followed him to his dreams.

***

Chapter IX

Jared sat on a bunk, observing the others who were crammed into the barracks with him. Earlier that morning, he'd simply walked in through the wide-open city gates and presented himself to the barracks with a few others. A short while later, he'd been assigned a bunk in a room that was crowded with nearly one hundred and fifty men, in a space designed for less than half that number.

All were from common stock and were now in training to join the Freestates army, assuming they didn't fall on their swords and kill themselves before such time.

They were a motley bunch, yet any man in time could be trained to wield a sword just like they could be trained to wield a sickle or hoe. Indeed, these men would likely have that time given the state of Daleth's injuries.

Yet Jared remained unconcerned.

Everywhere, men talked freely and the information he'd gleaned in such a short time was reassuring. The entire army facing Daleth would be no more than forty thousand strong and, whilst it did include seasoned and skilled warriors, it would remain hopelessly outnumbered.

It seemed many in his barracks had come here under the promise of coin for attending a recent celebration, but most had come due to the influence of two names that Jared was coming to hear spoken of more and more.

The first was the Lady Maya, and the second, Lord Commander Taran. These names were both familiar to him as they were to all the Rangers and officers, although their titles were new.

The End of Dreams

Once nothing but fugitives, these two were becoming a rallying call for many of the common folk and were spoken of with surprising reverence.

Jared couldn't wait to report to Daleth this night and thereafter find a suitable person to study and shift to. He pulled out his evening's food, some dried meat, bread, and an apple from inside his shirt, and started to polish the fruit on the dirty fabric.

'That's *my* apple,' a deep voice said.

Jared looked from under his greasy hair at the large man who stood next to his bunk, two equally oafish men standing at his sides.

Jared had taken advantage of weaker men his whole life and had risen through the ranks over many of their dead bodies. He was familiar with this situation, although certainly not from this perspective, and he quickly considered his options.

This was his first day, and the last thing he wanted was attention. Mind made up, he nodded nervously and dropped the apple into the oaf's huge palm, who sneered at Jared's apparent weakness. Much of the conversation had stopped as people watched what was obviously a ritual for the newcomers.

Jared kept his head down.

The man didn't move.

'I'll have your bread and meat as well,' he rumbled and reached out again.

Jared swallowed hard, his iron will wrestling with the desire to kill this fool. Instead, a genuine smile split his face as he handed over the food. The man looked perplexed as he turned away.

Jared had chosen his next victim. It wasn't an ideal first choice, but life shouldn't be without its small pleasures, and this would definitely be one.

He studied the big man who walked around the barracks like a peasant king. Yes, it wouldn't take long to learn how to emulate this fool, not long at all.

Two days at the most and revenge, sweet revenge, would be his.

***

Maya stared at Freeguard in the distance, and her hard-won feeling of contentment began to evaporate.

Escaping the city and returning to the forest was a way of denying her situation; a return to her youth. She smiled as she used that word, for although that past was but a mere few months ago, she certainly looked many, many years older.

Now, however, her escapade was coming to an end. She was returning from a successful three-day hunt with Ferris and his men. Their prizes of two deer and a dozen rabbits, prepared and smoked, hung across the back of a spare horse.

She hunted for the countryfolk, to supplement the meagre food they received from the city quartermasters who now provided for the growing alliance forces, and they needed every morsel.

Many farmers had been escorted back to local farmsteads now that it seemed fairly certain that no major attack would be forthcoming in the immediate future. It was now essential that everyone worked together, gathering supplies for the long winter, as the city wasn't ready to provide for the extra fifty-odd thousand souls that had descended upon it.

To make matters worse, Tristan refused to order the nobles and merchants to open their homes to ensure everyone had a roof over their heads. Come the first snows, those outside of the city would be at the mercy of the elements. Thus, the encampments of the desert men, Eyre, and countryfolk, were becoming more permanent.

As Maya, Ferris, and his men dismounted, they were surrounded by familiar and unfamiliar faces, laughing children and smiling women who greeted them warmly and with affection.

Maya felt more at home here in the camps than anywhere she'd ever lived. Here everyone was grateful for the food she provided, unlike back when she'd worked so hard for her settlement.

The bounty from the pack-horse was unloaded with the help of many willing hands. Maya sat down with some women and helped them ready a huge cauldron to make a stew. Nothing went to waste, for even the bones could be mixed with herbs, roots and vegetables.

As she worked amongst them, the children sang their songs, and Maya let their voices wash over her. They were so familiar, yet suddenly she stopped and listened, for the children began to sing a new one.

It started as a sadly heroic song of a man, a wandering soul, searching for a lost love. A man who'd walked into the arms of death to deliver a village from the soldiers of the Witch-King, suffering grave injuries whilst overcoming impossible odds.

Then it became happier for the song told that the gods approved of his deeds and guided his tired footsteps back to the one, the only one. It ended by describing how soon they'd be joined to light the heavens between them, and no king from the east or west could stop them.

Maya looked at a girl she'd not seen before, whose voice had sounded above the others, and smiled, seeing in her a reflection of herself when she'd been young.

The girl came over, surprisingly wrapped her arms around Maya's waist, and looked up. For a moment, their eyes locked.

'He saved my life,' the girl said, 'and all I could do was tell him of his death. Without you, he is lost. Without him, so are you. Go find him. Go find your Taran.' She pointed to the city.

Maya sat in surprise as the girl darted away, back into the crowd of playing children. Several women leaned over and gently took the knives from her, offering wet cloths for her hands.

Maya hastily cleaned up, then hurried toward the horses.

'My lady,' Ferris said softly as she quickly secured her horse's girth straps, preparing to ride, 'you have to tread softly,' but Maya ignored him.

Ferris took her by the shoulders, turning her, to better get her attention.

'I'm so sorry.' He snatched his hands away as she glared at him for laying them upon her. 'You saved my life, and it's been yours ever since, and the same for the rest,' he said motioning to the other soldiers.

'All I'm asking is that you tread softly. Tristan will be quick to take advantage of any mistake you or Taran make, and this is how you find yourself in your current predicament. It's known that Galain has two dozen loyal guards ready at all times within the palace, and one of the requisites for being in that unit is that no one had fought at Tristan's Folly.'

'Even a slow soldier like me can work out that there can be only one reason for that condition. It's so they've no conflict if ordered to arrest Taran or even execute him should he act rashly and give Tristan sufficient excuse.'

Maya's eyes widened as she took in what Ferris had said, and then she took his hand, squeezing it.

'Thank you, Ferris. Your loyalty humbles me. You're right to have made me listen, for my heart would have indeed made me act rashly. Now, stay by my side, and don't be afraid to remind me again if the need arises. I'm lucky to count you as my friend.'

Ferris beamed under Maya's praise.

'My concern now,' Maya continued, 'is that Taran doesn't have such a calm head and could well fall afoul of his emotions if Tristan says the right things. Taran's passion is a wonderful thing,' she said, sighing in memory, 'but it's now his biggest liability.'

Without further words, they all made ready before mounting and urged their horses to a canter.

It was nearing late afternoon as they finally reached the palace. Ferris accompanied Maya toward the gates as the other men went to stable the horses.

Ferris spoke softly, for there were dozens of retainers around, servants, and general staff.

'Let's not walk with haste. Let this be like any other day we return from a hunt. We know not whether Taran is even here. Let's take our time, and you can appear as disappointed as you always look on your return to captivity.'

Maya laughed.

'You couldn't be more apt in your choice of words, as this is indeed captivity for me. I consider myself cursed by my situation, but I'm still gifted compared to those souls on the hillside. Gifted with the power of wealth, position, and privilege.'

'Ah, my lady,' Ferris replied, 'indeed you are, but they still see you as one of them. Why? Because you, like them, desire none of it and see no worth in it. They see that you recognise the power of compassion, kindness, and consideration. But most of all, it's because you understand that the most powerful thing someone can have is, the love of another.'

The End of Dreams

Their conversation had taken them to the entrance, and as the doors opened before them, they walked along the corridor between the ever-present guards who saluted their future queen.

The doors to the audience chamber swung wide as she approached, and there sat Tristan with Ostrom, Dafne, and various other nobles.

However, another was seated at the table with his back to her, and she knew it was Taran. She could tell from the tilt of his head, and the wave of his hair even before she heard his voice or saw his face. Beside him sat Yana, for who else could be so radiant?

Maya swept into the chamber while Ferris remained at the entrance. Every fibre of her being wanted to run to Taran, to hold him and never let go, but she remembered Ferris' warning. There was also a look of anticipation poorly hidden on Tristan's face.

She saw him motion subtly to Galain, who moved off through a side door. Ferris' warning was sure to be correct.

All eyes were upon her as she moved quietly across the room, except for those of Taran and Yana, who were still unaware of her presence. She walked around the table toward the empty seat at Tristan's side, meeting the gazes of those assembled, nodding in greeting or recognition.

To her surprise, all the Freestates nobles bowed their heads deeply. It seemed they were still astounded by her disposal of Duggan, who'd disappeared since his fall from grace. His properties had been seized for the crown, and for a moment she wondered how he'd met his end. There was no doubt in her mind that his absence was fatally permanent.

But then Tristan rose, gesturing for her to sit by his side. As she did, she finally allowed her eyes to fall upon Taran.

She'd intended not to react and set the tone of any conversation so that Taran might pick up on the danger through her lack of emotion. However, the moment she saw his face, she let out a small cry and tears came to her eyes.

'My prince, what happened?' she gasped, starting to rise, her discipline deserting her in a heartbeat.

'He's not your prince!' Tristan roared. 'He is not royalty. He is Lord Commander, and if you're to address him at all, you can use that title.'

Maya sat down in shock, her eyes fixed on Taran's face, blinking furiously to clear the tears from her eyes. It was his face, but hardly the face she remembered any more, for the skin on one side was terribly burned. As her eyes darted over him, she noticed his arms were scarred and the skin fire-blackened.

Her eyes returned to his face, and this time when their eyes locked, tears flowed down her face unchecked, for when they gazed upon her, they held nothing, not a hint of warmth or love, barely even recognition.

'I'm sorry,' she said softly, 'It pains me to see my prince, sorry, the lord commander in such an injured state.'

Tristan waited, looking intently at Taran, unbelieving that where Maya had broken down, Taran's face had not flickered, and from everything he knew of Taran, he couldn't understand why.

Tristan slowly reached out, putting his arm around Maya's shoulders and kept it there despite her stiffening in revulsion at his touch. Even this caused nothing more than for Taran to look and smile in that mocking fashion as if he saw the game Tristan was playing and felt it too childish for him to partake in.

Tristan swallowed his disappointment, but at the same time also felt relief, for had Taran exploded, he wondered if the guards would've responded quickly enough.

'Right,' Tristan said, 'let's start this meeting. Lord Commander Taran, I can see you're still recovering from your ordeals and likely need several more days respite. However, I hope you've had time to consider our position further, and the different strategies that have been proposed. The last time you addressed us, you spoke of a glorious death. I hope this time you've something more valuable to present that warrants the rank bestowed upon you.'

As Tristan finished his address, everyone in the chamber leaned forward intently, their eyes fixed on Taran.

Maya struggled to hold her emotions in check as she saw Taran's scarred face twist in concentration.

Taran cleared his throat.

'Little has changed since I delivered my previous judgement,' he started. 'You're already well aware that we simply don't have enough soldiers to defeat Daleth and his horde. I considered the options that were previously tabled.'

'My king. You proposed we fortify this city and invite Daleth to siege us, hoping his forces could not penetrate the walls if well defended. There's no merit in this idea. It will fail,' he said bluntly.

Murmurs of disbelief met his announcement, not from surprise at his analysis, but from his forthright delivery.

'This city has one wall which is not even a third of the height or width of those at Tristan's Folly. We couldn't resist Daleth's assault for one day before it was overrun. He wouldn't even need to use siege engines if he was unconcerned about losses.'

'King Ostrom proposed we go seek battle, to use the strength and skills of his men in open combat, and indeed, that is where they would be best used.'

Ostrom puffed his chest out, grinning at Taran.

'Yet again, this tactic will not work,' Taran continued. 'Daleth's army can outflank, encircle, or outmanoeuvre our troops.'

Ostrom's grin quickly faded as Taran pressed on.

Taran turned to Dafne.

'Of all the strategies proposed, yours has the most merit. Yet, even so, it will end in disaster. At the start, ambushing or harassing enemy troops either in the field or behind their walls from afar with arrows will prove effective, but only until the moment that the enemy lancers decimate you to the last man and woman.'

Taran gazed slowly around the table, meeting everyone's gaze.

'The enemy has more spearmen, more swordsmen, more cavalry, in fact, their advantage in numbers is simply overwhelming.'

'Damnit,' Ostrom growled, striking his heavy fist against the table. 'You're simply repeating the arguments we've had for many days now. Is there anything we haven't heard that you care to propose?'

Maya watched Taran from behind her hair, and for a moment, she saw the old Taran, for the grin was mischievous, and there was a sparkle to his eye.

'We need to do just two things to win this war.' Taran stated, his demeanour serious.

'Oh, two things. Just two things,' Tristan mocked. 'What might they be?'

'Daleth needs to die.' Taran looked Tristan straight in the eye. 'I need to find a way to kill the king. It's something I've sworn to do, and trust me, nothing will prevent me from doing so!'

Tristan's face went white, for Taran had delivered his threat directly to him, cleverly worded, yet easily deniable.

Before Tristan could respond, Ostrom pointed a finger at Taran, looking decidedly unimpressed.

'How exactly do you propose we do that?' the desert king asked.

Taran turned his attention back to Ostrom.

'We must kill him along with his entire army in one final battle. It has to be decisive for there'll be no second chance and it'll set the course of this land, nay this world of ours for generations to come.'

'But you said we don't have enough troops to achieve that!' Dafne huffed in annoyance. 'The Eyre has no more to send, and I'm sure the same can be said for the desert tribes.'

Ostrom nodded in silent agreement.

'True,' Taran said. 'That's the second thing. We do need more, a lot more troops, and specifically, we'll need cavalry.'

Taran raised his arms wide as if to gather everyone into an embrace.

'We need the Horselords!'

***

Taran stood, his leg aching abominably.

The meeting had continued for some hours, but now, finally, it had drawn to a close. In fact, there was little of him that didn't hurt, with perhaps one exception ... his heart.

Yet when he'd seen Maya, for the briefest of moments his heart had beat so painfully, that it had taken all his willpower to withstand the initial urge to draw his sword and drive it through Tristan's throat. Fortunately, in the next instant, the influence of the amulet had smothered the pain like a heavy blanket, replacing it with hatred, with the desire for revenge. He hadn't been able to resist the veiled threat he'd aimed at Tristan, which he knew had landed, hard.

It had been a foolish thing to do, but it had still felt good to say aloud his thoughts and feelings that would one day find release, the gods willing.

The End of Dreams

Yana stood alongside him, and he noticed Maya's eyes were red and puffy as he looked around the table, but he didn't let his eyes linger, afraid that the amulet would let the pain through again.

Better to feel nothing than the pain of betrayal. Better the pain of his wounds than a broken heart. Yet her reaction had been strange, caring. He laughed disdainfully at himself. If she truly cared, she'd have never left him.

The pain of his leg was nigh on unbearable as he turned away from the table, for it hadn't healed well and could barely take his weight. He'd give himself a further two weeks to recover, but after that, he'd be in the saddle once again, so it needed to be strong, and for that to happen, it needed rest.

The doors to the audience chamber were held open for him and Yana, but as they approached, a painful spasm ran up his thigh. He moaned softly under his breath.

'Don't let them see your weakness,' Yana said, her voice low.

She moved in close, her arm snaking around his waist, and his went across her shoulder in return.

She grunted slightly as his weight hit her, but her heart thumped happily. This was the first time his arm had ever been around her, and it mattered not what the reason was. The doors closed behind them, and she looked up to see his face pale and beaded with sweat.

The residences that had been placed at their disposal were apart.

Taran's was within the palace grounds, while Yana's was in an apartment across the thoroughfare overlooking the palace that had recently belonged to the lord of the city.

'Come,' she said, 'lean on me till we get you back. I know you're not ill, but you'll not be ready to travel, let alone fight in two weeks if you don't take your rest more seriously.'

The two of them slowly worked their way through the palace grounds and gardens to Taran's small cottage. It was a homely place, and as they opened the door, a delightful aroma met them.

The fire had been lit, and fresh food and wine had been left.

It seemed rank had its privileges, and Taran's stomach rumbled as he gingerly sat down, leg out-stretched.

'Here, let me help,' Yana insisted, as she eased off his boots and then nibbled on some of the food before bringing it to him. She tasted the wine before turning her back and pouring him a large goblet.

She stood, tossing her hair, her smile dazzling in its brightness.

'I'd offer to take off your other clothes as well, but I'll wait till you're fit once again, Taran, heart-stealer!'

She winked, then left the cottage, pulling the door closed.

Taran laughed quietly, shaking his head at her audacity, and wolfed down the food, followed by the bitter wine. He thought back over the reaction to his announcement.

His plan had initially been met with disbelief.

The Horselords, everyone agreed, allied with absolutely no one. They kept to their grasslands as long as they received their yearly tithe of iron and other essentials. Freestates' kings had honoured this agreement, along with a promise never to enter their sacred lands for generations, ensuring an uneasy peace had existed between the two realms.

They were an insular, proud people who spent their nomadic lives seeking martial perfection and religious enlightenment. They looked down upon those who didn't share their heritage, code, and faith. Throughout the year they constantly fought amongst themselves for honour, rarely for blood, unless outsiders became involved, in which case ... it was always for blood.

But, irrespective of everyone's scornful dismissal of the plan, no one had any other ideas.

Taran had personally volunteered to journey south to seek the Horselords' help. This offer had been the catalyst for Tristan lending his support. Taran knew Tristan wanted him out of sight and on a dangerous mission that was just as likely to see him dead than return.

Not only would Taran need to travel unseen through lands now under Daleth's control, but it would soon be winter, and the Horselords were likely to kill him on sight before they even deigned to talk to him.

Taran anticipated recovering enough to ride in two weeks. Yet, even if his plan worked out, and he managed to convince the Horselords to join the cause, the question remained. Would it be enough?

He'd proposed that he only travel with one other. The smaller the number, the less chance of being spotted on route. He planned to go with Rakan, but if his father hadn't returned by the time Taran was ready to go, he'd travel with Yana, who was livid she hadn't been his first choice.

The journey to the grasslands would take at least four weeks, maybe more, depending on how much time was spent hiding from Daleth's soldiers and the worsening weather.

The Horselords were also nomadic and would likely journey further southward, where the winter snow was less brutal.

Assuming all went well, it would take another month or two to get the various clans on board and then the race to return before the spring thaw began.

The hardest part of the meeting had been to reach agreement on what would be offered in payment to entice them to join the war.

At some stage, Daleth would attack the Horselords anyway, but it was unlikely they'd agree to an alliance on this basis. They feared no-one and would deem it dishonourable to ally with others not of their nation. So Tristan had agreed that Taran could offer most anything, be it gold, steel, a higher tithe, whatever it took, to overcome their reluctance and have them come with all of their might.

It was estimated that they had nigh on thirty thousand heavy, mounted knights which, whilst not as versatile as lancers, could pack a mighty punch with a charge that couldn't be ignored.

If those thirty thousand joined, then the alliance would still be heavily outnumbered, but no formation would be able to turn their back on such a force. This meant they could tie up a similar number of spearmen to face them, even without drawing blood.

This would then leave around sixty thousand of Daleth's troops facing the forty thousand allied soldiers, and just maybe the gods might choose to favour the alliance.

Taran yawned, exhaustion washing over him, and from one moment to the next, with the soothing warmth of the crackling fire in front of him, fell asleep in the chair.

Not long after, the door to the cottage opened.

Yana slipped inside, closing it behind her, and smiled as she saw Taran had succumbed to the sleep weed laced wine. He might wake with a slight headache, but he needed the sleep more than he cared to admit.

Yana drew her sword as she walked toward him and then leant forward to kiss his forehead. She sat down in a seat opposite, facing the door with her blade across her lap.

Tristan desperately needed Taran, but she wouldn't put it past the king to send knives in the night after Taran's veiled threat. She'd had no ill effect from the food or wine before passing it to Taran, but would take no chances.

She'd stay till just before sunrise, then leave before Taran awoke. With luck, Rakan wouldn't return, and she'd be the one by Taran's side on the long journey to come. On the cold nights of winter ahead, she'd make her move, and he'd be unable to resist her keeping him warm.

She listened to Taran breathing and for any signs of an uninvited approach to the cottage. The fire began to die down, its flames casting shadows across Taran's scarred face.

She sighed. If only she could take away his injuries, his pain, like Maya had once done, and the thought annoyed her.

Then a smile spread across her face, for it had been revealed in the meeting that Maya was gifted no longer, and it was Yana's hands that treated and bound Taran's wounds now.

One day, if the stars aligned, Taran, who was once Maya's prince, would become Yana's king.

***

Maya sat in her room, wondering how she could be so foolish, so wrong, and yet this depressing thought only added to her pain. She'd spent all this time worrying about Taran, whereas it seemed he'd been pushing her from his heart.

The way he'd initially looked at her without emotion, then talked throughout the afternoon with barely a glance in her direction.

No actor, however consummate, would've been able to fake such a show. The only time Taran had displayed emotion was his tightly controlled anger when speaking with Tristan, and even that was disguised to be aimed at Daleth.

His injuries had changed him, not just physically, which wouldn't have mattered at all, but emotionally. She felt guilty, as undoubtedly her departure had added to that pain and hastened the dwindling of his feelings.

How could something that had burned so bright, so incandescent, be extinguished mere weeks later?

It was the obvious answer that brought Maya's heart close to breaking. The casual way Yana's arm had slipped around Taran's waist and his arm around her shoulder when they'd left the chamber had been like a dagger in Maya's heart. How quickly had he fallen into Yana's bed? Tears fell from her eyes as the pain of betrayal washed over her.

Had it all been a lie? No, it hadn't. It had been too good. But it had obviously meant more to her, whereas to Taran, she was likely just another woman in the long list he'd bedded when on the road.

But he'd given his life willingly to save her. If she hadn't meant the world to him, then why would he do that?

Back and forth, her thoughts crashed, confused and angry.

She moved across the room, took her weapon belt from a wardrobe, buckled it around her waist, and then flung open the door to the corridor.

Ferris was there waiting, and he looked up in surprise. His eyes flickered to the weapons at her waist.

'Are we expecting trouble?' he asked with a faint laugh.

Maya wasn't in the mood to joke and strode past him, leading him down the stairs as he hurried to keep up. She stalked along the warren of corridors toward the kitchens, surprising the cooks and servants who worked throughout the night as she entered.

They hastily fell to their knees, and usually, Maya would have bid them rise. Instead, she moved swiftly toward the cellar steps that led to where the food and wines were stored.

'No one is to disturb us, no one. Ignore this warning at your peril,' Maya commanded, as she took a flaming torch with her to light the darkness.

One by one, she lit the oiled torches on the walls until the stone floors and vaulted ceiling were awash with light. Maya spun to face the confused Ferris who stood wondering what had got into Maya's mind.

Maya drew her sword, swinging it in circles, loosening her wrist whilst pulling a heavy dagger free as well.

'What are you doing?' Ferris asked worriedly, as he backed away from the flashing steel.

'You're going to train with me,' Maya instructed as she squared off against him. 'Now draw your sword!'

Ferris shook his head vehemently.

'My lady, I think the king would have my head if I laid a blade on you, even by accident.'

Maya smiled coldly.

'The king isn't here to take your head.' She swung her sword at Ferris, who instinctively jumped back. 'But I am. So unless you want *me* to take your head, you'd better defend yourself.'

Ferris laughed as he drew his blade.

'I don't think I'm best placed to train you.'

Now it was Maya's turn to laugh.

'You survived the fall of Tristan's Folly, and you survived from thousands. You might not be the best swordsmen, but don't ever sell yourself short, for you're better than those who lay dead behind you.'

'You're the queen in all but name, so I'd best obey you,' Ferris agreed.

Maya's face turned cold at his words.

'Begin,' she commanded.

***

The torches were guttering when Ferris finally called a halt. His arms ached from two hours of swordplay. His jaw also hurt from a well-placed elbow that had caught him entirely off guard, spinning him to the floor earlier in the session.

Maya stood unsteadily before him.

'I'm not ready to stop,' she gasped.

Ferris shook his head, and raised a hand.

'If we're both tired, then one of us will get hurt. Using these will mean that mistake might prove deadly,' he said, indicating their weapons. 'If you want to train on the morrow, I'll find some wooden practice weapons. They'll be heavy and build up your strength and stamina, and mine, for that matter.' He stretched his arms, trying to ease his aching muscles.

Maya nodded reluctantly. The training had been therapeutic, her troubles forgotten for a while due to the pain of exercise. Yet now it was coming back again.

Ferris took her weapon as they moved up the stairs.

'The edge is notched and dulled and needs to be honed again,' he explained, as they moved through the kitchens.

This time, when everyone dropped to their knees, Maya stopped.

'I'm sorry,' she said to their astonished faces. 'I was so rude before. Thank you for allowing me to train. Would it be possible to eat here with you? I'm famished, and I believe good Ferris here will be as well.'

The look of disbelief mixed with joy on the faces of all those in the kitchen almost made Ferris laugh as everyone hurried to bring food, placing dozens of dishes and bowls in front of them.

Maya looked up, shaking her head, and everyone's faces suddenly dropped when they thought they'd done something wrong.

'No, no, don't worry,' Maya assured them. 'It's just that there's way too much for the two of us to eat alone. Come, all of you, sit with us. Let's eat together, and you can tell me about yourselves.'

For the next couple of hours, Maya's spirits lifted as the serving staff laughed and chatted as if she were one of their own. They demanded she tell them of her story, and whilst much of it was painful, she told the most of it, Ferris joining in as well.

Once Maya and Ferris finished their tale, a cook told the story of how Taran had saved the village where her cousin had lived.

'Your love has come for you,' she whispered.

'Hush,' another said. 'She's betrothed to the king. Saying that will cost you the lash or worse!' But suddenly the kitchen staff all started talking of the stories that had grown over the last weeks, of how true love would conquer all.

Maya didn't have the heart nor strength to tell them the truth of the matter and bade them all goodnight, as it was getting late.

It was past midnight when Maya returned to her room, and Ferris left her to retire.

As she closed the door, the smile slowly slipped from her face, and when she fell onto the bed, she pulled a pillow close.

'My Taran,' she sniffed quietly. 'I miss you, I really do. You would have loved tonight and would have captivated them all with stories of your own.'

She lay there, trying to control her thoughts. Perhaps she'd been too quick to judge Taran. Maybe there was more to his coldness and what happened with Yana than met the eye.

She'd find a way to reach him. She just needed to find the right moment. It had been a long and emotional day, and after the training session with Ferris, her body was as tired as her mind.

It wasn't long before exhaustion overtook her and she fell asleep fully clothed on the bed.

***

Chapter X

Rakan lay in the long grass on the brow of the hill, looking down into the small valley before him. The early morning air was cold, and the sun was creeping over the horizon. It was just bright enough for him to see in detail what was happening below.

Daleth's lancers had started the day early and now moved with impunity among a small, smoking farmstead they'd sacked the night before. The cooling bodies of the occupants who'd decided not to leave their homes lay strewn about as if thrown randomly by a child discarding its toys.

His face was grim, for the lancers' morning entertainment was toying with a farmer who was jostled between their horses. The lancers laughed and prodded with their spears, drawing blood as their victim screamed and pleaded for mercy.

Rakan and his men had arrived a day too late to save anyone, but that didn't mean he wasn't going to do anything about it.

Daleth's lancers were incredibly versatile. They excelled when used as scouts, covering terrain swiftly and gaining intelligence. In a battle, they could circle engaged enemy troops, charge from behind, and run down the routed unit.

Against swordsmen on foot, they could break a light formation, using their horses' weight to fling the line asunder. Their main weakness was spearmen and protected archers. Heavy cavalry could also decimate them, but the lancers' speed meant they could avoid any heavier foe.

He looked behind at the two centuries following him, a mixture of mostly spearmen and archers, preparing for the hasty ambush they'd planned. Even further down the hill were ten soldiers on horseback, plainly visible. He and they would be the bait that drew the eye and led the lancers to their deaths.

He eased to his feet, and head down, walked over the brow of the hill, whistling as if he didn't have a care in the world, waiting to be noticed.

'Over there!'

The shout carried to him, and he looked up to see the lancers spear the farmer through the chest, finishing with their prey, having discovered a fresh one.

Rakan pretended to panic, turned, and fell over his feet before running frantically up the hill.

The pounding of hooves grew louder as he pushed himself hard, running over the brow before disappearing from the lancers' view as he ran into the long grass, toward the distant horsemen who held a horse for him.

He was halfway down the hill when, looking back over his shoulder, he saw the lancers crest the hilltop in line formation as he knew they would. They were too disciplined to come over as an unruly mob.

Rakan's men on their horses below, stood in their stirrups, shouting and pointing behind him.

Seeing their quarry and how close to escape Rakan was, the lancers spurred their horses into a charge.

Rakan stopped running, turned, and drew his sword, watching as the century of lancers bore down upon him. It was, despite his planning, a sight that made him want to brown his trousers.

Instead, he raised his sword.

'NOW,' he thundered, to be heard above the pounding hooves, and in response, three ranks of desert spearmen rose from the deep grass. Their long ironwood spears were twice as tall as a man, and they grounded the butts in the soil, dropping the points. The lancers pulled frantically on the reins, trying to drag their horses to a halt, but instead, they only served to diminish the one chance they had.

Had they continued their charge, they might have broken through the thin line, but instead, as the horses slowed, their last chance slipped away. The ironwood spears were longer than the lances and plucked riders from saddles, or took the horses down as the spearmen pushed forward into their shocked foe.

The archers' bows sang, and the riders at the back of the faltered charge, trying fruitlessly to pull their horses around to flee, fell from their saddles as the arrows found their mark.

It was butchery, and as Rakan cleaved his sword through the neck of a downed lancer, he looked around, listening to the screaming men and horses, then stepped back for a moment.

Once, those sounds would have sent a thrill through his veins like a drug, yet now he looked at the flowing rivers of red leaching into the soil and felt tired, just terribly tired.

Two injured lancers were dragged before him once the battle was over and Rakan knelt down, staring into their eyes.

'I won't make you any false promises. You're going to die here along with your brothers, but how you do so is up to you. I can ensure it's quick or slower than you'd believe.'

Scared eyes filled with pain looked back at him.

'I have but one simple question for you. Where's Daleth and your army now?' Rakan asked as he held a dagger. 'Tell me and know peace,'

'We're operating from Freemantle,' one gasped. 'The army will winter there,' the other added.

Rakan nodded, and stood, motioning to a spearman.

Silence settled as the injured lancers were swiftly dealt with, and his men began looting the bodies and saddlebags of the dead for supplies to supplement their own. Twenty of Rakan's men had died, and several dozen were injured for a hundred enemy killed.

'Everyone, get ready to move out,' he commanded, having seen a thick copse of woods to the north, where he'd have them stationed as the final outpost.

During the afternoon, Rakan helped the men clear a campsite, during which he praised them, stressing their importance, reassuring them that they weren't alone out here. He joked it was a better place to be than having to bow to a noble every time they saw one.

Once basic defences were established, and the soldiers were busy building shelters, Rakan remounted and, along with the injured, turned east back toward Freeguard, secure in the knowledge that Daleth would winter at Freemantle.

A week of hard riding would have them back behind Freeguard's walls, but he wasn't sure that he wanted to return. That city was a nest of vipers, and he preferred the company of simpler men like himself.

Of course, a soldier wasn't the most educated individual, but for the most part, these were good men. Everyone got on because that way your comrades could be relied on to guard your back in a battle. It didn't matter what colour the skin, green, brown, or white, everyone was a brother. Thus, the comradeship offered by serving was a gift few outside an army appreciated.

However, what drove him back to Freeguard with haste was the hope of finding Taran there.

Rakan's eyes misted a little as he thought of his son. Then, of course, there was Maya, to whom he'd not had the chance to say more than a few words before he was dispatched on this mission.

If Taran was his son, then she was his daughter-in-law.

Damn, he thought, not if she marries Tristan, then she'd be his queen.

He'd seen love before, but nothing like that which Taran and Maya enjoyed. Yet now the cruelty of the gods had changed everything. His son was on a journey of revenge, and nothing good would come from that.

Rakan had to return and find a way to make this situation right, assuming they all lived long enough for it to matter.

It was almost as if his horse sensed his urgency, for even though he didn't seek to push hard, it decided to enjoy itself. Over the last eleven days, it had been forced to walk slowly to keep abreast of the infantry, and thus now it seemed to have limitless energy.

Rakan had to rein it back frequently, to help the less accomplished riders keep up, and to ensure that his mount had enough stamina left in case they came across further enemy lancers. Fortunately, luck was with them, for there was no enemy in sight and it would have been easy to enjoy the day had his burns and other injuries not been a constant reminder of the poor state he was in.

It now seemed certain that the final battle would be joined next spring. By then, he'd be back to full fitness, just in time to die a horrible death.

The End of Dreams

He laughed to himself as he thought of that and wondered how on earth they could have a hope in the nine hells of defeating Daleth and his horde. It just didn't seem possible.

He looked to the sky, noting the position of the sun. They were making good time, and he'd push them all a little harder so they could camp with another century he'd positioned near the road the day before.

With this in mind, he let the horse have its head again, and it cantered, tossing its head in joy at the freedom it was given to run.

He laughed out loud, shouting to the soldier trying to keep up next to him.

'Had I known riding could be so enjoyable, I would've joined the lancers in my youth, not the damned infantry!'

He leaned low, enjoying the fresh breeze on his face as the horse rose to the challenge.

***

Taran had awoken in the depths of the night to find himself still sitting in the chair where he'd fallen asleep with Yana sitting opposite him, a sword across her lap, eyes closed.

Initially, he'd been annoyed, but had then relented. Her persistence in trying to persuade him to join with her was frustrating, but she'd never betrayed him, not like Maya.

He'd carefully lifted her, gritting his teeth in pain as he went to lay her down on the bed in the corner of the room, then limped back to his chair. He'd moved it quietly in front of the burning embers of the fire and settled down once more.

His last thought was why Maya had been so upset when she'd seen him in the audience chamber, but then he'd fallen back to sleep before solving the conundrum.

Now, as he awoke again, a timeglass showed it was late morning.

Yana was absent, and the sun's rays shone through the gaps in the curtains while his stomach rumbled in hungry protest. There were plenty of leftovers from the night before, so Taran helped himself, shuffling carefully so as not to put too much weight on his leg.

Having eaten his fill, he gingerly removed his trousers, unwound the bandage there to inspect the wound, nodding with satisfaction that, despite looking and feeling painful, there was no sign of infection. Likewise, the deep wound to his shoulder, although having weakened his arm considerably, looked better. Yana had done an admirable job.

He re-bound the bandages and started to pull his trousers back on when Yana flounced in through the door.

'Oh,' she said gleefully, 'there's no need to put them back on for my sake. Quite the opposite, in fact.' She winked mischievously.

Taran shook his head and continued to dress.

Yana continued in the same vein.

'Don't be so coy and innocent, Taran, heart-stealer. I do believe you took me to your bed last night if I'm not mistaken!'

Taran couldn't help but laugh.

'You see,' Yana said, her heart fluttering, 'I'm not so bad, am I?'

'You're not just bad, you're the worst,' Taran chuckled.

Yana beamed, for he smiled as he said it. Then her smile turned to a frown.

'Would you believe that whilst you've been sleeping in, I was summoned to see Tristan? I've been charged with overseeing the setting up of a hospital near the west gate. Apparently, my work at the fortress has not gone unnoticed. I said I'd think about it. Tristan was furious, but I said my place was by your side unless Rakan was able to accompany you on your mission south.'

'You should try not to anger Tristan, he's the king after all,' Taran advised, 'and you have your title and privilege by his grace.'

Yana laughed, arching an eyebrow.

'I could throw that same advice at you. At least I didn't promise to kill him!'

Taran nodded, smiling wryly.

'Fair comment. But try to see it as an acknowledgement of your value. You've proven yourself to be skilful, and you deserve the recognition for all that you did at Tristan's Folly. All of those healers are likely to have returned here, and would follow your lead without hesitation.'

'Taran, I do believe you're becoming quite fond of me, bestowing so many compliments so quickly. Next thing you'll be asking me to become your betrothed!'

As soon as she said this, she realised her mistake. Yana's heart sank, for she saw the darkness fall over Taran's eyes and cursed herself for pushing too hard, too soon.

Taran might not care for Maya like he used to, but his anger, when roused over recent events, clouded every other emotion. Whatever warmth he'd started to show was now hidden behind a dark visage.

'I suggest you go to your new job,' Taran advised flatly. 'Close the door behind you.'

He turned his back on Yana, moving toward the small washroom at the rear of the cottage.

Yana thought for a moment to argue with his demand, to try and make amends, but instead did as Taran had bid. The best strategy wasn't always the obvious and direct one. She so wanted to accompany him on his journey south, but maybe he'd realise how much he needed her when she wasn't there.

She had faith in him that he'd succeed in his mission, but those cold nights alone, no caring hands to attend his injuries or prepare his food. Yes, she'd take his advice and keep Tristan happy. Not only because she'd make Taran proud of her achievements, but because after months of being cold alone, her warm body would feel like fire against his when she welcomed him home.

Her absence would definitely make his feelings grow stronger.

The amulet had done its job, suppressing his emotions for Maya, making him strong again. Now it was proving a hindrance, and she had to find a way to remove it on his return. Only then would his feelings and desires be able to flourish, and after being restrained for so long, she was sure he'd find her impossible to resist. Then she'd show him just how skilful she could be.

Mind made up, she smiled, closing the door gently, whereas a few moments ago she would have crashed it shut.

***

Jared had taken over the big oaf's form, and since then had been working toward the next step up the garrison soldier food chain.

He slowly picked himself up from the training yard floor, having been defeated by Tolgarth in the sparring that the captain took part in every day.

It hurt to let himself be defeated by one so unskilled, but fighting Tolgarth had allowed him to study his style, so that when he shifted to the captain's form, even his swordplay would be identical.

Tolgarth, it seemed, also enjoyed showing off to everyone, and found in Jared a good sparring partner whom he could beat whilst putting on a decent show.

Jared bowed his head, feigning respect.

'Your skill is incredible,' he said, noting how Tolgarth puffed up at his praise. He had to bite his lip briefly to stop himself laughing, such was the blatant lie, but instead, sincerity shone from his broad face.

He needed to get far closer to Tolgarth than he had to the oaf. The more important the person he shifted into, the more people would know him, and the more obvious any crack in his façade.

Of course, there were many ruses to overcome any unfortunate mistakes, and no one outside of his brother and Daleth knew of his gift. Even a slip of the tongue or not recognising someone could be covered by embarrassment and was unlikely to raise suspicion, and yet Jared would take no chances, none whatsoever.

He brushed some dust from his clothes while the small crowd of regular soldiers and peasants training amongst them applauded.

Tolgarth turned to Jared.

'I have to admit, you fought well. For someone who knew nothing but the plough until a short time ago, you're fast achieving a rudimentary level of skill.'

Jared beamed, nodding his head.

'It'd be my honour if I could buy you a drink, Captain. I know it's a huge favour to ask, but I have a few coins from my pay saved up. I can think of nothing more that I'd like to do than buy you an ale at day's end.'

Tolgarth looked as if he'd been hit, his face going white.

'You think that because you train under my barracks roof, and I give you a compliment, that you can ask to buy me a drink?' He spat on

Jared's boots. 'Have you any idea of the insult you've given me? The only reason your head is still upon your shoulders is because of a favour I'm doing for the Lady Maya. From hereon, respect your betters and don't speak unless you're spoken to!'

His voice rose to a shriek as he said this and Jared blanched in pretend terror. All the while, he noted Tolgarth's reaction, how his face moved and voice sounded when brought to righteous anger.

As Jared shuffled away, head bowed, he congratulated himself.

He'd learned as much in that exchange as during a boring drink with the captain. However, a drink would still be valuable, for drunken lips might spill stories that would give him the background to this odious man. Once in Tolgarth's boots, he could then pick his next target.

However, the shift wouldn't be without risk. He'd have to do it privately, out of sight, with Tolgarth alive but either unaware or incapacitated. Disposing of the body would also pose a problem.

The biggest challenge he'd faced so far had been dealing with the big oaf's body upon slaying him in one of Freeguard's dark alleys two days past. After taking the oaf's form, he'd quickly changed into his clothes before they became soiled. Then he'd stood looking at the body. There were no woods or drains to hide it in, so he'd had to cut off the man's face and disfigure his body to make it unrecognisable. It had been grisly work, but satisfying, for the man had been truly odious.

Now, as he walked back to the barracks, he considered how his food had previously been taken and thought to take it one step further. Maybe collecting a small tithe from his barrack mates would give him sufficient coin to provide him with an opportunity to buy his way into Tolgarth's favour. Then, in the next breath, he dismissed the idea. Taking food was one thing, but he could be arrested for taking coin.

However, winning it was a different thing altogether.

The lower ranks enjoyed playing cards for money, and till now he'd kept his distance, but from hereon he'd join in. Everyone saw him as slow-witted and brutal, which had been true of the original. Now he was just brutal.

He'd perfected reading people's features and facial movements and could tell whether someone bluffed or had a good hand with ease. Thus, with his legitimate gains, he could buy himself Tolgarth's favour, for nothing spoke louder than money in this land of the greedy, nothing at all.

Then, taking Tolgarth's form and killing him would not only provide him with a great deal of personal satisfaction, but a man of his rank and importance would have access to the palace, and he'd be a big step closer to his ultimate goal.

In the interim, life in the captain's shoes would be far more enjoyable than those of a mere foot soldier, and he could slow the training down of this bunch of misfits at the same time.

He couldn't wait to report his progress tonight, for Daleth would be pleased, and he warmed at the thought of the great king's praise.

***

Taran stared at his reflection in the silvered mirror, not recognising the face that looked back at him. He'd once been happy with his roguish looks, but now his face was marred with burns, and when he looked at his body, it was a lattice of healing wounds that would scar him like a patchwork.

Strangely, though, it didn't bother him, and in the back of his mind, he knew it was the amulet. But it didn't matter why, as long as it was.

He'd washed thoroughly and put on new clothes. His armour and weapons had been taken a short while ago by a retainer who promised to return them gleaming before the morning was out.

He still had Drizt's poisoned dagger concealed in its sheath on his forearm. He pulled it out, inspecting it, remembering his old friend, but there was no feeling of loss, just emptiness like a hollow where something had once been.

Replacing the blade, he considered the days ahead. He'd be heading out in two weeks, but in the interim would still be involved in meetings regarding the defence of Freeguard. Reports on the men's readiness, improvements to the wall, training, food supplies, new arrivals, and everything else required his presence.

He'd thought the siege of Tristan's Folly had been complicated, but that was just one fortress, whereas this was a city of over a hundred thousand souls before the alliance soldiers were even counted.

The End of Dreams

Most frustrating were the wealthy merchants and nobles pretending that the war was never going to happen and that it wasn't their problem. He'd push again for everyone to get involved in the effort to prepare, but Tristan relied on their support and was loath to order them to assist. Yet their wealth and stockpiles should be made available to everyone. Rations would soon be reduced for the soldiers to ensure there was enough stock to see them through winter, yet it was unlikely any merchant or noble would go hungry.

Thinking of this injustice made his anger rise, and he needed to relax. He was supposed to be resting, and his presence would be required in the afternoon. He had plenty of time on his hands, and in his state, he couldn't train, but neither could he sleep or sit still.

He was so used to Yana being around that he missed her company for a moment and considered going to find her, but cast the idea aside in the same instant. Some of his anger remained from her earlier comment. It was strange, but he felt a little lonely.

He hoped Rakan was alright and momentarily regretted his decision to not stay with him.

He opened the door to the cottage and stepped out into the vast palace grounds in which it was nestled. If the opulent building itself hadn't risen above the trees, he could have been in any forest in the land.

Next to the cottage was a large shed.

He walked over to open its door and peered inside to find tools neatly hung around the walls with a worktable in the middle. He spent a while examining the implements and the craft that had gone into making them, and his thoughts went back to his youth, working in the smithy with his father.

His anger soared for a moment but then diminished as he realised his father would have starved to death back in Daleth's old kingdom, and anyway, he had a new father. Rakan.

He turned a pair of large shears over in his hands, remembering having crafted similar items himself before the majority of what he'd fashioned had turned toward weapons of war. When his father had let him be, he'd enjoyed the physical challenge working in the smithy put him through. Pumping the bellows, lifting and striking with the heavy hammer again and again had been strenuous yet satisfying.

As the demand to produce more swords had soared, he'd become used to switching arms, resting one whilst the other continued pounding away. Because of this, he'd become balanced and strong, whereas many blacksmiths had one enormous arm and one smaller.

The constant sparks, heat, and knocks had hardened his knuckles so that when he began fighting, he'd been prodigiously strong, and had hardly ever hurt his hands during a fight.

He shook his head clear of the old memories, stepping back into the light and started to wander. He concentrated on keeping his gait level, ensuring not to favour his uninjured leg. Whether it was fighting with his fists, or fighting with weapons, balance and movement were crucial. A keen-eyed opponent could pick up and capitalise on any injuries with potentially lethal results.

The cottage was surrounded by tall trees, with a path that led to the main palace entrance, but there was another smaller path that led to a wrought-iron gate beyond which were ornamental gardens.

They looked worse for wear at this time of year, which was unsurprising, as it seemed he was now living in the groundsman's cottage. Where the man was didn't bother Taran. Unfortunately, the lack of care had changed what had once obviously been a beautiful oasis into a writhing mass of thorned vines, dying blooms, and fresh buds waiting to open before autumn was over.

Taran stood silently for a while, wondering where to turn next. It was still early, and he had a full day of rest before his presence was required at the palace. He retraced his steps, deciding to sleep as his leg was aching, yet found himself back at the shed once more, looking at the tools.

He shook his head at what he was thinking. Nonetheless, he gathered several and placed them in a handcart before making his way back to the garden. He lay them on the ground, casting his eye over the undertaking before him.

The gardens were vast, and he could only see this corner of them, but maybe he could make a small difference. With that thought in mind, he took the shears and started to cut away the vines that intruded upon the pathways in his immediate vicinity.

Something was satisfying, even calming, about such simple, manual labour, and like his smithying, he could see what he was trying to create in his mind take form under his hands.

It was only the rumbling of his stomach that made him realise that lunch had long passed, and the slowly setting sun made him down his tools and return to the cottage.

His back, legs, and arms all ached, but pleasantly, unlike lately when it had been the result of injuries sustained.

Fresh bread and meat had been left on the table, as well as water. His armour was hung neatly on a rack, and several pairs of fine new clothes and boots were there too. A heavy pouch sat on a countertop, and he opened it, finding coins inside.

He should have felt something akin to joy or fulfilment. He'd risen from being an outcast, a commoner making a living on the road without a place to call his home, to Lord Commander of the Three Nation's Alliance.

His armour, clothing, weapons, and now this pouch of coins, represented more wealth and power than he'd ever thought was possible for him to accrue in his whole lifetime. But as he let the coins fall through his fingers, he felt empty.

In the back of his head, a voice whispered, telling him nothing was worth more than the love he'd once known, but the thought disappeared before he could grasp it.

He changed into the tooled and embellished leather clothing, and examined the armour on the rack. The cuirass had been repaired, jewels that had been knocked free replaced, leather straps oiled, and it shone. A new helm, heavy kilt, forearm bracers, and greaves also gleamed, no less striking, and yet he left them there, instead just buckling on his weapons belt.

Force of habit had him hide the coins out of sight, and he helped himself to the food and water until he felt satisfied.

He'd been somewhat vain once and would have tried to do something with his unruly hair, but looking in the mirror showed him a face that was not unlike his soul. Turning one way, it seemed fresh and innocent, but the other showed a dark, ruined mess. How apt.

He threw some logs onto the fire to ensure the cottage was warm for his return and then left, closing the door behind him.

He almost turned back as he did so, for he'd have loved to remain therein, forgetting about the responsibilities he now had. With great power came great responsibility, but the more powerful, the more corrupt as well, he thought.

However dark his soul felt at times, he'd never become corrupt. He might kill, he might murder, but he'd never seek dominion over his fellow man at their expense.

He walked toward the palace, breathing deeply, working on keeping his anger in check. He'd play the game until such time as he was in a position to win it, or he was dead in the ground.

***

Tristan sat in the audience chamber, waiting for the others to arrive.

Only Ostrom, Dafne, and now Taran, really mattered, but he nonetheless invited merchants and minor nobles to maintain their support and furthermore, keep an eye on them.

Maya was on another of her hunts, and he wasn't unhappy to have her gone for a day or two. She'd failed to have the desired effect on Taran's emotions and indeed had caused no little embarrassment with her affection still remaining, and obvious to everyone.

Strangely, Taran's utter indifference toward Maya hadn't been feigned. He'd barely looked her way, and no sign of emotion had crossed his face. The way he'd put his arm around Yana when they'd left had made Tristan wonder if Yana had succeeded in her efforts to win him over. She'd certainly spent the last couple of nights at his cottage, according to Galain.

Yana. She was as devious as she was beautiful.

He was immune to her wiles, if only because he saw in her someone like himself. Someone who'd manipulate anyone to get the desired result. He'd appointed her to head up the new hospital to keep her mischievous mind busy, to recognise her skill, whilst at the same time giving the nod to the service she'd done him.

He knew she sought power and influence, and the handsome residence, the finest clothes, and a healthy allowance would keep those desires satisfied. Hopefully, Taran could look after her other desires.

The End of Dreams

The fact Taran no longer had an interest in Maya, and that he was willing to throw himself into danger once more to seek help from the Horselords, had given Tristan a great deal to ponder over. Taran was still useful, and so Tristan would overlook his veiled threat until such time as Taran was no longer required.

After much consideration and then inviting Galain to give a second opinion, he'd decided to deal with Taran like he would with any Freestates noble, merchant, or officer.

He'd bribe him.

As lord commander, the salary Taran would be paid, and the accommodation he could demand, was handsome by any standards. So, he'd arranged that Taran received at least some of what he was owed, intending to increase it to what was due should he be successful in his mission and his behaviour continue to improve.

The doors to the audience chamber opened, and Ostrom and Dafne came to sit alongside him, leaving a chair free out of respect for Maya even if she was absent. Others followed, taking their seats around the chamber, but only those of import sat at the table.

The doors remained open, leaving Tristan with a view down the corridor as Taran walked through the palace entrance. Tristan noted Taran's limp was less pronounced, and he wore some of the fineries that had been chosen for him.

Tristan smiled to himself, for those who dressed in the garb of the gods of greed would soon come under their influence.

As Taran sat, he bowed his head to Tristan and the others equally, and then various scribes and messengers came forward to present the day's news.

Galain hovered nearby, waiting to call upon the guardsman should Taran prove to be difficult.

Tristan caught Galain's gaze and gave his head a subtle shake, and Galain relaxed, seating himself amongst the merchants.

It seemed Taran might have been tamed for now.

Reports were presented on the state of the walls, the training of new recruits, and the accumulation of supplies. Several minor fights had broken out but with no serious consequences, but of note was that a body had been found severely mutilated beyond recognition.

Murmurs met this last announcement. Fights were not unusual, occasional deaths were acceptable, but mutilation was something new, yet as it was a one-off, it was decided there was nothing to be done. The nobles and merchants then took their turns, bemoaning the loss of trade and, therefore, the loss of wealth.

Once they'd finished and Tristan had placated them, he was about to call the meeting to an early end when Taran stood, and all eyes turned to the scarred figure of the lord commander.

Tristan opened his arms.

'You have the floor,' he said magnanimously, wondering what Taran would say, and as he spoke, Tristan's jaw dropped in disbelief.

***

Taran had sat through the meeting considering his options. He was tired, physically and mentally, yet as he watched the nobles and merchants speak as if world events shouldn't dare affect them, his anger rose.

For a moment, his mind played with the idea of mutilating one of them to see if they then found that news serious. Sadly, now was not the time to give way to his base desire, even if the amulet made the idea seem very appealing.

He stood, and Tristan invited him to continue.

'What if I told you, that you …' Taran pointed at a noble who'd been talking behind his hand, and as the red-faced man looked over, Taran continued. 'Yes, you,' he affirmed. 'What if I told you that you'll soon be dead? Your throat will be slit from ear to ear, and you'll die watching the silk shoes you wear soak up your blood.'

Gasps met Taran's announcement.

Taran didn't pause. He pointed to another.

'You'll die with your guts spilling from your stomach as you try to push them back in with your fingers. You behind him, you'll die suffocated by the weight of the dead bodies upon you that you try to hide under as you shiver in fear.'

Shocked silence met his words, and he pushed on.

'All of you will die in the most horrible of ways,' he said, encompassing them all with a sweep of his arms, 'for in war there's often no quick and easy death, rather it's a drawn-out agony. For Daleth and his men, listening to you cry for your mothers or beg for release will have them laughing in ecstasy.'

Shouts and cries of outrage suddenly erupted at his proclamations as the audience got over their shock, and many shouted for Tristan to have him thrown out.

Taran drew in a deep breath.

'SILENCE!' he thundered.

Such was the force of his command that no further sound was made. A guard peeked around a door, then quickly withdrew his head when he saw no blood had been spilt or weapons drawn.

'You think me impudent, rude, or disrespectful to speak so, and yet I speak the truth. The truly incredible thing is that each and every one of you who'll die could easily do something to stop it. Our king,' he said, nodding to Tristan, 'fought beside me, facing Daleth's horde, willing to shed his own blood.' He almost choked as he spoke the lie, but it needed to be said. 'He risked his life to protect his wealth and yours. What Freestates king could have done more?'

Tristan was stunned at Taran paying him such an undeserved compliment, unsure what would happen next.

'So I ask you all,' Taran continued, 'what have you done to not only protect your wealth, but your lives since news of Daleth's invasion turned from a nightmare to a reality?'

Taran held their attention with the force of his voice and the scorn it held.

'Your king spends the gold of the nation for he knows that it's required to save it, and you criticise him for it. Yet none of you have seen that with victory comes the spoils of war beyond what you can imagine. You cling on to your wealth with both hands, not even noticing that there is wealth to be taken that can fill both arms!'

This time, the voices that rose were not of anger but of excitement.

'Of what do you speak?' many cried. 'What are you not telling us?'

'All of you, you protect your money, and you complain about the loss of trade, yet this is the time to spend, not save. You should have your jewelsmiths craft weapons, you should empty your stables, giving horses to the army. You should share your stockpiles of food to keep our soldiers strong instead of letting it rot in your cellars.'

Taran dropped his voice, as if a co-conspirator.

'Yet why, why would you do something so generous, so risky, as to spend the wealth you've so cleverly hoarded?'

He smiled as everyone leant forward, trying to hear his every word.

'Because the rewards are beyond counting. The spoils of this war are limitless!'

Tristan leaned forward. *Tell us*, he was about to demand, then realising the ignorance it would convey, chose his words more wisely.

'Tell them,' he ordered Taran, his own excitement rising.

'If you give everything you have,' Taran continued, 'or, most everything,' he said, winking, 'when we win this war, not only will you keep your lives, but you'll have the chance to share in Daleth's wealth. The Ember Kingdom had treasure beyond imagining, accrued over centuries. Where do you think that wealth is? Daleth wouldn't leave it behind. What fool would do that? It must travel with his army!'

Shouts met his announcement.

Taran raised his hands.

'That isn't the all of it either. Beyond Tristan's Folly, a deserted kingdom with land and natural resources waits to be claimed. Those who help the crown, will be rewarded by the crown, and will be wealthier than the gods themselves!'

Even Taran couldn't silence the merchants and nobles who flooded forward, offering their wealth to the fight. Tristan's scribes took note of the promises of services, items, and supplies.

Taran turned toward the door, and as he neared it, Dafne and Ostrom accompanied him to the relative tranquillity outside.

The sun was setting, and the clouds burned red like fresh paint upon a canvas. Momentarily, Taran felt his heart react to nature's beauty, before the amulet dulled the feeling, replacing it with apathy. As he walked through the grounds, he waited patiently for his companions to speak, and Dafne eventually broke the silence.

'What you just did was simply amazing,' she said, taking his arm gently, turning him to face her.

Ostrom nodded.

'All this time, we've been trying to coerce those selfish fools to part with some of their ill-gotten gains, but the more we called them selfish, the happier they became. Now you come along and solve this in a moment.'

'Will this help turn the tide, do you think?' Dafne asked. 'Will it make any difference?'

Taran paused for a moment, looking at them both.

'You deserve honesty, so my answer is no. I didn't do this to enrich them, I didn't do this to save them either. I did this because, at least for the next few months, there'll be no empty bellies, and the inequality that I grew up with and now see at every turn will disappear. At least until next year.'

'Why until just next year?' Dafne asked, then laughed at her own naivety as realisation struck. The answer came from her own lips. 'Because that's when we die.'

Ostrom smiled unperturbed.

'If you can convince those greedy pigs to part with their wealth so easily, then I have faith you'll return with the whole Horselords nation. I reckon we might have a chance then.'

'It'll need all of them, that's for sure,' Taran agreed.

Dafne and Ostrom turned away, highlighted by the hues of the setting sun, and in other times they could have been mistaken for lovers, walking through the palace grounds.

A smile flitted across Taran's lips before pain drove it away. What was the point of love when it could be stolen from you at any moment?

With that dark thought, he limped further into the darkening gardens to find his way back to his cottage and sleep.

***

Chapter XI

Maya leant back, looking up at the colour-splashed sky, her gaze caught momentarily in wonder. Her heart ached both at the beauty and with the emptiness of having no one to share it with.

Taran crossed her mind, and she sighed wistfully, wishing she was by his side, but then angrily pushed him from her thoughts, tormented by the image of Yana's arm around his waist. She doubted he'd be looking at the sky when that vixen now shared his bed.

She used that anger to fuel her strength. Whereas before her limbs had felt heavy and she knew she couldn't fight on much longer, now the trembling in them ceased. The five men surrounding her circled her warily, respecting her skill with the heavy swords she held.

Taran's voice echoed in her head, a memory of time past, urging her to attack, for this was the best tactic to use against multiple assailants. Whilst she cursed him for coming to mind again, the advice was sound. Keep them off guard, not letting them coordinate their attack as one.

She sprang forward, attacking the soldier in front of her. He blocked her first sword blow, but her second found its mark on his side, and he fell away as she broke outside the circle. The falling man blocked the next to his left as she attacked the man on his right, constantly moving.

She spun left, then suddenly switched back, catching the man closing in on her off guard, and she ducked under his sweeping blow to slash her sword across his stomach. He fell with a cry.

Her breath became more ragged with every passing moment; her lungs hurt. Then, a tree root caused her to stumble, and her tired legs gave way. This momentary imbalance was all it took for a sword to crash into her side before another found her stomach. Her weapons fell from her grasp as she fell onto her back.

'Do you concede?' Ferris gasped.

Maya could only nod weakly in affirmation, for she could hardly breathe, let alone form words.

Her guard put down their wooden weapons and started stripping off the heavy padded-cloth armour they'd donned for the practice.

They left Maya to recover in her own time, and finally she sat up, wincing as the muscles in her side spasmed. Whilst the padding had absorbed most of the blow, the wooden swords were heavy, and she'd wear a bruise the size of her forearm along her ribcage the following morning.

They were a day's ride east from Freeguard, and whereas she usually hunted northward, Ferris had impressed the need to keep the city between them and any possible bands of encroaching enemy lancers.

So far, none had been seen close to the city, but that didn't mean it was worth taking the risk. Also, this trip wasn't really for hunting. The cellars below the kitchens weren't ideal for practice, and training on even ground, when almost all the fighting they could soon expect would be on the hills or plains outside of the city, just wasn't realistic enough.

In fact, this training wasn't just for her, for they all took turns to fight the other five, preparing for the time when they'd fight outnumbered against Daleth's horde. They also fought two on three, one on two, and one on one, learning from the experience and sharing with one another how they dealt with the various scenarios.

The hard physical exertion was just what Maya needed and staying away from Tristan, and now even Taran too, was best for her.

If only it didn't hurt so much.

The men kept the fire low in a hollow, for there was no point in announcing their position even if they were in friendly territory. There were plenty of farmsteads nearby in this rolling countryside and these were still very active, bringing in the last of the harvests for the autumn rains were already overdue.

As Maya skinned some rabbits she'd dispatched earlier with her arrows, the men played dice and left her alone, respecting that she needed her own space at times. She enjoyed preparing the meat for cooking, it was reassuring familiar, a ritual that she'd been doing most of her life.

The meat was soon crackling on spits over the fire, and the delicious aroma filled the air. Maya's stomach grumbled in anticipation while she boiled water in a pan for the vegetables and roots she'd gathered earlier on the outward journey of their trip.

Her keen eye could spot anything from berries to herbs, and she was always leaping off her horse to stuff her findings into a pouch. The men had initially raised their eyebrows, but after so many trips, they knew that she was a hunter-gatherer of incredible skill, and she could create a meal fit for kings from the land around them.

After they'd eaten their fill in companionable silence, Ferris took the first watch. Everyone else turned in, wrapped up in their furred bedrolls, for the weather was becoming colder.

Maya hated the time just before sleep, for she didn't know where to turn her thoughts anymore. During daylight, there was always something to be distracted by, something to do. When all was quiet, was when the hurt and pain returned.

What had been the best memories of her life offered no relief. When she thought back to her youth, it brought her now-dead parents to mind, her father's death still acutely painful. Her happiest moments recently had been in Taran's company, and yet even those memories were tainted by his apparent change of heart and current interest in Yana. Her gift, which had once brought her delight, was as distant as the stars, and she felt empty inside.

She didn't know how long she lay staring at the night sky, entranced by the moon's radiance. The fire had dwindled away, and yet there was still a red glow, but it wasn't from the fire or the sun that had set a long time ago.

Even as the thought registered, Ferris came around, kneeling beside them one by one, whispering, ordering them to gather their belongings and to saddle up.

After they mounted, Ferris turned his horse westward, back toward Freeguard, but Maya called softly for him to stop.

'We need to hurry,' Ferris urged. 'As sure as there are stars in the night sky, that glow to the north are farms burning. Daleth's lancers are abroad this night and have come further east than any of us would have guessed.'

Ferris urged his horse forward, signalling for the others to follow, but Maya cantered hers ahead, turning it to block them.

'No,' Maya spoke firmly. 'We need to investigate. We need to see if we can help!'

'Are you crazy?' Ferris hissed. 'There are but six of us, and you're to be the queen one day. We cannot fight lancers on horseback, we'd be slain in moments. We may ride mounts, but we're infantry, not trained cavalry.'

'Then we'll fight on foot,' Maya insisted. 'Let me remind you who you are. You're a soldier of the Freestates, and you swore an oath of allegiance when you donned the uniform. The Freestates isn't King Tristan, even if he thinks it is. The Freestates are the land, the Freestates are the people who live in this land. When you swore to protect the Freestates, you swore to protect them. Yes, I might well be queen one day, but a queen who deserts her people when they're in need is no queen at all. Now follow me!'

Maya led the group north, eyes straining as they rode under the silver moonlight. On reaching the valley's rim, they looked over to see two farmsteads completely ablaze, buildings engulfed, the smell of smoke thick in the air.

Closer to them, a third farmstead was surrounded by men on horseback with burning brands in their hands, whooping and calling as they swung them in the air leaving trails of sparks behind them. The buildings here were starting to catch fire but had yet to burn with full force.

Maya wondered if the poor workers had been slain whilst asleep, butchered in their beds, for of them, there was no sign.

'I count twenty,' Ferris said, and the other men agreed. 'We need to get back with this intelligence.'

Maya shook her head.

'No. A message is being sent to us by the lancers that the lands around Freeguard are no longer safe. We need to send one to the lancers that this land is no longer safe for them either, or they'll grow too bold.

'Follow my lead,' she commanded, and dismounted, unlashing her bow and quiver from her horse's back. The other men dismounted too and whilst they didn't have bows, they donned shields upon their arms and drew swords.

Under cover of darkness, they slunk down the hillside, keeping low, and came to within a hundred paces of the farmstead. They were now close enough to hear the lancers' laughter as they waited for the fire to fully take hold.

Maya took her arrows from the quiver, pushing them point down in the soil at her feet. There were twenty arrows.

'What do you want us to do?' Ferris whispered.

Maya smiled, teeth bright in the darkness.

'I want you to watch and see why they should be afraid of us, not we of them!'

As she spoke, with a whoosh, the fire finally engulfed the barn and the men on horseback were highlighted against the flames.

Maya's bow felt like an extension of her arm as she nocked an arrow without conscious thought, drew smoothly, and targeted her quarry. As she released her breath, the arrow sang from the bow.

Even as it punched a lancer from his saddle without a sound, she was loosing a second.

Laughter momentarily greeted the fall of the rider, whose friends thought he'd just fallen off drunk, but as the second arrow thunked home in the next victim's chest, he screamed, and shouts of alarm filled the night air.

The lancers wheeled their horses around, not sure from where the attack was coming and arrow after arrow found its mark, and then there were ten empty saddles as the remaining lancers turned their horses northward and fled in a panic.

'Now we leave,' Maya said as she gathered her unspent arrows.

They ran back to their mounts, and with blood pumping furiously in their veins, dug heels into the horses' flanks as they headed on the long journey back to Freeguard and safety.

***

The End of Dreams

Daleth's head pounded, and he reached for a goblet of wine beside his bed, savouring the smoothness of the alcohol as he swallowed. Tristan and his predecessors had undoubtedly the most exquisite taste in wine, which several hundred vintage bottles showed testament to.

This treasure and many others besides had been found in the extensive cellars beneath the palace. Although yet to be fully explored, they'd already given up all manner of wealth that the retreating forces had been unable to remove in time. The cellar entrance had been artfully concealed, but an inquisitive cat led a bodyguard to investigate its scratchings, and thus the hidden trove of wealth was revealed.

Daleth chuckled. A rat betrayed by a cat.

It was approaching midnight, and despite having slept, he hadn't rested, for this was the ideal time to communicate with his Rangers and overseers. The headaches were a small price to pay, for while spirit talking, he could see so much more of the world than his injuries currently prevented him from enjoying.

He listened to the wind howling outside and was grateful that his men were well sheltered, for this was becoming a lousy autumn, and the winter after would no doubt be even worse. Fortunately, his meticulous preparations meant this would have little effect. The army had plentiful shelter, food, and water, and the city was full of discarded supplies.

Likewise, Gregor and Julius' forces had already secured the cities of Freehold and Freemarch and advised there were plenty of provisions therein to last the winter. It would be an unfortunate consequence that the civilians who'd thought themselves lucky to have escaped death, would have it find them in the different guise of starvation. Both men were now readying to launch their attacks. Julius on the Eyre and Gregor on the Horselords.

Julius had the toughest job, but that was fine, for he was as tough as they came. The swamplands would be frozen by midwinter if he hadn't completed his task of subjugation by then. But he would, for the consequences of failure were somewhat final.

Gregor, being far further south, would enjoy milder weather for longer and might escape the worst of the big freeze. Even so, any snowfall would help him, for the enemy's heavy horse wouldn't fare well on sodden ground.

His last communications had been with seers embedded alongside the lancers, and overall, despite some losses, he was happy with their results. They were unable to hold any land, but they were now wreaking havoc up to and beyond Freeguard.

Their current role was to deprive the enemy of as much food as possible, spreading fear and destruction while keeping a wary eye for any large troop movements. It was exceedingly unlikely that the Freestates alliance would launch a raid, yet even a cornered mouse sometimes turned to bite the cat.

The lancers were so fleet that they could avoid any of the forces that Tristan could muster. How foolish that all Tristan's forces were foot soldiers. Even their mounted troops were just that, not cavalry.

Warfare wasn't like in the past, when two armies would lock shields and die in a battle of attrition and strength. Now it was about manoeuvrability and versatility, which was why his army combined different specialised units, although they all shared one common skill, killing efficiently without mercy.

The heavy knights of the Horselords were obsolete too. They could only be used for one thing, the charge. Of course, it could be absolutely devastating to swordsmen, but against heavy spearmen in deep formation, long weapons grounded, creating a bristling thicket of spears, any charge would be broken. First by the deadly spears, and thereafter by the falling bodies of the horses in front.

The first few ranks of spearmen would bear the brunt of the impact, but they were trained to fall back underneath their full-length body shields, which gave them a chance of surviving the crushing hooves and falling bodies.

The heavy sound of booted feet interrupted Daleth's thoughts.

His personal bodyguard tirelessly patrolled inside and outside the palace day and night, and he was grateful for their loyalty and diligence.

His panic over Kalas' apparent resurrection had abated. Were the daemon somehow alive, then it was unlikely he'd try to infiltrate a city of thousands of soldiers, and yet Daleth wasn't taking any chances.

In time, Jared, whilst embedded with the Freestates army, would become aware of any rumours surrounding Kalas, and he'd remember to ask him next time they communicated.

He walked to the window, and his eyes widened in surprise.

It was still late autumn, yet swirling around in the air were tiny flakes of snow. He rubbed his hands together in satisfaction, as the lancers' recent reports suggested many of the alliance forces and peasantry were still outside the city walls. They'd suffer terribly in the coming months, if not die, due to the greed of the very people they either served or came to protect.

Yes, he thought, let's hope this is a bad winter indeed, and almost as if in response to his thoughts, the wind howled like a wolf.

***

Maya sat with Ferris, opposite Tristan, Galain, Ostrom, Ultric and Dafne. There were no other minor nobles present, and she was glad Taran wasn't there. The realisation saddened her.

Tristan cleared his throat.

'I've called this impromptu meeting as, thanks to my betrothed, we're now aware that Daleth has his lancers circling north, and likely south around Freeguard to harass the peasant farmers. It's a strategy that ensures we're unable to collect all the harvests.'

'By harass, you mean slaughter.' Maya glared, annoyed at Tristan's choice of words, but he just smiled, unperturbed.

Dafne's voice interrupted the uncomfortable silence that briefly followed.

'Despite the sad loss of life, the good news is that it reinforces our beliefs that there'll be no major attack until spring. Why bother denying us food if we're to be attacked in the immediate future? It makes me feel assured that we're right in this assumption.'

Ostrom nodded.

'Agreed. But in some ways I'd rather have met him on the field sooner rather than later, for this will be a long winter for us all. My men are not used to the cold and will not fare well. I'd never seen snow until last night, and my men are fearful.'

Tristan started to laugh until Ostrom's glower silenced it before it truly left his lips.

Maya nodded in sympathy.

'We need to start getting all the people into the city from outside of the walls. It matters not whether they're from the desert, the swamps or from the fields, we must find them lodgings, and I mean proper lodgings.'

Tristan's eyes narrowed, but then he shrugged.

'Normally I'd have dismissed this proposal out of hand. None of the nobles or merchants would have supported the idea, and it would have weakened my position. Yet Taran has already eased the way for this to happen, although it might stretch the agreements somewhat. But we need someone to take this on board.'

Dafne smiled and thumped her hand on the table.

'I will do so. Ostrom and his men are more suited to rebuilding the walls, as they're larger and stronger. I'll have mine identify suitable properties that aren't on the main thoroughfare but near the walls, mainly warehouses and the like, so as not to upset the more important of the city's inhabitants.'

Tristan clapped his hands.

'Your understanding of our ways is appreciated. Galain will organise to have my seal affixed to an order, allowing you to requisition whatever property is needed in return for ample recompense.'

Tristan looked around the table.

'From now on,' he continued, 'do we agree only military units on patrol are to be allowed outside of the city?'

Ostrom and Dafne nodded.

'I might add,' Ostrom said, 'that we should have heavy patrols of my spears backed up by some of Dafne's archers up to half a day's march north, south, and east of the city to complement those Rakan took west. Lancers can't really cause mischief if they approach the city, but we don't want their appearance causing panic either if they're left undeterred.'

Tristan turned to Ferris.

'Lady Maya is your personal responsibility. I expect you to ensure that she remains in sight of the city walls from hereon.'

'It sounds like she's better off being let loose on the enemy,' Ostrom laughed, and Dafne joined in.

Maya smiled her thanks, but Tristan remained serious.

The End of Dreams

'All joking aside,' Tristan warned. 'Irrespective of her martial prowess, she's too valuable to me to be risked, and thus my decision stands. Ferris, I'd have a word with you later about this.'

Maya sighed. Her escapes to the countryside were exactly that. Escapes from this gilded cage that seemed to close in on her day by day. Sleeping under the stars, far from the city, was such a blessing, but nor could she escape the truth of the danger that now freely roamed the countryside.

Never in her life, since she was old enough to hunt, had she been inside her village walls for more than a day or two unless ill. She'd always felt more at home in the woods than under the thatched roof of her parents' cottage. Even the winter's snow hadn't stopped her from going out, however deep, to trap rabbits and small game in her snares. This would be a long winter indeed.

Galain whispered something in Tristan's ear, and the meeting was called to a close.

Maya walked dejectedly to her room, Ferris respectfully a few steps behind her.

'Don't worry, my lady,' Ferris said softly. 'We can still train outside the walls. We just can't sleep outside of them.'

Maya smiled gratefully over her shoulder.

'I appreciate the thought, Ferris, and indeed we'll train, but the saddest thing is, however hard we train, we'll likely lose. Yet, if we win by some stroke of fortune, then victory only furthers my incarceration.'

Ferris's face was glum. He understood her meaning, for he now knew her well.

'Then train hard, so that when the time comes, you can fight free of the chains that would shackle you.'

'Then let us start early on the morrow. Until dawn!' Maya bade Ferris goodnight.

'Until dawn, my lady,' he said, turning away as she entered her room. He nodded to another guard and walked away, sadness etched upon his face.

Tristan would never let her go. She was already in the cage, her wings clipped. Ferris felt a little guilty about pretending to still be her friend, but the gold Tristan now paid him to report her every move was simply too much to turn down. She might have saved his life, but

Tristan would ensure he could live the rest of it in considerable comfort.

The sooner she embraced the Freestates way, the sooner she'd accept her fate and worship the god of greed, revelling in the wealth she'd inherit. Nothing was worth more than gold, certainly not love.

***

Taran knelt beneath the weak sunlight.

It was going to be a bleak winter, people were starting to say, and some unseasonal snow had already fallen, although it hadn't settled.

This autumn was definitely far colder than usual, but at least his body felt warm. He'd put on some padded overalls and a hat he'd found within a chest inside the cottage, and the thick cloth protected him from both the cold and the plants' many spiked defences.

He worked tirelessly in the gardens each day, starting early as the sun rose in the sky, only stopping to eat or when Yana infrequently came by to check on him.

She teased him mercilessly, but not unkindly, joking that Daleth would quake to see the deadly enemy general pruning flowers. She didn't linger and would leave after checking his healing wounds.

He looked up at the sky, stretching his back, wondering how something as simple as gardening could cause him more aches and pains than fighting on the justice turf or weapons training.

His leg wound had healed enough to walk without much of a limp, and his shoulder felt mobile enough, despite the lattice of vivid and angry scars covering them. When he'd looked at himself in the silvered mirror in the morning, it looked as if he had been sewn together from different bodies.

He also knew he was weaker than he'd been for many years and was amazed at how his muscles had atrophied from lack of real use. He needed to get back to fitness and start honing his weapon skills. His trip to the Horselords would be fraught with danger and hardship, and in his current state, he'd likely fall at the first challenge.

Two more days of gentle torture in the garden to get that in shape before he started on himself.

The End of Dreams

He surveyed the work he'd done, evaluating the results of his endeavours. It wasn't as though he saw the beauty of the garden, but the order and neatness somehow settled him. Beforehand, the chaos of the tangled vines and the dead blooms had somehow reflected his inner feelings.

What would he feel if he looked upon the world again without the amulet? His fingers strayed behind his neck to the chain, but hastily he pulled them away as a feeling of panic and nausea swept over him.

He leaned forward once again, turning the soil with a small hand fork, removing weeds and stones that somehow upset his calm with their encroachment.

As he toiled, he heard footsteps slowly approach without purpose or direction, and for a moment, he froze in embarrassment. This was his secret, his place, and he willed with all his might for this intruder to move on. But, his gift was long absent and simple force of will was not enough.

The footsteps were not stealthy, nor heavy, and had obviously come across him through bad luck. Taran didn't perceive any threat as they stopped some distance short of him, so he continued to work with his head bowed, wondering how long it would be before the person moved on.

'You're doing such a wonderful job,' Taran heard, and his heart almost stopped. He froze for a moment, before carrying on diligently.

'This place was so overgrown and unloved, and you've transformed this part wonderfully. What a gift to have such a way with the land. What's your name?'

Go away, Taran wanted to shout, but instead, he ignored the question, his shoulders hunched as he cast stones from the soil as if this would somehow cast the unwelcome visitor aside as well.

'Are you hard of hearing, or just a little rude?'

The question betrayed a hint of annoyance in the voice.

'You know, I could order you to talk to me if that were my wish, but I'd far rather you do so out of courtesy.'

Taran felt anger course through his veins as he knelt there, unable to contain his temper anymore.

'Once a simple wish from you would have seen me cross oceans,' he snapped angrily, turning around. 'But that was when you were like me, a commoner. Now, however, as you're soon to be queen, there's nothing you could order that I'd obey. Save one perhaps, that demanded I never see you again!'

Maya staggered back as if struck.

'Taran,' she whispered incredulously. She went to say more, but Taran raised his hand, so obviously furious that she swallowed her words.

Taran rose to his feet and stalked away, leaving his tools where they lay, dark emotions threatening to overwhelm him. How dare she intrude on his solitude, his place where he could find serenity!

Thankfully, Maya didn't follow, and he soon found himself back at the cottage. An axe stood embedded in a trunk, and he pulled it free. Taking a block from the woodpile, he angrily swung the axe and split it in two.

Yes, he thought, that will be you, Tristan. The next one was Daleth. Yet, however hard he tried, he couldn't bring himself to picture Maya as he split the wood. Still, the exercise felt good even if his shoulder complained painfully. He split enough wooden blocks to last the coming winter, even if he wouldn't be here to see it.

He'd have to rise earlier tomorrow and finish by lunchtime so he didn't bump into Maya again and he'd start his training then too instead of waiting any longer.

There was a small well at the back of the cottage, from which he pulled up a bucket of water and cleansed, rubbing himself down with some herbs he'd pulled from the garden that turned into a nice lather. How did he know these were good for cleansing with?

Then the memory of him washing in the crystal waters of the woodland pool with Maya came to mind. Tears welled in his eyes, but the amulet as ever quashed the emotion before it took hold.

At least something useful had come from their relationship, he thought, as he scrubbed himself clean before going inside and closing the cottage door behind him.

He was so focussed on his own thoughts that he never saw Maya turn away, walking sadly back whence she'd come, tears in her eyes as well.

***

The End of Dreams

Yana nodded in satisfaction as she surveyed the beautiful building with its columned entrance.

Lord Duggan's fall from grace and likely death at the hands of Tristan's men had seen her not only presented with a beautiful house overlooking the palace but also this enormous property with an attached apartment to turn into a hospital along with the funds to do so.

The last few days had been a blur, having spent her time gathering together all the skilled physicians, healers, apothecaries and volunteers she could find. She'd then sourced herbs and ingredients and had carpenters make bunks to replace the exquisite furnishings and furniture of this grand house.

She'd taken care to keep the rarest pieces whilst exchanging the other items, which were still of amazing quality and value for the things she needed. This had allowed her to keep most of the funds from the crown treasury, increasing her wealth dramatically.

What better way to curry favour with the merchants and lesser nobles than by allowing them to profit handsomely from her enterprise in exchange for their pledge of support in the future should the need arise.

She appeared virtuous to all, whilst her motives were anything but.

Of course, no one had any idea that her goals extended to being the queen of this land, but it wouldn't matter, they'd find out in due course. In the interim, her name was spoken of highly, securing her importance and position.

Once the hospital was finished, she planned to help not just the wealthy before the continuation of hostilities, but the needy, and ingratiate herself with those of the lower classes. Of course, some peasants might have to die here and there as she experimented with different herbs and concoctions, but that was the price of progress.

Excitement filled her veins as she allowed herself a moment to remember the lives of the soldiers who'd slipped away while under her care at Tristan's Folly.

People were so easy to manipulate. Everyone she dealt with saw her as a creature of beauty and intelligence, sharp yet understanding. She was becoming adored and admired by all, except by one.

The king to her queen.

Whilst the last few days had been rewarding, and two or three more would see the doors to the new city infirmary open, she'd missed spending time with Taran. Her hope was that he'd realise just how good she was for him, having missed her tending to his wounds, as she'd done for so long.

With a final glance and a nod to the foreman who was in charge of the myriad of workmen on-site, she turned away.

It was time to find her king.

The city still amazed her as she walked through the busy streets, although she was careful to not let this show on her face. She'd grown up thinking Ember Town was important, but now realised its utter insignificance. This was her world now, and she wanted it all.

She'd taken to wearing far more expensive clothing, finely cut so that it accentuated her figure, revealing, but not so much as to be scandalous.

Merchants and minor nobles walked the streets, as well as servants and soldiers. The merchants talked in groups, sneers openly visible on their faces as those of lower stature passed them by. Yet Yana was happy to note that when their gaze fell upon her, they looked with curiosity if they didn't know her, or respect if they did.

Several times she was invited to join in their conversations, and by the time she bid the merchants goodbye, she knew she'd made potential allies.

She even enjoyed the looks the soldiers and others of lower station gave her as she made her way toward the palace.

Her reputation was growing.

Halfway to the palace, she stopped at a merchant's stall to buy some food. The merchant protested that someone so important could enjoy the food for free. It was a game, of course, and one she intuitively excelled at. In a city of the greedy, only a fool with no understanding of the culture would think anything came free, and thus she paid and was respected the more for it.

It was the afternoon by the time she made it to the palace grounds, and despite the walk, she felt cool. The previous night had seen the first few flakes of snow, and the sun was weak in the sky, but on such a still day it provided enough heat if one were active.

The End of Dreams

The guards at the gate saluted her, and after being admitted, she wandered toward the palace. Courtiers entering and leaving nodded to her, and she revelled in their acknowledgement.

She enquired at the entrance as to whether Taran was within, but it transpired he'd yet to be seen. Her heart beat a little faster as she ambled across the palace grounds. The path she chose led through a small copse of woods, and as she neared Taran's cottage, the clash of blades chimed harshly on the air.

Her hand went to her side, and she cursed for dressing in such a fashion, having left her weapons behind, and vowed never to do so again.

She picked up a fallen branch, hefting its weight in her hand and stealthily approached through the trees to see three men fighting one other with two more, and a woman, standing aside.

She relaxed when she realised this was a training bout even if the weapons were of steel, for despite the looks of concentration, there was no hatred, fury or malice on the faces of any. Even Taran seemed calm despite the amulet as he spun and turned, parrying each blow as if he knew they were coming before they were even made.

She let the branch fall from her grasp, her insides warming, her heart pounding, for it was as if he danced for her.

For a moment, she was reminded of her uncle, Kalas. On one side, Taran's face was boyishly handsome, but on the other, it was almost daemonic in its scarring.

It thrilled her to see him training once more. No longer grubbing in the soil like a farmer, but fighting like the warrior he was and the king he'd be one day. He sparred with two men from the desert, while a woman from the Eyre and a further two men from the Freestates observed.

She smiled at his choice.

Whether it was purposeful or intuitive, Taran would be spreading his reputation amongst the different factions of the army just as she was doing with the merchants, nobles, and shortly the commoners.

He was still heavily favouring one leg, and as they took a break, he started to stretch it.

She stepped forward from the trees, and the men smiled in recognition and bowed slightly as she approached.

Taran looked up, his face splitting into a grin, and Yana felt her heart skip a beat.

'Here, let me help,' she offered, and indicated for Taran to sit.

He did so with his back against a tree, and she stretched his leg out and started expertly massaging the muscle, barely controlling her hands as they desired to travel up his thigh.

'You have strong hands,' Taran grunted.

Yana continued until she felt the muscle relax.

'Move forward a little,' she instructed, then knelt behind him, her hands working on his shoulders. Taran closed his eyes, and Yana felt like purring.

Yes, he'd certainly missed her and now appreciated her skills. But if this was the key to him coming to appreciate her, then she'd need to play this strategy a little longer. Only the highest peak had the perfect view, but the journey to the top should never be rushed, or tragedy could strike.

She rose, tossing her hair. One of the other men called over, complaining that his leg ached too, and she laughed, flashing him a smile as she turned to look down at Taran.

'You see how sought after I am? But my hands, skill, and heart are being saved for one person. However, from now on, that person will have to ask so that I feel appreciated.'

She smiled sweetly before turning away.

Yes, let him come to her in time. There would be so much pleasure after such anticipation.

***

Jared looked down upon Tolgarth's corpse and sighed.

He hadn't intended to kill him so soon, but sometimes life didn't quite turn out as you expected. It certainly hadn't for Tolgarth.

Jared had won a considerable amount of coin from his barrack-mates and having studied Tolgarth's habits, knew him to be a lover of Eyrean wine. This was made from swamp berries, which at different times during the fermenting process, could range from a sweet delicacy to a deadly poison.

The End of Dreams

It was expensive and hard to come by, and Jared had procured a bottle. He'd asked Tolgarth for a moment of his time during one of the training sessions and mentioned he'd purchased a gift born of admiration.

Jared had gone by arrangement to the captain's quarters and had humbly presented the wine. He'd asked as a favour if Tolgarth could spare a little time to tell of his exploits and share his wisdom regarding the city and those within it. It would have been invaluable to learn, observe, and understand Tolgarth's allies and detractors.

Tolgarth's response had instead been a withering dismissal, advising that a peasant bearing a gift was still just a stinking peasant and Jared should remove himself from his presence immediately.

Unfortunately for Tolgarth, Jared's anger and impatience had gotten the better of him. His huge hands had found Tolgarth's neck and squeezed the life from him. The horrified look in the captain's eyes, as he witnessed Jared shifting, had been exquisite to behold before the life faded from them.

Now he turned and locked the door quickly, for it was at times like this, in a situation that could never be explained, that he was most vulnerable.

A chair had been broken in the furious struggle, a desk overturned and papers strewn everywhere, but it was the body that caused him most concern. He hadn't killed Tolgarth in some dark alley where he could just mutilate the body, or throw it down a sewer. He stood in Tolgarth's own quarters, and there was no way he could simply carry the body out unobserved.

He stripped himself naked, then did the same to the corpse before dressing in the captain's clothes.

What to do with the body?

Casting his gaze around the room, he spied a large chest at the end of the bed. He lifted the heavy lid and found it full of neatly folded uniforms and casual clothing. He set the table upright and put the garments on its wooden top before dragging the heavy chest to the washroom at the back.

Returning, he knelt, grabbing Tolgarth's cooling hands before dragging him back to the chest. It took some time, but after much effort, he managed to squeeze the body in, then closed the lid and locked it shut with a padlock that thankfully hung open on the hasp.

No sooner had he returned to the main room and started picking parchment from the floor than there was a banging on the door.

The voice of the corporal, Rafeen, called out.

'Captain, are you all right?'

The hammering continued.

Jared took a deep breath and opened the door, a perfect sneer on his face as he thrust his chin out.

'What on earth gives you the right to pound on my bloody door?' he demanded in that menacing whisper he'd heard Tolgarth use.

Rafeen blanched, stepping back.

'I'm … I'm sorry, Captain. Me and the lads heard banging, and we'd seen that big oaf come over and wondered if there was some kind of trouble afoot?'

'Have you been drinking?' Jared squinted, leaning forward. 'Do you see that fool in here?'

He stepped to one side to give Rafeen a view of the room.

'Do I look like I couldn't handle some common scum if he wanted to give me trouble?' His voice rose to a shout.

Rafeen backed away, bewildered and somewhat horrified.

'I'm sorry, Captain. We made a terrible mistake. I can … can see everything is all right,' he stammered and stood to attention, saluting.

Jared sighed and waved his hand dismissively.

'At ease, Corporal,' he said in a softer tone. 'Your apparent concern somewhat alleviates the crime of your stupidity. Indeed, you might have heard banging, but if so, it's because the chair I was on broke. Come in for a moment.'

He stepped aside, and Rafeen, looking even more flustered, followed Jared into his quarters.

Jared sat on another chair and poured himself a goblet of wine, looking at Rafeen carefully, making him squirm a little under the scrutiny.

This was a test for himself, and so far, he was doing well. By inviting him in, he ensured Rafeen had no doubt that his captain had been alone unless someone was hiding under the bed. Now, with the immediate danger past, it was time to make the best of this situation whilst buying himself a little more time to become accustomed to his new apartment.

Jared rubbed his chin as if deliberating, then hit his palm against the tabletop, pretending to have come to a decision.

'Rafeen, I've been considering you for promotion, but I want to hear how well you know the men you'd command and what you believe their strengths and weaknesses are before I make a final decision.'

Rafeen puffed up, barely able to conceal the smile that threatened to break out over his face.

'I don't know how to thank you, Captain.'

'Well,' Jared said, 'first, you should go get us some decent food, and then we can eat and talk together like civilised men.'

Rafeen's head bobbed up and down as he turned toward the door.

'Oh,' Jared said, raising his hand. 'Keep your pending promotion quiet. We don't want to make anyone else jealous, do we?'

Rafeen shook his head so hard that Jared thought it might fall off, before hurrying out of the door.

Jared smiled to himself. He'd gotten away with Tolgarth's killing, and now had a new loyal lapdog who'd fill in the blanks about many of the people Jared should know.

In Tolgarth's form, he'd have access to the palace. Caution would be paramount for a while. He'd have to tread very carefully, filling in the holes of his knowledge, but he was a master, and no one had any idea he was here and of his gift.

Once he'd learned as much from Rafeen as possible, he'd repeat the tactic with some of the other ranks, ensuring that his disguise became flawless before he exposed himself to the scrutiny of those higher up.

He looked closely around the room and noted with interest stacks of ledgers on the shelves. He took his time going through them, impressed at the detail of Tolgarth's operations therein, from guard rotations to his accounts at the local merchant's bank. Yet the best find of all was a daily journal, and Jared sat down to read this treasure trove of personal information. Tolgarth had been most helpful.

Daleth would be pleased, and Jared couldn't wait to advise him of his progress.

***

Chapter XII

Taran yawned and rolled out of bed, feeling better than he had for as long as he could remember. He peered out of the window, seeing a gentle glow in the sky. The sun would be rising soon, but not for a little while yet.

The last week had seen him train hard every day, and he was slowly returning to fitness. His leg felt stronger, his shoulder mobile, and as he stretched in front of the fire's glowing embers, he considered the day ahead.

He had a free morning and afternoon, with a meeting scheduled for the evening, ahead of his departure to the grasslands of the Horselords in just two days. He'd also received word that Rakan had returned late the night before, and was looking forward to seeing him. It had been too long.

He dressed in rough clothing, not the finery nor the leathers that he would wear beneath his armour, but in the clothes he wore when he tended the gardens.

He'd avoided his new hobby this last week, wanting to ensure there was no chance of running into Maya, and had instead trained from dawn to dusk. But he found himself missing the simplicity of the work and the sense of accomplishment he felt in turning the chaos of growth into a semblance of order.

He finished off the leftovers of dinner for breakfast, washing it down with water, then put the pouch of gold that was left every day behind a loose wooden panel in the wall alongside the others.

The End of Dreams

If he survived this war, he'd take to the road once again, he thought. Put this ugly city behind him, but not until he'd buried Daleth and then Tristan in the cold earth.

He walked to the shed, collecting the tools that now shone, their edges honed by his careful hand, oiled and well cared for. If the gardener ever returned, he'd be in for a pleasant surprise at the state of his equipment.

The sun edged above the horizon as he started his work, trimming the hedgerows with shears, shaping some into serpents and winged creatures. He had no idea where the creativity had come from, but his hands that had such skill with weapons found these blades no different as he wielded them.

He worked tirelessly, first on the hedgerows, then on the rose gardens, clearing up after himself. Despite the amulet, he felt saddened that almost all the blooms had now fallen with the early onslaught of wintery weather but recognised that winter was as necessary as summer.

Balance was everything, without one, you couldn't truly appreciate the other, like knowing emptiness after having experienced love.

He cursed, annoyed that his thoughts had led him to that conclusion and redoubled his efforts, sweating in the weak sunlight.

'You missed your calling it seems, for you've a gift of shaping nature to your will,' a voice said softly, and Taran froze.

Why would she have come here?

He raged inside, but with the enemy lancers known to be marauding in the local countryside, it was unsurprising that she'd spend some time here.

For a moment, he thought to walk away, but even if he felt anger, it wasn't for him to leave. This was his place, and he hadn't finished what he needed to. Yet he also realised he needed to say the things that were on his mind.

He turned, and his heart beat painfully as he looked at her.

'I find solace here,' he explained. 'I don't know why, but it helps ease the pain that I feel daily.'

'Your wounds are healing, are they not?' Maya asked softly.

Taran's hand went to his face, feeling the burned skin, and he grimaced.

'Yes, the wounds on my body are all healing well enough, although some have further to go than others.'

There was an awkward silence for a moment, and Taran started to turn back to his work.

'Why are you so angry with me?' Maya asked hesitantly.

The feelings that Taran had suppressed roared like flames fanned by the wind, and he turned back, smouldering.

'Why am I angry? What on earth could I be angry over? Perhaps the betrayal of the king I gave my allegiance to, or the betrayal of the woman to whom I gave my heart? Choose whichever one you wish, but it's in the past, and every day brings me closer to forgetting.'

'Yes, I've seen how you help yourself forget,' Maya snapped. 'It didn't take you long to fall into the arms and the bed of another woman! You claim to have given me your heart, but you were just as quick to give it, along with your body, to Yana the moment you had the chance!'

As she said this, she spun away, leaving Taran open-mouthed ready to deny the ludicrous accusation, but she was already gone.

The amulet warmed against his chest, and his anger slowly settled. She'd understand loss when he took Tristan from her.

Yes, she'd made her choice, but her choice wouldn't live to enjoy it.

He cleared up and packed his tools away, his thoughts full of blood. Returning to the cottage, he donned his fighting leathers and stalked outside.

Time to practice some more. Even if this mission wasn't a success, he'd damn well live to return and make sure Tristan met a grisly end before he did.

He stalked between the trees toward the palace to find some sparring partners. The gods help them if any looked like Tristan.

***

Rakan walked tiredly toward the palace.

He'd arrived at Freeguard late the night before and had spent a little time ensuring the wounded who'd accompanied him were well looked after. Several were unlikely to make it, but at least they were now looked after in a new hospital a short way from the city gates.

The End of Dreams

When Rakan had approached, he was surprised to find Yana was in charge and spent a while in her company. He'd wanted to know how Taran was faring and if there were any developments he should be aware of.

He wasn't exactly trusting of Yana, but he'd known her longer than most everyone else in this country. She'd been forthcoming, and thus armed with the knowledge of Taran's impending departure and likely his own again as well, he'd returned to the barrack's bed he'd claimed the first night he'd arrived to bunk down.

Now, after a night of poor sleep, he took his time returning to the nest of vipers at the palace. Yet however slow his footsteps and however busy the streets, it eventually hove into sight.

He approached the western palace gates, and the guards saluted.

As he entered, he was surprised to receive a warm, genuine smile from Tolgarth, who passed the opposite way.

Rakan wondered for a moment what on earth could be going on as he looked over his shoulder at the departing figure.

Of all the emotions he'd have expected to see on Tolgarth's face after the beating he'd served him those weeks ago, this was, without doubt, the last one.

If Tolgarth could change from being a pompous ass, then there was definitely hope for the rest of the people in this place.

He walked into the palace, greeting familiar faces as he headed toward the kitchens, his stomach grumbling in empty protest. As he entered, he heard the unexpected sound of combat.

None of the serving staff seemed concerned, so nor was he, but he was intrigued to hear such sounds when he'd expected to only hear the banging of pots and pans. So, following the noise, he descended the steps leading down into the cellars.

Torches illuminated the scene, and their flickering made the combat in front of him look almost otherworldly as Maya fought against Ferris and four other soldiers.

They were engrossed, and because it would have been dangerous to interrupt them, Rakan sat on the bottom step, watching with a critical eye as the duel continued. He nodded in appreciation, for Maya's skill had improved dramatically, and her awareness of the multiple opponents and positioning reflected hours of good practice.

Physically, she looked stronger, fitter, and her white hair was bound back from her face. In the flickering light, her features at times looked young, then old, but she moved as one still in her prime. Yet there was something else. As Rakan looked closer, he realised that where once there'd been nothing but light and wonder in her eyes, they now showed a fierceness that did little to hide the sorrow behind them.

Rakan raised his hand during a natural pause in the combat, and Maya caught the movement. She'd squared off against Ferris but stepped back, and a smile swept across her face.

Rakan stood as Maya cast her practice weapons to the floor, ran toward him, and then slowed, almost unsure that such warmth was the right reaction. Decision made, she threw her arms around his neck and gave him a sweaty hug.

'Rakan, it's good to see you,' she sighed, casting a look over him, noting his healed burns and that there were no new injuries.

She glanced over her shoulder.

'Thank you, everyone. Let's break for today, I need to catch up with my old friend here.'

She took Rakan's arm and led him up the stairs to the kitchens.

'I'm famished, are you?' Maya asked, as the staff hurried to make room for them at the end of a long wooden table.

Rakan nodded in agreement.

They remained silent for a while as people hurried around them, laying out platters of bread, honey, meat, and cheeses.

Rakan noted the love that shone from the eyes of all of those who served Maya. She smiled at them all, nodding thanks, gently touching arms or hands to reinforce the genuine appreciation she felt at their care, and they loved her for it. She might have lost her gift of healing, he thought, but she'd always have her gift of making people feel valued and special.

They ate silently for a while, neither quite sure how to start the conversation.

Maya sighed.

'Tell me what happened after I left. I want to hear it from you. Tell me everything, leaving nothing out, so I can understand.'

Rakan finished a mouthful of meat, then nodded.

'That's a good a place to start as any.'

He spoke then of their discovery of her absence, of Taran's sadness at her leaving that had turned into depression and blinding anger when they'd heard of her betrothal. He spoke of Astren's death at Kalas' hands and how Kalas had sought redemption. He spoke of Drizt and Trom, the fortress' eventual fall and then the long journey east to find sanctuary.

Finally, he told how Taran's heart was darkened by thoughts of revenge on Daleth and Tristan, and how he sought to dampen and ignore his heartbreak by wearing one of Daleth's amulets.

Maya gasped, her hand going to her mouth in dismay.

Rakan nodded, his face grim.

'It helped him deal with everything. It was the only way. But as I would know, it left no place for the light in his soul. After you left with Tristan, I think if it hadn't been for the amulet, I fear he'd have taken his own life or thrown it away on the walls.'

Rakan reached out to hold Maya's forearm.

'Now, tell me, why did you cast him aside? You two had something the like of which no one had ever seen, and look at you now. Your gifts have deserted you both, and surely that's no coincidence. I find it hard to believe the riches of being Tristan's wife could lure you. I have my suspicions, but tell me the truth now, you owe me that, at least.'

Maya's head was spinning as she took on board everything Rakan had said. There'd been no mention of her note under Taran's pillow, no understanding of her sacrifice. So, she, in turn, told Rakan all of what he didn't know, starting with Tristan's price for saving Taran's life.

By the end of it, Rakan gripped the hilt of his sword so hard his knuckles were white, his face a mask of anger.

'The devious, greedy bastard,' he said. 'I'd thought this might be the case but didn't want to believe it, yet it all makes sense. Whereas before, I was unhappy with Taran's constant desire for revenge on Tristan, he was right all along, especially now that I understand the truth of what lies behind your departure.'

Rakan took Maya's hand, tears in his eyes.

'Forgive me, for I doubted you at times too. It broke my heart to see Taran brought so low, and my own grief at his sadness clouded my judgment. No wonder Tristan sought to keep us apart for as long as he did, to ensure this secret stayed hidden. The problem is what to do next.'

Rakan rubbed his face with both hands, as if trying to wipe away his indecision.

'I want to tell Taran immediately, but I'm concerned with the amulet's effect on his reactions. He won't be indifferent, even if it suppresses his feeling of love for you. Instead, it will ignite his anger and thirst for revenge so brightly, that he'll seek Tristan's life without thought of consequence.'

'By all accounts, we're to leave the day after tomorrow on a mission to the Horselords. If he discovers this, then blood will be shed, and whatever small chance we'll have of success will disappear as if it never was.'

'So, what good will it do to tell him at all?' Maya asked. 'It sounds better for everyone that he continues to believe what he believes to be true and carries on hating me while we still live. I might not like the position I find myself in, but I gave my oath in exchange for his life. I might hate where it has led us, but he's alive, even if unhappy. I swore never to tell him. It seems I should keep it that way.'

Rakan's held Maya's gaze with his own.

'Listen to me. I'm a man of my word, and I know your word means as much to you as mine does to me. You swore an oath to save Taran's life and to keep Tristan's price secret, but you swore it under duress. In my eyes, there are some decisions we make, some oaths we swear, that the gods would not be supportive of. Do you frown upon me for breaking my oath to Daleth, for example? To serve him till death, to deliver you unto his hands?'

Maya shook her head.

'Then where is the difference? I broke my oath for my growing love of Taran. If you're to break yours for the same reason, then, just like with me, whether we can escape the consequences is all that matters. It should be you and Taran forever, Tristan be damned. We needed him back then, just as he needs us now. We win this war somehow, then we part ways, and it'll be down to him whether it's with friendship or enmity, whether we walk away in peace or over the bodies of those who try to stop us.'

The End of Dreams

Maya quietly considered Rakan's words and her choice of action. Mind made up, she nodded decisively.

'I'll talk to Taran. All that has happened, he needs to hear from me. I'll find a way to have him listen, but first, I'll ensure he removes the amulet so he can think clearly.'

Rakan drummed his fingers on the wooden table.

'Yes, that's going to be the most important but hardest part. I wanted to kill Taran when he took my amulet from me until my thoughts cleared. You must be careful.'

Rakan stood decisively.

'I'll go see Taran now. It has been too long since I embraced my son, and we've much to discuss. We also need to prepare for our journey.'

With a final squeeze of Maya's hand, he walked away.

Maya sat deep in thought for a while. Her heart ached with relief to know that her fears of Taran being with Yana were baseless. She'd make Taran see the truth and calm his thirst for blood when it arose. Then, they could plan a way out of his mess, as had been her desire all along. She took a final gulp of wine before rising to return to her room.

Ferris waited a while himself, finishing his food.

Neither Maya nor Rakan had noticed him quietly sit down close behind, mid-conversation, such had been the intensity. He now had news to deliver but had to ensure Tristan's anger didn't cause the messenger to befall a terrible fate.

Yes, this had to be handled carefully, but the rewards would be well worth it.

***

Jared sat across from Galain and raised his goblet.

'May the wine never run dry,' Jared toasted.

Galain laughed, repeating the toast.

'Nor the gold,' he added, as was tradition.

Jared savoured the fruity taste, enjoying the rush it brought. In this guise of Tolgarth, he had access to the palace, but not directly to the king. Whilst he was responsible for the palace guard's rotation, it soon became apparent that he needed another way to get closer.

'I know why you're plying me with wine,' Galain confided, a crafty look on his face.

For a moment Jared felt a twinge of unease in his stomach but allowed Galain to continue uninterrupted.

'You want to know if your name is still tainted because of your association with the late Lord Duggan,' Galain whispered in a quiet voice. 'Well, let me tell you, at first that might have been true. However, the fact you're so judiciously training the commoners to join the ranks at your own expense without complaint or manipulation has helped Tristan see your genuine contrition.'

Jared breathed a slight sigh of what Galain thought was relief but was, in fact, understanding as he pieced together Tolgarth's recent past. Every day he polished his guise, while at the same time got closer to and studied his next victim.

'You should know, Tolgarth,' Galain continued, 'that it'll take more than just a few drinks over a few nights for me to say the right words in the right ears. But, as I can tell you're an ambitious man, I'm sure you'll do what's required for this to work in both our interests.'

Jared grinned.

'I appreciate the offer. Be assured that your friendship carries no price I'm unwilling to pay.'

He poured another goblet of wine for the beaming Galain.

'I bet you're glad to see the back of Rakan,' Galain laughed softly, keeping his voice low. 'I know it must be a sore point, but with any luck, that one will meet a sticky end on his mission.'

'What do you mean?' Jared asked carefully.

Galain leant in close, grasping Jared's forearm.

'It's been spoken that Rakan beat you soundly when he arrived. There's no shame in that. He was one of Daleth's finest by all accounts.'

Jared almost choked, firstly at Galain's *finest* comment, but also at how easy it was to trip up however close he got to know someone before shifting.

He'd greeted Rakan politely with a smile from a distance and had wondered why he'd seemed so surprised, yet now that made sense too. Good thing they hadn't spoken. Tolgarth's journal had omitted that event for obvious reasons.

Jared recovered his thoughts, posing his next words carefully.

'I appreciate your sensitivity. But I do carry shame for what happened, although knowing he was one of Daleth's finest lets me carry it a little easier. Now, however, you've intrigued me. What mission do you speak of that might see this uncouth turncoat meet his deserved end?'

Galain looked theatrically around the room in the back of the wine house in which they sat, then smiled conspiratorially.

'He and the other upstart, our dear Lord Commander Taran ...' he snorted with disdain, '... left tonight on a mission to the Horselords to try and recruit them to our cause.'

'Unbelievable, that two such uncouth fools should be given such a mission,' Jared murmured.

'I shouldn't wish their death so soon,' Galain continued, 'for without the Horselords, it's said we have little hope of defeating Daleth. So, let's drink to them succeeding on their mission but meeting a grisly end upon their return!'

Galain raised his goblet.

Jared returned the toast, laughing, still assimilating this interesting news.

Not only was Galain to be his next victim, but he was already proving to be a source of incredible information. Jared knew of his brother Gregor's mission to defeat the Horselords and was in awe of Daleth's foresight in having ordered this before an alliance could be formally sought. Rakan and Taran's mission was doomed before it had even started.

More importantly, with this knowledge, the two fugitives would be too, for he'd forewarn his brother and Daleth. Between Gregor and the other Rangers that Daleth would unleash on the hunt, these deserters would finally be run to ground. The justice that would be brought upon them would be righteous in the extreme.

Jared kept Galain drinking long into the night, carefully concealing that he only pretended to fill his own goblet. Jared marvelled at Galain's knowledge of strategy, his ability to remember the numbers of troops and the amount of food required to feed them through the winter. Galain talked and talked, happy to share anything and everything whilst the wine kept flowing.

However, the alcohol began to take effect, and Galain yawned, looking at the hourglass the owner had just turned in the corner of the room.

'Time for me to return,' he said, staggering to his feet, thrusting out his hand to pump Jared's. 'Why not give me a report tomorrow on how the peasants are doing with their training, and I'll make sure I pass on the news to Tristan. Shall we meet here for dinner?'

Jared smiled.

'Of course, but only if you let me pay, for the favour you do me deserves such gratitude!'

They said their goodnights as Galain stumbled from the room.

Jared smiled at the proprietor as he looked over.

'Give me a short while to rest my eyes, my good man, and then I'll be taking my leave.'

He leaned his head back.

'My king,' he whispered silently. He waited patiently but a few short moments.

'Tell me, my favourite son,' Daleth's deep voice resonated in Jared's mind. 'Tell me everything.'

***

Dusk had fallen by the time they rode from the city, and Rakan glanced over his shoulder.

Taran looked at him inquiringly, but Rakan just shook his head, keeping his thoughts to himself. There'd been no sign of Maya since their earlier meeting, and Rakan was worried. She must have had second thoughts and decided to wait for their return before approaching and talking with Taran.

They were both dressed in dark clothing, dark leather armour, their faces blackened with soot, and on black horses. The plan was to only travel at night, for with the lancers abroad in the countryside surrounding Freeguard, they'd be easy prey if spotted.

Stealth and darkness would be their ally, and there was enough time to take their time.

There was a spare horse each, burdened with supplies and gold, although Rakan didn't feel the gold would do much good. What was more valuable was the letter signed by Tristan with the royal seal stamped upon it, giving Taran full rights to negotiate an agreement on the crown's behalf. Whatever it took to get the Horselords to assist without giving away any of the Freestates was the mandate.

The Horselords were notorious for killing strangers on sight within their sacred grasslands, and that is where they needed to go.

They'd both been given a culture lesson about their targets and knew that the clans would be heading south to the warmer climes at this time of year. There was a sacred site where the clans would congregate for the winter and meet in peace before once again going their separate ways come spring.

It was the ideal time to approach them, otherwise, they'd be spread out so much that recruiting any meaningful number would have proved impossible. During this congregation, the senior knight commander maintained order and had the power to make decisions on behalf of all the clans.

Rakan hoped the gold and the seal would prove who they were and the sincerity of their mission, but the real challenge would be to remain alive long enough to present it. The idea of taking more men had been discussed, but ultimately two had more chance of evading notice and capture.

Rakan had reunited with Taran only the day before, and whilst he'd wanted to tell him of his discussion with Maya, he'd kept it to himself, expecting Maya to appear. Instead, he'd simply enjoyed the time they had, quietly surprised at Taran's newly acquired skills as they walked the beautiful gardens, shared food and told tales of the last weeks since they'd seen the other.

They both knew there'd be little time for talking when they started on their mission, for they'd need to be alert at all times. So they rode in silence, heading directly south. This would lead them to the southern peaks, and from there they'd turn west, following the mountain range until they came close to the city of Freemarch.

It was assumed this would now be under Daleth's control, for nothing had been heard from the city, but if not, they could resupply before crossing the border.

From Freeguard to Freemarch, travelling slowly and carefully at night would take maybe three weeks, then another three heading southward. So, approximately one and a half months to reach the Horselords and the same to return. Assuming negotiations went swiftly, they'd hopefully have a month in hand before spring arrived and hostilities resumed in earnest.

Thirty thousand heavy cavalry could possibly make the difference in the final battle even if the alliance forces remained outnumbered, for if their charge wasn't checked by heavy spearmen, they could run down light or medium infantry with ease.

The key was to keep this new alliance secret from Daleth and the Horselords' presence hidden from the battlefield until a pivotal moment. But to do this would require a huge amount of luck, for there were so many lancers scouting abroad. Their hopes rested on a harsh winter that would drive the lancers back to the safety and comfort of Freemantle, allowing the Horselords to move north unseen.

Rakan shook his head. There were so many things that could go wrong.

He coaxed his horse to a trot, and Taran followed.

Caution was important, but so was speed. They were more likely to be spotted the closer to Freeguard they were, so the sooner they put distance between them and the city, the better.

Rakan couldn't help but feel vulnerable as they left the city walls behind them, and it was not a feeling he was used to. Then he chuckled softly, after all, what was there to worry about? It was just two men against the wilderness, the oncoming winter, and thousands of enemy troops between them and a potential ally. Not forgetting this ally would initially be hostile and would probably kill them if they got that far. Why on earth should he feel vulnerable?

'You seem in good spirits,' Taran remarked.

Rakan explained his humour and was pleased to hear Taran laugh softly in return.

'Father, it's them that should be fearful of us. But if we go to our deaths, I'll die content, for you're the only person I'd want beside me to face what lies beyond this world.'

Taran leaned over, extending his hand.

Rakan grasped his forearm. He was touched by Taran's words, his use of the word father, but also saddened. Once Taran would have wanted Maya beside him too, but maybe that day would come again if they lived long enough.

'Come,' Taran said, 'the moon's bright. Let's hurry whilst it lights our way.' He urged his horse into a canter.

It was risky, but so was travelling too slowly.

Rakan followed suit, and soon the walls and the torches upon them faded from sight.

***

Daleth sat drinking another bottle of Tristan's wine. He'd soon have to stop enjoying the plentiful luxuries the palace offered, or he'd end up resembling the fat gods of greed. Every ceiling in the palace was adorned with depictions, showing their bulbous forms raining coin down upon their worshippers below.

His forces based within Freemantle were busy, scavenging supplies, harvesting timber, training and then training even more. His lancers were out ravaging the countryside and were keeping a close eye on Freeguard, ensuring the surrounding farms and countryside were pillaged and burned, putting the city's food sources under pressure.

He helped himself to another goblet and smiled. This was definitely a celebratory drink. He'd heard from Jared, and his faith in the Ranger had been rewarded beyond all expectations. Not only had Jared confirmed that Kalas was indeed dead, but the exact numbers of the alliance forces. He was also getting closer to Tristan, and this had provided a real gem that put a smile on Daleth's face. The two elusive fugitives, Rakan and Taran, were heading south to seek an alliance with the Horselords.

He laughed, for they obviously had no idea that Gregor would soon be putting their hopes to the sword before they even arrived. Now, of course, their arrival was unlikely to happen at all.

Upon receiving this news, he'd given his Rangers a challenge ... a competition to hunt down and finally exact justice on those two deserters. The Rangers to a man had been ecstatic and would vie for the honour delivering death to the targets would bestow upon them.

Daleth would have liked to see the life slowly fade from Rakan and Taran's eyes after weeks of torture, but he wouldn't allow his petty desires to overrule common sense. To capture them alive would cost more of his Rangers' lives. They were irreplaceable, so why even risk it.

He just wished he could let Taran and Rakan know of the fate that awaited them, to observe them fleeing in a panic once they knew of the unstoppable forces unleashed upon them. They'd be so terrified that they'd likely miss the subtle honour that was hidden in the kill order.

Daleth stood, unaided by sticks or support, and breathed in deeply, feeling his weakness fading as his strength returned. He'd be fully healed before winter's end and would start training long before then. He'd walk amongst his men, build morale, pride, and their hunger for blood and death. When they were finally unleashed in the spring, they'd be fearless and unstoppable.

Daleth returned his attention to the ceiling, studying the gods that for so long had showered immeasurable wealth upon the Freestates.

What would the gods who'd bestowed his gifts look like?

Maybe if he pleased them enough, they'd show themselves one day or perhaps invite him to sit by their side.

For a moment, thoughts of Alano slipped into his mind.

If only he'd had longer to find out about the gods before Alano's passing. Still, once this campaign was over, he'd have centuries to find out whilst he continued his conquests, and one day, he'd discover the way to become one.

He reached for the wine jug, but this time he walked over to the fire, pouring it slowly over the hot coals that hissed and let forth a fragrant steam that filled his nostrils.

Time to become strong again, time to become a god.

The God of War.

***

Chapter XIII

Maya's gift had deserted her so completely of late that she was shocked and exultant to find herself looking down upon her sleeping body as she sat on the side of the bed.

Her spirit felt heavy as she stood, so there was no point in trying to fly. Instead, she thought to go look upon Taran if her spirit state lasted long enough.

She left her room, passed a guard outside, and walked slowly down the corridor. Each step took so much effort that she almost gave up, but her willpower prevailed and kept her moving.

She encountered several people, entirely oblivious to her spirit presence, mainly servants with food brought from the kitchens. Occasional guards followed their allotted routes, boredom etched on their faces, and she continued by.

As she approached the main palace entrance, wondering if she had the strength to walk through them, Ultric ghosted through the doors like mist in the opposite direction.

His face lit up, and Maya was amazed to see that in his spirit form, his eyes were wide open and alert, as sure sighted as she was.

'Well met, Ultric.' Maya beamed. 'Where have you been this evening?'

For a moment, Ultric looked a little abashed.

'Normally I'd respond that I simply ventured outside to enjoy the crisp night and to view the stars, but with you, I'll tell the truth. I act as my king's eyes and ears, and my duty is to keep him informed of all that happens in this city so that he's never caught unawares. Being denied my sight has given me the most amazing ability to hear the tiniest whisper. Thus I listen for the softest spoken word, the one that is meant to be only for the ears of one other, and then I investigate.'

Maya was thoughtful for a moment.

'I guess lovers should be wary when a voyeur like you is abroad.' She laughed, hoping her joke was appreciated.

Ultric chuckled.

'You're right! Now, where do your travels take you this night? Be assured, the fact you've managed to use your gift when of late it's been denied you will remain firmly between us.'

This time it was Maya's turn to pause, but Ultric had shared, and she felt he could be trusted. They might not yet be friends, but he could easily follow her and discern the truth himself, and thus lying would only likely make a rift between them. So she spoke truthfully.

'Whilst my gift allowed,' she replied, 'I sought to look upon Taran, for on the morrow we need to talk. We've only spoken angry words to the other and were close once, and he's soon to leave on a mission.'

Ultric looked confused as she spoke and raised his hand, forestalling any more explanation.

'I will choose my words carefully, for I wish no offence. First, I can tell from your voice that you're not telling me everything, and in many ways, I blame you not. But let me point out the obvious. It's common knowledge that Taran used to be your lover before you decided to marry Tristan. If the stories and songs that I hear daily are anything to go by, he was your true love and seeks to reclaim you whosoever opposes him.'

When Maya said nothing, Ultric smiled and continued.

'What I don't know is how much of that song is true, but I can see there's no love lost between him and Tristan. In fact, Taran's heart beats with barely restrained rage whenever he addresses him. I would discern he's always but a mere heartbeat from violence when in the king's presence.'

'It isn't quite as simple as that!' Maya interrupted.

Ultric nodded.

'I haven't finished yet. I don't blame you for not sharing everything, and I know already far more than you wish to share. Instead, what concerns me is your intention of talking to Taran on the morrow.'

Maya's brow furrowed, and she looked fierce.

'Don't seek to stop me,' she said, voice lowering, her opinion of Ultric starting to change.

'No, no!' Ultric assured, raising his hands. 'That's not what I'm implying. But unless you can find him and project yourself, which I believe is beyond your talents, you'll be unable to do so, for he left two nights ago with Rakan.'

Maya shook her head, somewhat bemused.

'What are you talking about? I only spoke to Rakan earlier today.'

Ultric's slowly shaking head and face convinced her he was somehow telling the truth.

'I wondered where you'd been these last two days,' he said, 'but I was told you weren't well when I enquired. Now I wonder if there isn't something more sinister afoot.'

Ultric took Maya's hand.

'Come!' he said, 'we should go to your room.'

He pulled Maya slowly after him, aware of how tired her spirit form looked.

It took a while to return as Maya's feet felt like stone. As they entered, she could see her body asleep upon the bed, motionless other than for her chest rising and falling.

Ultric looked closely at Maya's sleeping form, then started looking around the room. As he did so, the door to the room opened.

Maya and Ultric both jumped, even if they couldn't be seen.

To Maya's surprise, Yana was ushered into the room by Ferris and on her hip was a healer's satchel. As they watched, open-mouthed, Yana came and sat beside Maya and pulled some sleep weed from her satchel, which she carefully crumbled into a goblet of water that sat on a bedside table.

As she let the sleep weed disintegrate, she idly stroked Maya's white hair back from her face.

Maya flinched even if she couldn't feel the touch.

'I'm only supposed to keep you asleep,' Yana said softly, her face showing regret.

Ferris chuckled.

'Make sure you do that, because if she wakes up too soon, both you and I are in trouble.'

Yana stared at Ferris.

'I think you'll be safe. You've earned Tristan's favour, not just his coin. Informing him of her intention to tell Taran everything of their bargain was masterful. Who knows what Taran's reaction would have been?'

'I can't believe it,' Maya gasped, her hand flying to her mouth in shock. 'Ferris betrayed me. He must have overheard my conversation with Rakan.'

Ultric turned to Maya.

'Now we know why you've been absent these days. Yana's obviously doing this by order of the king and possibly against her will, although she doesn't seem too shocked by developments.'

Yana was singing softly to herself as she stroked Maya's hair. As the last words of the song left her lips, the conflicted look left her face. She picked up the goblet and gently lifted Maya's head, carefully trickling the liquid into Maya's mouth drop by drop.

'What can we do?' Maya cried, collapsing to her knees. 'How long will they keep me here like this?'

Ultric knelt beside her.

'I don't care whether Tristan is king, and you his betrothed. This is wrong,' he growled. He paused briefly, thinking, then continued. 'Yana has no choice and will continue doing his bidding for as long as she's ordered. If they feed you broth, you could remain like this for weeks. While the liquid remains in your stomach, you'll continue to sleep, so we need to get rid of it. I can help awaken you briefly, but you'll have mere moments to make yourself sick before the infusion overcomes you again.'

They waited until Yana and Ferris left.

'Sit on the bed,' Ultric ordered.

Maya sat next to her sleeping self.

Ultric reached out a hand.

'Are you ready?'

Maya nodded in response.

'Awaken,' Ultric commanded, tapping Maya firmly on the brow with his fingertips.

Maya felt her spirit self merge with her physical one, and her eyes opened. The room span, disorientating her, and she fought the urge to close them, fighting to stay conscious. With her strength fading rapidly, she rolled onto her stomach and twisted her body, so her head hung over the edge of the bed.

The nausea was overwhelming, so that when she pushed her fingers into her throat, she vomited immediately, her stomach cramping again and again.

Ultric watched as Maya's eyes closed, her body going limp as she fell asleep once more. Looking at the amount of fluid on the floor, he hoped she'd done enough. There was nothing more he could do without putting himself at risk.

There was so much to tell Ostrom in the morning, but the night was still young. Maybe he should spend more time looking at those closest to the palace, for it seemed nothing was quite what it seemed.

He hoped Maya would be alright. But what would she do? In their haste to try and awaken her, he hadn't discussed any kind of plan. He'd like to be there on the morrow if she stormed into the audience chamber. That would be a sight worth seeing, or in his case, he'd just have to listen.

Perhaps an early night was indeed in order, for he wouldn't want to miss this, and neither would Ostrom. Tomorrow would be an interesting day indeed. So with that in mind, he returned to his body, merged with his physical self, and finally fell into a resting sleep.

***

Gregor, with his army, had journeyed forth from Freemarch after putting many of its inhabitants to the sword. He left behind a substantial garrison of a thousand soldiers to ensure compliance from those civilians remaining who now faced the grisly task of burying their dead.

They'd travelled for a week into the grasslands and at last battle was soon to be joined.

He was aware that the clans moved south in winter to meet at the Shrine of the Moon Goddess, or some such weak deity. Yet this clan seemed to have been slow in following their brothers south. Whatever the reason, now they were faced with foreign feet upon their soil, they were honour bound to defend it.

He stood tall in his stirrups to get a better view from his position behind the spearmen's main line. The sun shone momentarily between the clouds, long rays of light shining down as if the gods themselves had parted them like a curtain to witness this battle. He shook his head in recognition of both his opponents' bravery and the abject stupidity for what they were about to do.

He had over thirty thousand men, and the opposing clan numbered less than a thousand, many of them women and youths. Even as he watched, they were forming a wedge, preparing to attack his position head-on.

The Horselords could have run. He wouldn't have risked his lancers in tackling the heavier foe, but honour forbade them from doing so. Now they were only moments from death.

The Horselords' combat was stylised, full of tradition. Amongst each other, they jousted for honour and prime pasture. Their enormous horses, covered in mail, blew clouds of steam from their nostrils. The knights astride them carried heavy lances, large shields, and long swords.

The early morning sun shone down on the Horselords, its rays shimmering and flashing from their polished plate armour. Pennants fluttered in the breeze from their helmets and lance tips, depicting their clan. Upon the air, a horn sounded from within the knights' ranks. Lances dipped in unison, saluting, before rising once more and then the horses started to walk forward, urged by their riders.

Gregor had positioned his spearmen in the centre of the line, with the archers stationed close behind. Lancers moved about the flanks, well away from the heavy horse, but ready to encircle, once the knights committed to the charge.

There would be little strategy of note employed in this battle. The knights' archaic code of honour dictated they face their enemy at the strongest point, and thus they lined up against the massed ranks of spearmen.

The horn sounded again, and the knights' chargers broke into a trot. Even from this distance, Gregor could see the billowing clouds of steam rising from the nostrils of the enemy steeds as they picked up the pace. The front rank of his spearmen knelt, lowering their long weapons to rest in the forked stakes they'd pummelled into the ground in front of them. The following ranks also lowered their weapons, creating a bristling, impenetrable hedge of wickedly pointed spear tips attached to their ironwood shafts.

The horn sounded once more, and the heavy horses broke into a canter. Gregor found himself holding his breath, as even from this distance, he could feel the hard, cold earth tremble under the impact of their hooves.

He watched as his archers drew back their bowstrings. He didn't need to issue any more orders, for his captains had been briefed a hundred times on how to react, and he watched in satisfaction as the archers held their fire.

The horn blew a final, long, mournful note, and the very ground shook as the heavy horses broke into a charge. It wouldn't be sustained for long, the horses, their riders and equipment were simply too heavy, so they timed the charge for when they were no more than two hundred strides distant.

As the densely packed wedge surged toward his spearmen, the archers loosed. The arrows arced low over the heads of the spearmen, and horses went down. The chargers were protected with mail, so compared to the thousands of arrows that rained from the sky, it wasn't many. But that few were enough. For every horse brought down, others behind were fouled, often tripped by their falling brethren.

By the time the charge reached his spear line, it was no longer a solid mass of destruction. Nonetheless, the sound as it hit was like a thunderclap, deafening even from a distance, and then the screams of horses sounded high in the air. He watched, mesmerised, as the first two rows of his spearmen went down under the weight of the charge before the lines behind held and the massacre began.

He knew casualties from the first two rows of spearmen would be minimal as they'd fallen in unison under their heavy shields a bare heartbeat before the charge struck. It was a well-drilled skill that would keep many unharmed until they were helped from under the piles of bodies after the battle was won.

The sound of screams continued to rise, some high pitched from the women and youths. They'd been in the later ranks of the charge, and followed the men onto unforgiving spears that didn't discriminate but drew blood and life with equanimity.

He felt strangely disappointed.

If all the clans died in such a fashion, where would be the challenge?

Despite knowing Daleth would disapprove of his actions, he decided to slow his advance in the grasslands a little, allowing the clans to group before he fell upon them. To face them all at once would surely be wondrous. The sound of that battle would have the gods watching from the heavens and the daemons from the hells too.

He smiled. He'd report to Daleth tonight and couldn't wait to receive his praise. The first battle was already mostly over, and he doubted he'd lost more than a few dozen or so men.

'Let's make sure there are no survivors,' he told the captain of lancers who hovered nearby before urging his mount forward, drawing his sword.

He'd sleep soundly tonight, and dream of the glorious battle ahead.

***

Maya awoke to darkness, the taste of vomit strong in her mouth and the stench of it in her nostrils. Yet that was nothing compared to the headache and nausea that threatened to overwhelm her.

Light from the moon outside lit the room with a silvery hue as she struggled to sit. Every movement sent spears of pain behind her eyes, but the positive side to this was there was no chance of falling back to sleep. She reached for the goblet of water on the bedside table, only to realise just in time that it was infused with sleep weed.

Desperate to drink due to her parched throat and the horrible taste in her mouth, she looked around her room. As usual, there was a vase of nearly dead flowers on a table. She couldn't understand why they were never fresh, but now wasn't the time to ponder.

Quietly, she moved to the vase, pulling out the blooms, and was grateful to recognise them as the desert rose that Ultric had identified. She gulped water from the vase, thankful it relieved some of the nausea and didn't taste as foul as she first feared.

She sat for a while, pondering what to do. She could wait, gather her senses, then raise all kinds of hell, and her fury was such that Daleth would hear her voice all the way over in Freemantle. Then another thought came to mind.

Taran.

Tristan might have bound her with the oath she'd sworn, the contract she'd signed, and the threat of death if she broke it, but now it was time to find a way to rewrite those terms. Taran wasn't in a position to help her, so she needed to be strong enough to save herself and Taran in the process.

Confronting Tristan now in the seat of his power would achieve little, and there was nothing to stop him from having her drugged again or, failing that, imprisoning her should he choose fit.

If that happened, she'd spend the winter under guard, or worse.

The path she had to take finally became clear. The happiest time of her life had been when she'd run, evading death with Taran and Rakan. The choice between captivity and running from both Tristan and Daleth was now a simple decision to make.

Taran and Rakan might have several nights' head start, but she'd been hunting all her life and could find a trail even if it were days old, especially from someone as bearish as Rakan.

Mind made up, she moved quietly with a purpose, knowing a guard was likely outside, although what with the hour and the fact she was drugged, it was possible he might be asleep.

She still wore the night-gown from the night she'd seen Rakan, and wondered when she'd been drugged, but it didn't matter now. Likely it had been the fruit water she drank before bedtime, for that would have masked any taste.

Opening the wardrobes, she breathed a sigh of relief.

They were full of finery, but she'd ordered winter hunter's clothing to be fashioned, and they'd been completed and now hung at the end along with her old leathers. More importantly, her weapons, backpack, and gathering pouches were within. Carefully pulling out the items she needed so as not to make any noise, she laid everything out on the bed, then changed quickly.

There was no way she could just walk out the door as any guards would obviously raise the alarm, and she wasn't willing to kill anyone whilst making her escape. So, to avoid detection, she moved to the window and, praying to the gods that it wouldn't make any noise, carefully opened it, looking down to the ground, two stories below.

She paused, willing the horrible rolling feeling in her head to stop. She was dizzy and weak, and it was a long way down, but she had no other choice. She wrapped her weapons belt, sword and dagger, as well as her bow, quiver of arrows and backpack in a bedsheet, and looking around to ensure no one was about, tossed them to the ground below.

They landed with a muffled thump that seemed as loud as her heartbeat, but when no one came to investigate, she lowered herself over the edge of the sill, her feet finding purchase between the great blocks of stone that formed the palace walls.

Her fingers and arms trembled as she lowered herself down to the balcony on the floor below, and sweat trickled down her brow. From here, it was easier, for a decorative trellis supporting vines stood against the wall, and she made quick progress to the ground. She gathered her weapons before balling up the sheet and covering it in loose soil.

Her head swam, and she stumbled. She needed to not only eat and drink to regain her strength, but to gather supplies that would enable her to travel as quickly as possible, without the need to stop and hunt.

She crouched low and hurried through the gardens under the light of the moon. It was eerily beautiful as she moved like a ghost through the night, passing from shadow to shadow until she eventually came to the cottage Taran had occupied.

She quietly approached the door.

Would she open it to find Yana keeping Taran's bed warm for his return? She berated herself, for she knew her worries were unfounded, but the thought nonetheless brought knots to her stomach. She slowly lifted the latch to find the cottage door unbolted, and cautiously ventured inside.

The open shutters let in a faint light, and Maya paused, allowing her eyes to become accustomed to the gloom before she finally made out the cottage was empty, the bed vacant.

She removed her backpack and searched through the cupboards, finding dried and stale bread as well as cured meats. Thankfully, no one had come to clean the cottage, and she tucked in, suddenly realising how ravenous she was. It felt somewhat comforting to be in Taran's cottage, and it even smelled faintly of him, and she smiled while draining a large flask of water.

She felt stronger, in mind, body, and resolve. She had a difficult task ahead of her, and time was crucial, for she had to be gone from the city before her absence was discovered. The gates at night were now always closed, so she had to find a way to escape, then put sufficient distance between herself and the search parties who might pursue her anticipating her direction.

Her white hair shone as she stepped into the moonlight and she took time to strap her sword and bow to the backpack. She put the quiver inside and lightly bound the protruding arrow shafts with a dark cloth to ensure they wouldn't rattle and come loose.

She wouldn't be fighting tonight and needed to move fast.

Having finished preparing, she crouched low and headed south through the woods. On reaching the edge of the palace grounds, she climbed over the iron railings, careful to avoid the night watch.

The city streets were patrolled continuously at night, and Maya couldn't afford to be spotted. She looked up to the sky and smiled, for who would think to look up.

She ran across the cobbled street and leapt, hands reaching to the low rooftop of the nearest building. It was many-storied, but Maya made short work climbing to the highest roof. The city's design would help her now. The beautiful stone buildings on the main thoroughfare sat close together in a perfectly straight line toward the southern gate. She ran across rooftops feeling as if her gift had returned, she was so high and close to the clouds.

She almost laughed loudly in exultation. Despite her incarceration, she hadn't realised how much her spirit had been imprisoned till the moment she escaped.

***

Yana awoke with a start.

The pounding on the front door matched that of her heart as she leapt from bed and pulled on some clothes. Although it was light outside, a quick glance at the timeglass on her table confirmed it was still early morning.

'Open the door in the name of the king,' a voice shouted.

She straightened her hair quickly as the pounding continued.

What could they want? She'd been tempted to give Maya too much sleep weed so that she'd never awaken, but had known Tristan's wrath would be inescapable. So, she'd carefully administered just enough to see Maya through to noon and the next dosage.

She hurried down the stairs and hopped across the hallway, pulling on her boots as she did so, not wanting to be dragged from her apartment barefoot if that were to happen. As she reached the door, she drew in a breath, composing herself.

She slid open the viewport in the door to see a contingent of Freestates guardsmen. There were several bolts on the door, and once they were slid back, she fixed a disgruntled frown on her face.

'What do you want?' she demanded, swinging the door open, using the authority in her voice to gain the upper hand.

It gave the guardsmen pause.

'Well? You've woken me by demand of the king. Tell me what it is I can do to help whilst you escort me to his side!'

Pulling the door closed behind her, she strode through the middle of the eight soldiers, pushing them aside.

'We don't know,' a sergeant stammered.

'We don't know, *my Lady*!' Yana snapped, glaring at the sergeant. 'You do understand that's my title, do you not?' She turned away from the guard's horrified face.

'Where's the carriage?' she asked. 'Oh my, you come here demanding my presence with all urgency, and what, now we walk to the palace? Are all of you men daft as well as discourteous?'

'Quickly,' she ordered, and strode off toward the palace. 'Let's hope the king forgives your stupidity.'

Despite her bluster, her heart quailed.

Why was she being summoned? Maybe the king was ill, maybe Ostrom or Dafne, but in her heart, she knew it had to do with Maya. Whatever the reason, it wouldn't be good.

It took far too long to walk to the palace, for she'd been staying at her apartment by the hospital after a long day's work, and she knew

The End of Dreams

keeping Tristan waiting would only serve to anger him. As she finally approached, the guards stood aside, first at the iron gates to the grounds, and then the main palace doors themselves.

Even before she got close, she could hear Tristan shouting in anger through the audience chamber doors, and her heart sank. The doors swung open, and she was ushered in. They closed with a final-sounding thump behind her. Inside, there was Tristan, Galain, Ferris, and several guards.

Tristan's face was mottled red as he turned to her and Yana knelt, such was the fury in his eyes and her wish to placate him.

'All you had to do was give her the right amount, and it would be safe, you promised. You lied, and now she's gone,' Tristan screamed, his voice breaking. 'She's gone!'

Yana couldn't believe her ears. Maya was dead! She thought for a moment and wondered how long it would be before she felt the bite of a guardsman's blade.

Before any more was said, the doors to the chamber opened, allowing Ostrom, Ultric, and Dafne to enter.

'This isn't a good time,' Tristan shouted, but to his disbelief, they continued to their seats and sat.

'Whatever causes you such distress is cause to alarm us all,' Dafne stated. 'Let's share in the problem so that together as the allies we are, we can solve it together.'

Ultric leaned in, whispering softly to Ostrom.

Tristan, already at the end of his temper, couldn't help himself.

'If we're here and all about sharing, why is your blind helper whispering in your ear? Perhaps you'd like to share what he just said?'

Ostrom sat stony-faced for a moment, angry at Tristan's tone, but then pulled a smile.

'Of course, my fellow king, there are no secrets here.'

Ostrom placed a hand on Ultric's shoulder.

'Be a good fellow. Please tell everyone what you just told me.'

Ultric stood, bowing slightly to Ostrom before turning his white gaze toward Tristan.

'King Tristan. I simply shared with my king that the only time I ever saw him as angry as you, was when he'd argued with his late wife. I suggested that maybe your troubles were of a similar vein. May I take it from the absence of Lady Maya these last few days that my guess is correct?'

Silence fell upon the room as Tristan's mouth opened and closed like a fish out of water.

'It seems Ultric is on the mark, to have left you so speechless,' Dafne said. 'Perhaps, as a woman, I can help by talking to the Lady Maya and try to reconcile the both of you?'

Tristan shook his head, eyes wide.

'She's gone,' he whispered.

Yana fell to her knees, hands clasped together.

'I'm sorry. I didn't mean to kill her,' she sobbed hysterically. 'As you commanded, I just gave her enough to keep her unconscious. Ferris was there. He can testify to that.'

'The Lady Maya's dead?' Ostrom shouted, rising to his feet. 'What did you give her, girl?' But he already knew the answer, for Ultric had told him everything that morning.

'No, no!' Tristan cried. 'She isn't dead. She gone, disappeared. She's escaped!'

'Oh, thank the gods,' Yana cried. 'Thank the gods.'

'What do you mean, escaped?' Dafne demanded. 'She's your betrothed, and you say escaped. Now the Lady Yana here is talking about killing her. What on earth is going on? Was the Lady Maya your captive against her will?'

'I've heard stories and songs,' Ostrom rumbled. 'They talk of you forcing the Lady Maya to accept your betrothal to save the love of her life. Tell me this sordid tale isn't true!'

Tristan couldn't believe how this conversation had turned, from him being in righteous anger at a prized possession escaping, to having to defend himself for his actions.

'I don't have to answer to you, to any of you!' he spluttered, waving his hands around. 'What I do with my possessions is none of your business, none whatsoever!'

He jabbed a finger at Yana and Ferris.

'Get back to your duties,' he shouted, 'We'll continue this conversation later once I've decided what to do with you both.'

Tristan's chair fell over as he stood abruptly.

'There'll be no meeting today,' he called as he strode from the chamber, Galain frantically trying to keep up.

Ostrom turned to Ultric as he watched Tristan disappear out of the palace entrance.

'An interesting morning indeed,' he laughed.

Ultric laughed with him.

Dafne looked across.

'Did you two know this was going to happen?' she asked.

Ostrom thought for a moment before smiling.

'Yes,' he admitted. 'It seems our Lady Maya was drugged unconscious as a means to keep her under control, yet she somehow managed to escape her imprisonment.'

'In which case,' Dafne smiled, 'I hope she finds herself back in the arms of our Lord Commander Taran.'

Now it was Ostrom and Ultric's turn to look shocked.

Dafne laughed, tapping her nose.

'You two are so funny,' she said. 'Your pet spy here isn't the only one with his ears to the ground, and let's be honest, she hardly kept her feelings secret when she saw how injured he was.'

Then she leant forward, looking around as if afraid to be overheard.

'Oh, and don't worry, we won't be deserting the alliance anytime soon either,' she whispered, winking at Ostrom. 'I think Ultric here is worried we might leave.'

Ostrom and Ultric's laughter followed her all the way to the palace entrance.

'Never marry someone as clever as her,' Ultric said softly to Ostrom.

'I heard that!' Dafne shouted over her shoulder, and their laughter started all over again.

***

Chapter XIV

Taran cursed softly, and Rakan's own choice comment wasn't far behind.

The first week they'd made good progress, but then into the second, one of their horses went lame. Sadly, it had to be put down, so they'd had to share the burden of its equipment upon the remaining three, slowing their progress considerably. Then the moon, which had initially shone brightly, seemed to be veiled continuously behind thick clouds, making their night-time progress painfully slow.

Now their luck was turning from bad to worse.

Taran watched as a century of lancers carefully searched a wooded copse across the other side of their shallow valley.

'I'd bet the good side of my face that they're searching for us,' Taran muttered, turning to Rakan as they knelt low amongst the thick brush.

The bright rays of the early morning sun were in direct contrast to the darkness of their mood. They were exhausted from their night's journey and now, just when they'd been about to set up camp, the whinnying of horses had alerted them to the danger nearby.

'I don't see how,' Rakan grumbled. 'How would they know we're heading this way? It could be they're after some unlucky farmer who's given them the slip, that's all.'

Taran sighed, and shaded his eyes as he kept watch on the lancers.

'You might be right, but the last evidence of farmland was a good three days ago, and I'm sure anyone fleeing would head toward the city, not away from it. Whether I'm right or wrong matters not, they'll be just as happy to catch us.'

Rakan chuckled.

The End of Dreams

'We need to put a lot of distance between them and us. Moving at night is too slow, and when everything is so quiet, we can be heard quite clearly. Who knows, we might even stumble onto their camp if they're not lighting fires. But with them searching for us, travelling during the day will also be too risky. Soon their search will find us napping and we'll die forgotten, rotting out here in the middle of nowhere.'

Taran stared hard into the distance, taking in Rakan's words, then a smile slowly crept across his features.

'You pick the strangest of times to show your human side again,' Rakan observed, pleased to see the smile. 'So tell me, other than riding over and slaughtering them, which is what your amulet is probably encouraging you to do, please tell me something else is making you smile.'

'You gave me a great idea,' Taran said. 'Where are they least likely to find us?'

'A riddle?' Rakan shrugged. 'Let me think. Drinking wine with Daleth?'

Taran laughed softly.

'Not quite, although I admit they're less likely to search there. The last place they'll look is where they've just searched. All we need to do is follow them as long as they head south. Hopefully, they'll never think to turn and look behind them, let alone search the last place they've been.'

Now it was Rakan's turn to smile.

'That's devious, and I'll be damned if it doesn't work.'

As the sun crept ever higher, the lancers finished conducting their search, and as Taran watched, they mounted, heading toward the next large piece of woodland in the distance.

'Now?' Rakan asked.

Taran wagged a finger.

'Let's wait a little longer.'

Sure enough, the lancers continued on their course and Taran turned back into the woods, followed by Rakan, and guided their weary horses from the trees before stepping into their saddles.

'Sorry,' Taran said, leaning forward to pat the horse on the neck. 'There's no sleep for any of us this day.'

He dug his heels in, and the two of them rode, keeping low, galloping across the shallow valley before dismounting and leading the horses into the thick copse.

They led their mounts through the disturbed undergrowth, taking their time until the trees started to thin on the far side. Tying the reins off on some branches, they crept to look out over the open grassland beyond. There in the distance, the lancers' horses were held by several riders, whilst the remainder searched a larger woodland area.

'From the size of that wood, I guess they'll be a while,' Rakan suggested. 'We need to use this time to get some sleep, or before long we'll make a stupid mistake if we're too tired.'

Taran grunted in acknowledgement.

'Let me guess. You'll take first watch?'

Rakan smiled, his teeth white against his sun-browned skin.

'By your order, Lord Commander.'

Rakan pulled some dried food from his pouch and started chewing.

'How can a man sleep when you're so noisy?' Taran complained, but as soon as he leaned his head back against a tree, he fell asleep.

Rakan looked at his son and smiled sadly. They'd had so little time, and it pained him to see the enormous physical and mental changes that had aged Taran beyond his years.

He was tempted to try and remove the amulet while Taran slept, but paused as he shifted his weight to do so. Whilst removing it would be beneficial in the long term, he had no idea what Taran's mental state of mind would be if he succeeded. If weakened, it could lead to their deaths even sooner. He settled himself back down again, reflecting on how he'd changed since Taran and Maya had come into his life.

It was a shame Maya had experienced a change of heart, but likely she'd weighed up the downsides of trying to remove the amulet just before the mission and arrived at the same conclusion.

The need to sleep weighed heavily on his shoulders, so to help keep him awake, he pulled out his dagger and stone and began sharpening the already razored blade. He didn't even need to look at what he was doing, and it put him in an almost meditative state, awake but resting. This was his secret on how he could keep watch and still keep going longer than most men.

The End of Dreams

It had passed noon before the lancers emerged from the trees and mounted up.

Rakan gently kicked Taran's foot, and his son's eyes snapped open, sharpening as the blood rush kicked in.

Taran's gaze immediately locked on to the lancers in the distance through the undergrowth.

'Let's see if we can employ the same tactic again,' Taran said, then laughed in relief when the lancers skirted the woodland before heading southwest.

'We have our own scouts,' Rakan observed. 'They're ensuring no vagabonds await to ambush in our next choice of camp.'

He stood as did Taran, moving over to talk softly to the horses, steadying them so that they made no complaint when mounted.

'Hopefully, they've trodden down the underbrush so I can enjoy a good sleep on some flattened ferns,' Rakan muttered.

'I just hope they don't hear you snoring in the distance,' Taran chuckled. 'I swear if a bear drops by looking for a mate in answer to your grunts, I'll move aside and let it bed you.'

Rakan laughed.

'Like father, like son.'

They carefully moved into the light before mounting and spurred their horses across the open ground.

***

Shinsen, of the Red Scorpion Horseclan, was a knight of the first rank, only one below that of a knight commander. A rank that had been hard-earned over the forty years of his life. Over two hundred victories in single combat lay behind him with the lance and nearly as many with the sword.

His reputation was such that, across the clans, his superiority in individual combat was undisputed. Yet despite this, the highest rank eluded him. It had to be earned by diligently following the ways of the clans' goddess, in dedicating oneself to the lore, knowledge, and prayer that Shinsen had never been interested in. Because of this failing, he had remained quite happily, at the first rank, knowing in his heart that there was only one ranked above him in this land.

Except that now, this was no longer the case, for the knight commander lay dead, and only Shinsen's fearsome reputation and rigid discipline held the two thousand knights at his back from attempting to take revenge. Of the two thousand, three hundred were youths, still to be bloodied in contest, sharing the saddle with their mothers or fathers.

As he rode, numb with shock, his mind replayed the day.

His clan, the Red Scorpions, had been half a day ahead of the following clan, the Green Serpents, who were the eminent clan in the land led by the knight commander.

The Serpents were legends, numbering nearly four thousand, and Shinsen and his people had laughed good-naturedly as they'd forced the larger clan to eat the dust kicked up by their chargers' hooves. It was the only time they'd be ahead of the Serpents in anything.

They'd been riding under the weak midday sun, following the wide trail left by the clan's herd of cattle and horses, driven this way a week earlier by some of the clan youths. While drinking from his waterskin, he'd heard above the jingle of tack, harness, and mail, the sound of distant shouting. He'd stood in his stirrups and turned around to witness something he'd never thought to see ... enemy horsemen.

He'd been shocked and confused.

The Freestates had kept the peace for time immemorial, and they'd never fielded cavalry. So where had these corruptors of their sacred land come from? It mattered not, however, for whosoever these interlopers were, they needed to be put to the sword or lance before they sullied this sacred land.

Shinsen had felt both jealousy and respect as both clans turned to follow the lighter mounts of the invaders. Jealousy that the Serpents were closer to the foe, therefore claiming the battle for themselves and respect at the discipline and skill with which the Serpents had wheeled and formed the wedge attack formation so fluidly.

They'd been travelling through a shallow, winding valley and as his Scorpions had followed the Serpents, he'd ordered his clan up the east slope, gaining higher ground so he could better witness the invaders' destruction. It was doubtful the Serpents would need help, but if they did, a downhill gallop would add tremendous weight to the Scorpions' charge.

The End of Dreams

He'd gained the crest and pulled on his reins, not believing what was plainly in front of his eyes.

There, spread across the valley below, had been an army of a size he'd not believed possible. The lighter horse formation he'd seen baiting the Serpents rode around the flanks of a long line of heavy infantry with spears twice as long as Shinsen's own lance. Behind the spearmen looked to be lighter troops, although it was hard to make out their type.

Ice-cold fingers had grasped his stomach as he'd realised this army was almost as large as the combined might of every clan. There before the enemy ranks, in the middle of the valley, the Serpents had stopped, pennants flapping in the wind, armour shining. The Serpents' overall cohesive strength, which Shinsen had always felt in awe of, seemed puny compared to this lumbering beast of a horde.

His second, a knight called Harshen, had come up next to him asking to form the clan into an attacking wedge, and Shinsen had listened in disbelief.

'We don't want the Serpents to take all the glory,' Harshen had stressed, sure in his mind that the defeat of the enemy was inevitable.

Shinsen had been dumbstruck. This was what was wrong with the clans and the *true believers* ... unshakeable, blind trust in the Moon Goddess which assured victory on the battlefield.

The sole reason he'd never achieved the highest rank was he couldn't bring himself to blindly follow faith. As he'd looked at the black stain of men slowly moving across the valley floor, he'd shaken his head, turning to Harshen.

'No,' he'd replied. 'We do not engage.'

Shinsen remembered the turmoil on Harshen's face. The desire for combat, to charge, to kill these heathens and to disobey the order, but duty and years of unquestioning obedience had won over.

'Yes, sir,' he'd said with a salute. 'We let the Serpents have the day.'

Even as those words had left Harshen's mouth, the distant sound of a horn had echoed along the valley. The eyes of everyone in his clan had looked down as the Serpents did what Shinsen knew they'd do, at what the Scorpions should have been doing.

They'd attacked.

From trot to canter, from canter to full gallop, the wedge held perfect formation until suddenly a cloud appeared above the enemy ranks and arrows rained onto the charging horses. Many fell, yet the Serpents' knights were glorious, skilfully avoiding falling horses, maintaining discipline. Shinsen had held his breath as the infantry stopped, awaiting the charge, long spears lowered.

It was as if the gods had clapped their hands, the crash had been so loud, and everyone held their breaths as the immortal Serpents hit the enemy line and for a moment it looked as if they'd break through. Then suddenly it was as though a mouth closed over them, and the thick line of infantry had appeared to swallow them up.

Shinsen didn't know how long it had lasted, the clouds had barely moved across the sky, but as cries of disbelief sounded from all those around, Harshen had turned, eyes accusing.

'We should've been there,' he'd cried. 'We'd have turned the battle. We need to charge, we need to kill them all. We need to avenge our brothers.'

Shinsen had shaken his head. He'd clutched the Red Scorpion pennant, raising it in his gauntleted fist, and had swirled it high in the air, then turned his horse to lead his people southeast, away from the battle site.

The cries at seeing their brothers defeated were then almost drowned out by those of disbelief. Shinsen had closed his mind, hardened his soul, for just like them, he wanted to wreak revenge on this invading army. Unlike them, however, his mind wasn't clouded by faith, and he knew they'd die like an insect beneath a boot if he followed the Serpents' lead.

His horse snickered, and Shinsen shook the terrible memory aside and turned, casting his gaze back toward the horizon behind him. He breathed a sigh of relief that only his clan could be seen stretching into the distance.

He needed to rally all the remaining clans, have them all work together, and even then, he wondered if they could defeat this foe. Perhaps if they coordinated separate charges from all sides, they'd succeed. Yet even that seemed doomed to failure. The enemy didn't fight like they did. There was no tradition, no honour, no formal exchanges. It was butchery, like slaughtering a deer, and the enemy were happy to kill from a distance as well, using arrows.

He needed to get to the Shrine of the Moon Goddess as soon as possible, to warn the other clans and ensure no more were swallowed up by this behemoth.

He flicked the reins, and his horse broke into a canter, and his clan followed suit moments later, not understanding, but obeying as was their duty.

Their heavy horses would suffer for this, but they needed speed and time, and yet Shinsen knew they had neither.

He didn't believe in the Moon Goddess, but they'd need all the help they could get. So, as he rode, he sent a silent prayer to the sky for the first time since he was a child.

Moon Goddess, come help your people in our time of need.

***

Maya knelt, studying the tracks at her feet, and scanned the horizon briefly before looking back down. She'd been steadily gaining on Taran and Rakan over the last week, having picked up their tracks the morning after leaving Freeguard behind.

That first night, escaping from captivity, had been both frightening and exhilarating. The invisible shackles that restrained her had fallen away as she ran and leapt from rooftop to rooftop, reaching the city wall with the prize of freedom just beyond.

Fortunately, that obstacle had been easily overcome. It wasn't high, and along her route, she'd commandeered several clotheslines. It had only taken a matter of moments to weave them together to create a sturdy, makeshift rope that she'd looped around a merlon before lowering herself halfway down the wall. She'd then released one end of the rope, letting herself fall, rolling as she hit the ground.

She'd stood, the night air fresh in her lungs, for a moment overcome with relief, but there was no time to waste nor celebrate. Quickly recovering her equipment, she'd run south under the moonlight and with every step had found her true-self returning, not the Lady Maya, but the huntress.

Speed had been her ally. Despite these last months, her fitness and stamina remained, perhaps from her training with Ferris, and she cursed his name. No, she thought, it was because her whole life, as far as she could remember, had been spent doing this. Her body had evolved to the demands placed upon it and was now everything it needed to be to excel.

Her feet felt light as they landed, her long legs effortlessly carrying her swiftly while hardly raising her pulse. She moved like an animal, constantly alert, using her senses, hearing, sight, smell, and even taste.

As she'd run free for the first time in so long, she felt like whooping from sheer happiness, but the seriousness of the situation had provided a counterbalance, kept her focussed.

The day after her escape, she knew that to make up the lead the others had on horseback, she'd have to travel by day. Having mastered the art of camouflage many years ago, weaving long grasses into all her equipment took no time at all, and from a distance, she now looked like a bush. It had been time well spent for several times she'd knelt, unmoving, as columns of enemy lancers passed on nearby ridgelines, and whilst in plain sight, they'd never once suspected she was there.

Now, as she examined the disturbed soil, she smiled.

Taran and Rakan's tracks followed those of a large group of horsemen, and she knew exactly what they were doing. They were evading danger by staying in the footsteps of a large predator, and this predator was searching for something or someone. Almost every copse or tract of woodland she'd come across had been scoured, and it amused her to think that what the lancers possibly sought, was just behind them.

She listened carefully, fingers lightly touching the soil, but there was no gentle vibration, no indication of movement nearby. She continued her run, eyes ranging, taking in everything from the ground at her feet to the horizon all around. She was getting closer, for the tracks were fresh, only a day or two depending on their current speed.

The thought that she'd soon catch them unconsciously quickened her pace until something suddenly tweaked her senses, and she stopped to look carefully at the trail.

How long she'd run without noticing she didn't know, but she thanked whatever gods might have given her good fortune. As she studied the flattened grass and the scuffed ground, she discovered there were others following Rakan and Taran.

The tracks were light and made by men on foot, running as she did, and yet the strides left little to no imprint. She moved slower, fully focussed on the ground until she found some barer soil, and then her insides went cold.

There were five sets of bootprints, and she knew now the type of men who travelled in fives. Taran and Rakan were being tracked by Rangers and would soon find themselves with demons at their backs whilst they were following the jackals in front. All the residual happiness that Maya had felt disappeared in that moment as she picked up her pace again.

Taran had been able to defeat two Rangers at the fortress, but that had been one on one when in his prime. Now he was still recovering from who knew how many injuries, and Rakan was the same.

Five against two.

No!

If she picked up her pace enough, it would be five against three, and she'd make sure the Rangers didn't see her coming, as long as she could get there in time.

Her stride lengthened, and her brown eyes scanned ahead. This was not the time to be cautious of the lancers, there were more dangerous predators afoot.

But whilst she was behind the Rangers, she was hunting them, and an unsuspecting prey fell easiest.

**

Lorax and his men lay amongst some brush, staying low, almost invisible.

His gift, for no man could become a Ranger without one, was his ability to track and never lose his prey. This gave him a clear and unfair advantage over his fellow Rangers in the competition that Daleth had set. Not only that, they'd already been ravaging south of Freemantle when he'd heard from the king, so they were days, if not a week ahead of his brethren.

Whilst he and the Rangers around him felt supremely confident in taking down these two fugitives, they'd be anything but complacent in their approach.

It was known throughout the ranks that Taran and Rakan had been personally responsible for the deaths of nigh on twenty of their brother Rangers. That alone earned his respect, albeit tinged with disbelief. Even their current strategy of following the very lancers that searched for them earned his admiration further.

Yet the more he studied them, the more he realised that, although they had the advantage of being mounted, they were tired, injured, and would likely be easy prey. They would put up little resistance to his men, who were in peak condition and were skilled beyond belief.

Initially, he'd thought to fall upon them at night, but the fugitives were cautious enough to rest amongst thick undergrowth in whichever part of the woodland they chose to camp. Despite all his woodcraft and skill, there'd be no way they could approach without giving themselves away, especially as they'd come across snares set to give an early warning of intruders.

The risk would be that if the Rangers gave themselves away in the quietness of the night, the fugitives might have enough time to make good their escape on horseback.

So, shortly they'd circle the copse the fugitives had entered and work their way south, approaching carefully just before dawn. That way, when the two of them led their horses from the woods, their way would be blocked. Trees at their back, Rangers to the front, and if they tried to mount, they'd be dead before they even reached the saddle.

His fellow Rangers discussed the plan after he explained it to them.

He might act as their leader, but they were all equals, and he respected their skills as they did his. It would be a long, chill night hiding in the grass, but they all agreed it was the best way to ensure their prey didn't escape the snare.

They all hunkered down, waiting for the sun to set so they could make their stealthy approach under darkness. Fortunately, with winter nigh on upon them, the sky was dark with heavy clouds, and there was no chance they'd be seen. The surprise would be absolute.

In some ways, it would be a shame to finish the hunt so early, but Lorax knew any injured bear could still be dangerous and kill, so better to put this pair down swiftly.

'Let's get some rest, lads,' he murmured, and closed his eyes, dreaming of the praise and recognition they'd earn from their beloved king.

***

Daleth lowered the practice sword, sweat beading his brow and soaking his clothes. His chest burned, his arms ached, and his legs were sore beyond belief as he leaned against a table for support.

He'd spent the early evening shadow fighting, sweeping his sword slowly through the air in intricate patterns, wrist loose, emptying his mind. Carefully at first, then as his confidence grew, with more intensity so to test his healing body, and he found it wanting.

He grabbed a goblet of water from the table and drank deeply as his breathing slowed, cursing as he struggled to keep it down. True, he was recovering faster than any other mortal man, for any other man would likely be dead or never to walk or fight again, but to feel so weak was disgusting.

A platter of meat and bread had been set, and he sat, chewing slowly, swallowing forcefully, before following it with more water. He closed his eyes and tried to relax, waiting for both his breathing and heart rate to return to normal.

There was a tugging on his mind, and he opened his thoughts to find Lorax whispering his name. Lorax, who amongst the Rangers, had a gift that others quietly derided behind his back, for it didn't make him a more effective killer. Yet now, after all these years, his gift would see him elevated above his peers.

'Tell me,' Daleth commanded, and his hopes were rewarded as Lorax spoke of having found the fugitives and his plan of confronting them as they arose, still groggy from their night's sleep.

'Wait,' Daleth commanded, severing the link, reaching out to the other groups of Rangers, to find the closest still four days away.

It was frustrating, for even if it meant delaying the kill, he'd rather have waited for more groups to join Lorax to ensure there were no mistakes. Yet, as Lorax had explained, who knew what might happen if they waited. A storm that saw all tracks washed away and Taran and Rakan disappearing from his grasp?

Of course, they'd fall into his clutches again in due course. The fugitives were, after all, heading toward Gregor and his army, but killing them now would be one less thing to worry about, and indeed it would be one good thing to savour.

He reached out again to Lorax.

'I have the utmost faith in you and your fellow Rangers. Make me proud, make me celebrate the day you all joined me and return as favoured sons when you do this deed.'

Lorax's devotion shone as Daleth severed the link again.

For the remainder of the evening, he reached out. First to Julius' seer, who explained that Julius, and his men, had pushed deep into the land of the Eyre. So far, the only casualties to Julius' forces had been to traps and poisonous animals. The remaining people of the Eyre had decided not to fight at all, merely choosing to withdraw ever northward, further and further into the swamps.

Julius was now turning back, torching everything that would burn, which was difficult in the dampness of the swamp. But he'd found and plundered many of the swamp people's stores, ensuring that the Eyre would either have to come forth and capitulate or face possible starvation and freeze in the cold of the coming winter with their homes in cinders.

It was a prudent and bold move by his commander, for many men might have simply pushed onward, thirsting for blood, thinking that was what Daleth wanted.

No.

He wanted men who made good strategic decisions. With little to gain in advancing, Julius had seen that returning to Freehold outbalanced the reward of chasing an enemy he'd unlikely run to ground.

Next, he called out to Gregor and waited a while for him to respond. However, it didn't frustrate him for a commander in the field who ignored his men's needs, simply to curry favour with his king, was again not the commander he wanted.

The End of Dreams

It was worth the wait, for when he'd finished receiving Gregor's report, and seen in his mind the images of the two battles he'd fought, he felt his own blood stirring. To see a full charge of heavy knights against his men, hear the crash, the screams, the shouts of victory, had been glorious.

Gregor had already been forewarned by his brother of the fugitives heading his way to enlist the Horselords' help, and they shared the warmth of laughter over the impending failure. Even if the fugitives completed the journey, they'd only find dead bodies to recruit.

It was a desperate fool's errand destined for failure.

Finally, he reached out to Jared but received no response. He knew Jared was currying favour with Tristan's closest advisor and thus his nights were spent entertaining his next victim, learning every minute detail. Jared would report when he could do so, and Daleth knew he'd be as happy with his progress as he was with Gregor's.

He'd been right to show these two favour above the others all these years. It was a shame that, like all the other mortals, they'd grow old, outliving their usefulness and die discarded, wondering what they'd done wrong. Fortunately, others would always rise to replace them. Except, of course, without Alano to train them, they'd no longer be quite so deadly ... not like now.

The loss of Alano had been a terrible blow.

I doubt your soul is resting easy, old comrade, he thought, and then smiled as another thought struck him. If Alano had ended up in the fires of the nine hells, he wondered who'd be the one being tortured. It was likely Alano was making any demon's life a true hell, and the thought strengthened him.

He arose, hefting the heavy practice sword once more.

In many thousands of years, he might have to face Alano and those very demons himself, and he wanted to be ready.

***

Rakan nudged Taran with his foot. Dawn was approaching, the sky to the east growing brighter.

The lancers they'd been following had turned west a day before, but the plan was to continue further south, to meet the mountains before circumnavigating them to the grasslands. It made the journey simpler, and they'd also return to travelling at night again once they made it that far.

Taran opened his eyes, nodding. They kept conversation to a minimum. The dawn was a time when sound could travel, for the creatures of the night were starting to sleep while the creatures and insects of the day had yet to rise, so getting ready was done mostly in comfortable silence.

They saddled the horses, fed them, checked their hooves and made sure they were looked after first. The horses were pivotal to their survival and needed to be kept healthy and strong. Then it was themselves ... tough meat and bread they could almost break a tooth on, softened and washed down with water.

Rakan watched as Taran went through his morning stretching and was pleased to see him looking stronger despite being so battered. Rest, food, and thankfully no additional injuries had finally allowed him to regain much of his strength. It was such a shame his gift was denied him, for it would certainly have come in useful should they meet any Horselords.

Taran finished and looked at Rakan.

'You should stretch a little too, old man. How long has it been since you could touch your toes?'

Rakan laughed softly.

'What's the need to touch my toes when I never change my socks?'

He was pleased to see Taran smile by return. From memory, the only thing Rakan had smiled about when he'd worn an amulet had been the undertaking of violence, drinking, whoring or similar.

'Since we've lost our escort,' Rakan said softly, 'I think we can push a little faster. I don't think we'll see any more lancers this far south.'

'You might be willing to take risks in your old age, but some of us have a whole life to live ahead of us,' Taran replied, and for a while, the conversation and banter flowed quietly back and forth.

From Taran's stories, Rakan knew his son had spent his few adult years travelling alone between villages, and it seemed being on this journey, just the two of them, was just what Taran had needed to rekindle some of his old spirit.

The End of Dreams

Rakan was tempted to bring up Maya, to disclose the facts as he knew them, but he was a man of his word, or at least as much as he could be. He'd broken it several times in his life, but he couldn't break it with Maya. He realised that it was who you gave your word to that mattered more than anything.

'Are you ready, son?' Rakan asked.

'Yes, grandfather,' Taran said with a wink, and the two of them led their horses and the pack animal carefully out into the weak light.

Barely a whisper of wind stirred the long grasses in front of them, and then, as if rising from the grave, five black-clad Rangers rose like wraiths to claim their souls.

Empty eyes stared with such malevolence that it was like a physical blow, and the smiles on their faces were cruel and snide. A raven cawed noisily at this intrusion, breaking the morning silence before angrily flapping off.

'I don't think you'll be needing those horses,' the leader said, sneering. 'In fact, you'll not have use for anything beyond your next few breaths, so use this moment wisely.'

Taran looked to Rakan as he drew his weapons. At his peak, his gift at his fingertips, he'd managed to beat two Rangers, one after the other, and still he'd been badly hurt. Rakan, on the other hand, whilst he'd injured Darkon all those moons ago, had nigh on died to his blade.

Here they were, both below their prime, against five all at once.

He reached out his hand, grasping Rakan's forearm.

'You became the father I always wanted,' he said softly.

'You're the son I never deserved,' Rakan replied. 'Now let's see if we can take some of these whoresons to the grave with us.'

Taran looked up, meeting the leader's eyes and suddenly smiled, a genuine smile.

'It's a good day to die. A good day for you to die.'

'Not by your hand,' Lorax replied, his eyes narrowing, swords held loosely in his hands.

'You're right,' Taran said. 'Not by mine. Not by mine.'

***

Chapter XV

Maya had taken the whole night to get into a position she was happy with and had made it there just before dawn. It had been a night where her nerves had been tested the whole time. She hadn't slept, afraid that if her eyes closed for even a moment, the one chance that presented itself might be lost.

She approached under the dim light of a moon that stayed mostly hidden by the clouds, pushing herself faster than was prudent, but not as fast as her heart wanted her to.

Years of rising before sunrise had developed her sight to a level whereby she could follow the Rangers' tracks through the long grass on such a night. She was worried she'd arrive too late and had been surprised to find them circling away from the copse toward which Taran and Rakan's tracks had pointed and had paused, wondering on what to do.

Without knowing where the Rangers were, it would be impossible to know with certainty which way to flee, and this made the decision for her. This was not the time to be the prey. To remain the hunter, she needed to be the one who surprised, full in the knowledge of her target's location.

A poor hunter killed their prey on the run, once it was startled, having caught scent or sight of the hunter. Panic-stricken, its sinews pumped with blood, a deer brought down in such a fashion not only knew the terror of death's approach but would be tough to eat. A true hunter could deal death without the prey knowing it had died from one heartbeat to the next, clean and without pain, a calculated execution.

The End of Dreams

So she'd slowed her approach, inching forward, knowing the tracks would lead to the Rangers' camp and that to stumble into it would mean her immediate death. Every few steps, she'd stopped to listen.

She knew she'd found their camp before she got too close, not because of any noise, but more the absence of it. The grasses whispered in the subtlest of breezes, but where the Rangers lay, hidden comfortably in the grass, the symphony of sound was interrupted. They'd positioned themselves some way south of the tree line and would confront Taran and Rakan on their exit.

She'd backtracked a little, then circled the Rangers, quieter than a mouse. She'd tested each step, knowing that her prey might also be sensitive to a disruption in the song of the night. Her skill, however, was such that she'd remained unnoticed.

One hundred paces south, she'd distanced herself and then settled down, knowing she'd made the right decision. Had she warned Taran, even with the three of them facing the Rangers, it would have still led to their deaths. Had they tried to escape during the night they'd have been discovered, for neither Taran nor Rakan had the skill to move unheard or they'd have run straight into the Rangers had they chosen the wrong direction.

Now the waiting was almost over. It would soon be time.

She carefully unwrapped her bow, then discovered how difficult it was to string it lying down. But perseverance got the job done. Next, she pulled her arrows from the quiver, assessing their trueness by touch, choosing six that she pushed gently point down into the ground. Quietly as possible, she flattened a small circle of long grass so that nothing would interfere with her draw and then knelt, waiting for the sunrise.

In her mind, she played through different scenarios.

She could shoot one Ranger in the back, leaving four, because even a Ranger couldn't block an arrow he didn't see coming. From that moment, one would come to kill her, and three would stay to kill Taran and Rakan. This wouldn't work.

If instead, after killing the first Ranger, two turned for her, then Taran and Rakan might hold against the two who stayed to face them. However, once the two Rangers killed her, again, the outcome would be the same.

No, the only sure chance to win was if she killed three, right at the beginning, leaving the Rangers outnumbered. It was the only way.

Having just come to this conclusion, a raven flapped overhead, disturbed from its roost. Her heart almost stopped as she stood slowly to see the Rangers further distant than they'd been when she found their camp. She cursed herself that she hadn't considered that they'd push closer to the woods, ensuring there was no place for Rakan and Taran to run.

They were spread out in a curved line as she lifted her bow, positioning herself behind her arrows, reaching down, finding one where she'd knew it would be without looking, before plucking two others as well which she let hang loosely from her draw hand.

She looked at her targets, the Ranger in the centre and the two to his left, five paces apart, one hundred and eighty-six paces distant. There was no doubt in her mind as to exactly how far away they were, and it was far further than she'd wanted. Fortunately, not a breath of air moved the long stalks of grass between them.

She raised her bow, the arrow pointing high into the sky and released, instantly nocking and releasing the second on a slightly lower trajectory before loosing the third, lower still. All within two heartbeats.

She reached down, grabbed the last three arrows, and started to run.

***

Taran stood still, keeping the Ranger's gaze firmly fixed, stretching the moment, willing him and his men to hold position. until …

Lorax grunted, and within the same heartbeat, two men to his right were spun off their feet, crying out. Lorax looked down incredulously at the bloody arrowhead jutting from his throat before his eyes rolled back and he fell.

There was a high, distant war cry, and then Taran leapt forward with Rakan, engaging the two remaining Rangers to take advantage of the situation. Yet the Rangers, whilst shocked by the sudden downing of their brothers, stood resolute, and within moments both Taran and Rakan were being pushed back.

Taran defended well, parrying the flurry of blows raining down on him, but he heard Rakan cry out in pain as a Ranger's sword found its way past his guard, slicing his arm. Rakan had dropped his dagger and was now only armed with a sword.

The war cry sounded again above the clash of steel, and the next moment Maya ran into view, bow drawn and loosed an arrow into the leg of the Ranger who'd injured Rakan. She tried to do the same to the Ranger attacking Taran, but the man leapt, avoiding it, so it thunked into the ground.

But the distraction was enough, and Taran's lunge went deep into the Ranger's side. For a moment, those cold, black eyes held Taran's gaze before rolling back as blood gushed from the deep mortal wound.

Rakan's opponent struggled to stand, hatred and pain etched on his face as he faced Rakan and Taran, but Maya moved behind him and planted another arrow between his shoulders, and he pitched to the floor.

The two mortally injured Rangers, pierced by Maya's initial volley, moaned in pain. Rakan moved over to them, and soon the sound was replaced by silence, leaving Taran, Rakan, and Maya looking at one another.

'I found you in time. I knew I would,' Maya whispered, tears starting to flow down her face as she looked at Taran. 'Remember what you told me? We have something worth fighting for, something worth dying for, but something worth killing for as well.'

Taran looked back, staring into her eyes as she raised her arms wide, moving toward him, her face breaking into a smile, filled with love.

'I was wrong,' Taran said coldly, and turned away, back toward the horses. 'Come, Rakan, we need to get moving.' He swung up into the saddle. 'Keep up or go home, preferably the latter,' he said to Maya as he rode past.

Rakan took Maya into his arms as she sank to her knees, pulling her upright.

'No lass, be strong. Remember the words you just said. You're right and so was he when he said them to you. Let's make him remember, together. This is not just your fight, Maya, this is ours. Let's get that damned amulet off him and have our Taran back.'

Maya's eyes met his.

'He once said he'd love me in this world and the next. Maybe it should be the next.'

'No,' Rakan stated firmly. 'Take what's good in this life. Don't wait, don't let anything stop you. You're a hunter, now go capture your prey. If you can slay three Rangers, then what's one man's heart compared to that?'

Maya looked unconvinced.

'We'd better keep up,' she said. 'Mind if I borrow the spare horse?'

She leapt into the saddle.

Rakan followed suit a little less dynamically.

'You saved my life with your touch, Maya,' Rakan said. 'Now, let's go save yours.'

Together, they turned after Taran, leaving the motionless bodies of the Rangers behind them.

***

Shinsen sat by a low fire pit, eyes searching for a clue as to the thoughts of the ten other clan leaders before him.

They sat within the one permanent settlement in the whole of the grasslands. It was a common home to all the clans' youngest and eldest. Almost a thousand of them lived there in peace at any one time.

The children of the different clans grew up together, bonding, learning the ways of their goddess from the priests who lived there. The eldest of the clans lived out their final days here too. They raised the children, teaching them of the demands of knighthood, and passed on centuries of acquired knowledge of riding, sword, and lance. Then, when the children reached their twelfth winter, they were ready to leave and ride alongside the knights.

It was their holy place, where the shrine to the Goddess of the Moon stood alongside the sacred tree of their goddess, an enormous moonwood tree. One of a kind amongst the entire grassland plains.

Everything about it was silver, from the trunk to the branches and twigs. It shone with a lustre under the night sky when the moon smiled down brightly. It was a place of peace among the clans who constantly fought for supremacy over the grasslands' prime pasture. A place where every winter they'd meet and recount the great jousts of years past. Those of all ages would join the knights around the fire, and families would be reunited after being apart the past year.

It was beyond anyone's recollection as to when the tree had last blossomed, let alone grown leaves, and yet it stood tall, strong, healthy, and proud like the clans themselves.

'I find it hard to believe the words you've spoken,' Krahlen said solemnly, the grey-haired leader of the Dagger Clan, and others muttered in agreement. 'Yet two of our people's clans are absent from this meeting, and the most convincing aspect of your tale is you admitting to cowardice.'

Shinsen stood, fists clenched at the insult.

'If we weren't seated under the tree of our goddess, your blood would surely be spilt to the last,' he snarled. 'I am no coward, and I've proved that against you and yours many times. Be careful of the words you speak, Krahlen, tread warily.'

'You show strength now when you should've shown it before!' Krahlen retorted, 'and you reference our goddess when you've never truly believed yourself. If you did, you'd have helped the Serpents to victory instead of leaving them to die!'

He sat down, leaving the floor to Shinsen.

Shinsen's face was still mottled red with anger, but he held it in check.

'At least you spoke one true word there. I don't follow the Moon Goddess blindly, yet nonetheless, I believe I honour her with my victories, not with my prayers, but it's not my faith we're here to debate.'

He looked around, but no one challenged his words.

'Trust me, when I say,' he continued, 'had my clan, or all of ours together, faced this beast, we would have perished. What then for our land, our faith, and our children to come?'

Drayden, who was a huge man, stood and spoke.

'I don't believe what you say. With our forces combined, there's nothing that can withstand our strength. These lands have been ours since the rising of the first moon, and we must visit the wrath of the blood moon upon all those who trespass on our soil!'

Voices rose in agreement and shouted words flew back and forth for a while.

Shinsen was relieved to see two of the clan leaders shaking their heads, and turned to them.

'You disagree with Drayden? Stand tall and strong like the tree that shelters us. Come, speak with your own voice.'

Nadlen spoke first.

'You're the eminent warrior of all the clans, even if not the most pious. In battle, I'd follow you and trust your lead, knowing you've known only victory since you first stepped into the saddle. So I ask myself. If someone who had only ever known victory truly sees defeat, then I want to listen with a mind of logic and not just a heart of religious fervour.'

Chochen then stood.

'Nadlen speaks wisely. All of us have faced Shinsen. When has he ever not seen the truth of the fight before him? How do we continue to serve the goddess if we meet these invaders and die, leaving them to desecrate our lands unopposed for all time to come? Like Krahlen, my heart says we ride to meet them tomorrow, but my mind says we should learn of our enemy and gauge his strength first. This is what we do when we face each other in combat. Where's the difference?'

Krahlen stood again, pointing a shaking finger at Shinsen.

'Can you not see that he's infecting you all with his words, with his lack of belief? By all accounts, the invaders are likely only four days away, and yet we sit here trying to find courage in our hearts. The shame of it! We should be planning to leave in the morning while celebrating the coming righteous death of these weak unbelievers!'

'Those *weak unbelievers* destroyed two clans to a single man, woman and youth!' Shinsen stormed. 'If the Serpents, our most eminent clan, with knights of the utmost experience, strength, skill and cohesion, couldn't stand against them, then none can. So, let me assure you, the invaders are not weak, for if they are, what does that make us? They swept aside the Serpents as if a fly! If we face them one clan at a time, we'll die. If we face them together, head-on as our goddess demands, we'll die. This time we need to fight another way!'

Krahlen, knowing he had the support of seven of the clan leaders against Shinsen's two, stood hands on hips, facing him.

The End of Dreams

'You seek to change tradition, an edict from our goddess, that's lasted since the dawn of our people's time. I tell you this. Faith is what you lack. You may not be a coward, but you have no faith, and your hubris is that you think you know better than our goddess.'

Krahlen swept his arms wide.

'We don't need you, your clan, and nor yours if you have doubts,' he said, nodding to Chochen and Nadlen, 'for we're stronger without your faithless, weak souls in our midst.'

The other clan leaders shouted their agreement, and Krahlen stood tall, strong, the look of eagles on his face.

'Tomorrow, we'll ride, and return victorious with the sigil of the blood moon on our foreheads, and when we do, you and yours will be banished from these lands, never to return. You'll die in time without a home, without a goddess, and without honour!'

With that, he and the other seven clan leaders rose and stormed off, leaving Shinsen, Chochen, and Nadlen alone.

Shinsen looked at his hands, turning them over before him. Hands that knew the shape of his weapons better than the body of his wife. The silence was only broken by the crackling fire, and the sound of distant, cheerful voices, belonging to those who knew not that death awaited. He lifted his gaze to meet those of Chochen and Nadlen.

'You might not know it yet, but you might very well have saved the lives of everyone in your clans.'

Nadlen nodded, his expression sombre.

'That may be true, but in doing so, I've taken the very souls from their living bodies and thrown them into the fire. So, tell us, what can we do? How do we fight these invaders?'

Shinsen shifted uncomfortably.

'In truth, for now, we should avoid a fight entirely. Their weakness is that the majority of their army are spearmen and archers. Their light cavalry cannot harm us, for if they got too close, we'd crush them. Perhaps not fighting is the way forward, for they cannot engage with us unless we go to them.'

Nadlen and Chochen looked aghast.

'Running was not what I thought you had in mind, Shinsen. I must reflect on this,' Nadlen grumbled, his disappointment obvious.

Chochen nodded.

'Nor I. I thought you'd have some strategy on how we could fight them.'

Shinsen raised his hands, stalling their exit as both men rose to leave.

'Please remember what you said earlier, Chochen. What do we do before we fight? We seek to learn each other's strengths and weaknesses. We circle one another, looking for an opening. You say we are running, I say we are circling, looking for that opening.' He was relieved to see their looks change to one of thoughtfulness.

Both Chochen and Nadlen made their way into the darkness beyond the fire, the meeting having come to its conclusion.

'Until the morrow, my brothers,' Shinsen called after them.

He sighed, sitting there. Never had he run from a fight, nor dreamt a day would come when he'd have to. Yet that day had arrived. They would run, not circle. To survive, he'd have to lead his clan, and maybe those of Chochen and Nadlen, away from a fight for the first time in their lives.

His footsteps and heart had never felt so heavy as he returned to his clan's camp outside the settlement and entered his tent.

His wife, Shinmata, met him, and they embraced.

'What now, my lord?' she asked.

Shinsen smiled. He might be the head of the clan, but she was his equal. Yet she was more pious than he and adhered to the old ways of address.

'Tonight we should try for another child,' he replied, 'for tomorrow and in the days after, we'll need many more if we're to survive as a people.'

'As ever, our thoughts are aligned,' she replied huskily, and taking Shinsen's hand, led him willingly to bed.

***

'If you hadn't both proved yourself so valuable before, you'd have disappeared like Lord Duggan,' Tristan hissed, his eyes dark, the threat obvious.

Yana and Ferris knelt before him, heads bowed.

The End of Dreams

The fact that they'd offered this sign of fealty placated Tristan a little, but he wasn't sure as yet whether they'd keep their heads. A guard stood behind each of them, swords drawn.

Tristan turned to Galain, who stood beside him.

'What did Captain Tolgarth deduce as to the likely whereabouts of Lady Maya?'

Galain cleared his throat.

'Tolgarth showed me a woman's tracks from Lord Commander Taran's cottage that led south to the perimeter of the palace grounds. He deduced she climbed over the rooftops toward the southern wall to evade the night watch. His tracking skills are far beyond what I would have credited a captain of guards with. Whilst I could only take him at his word, I'm confident he tells the truth.'

Galain drew a deep breath.

'From her direction of travel,' he continued, 'it's apparent she's trying to catch up with Taran and Rakan. Tolgarth was keen to pursue, but with so many enemy lancers abroad, it would've been foolish to do so, and I forbade him from going.'

Tristan's face was red with restrained rage, and he didn't say anything for a minute, until finally, he nodded.

'Lucky for him and for you that I agree with that judgement. Should a search party have been intercepted, it could have put the Lady Maya and the mission in jeopardy. Never make a decision like that without consulting me first if you value your head. This has both embarrassed and weakened me. My betrothed, potentially the most valuable asset to my realm, has run off like the stupid, love-struck girl she is.'

Tristan slammed his palm on the tabletop.

'Gossip already abounds! A king who can't keep hold of his prospective wife is unlikely to be able to keep his wealth or kingdom safe. Thankfully, the more ambitious nobles are too wary of what happened to Duggan to make any overt moves, but I know some are plotting.'

Tristan leant forward, his face twisted by anger.

'Now, that brings me to you, Yana, for you've been part of this tale from the beginning. How on earth, when you've shown yourself to be so sharp, did you allow yourself to fail so miserably in just keeping her asleep?'

Yana kept her eyes lowered.

'I know my craft, and for two days, Maya slept as you wished. She'd used sleep weed before, so I can't understand how she reacted unfavourably to my infusion. It's apparent that her vomiting it over the floor allowed her to awake, realise her situation and escape.'

Tristan clenched his fists, then slowly relaxed them, in control once more.

'Gah. It makes sense, and you've nothing to gain, and absolutely everything to lose from her departure. Taran matters to you as much as Maya does to me, and thus, this hurts us both.'

Tristan tapped his nose.

'But that poses the most interesting questions. How did she even know what day it was? How did she know that Taran and Rakan had left and had the presence of mind to leave immediately on their trail?'

Tristan's eyes flickered to Galain, who nodded to the guards.

'There's only one possible explanation, one only,' Tristan continued. 'It seems that Lady Maya's favourite bodyguard has been playing both sides in this game. That's the only explanation that fits.'

Ferris' head snapped up.

'My king …' he started to protest, rising to his feet.

But as he did so, the guard behind him thrust down with his sword, through the back of Ferris' neck, killing him instantly.

Yana knelt, shaking, as Ferris slumped to the floor, his dead eyes staring, blood coursing across the floor toward her.

'Get up and get out,' Tristan growled. 'Don't forget that the cost of betrayal or failure can be one and the same! Now, go do what you do best. You've gained a strong reputation in the city for your work in getting the hospital ready. It would be a shame for you to end up in the very beds you procured if I have both your legs taken off at the knee for any future mistakes.'

As Yana hurried out, others came in to take away Ferris's body and clear up the mess.

Tristan turned to Galain.

'This Tolgarth is a skilled soldier, you say?'

Galain nodded.

'With Taran and Rakan gone,' Tristan mused, 'we need a military voice speaking on behalf of the Freestates' forces when we meet with

Ostrom, Dafne, and the other nobles. He was once Duggan's man, but if you think he'll be loyal to me and can be trusted, then he could prove valuable. What do you think?'

Galain kept his face neutral, but inside, he was jubilant. Brokering this deal carefully would make him wealthy and garner Tolgarth's favour.

'Let me talk to him in confidence, my king. I'll also ask around the court and see what people think. The worth of a man isn't just about how he wields a sword. Just look at Lord Commander Taran.'

Tristan nodded, a smile slowly replacing the frown.

'Wise words indeed. Again, you show yourself worthy of my trust. We need to keep close only those who are totally loyal to me and the Freestates' way. People who'll obey without question, kill my enemies without question and, if we are to lose this war as it still seems we might ... die for me without question when it's time to escape.'

'Fear not,' he added, looking at Galain. 'If the times comes to escape, you'll be alongside me if you continue to serve as you do.'

Galain nodded happily, his future secured.

'Now, let's meet with Ostrom and Dafne, Tristan ordered.

'Oh, leave a little blood on the floor,' he said dismissively to the servants, who were frantically cleaning it up.

It would be good to remind his allies that the king of the Freestates could be as dangerous and ruthless as any.

***

Jared sat opposite Galain and leant forward, pouring him a drink.

Things were going well, and tonight it looked like things might get even better, for Jared could read a man so acutely that nothing escaped him.

His daytimes were painful, trying to find the right balance between slowing the common recruits' training, whilst ensuring there was just enough progress so his efficiency couldn't be called into question.

He'd assumed the guise of Tolgarth long enough to feel comfortable, and if there were any subtle differences to his personality, well, the coming war was changing everyone. If he seemed a little forgetful at times when he met an old acquaintance, he explained that it was due to the huge responsibility he shouldered in training five thousand new faces.

His position also allowed him to accrue no small amount of wealth. He was responsible for tax collection, which, of course, wasn't *all* accounted for. With very little effort, his personal wealth was growing, even if he had to pay for all the training. That was a surprise discovery that had momentarily left him floundering.

But he was a consummate actor, and with everything running smoothly, he'd eased himself into spreading his influence. He would take the time to walk the streets, greeting the wealthy with humility, sympathetic to their frustrations over this likely avoidable war and the pain reduced trade inflicted on them.

Sow gentle seeds of division without saying anything damning. For merchants always thought of their profits first. Now he was greeted with respect wherever he walked.

Whereas before he'd had to seek out Galain for his company, it was now the other way around, and yet still Jared deferred to him, knowing Galain's ego was such that this was the best way to deal with him. Allow him to believe that *Tolgarth* looked up to him, grateful for his patronage.

'What's on your mind, my friend?' he coaxed gently. 'Is there anything I can do to help you? Something consumes you, and what are friends for if not to help one another? Did you receive the wines I sent with those amazing cheeses? I only ask because you can't trust too many people these days, and it helps to know who can be relied upon.'

Galain nodded enthusiastically.

'I did receive them, and they were exquisite. You have a perfect taste in flavours that matches your choice of perfect friends.' He smiled broadly, then rubbed his hands together. 'I've been eager to share an opportunity with you the last two days,' Galain confided, lowering his voice, 'but I've had to spend so much time and money ensuring that we had support, that I had to be patient before I did so.'

'You've spent money on me?' Jared asked, feigning shock and gratitude, reading the lie on Galain's face. 'This cannot be allowed to go unrepaid, whatever the opportunity is! Tell me first, how much do I owe you? I'll not have you out of pocket, whatever the reason. We're men of the Freestates, and nothing should ever be for free.'

The End of Dreams

'Three, three hundred gold pieces,' Galain said tentatively.

If Galain had lied badly before, this was so obvious that Jared almost felt embarrassed for him. He shook his head with a smile and look that conveyed gratefulness and wonder.

'You've taken a great personal financial risk for me, and no doubt staked your reputation too. I'll have that money moved to the merchant bank where you hold your money first thing on the morrow. Now tell me, for I'm fit to burst. What opportunity is worth such?'

Galain leaned forward, grasping Jared's arms with sweaty hands, clasping them in apparent affection.

Jared swallowed the urge to kill him.

'I've managed to get you a seat at the king's table,' he gushed, eyes gleaming as he delivered the news.

This time, the shock on Jared's face was genuine, and he laughed so joyfully that Galain couldn't help but join in.

'Your tracking of the Lady Maya and unravelling her intentions brought you much favour, and with my not inconsiderable help, Tristan wants you at his side. He needs an advisor on things military in the absence of Lord Commander Taran.'

Galain looked around, ensuring they weren't overheard.

'The king needs people around him he can trust totally,' he said softly. 'Those who'll put the Freestates and its rightful king above all previous loyalties. He doesn't enjoy that relationship with Taran or Rakan, whom I know you hold no affection for. He needs them for now, but let me tell you this. The day might well come when he doesn't, and I need to know where you'd stand on this matter.'

Jared couldn't believe his ears, his heart only ever beat this quickly during combat.

'The king can trust me as much as you can, my friend. You know me, you know who I am. Tell him I'm his man and will gratefully serve him!'

Galain almost leapt from his chair.

'I'll go give him the good news and will send one of the palace retainers to give you the details of our next meeting.'

As Galain left the tavern, Jared watched the door close, and this time drank deeply of the wine, whereas normally he only sipped. The gods had favoured Daleth once again by putting Tristan's neck that bit closer to the edge of Jared's sword.

Oh, he'd serve Tristan. He'd serve his head on a platter to Daleth.

***

Daleth sat deep in thought, fingers steepled, controlling his breathing and emotions.

In war, it was rare that the original plan lasted throughout. There were simply too many variables, and thus a good commander had to accept the ebb and flow of conquest. It was how well a man overcame adversity that showed the individual's true greatness, or so he told himself.

Even so, setbacks angered him, for he should have foreseen them.

First, the long delay in taking Tristan's Folly, then his injury preventing him from moving on to conquer Freeguard where the unforeseen obstacle of an alliance awaited him. Then there was the loss of so many irreplaceable Rangers in pursuit of those damned fugitives, deserters from his army.

He'd not heard from Lorax in three nights now, and he'd known the first night something had gone awry. Now his worst fears were confirmed, as the other Rangers following the trail had reported discovering Lorax's corpse, torn apart by animals on the open plain.

To make matters more interesting, tracks had been found that showed a third person joining Taran and Rakan, an archer of some consummate skill who'd turned the hunters into the hunted.

Now having communicated with Jared, he knew exactly who this hunter was.

Maya.

Once, just a peasant girl from a village with an interesting gift, who'd escaped his clutches, she'd somehow become the future queen of the Freestates. Now she was apparently throwing it all away, chasing after her lover who'd originally saved her, Taran, who'd become Lord Commander of the Freestates forces. Now she'd saved him again, as proved by the dead bodies of Lorax and his men.

It was nearly impossible to fathom how a peasant and a deserter had become such key players in this game of war. They were so adept at it that he wondered how on earth he'd overlooked such skill within his kingdom.

The End of Dreams

Yet, however fortunate they'd been before, their luck wouldn't continue. Previously, they'd always run from his Rangers, fled away from the danger with it chasing behind them, yet now, unbeknownst to them, they were running toward it. No amount of luck would save them, nor individual skill with which they were obviously gifted.

No, their story would soon end, whereas his was just beginning.

***

Maya sat in near darkness, looking across at Taran.

They'd called a halt to their day's travel after the final horse went lame. It had been hard to slaughter it, but having it limping in plain sight was as big a sign as any pursuer could ask for, and they knew without question they were being pursued.

They were now on foot, but this suited Maya. She'd spent her whole life with feet upon the earth, close to the ground, where one would miss nothing if only you knew how to listen and feel.

She'd chosen the campsite, her knowledge of the land far eclipsing that of Rakan or Taran, and as the temperature started to plummet, they'd risked making a small fire to avoid illness from the cold.

They were in a hollow, and Taran had excavated a fire pit in quick time. He was efficient, purposeful, and emotionless as he went about the task of gouging out the soil, then finding stones to line the pit. Stones that would not only stop the light from spreading, but that would also hold the heat and could then be wrapped and put in a bedroll.

If only she didn't need a stone, she thought, looking at Taran.

He hadn't said anything to her since the fight with the Rangers, and that had been days ago. It was left to Rakan to communicate anything vital. Whenever they camped, Taran turned his back to her, almost as if by denying her presence, he could avoid whatever conflict was going on in his head.

But this had gone on long enough, Tonight was the night.

Rakan nodded subtly at Maya.

'We all need to talk,' he said softly. 'There's much to be said, for who knows whether we'll have the chance tomorrow or the days after, for we're as likely to meet death as we are to see the next sunset.

We're now on foot, we know we're hunted and whilst we're running from what's behind us, we cannot run from our past, for they're two different things. What I'm trying to say, son, is that you need to speak with Maya.'

Taran shook his head.

'I don't have the need, Father,' and the title he bestowed didn't have the usual warmth to it. 'We have a mission, you and I, and she decided to join us, uninvited. What's in the past can remain there. I'm not running from it, but nor do I wish to look back at it either.'

Taran lowered his head, wrapped himself in a blanket, and turned his back.

Maya sighed.

'Then if you've no wish to speak, then I shall, for what I have to say, needs to be heard.'

Rakan nodded encouragingly, and Maya forged on.

'I knew a young man once, and he held no high station. In fact, he wore the uniform of my enemy. Yet there was something about him that made me want to know him better, and it wasn't out of desperation because I was being taken to my doom. No, it was because despite being born far apart, despite never knowing the other's life, there was something about him that resonated within me. Maybe his stories, perhaps his laughter, or something intangible I couldn't put my finger on. Whatever it was, I knew within him there was a pure spirit.'

Maya wiped an errant tear away, then steeled herself to continue.

'That same young man who hardly knew me, when the terrible time came, offered his life. He did so knowing he'd lose it, just so that I wouldn't die alone. What kind of man would do such a thing? Who could be capable of such an action?'

'Let me tell you,' she said, raising her voice. 'He's the man who I gave my heart, body, and soul to. The man at whose feet I lay my dreams. The man who gave me the same in return without hesitation or question. He knew that somehow, in this world of ours, we'd managed to stumble onto that most powerful gift that everyone wishes for, hopes for their whole lives, but often never finds. True love.'

Maya's voice broke a little, choked with emotion, and she cleared her throat.

The End of Dreams

'I didn't take back this gift, for once given, it was not mine any longer. In your hands, you still hold everything that is me. Your fear and pain are born of misunderstanding, for nothing creates more horror than the unknown, and till now, you've not known what led us to where we are today.'

'Our hearts are broken in half, yet now, sitting right beside one another, they're ready to be made whole, ready to be forged anew in the fire of our love.'

'My prince. I never betrayed you. I gave up my life, my happiness, for yours. You lay at death's door in the hands of our enemy, and Tristan demanded, as payment for your release, my oath, on pain of death that I'd be his. I gave it, for I would and always will do anything to protect you.'

'I never realised we'd still both die that day. I don't regret what I did, I just regret it has taken so long for you to know the truth of it, to hear it from me. I wrote a letter to explain everything before I was taken away. I healed you and left it under your pillow so that when you awoke, you'd understand everything.'

'I know not what happened to it, but my prince, hear my voice and know that the words I say are true. I broke that oath, as you now know. I ran from Freeguard to be with you, knowing that Tristan will seek his revenge. But I realised that I'd rather live a week in your company, than a lifetime without it.'

'I'm not the future queen of the Freestates. I'm your princess, a common village girl who loves you with every fibre of her being.'

Taran turned slowly, looking at Maya's face glowing softly from the fire's embers. Even her white hair shone with a sheen. For the first time since he'd seen her in Tristan's audience chamber, his eyes met hers and yet still they were devoid of emotion.

'I hear what you say, and I know it should reach me, but I chose a way to deal with your loss, and I'm afraid to tell you what it is.'

Maya nodded.

'I already know, and you needn't be afraid.' She stood, moving around the fire to kneel behind him. 'Here, rest your head on my lap,' she said, and her fingers gently stroked his hair, brushing it back from his terribly scarred face.

Her heart beat so rapidly that her hands shook, but Maya didn't rush, for she could tell from Taran's rigidity that he was barely holding himself in control. So instead, she did nothing more than gently caress his face with her hands, her hair falling upon his face as she leaned over him.

'Just relax,' she murmured, starting to hum as she used to do when she once used her gift. It surprised her, for it had been so long since any kind of melody had come to her mind, and yet it came naturally, unbidden. Her fingers moved, gently massaging Taran's scalp until, at last, she felt him start to relax.

His breathing began to deepen, and then his eyes closed as he drifted toward sleep.

Maya lifted her eyes and met Rakan's, whose face shone with hope even in the darkness, but she didn't dare stop her fussing, not yet. It wasn't until the moon was high in the sky that her hands moved ever so slowly toward Taran's neck to find the clasp of the amulet.

As her fingers touched it, Taran's eyes snapped open, and his hands reached up to grab Maya's. She froze, for the danger in his gaze was frightening, but he clenched his eyes shut, releasing her hands suddenly.

'Do it,' he gasped, shaking.

With a wrench, she pulled the clasp apart and tossed the amulet away.

Taran's cry as she removed it howled out into the night, but in the next moment it was silenced as he pulled her close, so hard she could barely breathe. But her hold on him was just as tight, and their hearts beat as one once again.

'We have a love worth fighting for, worth dying for, but especially worth living for,' she whispered.

As they finally fell asleep in each other's arms, Rakan stood watch, tears in his eyes the whole night but with a smile on his face brighter than the moon.

***

Chapter XVI

We owe it to them to bear witness. That way, we can acknowledge our cowardice and lack of faith should they return victorious through bravery and belief. I pray that's the case, for otherwise, whilst we're absolved, there will be no victory or celebration in us being right.

The words that he'd spoken to Chochen and Nadlen earlier in the day sounded in his mind, as the three of them watched uncomfortably from within a tree line on a small hill. They skulked as if children and the word cowardice echoed loudest in his thoughts.

Shinsen knew the other two were likely thinking something similar. Their commitment had wavered as they regretted their decision, but nonetheless, they'd set out to follow the eight clans who'd chosen to destroy the invaders.

They'd travelled alone, without their clans, leaving them at the shrine with strict and simple orders to stay there unless attacked, and that to leave would invoke being made outcast, clanless.

Had they known that this was the fate already placed upon them, should the knights under Krahlen prevail, they might well have chosen to join the fight. Fortunately, they were unaware, and discipline within the Horselords was paramount, and thus they'd stayed.

For three days they'd travelled northward, following the other clans at a distance, not wanting to be subject to the barrage of insults and threats that were aimed their way were they to come too close.

Never in his life had Shinsen, or the others, faced such hostility until now. Both on and off the field of battle, knights faced one another with honour and respect, yet this courtesy had been stripped away overnight.

Now here they were, witness to what was about to happen, and for once in his life, Shinsen hoped with all his heart that he was wrong. If only it was his lack of belief, his lack of strength, that was at fault, for if so, then the clans would survive, and the intruders would be punished.

He'd even welcome his banishment and do his best to ensure his clan's people somehow avoided sharing his fate, even if he had to take his own life to do so.

'They look so magnificent!' Nadlen murmured beside him, heart torn, as he looked down upon the clans massed below their vantage point. 'I can't believe how they can be stopped. Yes, the enemy outnumbers them, but the power of our warhorses, the strength of our armour, our skill in combat … we were fools to listen to you.' Nadlen's voice was tormented as he tried to hold back on his emotions lest he say something unbefitting of a knight of the first rank.

'I hope you're right,' Shinsen said, voicing his private thoughts. 'I pray to the Moon Goddess you're right.'

'You don't even believe in her,' Chochen scolded, 'so why even invoke her name? Nadlen is right, we should be sharing in this glory. I foolishly held you in too high esteem, having been unseated by your lance many times without reply.'

'What are they waiting for?' Nadlen asked. 'How long will they simply face one another? What's Krahlen doing?'

'He's waiting for fear to eat away at the invader's hearts so that they'll break the moment the charge starts. The clans will run them into the ground without any significant loss,' Chochen responded.

Shinsen shook his head.

It was as if both armies were simply content to wait, for they'd faced one another since noon and now the sun was approaching the horizon. Suddenly, Shinsen realised that whilst Chochen was correct in his thoughts, the advantage was shifting to the enemy, a shrewd move to accept the delay by the enemy commander. The valley ran northeast to southwest, and with the clans to the east, the slowly setting sun was shining into the knights' eyes.

'The sun is dropping behind the enemy,' Shinsen said, 'they now have that advantage.' A plume of mist rose from his mouth, for the air was so cold, and whether he shivered from premonition or the chill, he didn't know.

The End of Dreams

Almost as soon as he said it, horns sounded amongst the clan ranks. Krahlen had recognised his mistake and sought to minimise the effect by sounding the advance before the sun dropped any lower.

A knight on horseback looked enormous, and the enemy further away from them looked tiny in comparison, even if their line was long and deep. Despite the distance, Shinsen could see the lancers moving around behind the enemy lines, content to stay away from a foe they couldn't beat, leaving it to their slow brothers on foot.

Nadlen went to urge his horse forward, but Shinsen raised his hand.

'It's too late to join them. We're too far away, and they'd not want you there. However much I want our brothers to tear this enemy asunder, they are lost.'

If it wasn't the words that stopped Nadlen, then the sadness and finality dripping from Shinsen's voice somehow reached him, for he paused as the second horn sounded and the trot became a canter.

Sounds echoed along the valley, the jingle of harness and mail, the metallic ring of lance against shield, and the shouts of men laughing, exhorting, gleeful as they urged each other on. All this and more reached them clearly on the soft breeze, the rumble of the horses' hooves a contrasting undertone to the lightness that exuded from the Horselords who rode into battle.

The enemy lancers fanned out, up the gentle valley's sides, rising above the large wedge of clansmen below. Then, as the horn sounded to order the final charge, the lancers swept down.

'They've timed it too late,' Chochen cried joyfully as the lancers swept behind the wedge by some distance.

Shinsen shook his head, his eye narrowed as he recognised their role.

'They chose not to engage. They'll close in from behind to ensure none escape,' he murmured.

Suddenly the sound of the wedge hitting the enemy line reverberated back down the valley, the cries and screams of men and horse sounding high pitched in the distance. The dust clouds thrown up by the hooves were thick and high, and without being able to see anything, all Shinsen, Chochen, and Nadlen could do was wait. The sound intensified, washing back over them in waves before slowly fading away. Then suddenly nothing, as if a god had waved his hand, casting a spell of silence across the land.

Not an insect rustled, nor a bird flew across the sky as the three of them sat mounted, waiting as the sun set, waiting for the dust to fall, but it didn't fall quickly enough.

Darkness began to spread, and still, nothing came from the valley.

'We should go and witness the outcome,' Chochen insisted.

Shinsen again shook his head.

'We'll wait until the morning to observe the fate of our brothers and the enemy. I pray we witness Krahlen and our brothers victorious.' The words rang hollow for he knew them to be false even as they passed his lips.

They made a makeshift camp a short way within the tree line and settled down for the night. They lay silent in the cold and dark, each with their own troubled thoughts, until one by one, they fell into a restless sleep.

***

Shinsen awoke shivering, to find the land had turned white overnight, leaving the forest around him highlighted in stark detail. It wasn't the cold that had woken him, for his body was used to it, even when encased in metal, rather it was the noise, a strange rhythmic crump.

He lay still for a moment, until he realised what it was, the faint sound of feet marching through the newly fallen snow. He quietly sat to discover both Nadlen and Chochen absent from their bedrolls.

He followed their bootprints to the tree line, and found them crouched, cloaks pulled around their shoulders as they knelt, peering through the foliage at the army passing below at the base of the valley.

Despite their vast number, the snow had the effect of deadening the sound of the enemy. With their breath blowing vast clouds of steam into the air, it was as if they were an army of ghosts marching by. Even the lancers on their horses looked ethereal.

Lightly mailed archers walked amongst the thistle of spearmen, bows unstrung and covered to protect them from the cold and moisture. Dozens of wagons trailed the fighting men, full of supplies and covered in stretched hide.

The three of them crouched there as the army slowly moved by, and Shinsen quietly counted the units as they passed. It seemed to take forever until the last man had disappeared around a bend in the valley, yet they sat silently, just in case there was a rearguard. None appeared, perhaps because the invaders already knew that they were the predator, not the prey in this land.

Finally, Shinsen broke the silence.

'How many?'

Nadlen answered without looking away from the sight before him.

'I think around thirty thousand, but that cannot be right. You estimated near that amount when you first spied them.'

No further words were spoken as they returned to tend to their horses, not rushing despite the urgency in their stomachs. Finally, they led the horses clear of the brush, mounted, and rode down into the valley.

It wasn't long before they came across the abandoned enemy camp, and despite the cold, there was no sign of campfires. Shinsen nodded to himself. Even in his superiority, their commander took no chances of highlighting his camp at night, knowing that was when his troops were most vulnerable.

He cursed out loud, and the others turned to him.

'They'd have been vulnerable in the night to our charge,' he said, realisation hitting him too late, cursing his lack of strategic foresight.

Nadlen laughed out loud in ridicule.

'What are you saying? We've never fought that way. How could we hold cohesion in the dark?' But even as he said it, his voice slowly died away as he considered Shinsen's comment further.

'Their spear line is too strong. Had we in our entirety caught them unawares at night, with no formation, no cohesion of their own, we would have run over their camp,' Shinsen said, but even as he spoke the words, he dismounted to inspect countless holes in the snow. 'Damn them, they've even thought of that,' he spat. 'Look, these are holes from where they planted stakes or spears to help protect their camp from a charge.'

'It seems your idea had some merit then,' Nadlen conceded. 'Even so, Krahlen would never have agreed to fight in such a dishonourable way. Killing in the night? He'd not have listened.'

'I could have made him had I thought of it earlier,' Shinsen cried, but knew the lie of his own words.

Nadlen spoke the truth, and it wouldn't have been just Krahlen opposing the idea. None of the others would have agreed to spill blood under the moon. To win in a dishonourable fashion while defiling the goddess? Never! Unless, of course, it had been a blood moon, and one was not destined to rise for many a year.

They continued in silence but then paused, gently tugging on reins, as in front of them, in the middle of the valley floor, was the battlefield.

They dismounted, letting the reins drop, for the warhorses were so well trained, they would stand in place till they died should their masters not return.

Shinsen wasn't sure whether the snow helped conceal the horror or somehow added to it. The snow was tinted red from the blood that had seeped into it before it froze. Everywhere he looked, hands, arms, legs, and heads pushed through the snow as if the ground was giving birth in some macabre fashion.

Not a single horse stood, nor pennant fluttered, above the silent, eerie battlefield. They searched through the snow until midday, finding in their wintery graves, ten dead from the clans for every one of the invaders, the latter stripped of uniform and equipment.

'Why do they dishonour their dead in such a way?' Chochen wondered as they looked at the cold, dead eyes of a corpse.

Shinsen thought, rubbing his chin.

'It's because they waste nothing, and take everything that's valuable. Their armour and weapons are as precious to them as ours are to us. These are men who have trained to fight just like us, and to fight is their purpose. If they're collecting armour, it's because they have many battles before them yet to come.'

Nadlen and Chochen looked at one another, then dropped to their knees in front of Shinsen, drawing their swords, lifting them in fealty to him.

Shinsen stepped back in surprise, for it was something a young man attaining full knighthood would do to their clan lord. It promised obedience, unswerving loyalty, and was never something another clan leader would ever do, for in doing so, all below them were bound by their leader's oath.

The End of Dreams

'We talked whilst you slept,' Nadlen admitted. 'Everything you said would happen, has happened. At times we doubted you and slighted you, and we realise it was not cowardice that drove your decisions. You saw the truth, and perhaps, after all, you are favoured by the Moon Goddess, for she helped you to see what would happen.

'We pledge our lives, our swords, our honour, and those of our clans to you. Let there be no more separate clans, let there be just the one. But this is on one condition,' Nadlen finished softly.

Shinsen raised his eyebrow.

'You must do whatever it takes to find a way to kill them all,' Chochen continued, looking up.

Shinsen took the hilts of their swords in either hand.

'I accept your pledge of fealty, and I accept your condition. I will find a way, of that you can rest assured.'

Chochen and Nadlen stood, brushing the snow from themselves and together they walked back to their horses and mounted.

They had to overtake the invading horde and return to the shrine quickly, to tell everyone that their way of life and world as they knew it was over.

***

'There are at least six groups north of us now,' Maya puffed as they ran, 'and another four to our east.'

The fact Maya was slightly out of breath was surprising, for her stamina and ability to run without pause was unmatchable. But they'd pushed the pace fast, faster than they should have, and it had been a mistake, for now, they had to slow right down.

The chase had been on for over a week, and they'd dropped everything unnecessary. The first had been the gold they'd carried and whilst there was fear in all of their minds, they'd laughed as they tossed aside the heavy pouches each of them carried.

'I've just thrown away more gold than I'd ever seen in my lifetime,' Rakan had quipped, and yet there was no feeling of loss, just relief to feel lighter.

They still wore their packs, holding bedrolls, food, and water, but now they felt like the weight of the world was on their shoulders. Snow had fallen the last few nights, and whilst not yet too deep, it was draining their energy.

'We should ditch more weight,' Rakan gasped, vapour clouds rising from him. 'We could travel faster.'

Taran shook his head tiredly.

'Not yet, there's something strange going on here. Burdened and tired as we are, they're not closing the distance. However fast or slow we move, they're not closing in for the kill.'

'If that's the case, let's try slow,' Rakan begged, who was suffering the most,

'Let's try it,' Taran said, and sure enough, when they slowed to a walk, the distant pursuers matched their pace.

'Why didn't you notice that earlier?' Rakan grumbled, his head turning, trying to keep an eye on the groups all at once. They were easy to see, for against the white snow, their black garb made them stand out even at a distance.

'Maybe I've been a little distracted,' Taran chuckled, and he pulled Maya in for a brief kiss.

'Ye gods,' Rakan moaned. 'I'm glad you two are happy again, but how can you be like this when death is all around us?'

Maya laughed, the sound uplifting in its purity.

'You should understand, Rakan. Taran and I fell for one another, running through the woods when first we escaped, and here we are all over again. We've been given this time, however short, to enjoy each other once more. So, whether it's running, talking, holding hands or indeed kissing,' and she took Taran's face in her hands to emphasise the point, brushing her lips briefly against his, 'I intend to make the most of it.'

Rakan couldn't help but laugh.

'I've lost count of how many times I thought I'd die since I met you two. Now there are at least fifty Rangers out there just for us,' he said in wonder. 'I don't know what I feel the most ... scared out of my wits, or rather proud they think they need that many.'

'That's it!' Maya gasped, snapping her fingers, and both men turned to look at her.

'You're right, Rakan. Think about it. Since you two first rescued me, we've evaded, killed, or caused the death of how many of their finest?

The End of Dreams

We've constantly killed the unkillable. I'm not sure how, but the fates always smiled upon us, and we made our escape. Since then, Taran here killed two in single combat, and then we defeated another five when they felt your death was assured.'

'Where are you going with this?' Rakan asked, scratching his bristled chin.

'They still intend to kill us,' Maya continued, 'but this time Daleth's making absolutely sure there's no miraculous escape, not a single chance of us taking one group down after another. So, I think they're herding us, making sure we journey along our original course to the south-west. Then whether it's today, tomorrow or next week, we'll run into another fifty or more coming from the other direction, and that's when we'll die, surrounded, without a chance of escape.'

'What I want to know is how they know where we're heading?' Rakan demanded. 'Someone must have been passing information from within Freeguard. Why else would we have first encountered those lancers, and now have all these Rangers hunting us down?'

'It doesn't matter,' Taran murmured, peering at the distant figures. 'We're here, and so are they. We can't turn to face them, for we'll die. If we continue our journey, I've no doubt that, as Maya surmises, we'll become encircled and meet our end. A few days or maybe a week from now perhaps, but still we'll die.'

They continued in silence for a while, yet as they walked, Maya slipped her arm around Taran's waist and his encircled hers by return. She leaned her head into his shoulder, and onward they continued, strides perfectly matched.

'How is it that we're so close to death, and yet I've never felt happier?' Maya sighed, looking up at Taran with her large brown eyes.

Taran smiled, and from where she stood, she couldn't see the terrible burns on the other side of his face, and he looked so handsome that her heart skipped a beat.

'Perhaps because when we're about to lose what we value the most, we cherish it more than ever before. Especially that we've only just found it again,' Taran explained.

'Come, let's run a little,' Maya laughed. 'It's a beautiful but cold day, and I think we should make those Rangers work a little harder for their pay!'

She started running, her hand pulling Taran along, who groaned and rolled his eyes at Rakan as they ran past.

'If she carries on like this, then I'm taking the easy way to death. I'm going to meet the Rangers instead,' Rakan complained as he jogged on after them. 'Not everyone is as young as you two.'

The day passed quickly, the clouds becoming heavier, the sky turning angry and dark. By contrast, even in the sun's absence, the bright, fresh snow on the ground hurt the eyes.

Finally, as the sun began to drop, Maya called a halt.

'I can see you're almost fit to drop. Forgive me for pushing so hard,' she apologised to Rakan. 'Perhaps if we went slower, we'd meet our fate later. I think we should stop and make camp, eat and rest as much as the weather and our distant neighbours allow.'

Rakan's face suddenly lit up.

'I've been thinking while we ran. What about if we try and push northwest toward Freemarch? We might find it still unoccupied and lose ourselves in the city.'

Taran considered Rakan's words.

'It's the best idea you've come up with, and maybe that's because it's the first.'

Maya laughed, and Rakan rolled his eyes.

'But I think we all know,' Taran continued, 'that we'll run into Rangers if we go that way. It's almost certainly fallen to Daleth's forces. There's no way he'd leave such a large Freestates city unoccupied.'

Rakan's face fell, but Taran reached out, taking his shoulder.

'Father, *if* I can think of nothing better, then any plan is better than none. So, in the morning, if we still breathe, let's see if our escorts will allow us to change course a little.'

Rakan nodded, and as Maya started cleaning the ground for a camp, he pulled Taran to one side.

'I know you're right, son. I just want to keep Maya's hopes up. It's good to see her so happy, so radiant,' and then he dropped his eyes. 'It's also good to have you, the real you back too.'

Taran smiled warmly and went to speak, but Rakan hadn't finished.

'You say you two fell in love and found one another when we escaped all that time ago. Well, I found my soul, a son, and a daughter to boot. I might tease you two for the affection you show one another, but it does my heart good to see something so bright in this dark world of ours.'

Taran nodded, his eyes moist, and went to turn back when Rakan gently restrained him.

'It'll be a cold night,' Rakan noted. 'It's going to snow again, and we don't know if this will be our last night or the last morrow. So, tonight I'm going to walk away a little yonder,' he said, nodding out into the snow, 'and I'll take watch, and you …' Rakan blushed a little. 'Well, you and Maya can have a little privacy if you so wish.'

Before Taran could say anything, he stamped away, embarrassed.

Taran returned to Maya, who'd cleared a small circle of snow and had used it to create a low wall to provide a little shelter from the wind. Taran looked at her handiwork for a moment, shaking his head.

'You've many gifts,' he laughed, 'but building with snow is not one of them.'

Together, they made it higher and thicker, and Maya smiled at him as they worked.

'I have fewer gifts than before, but trust me when I say the one that matters the most has returned to me.'

She kissed Taran deep on the mouth before pulling back, breathing hard, looking away, her white hair covering her face.

She laid out the bedrolls, taking out some food from their packs and they sat close together, the bitter night air starting to chill them now that they'd stopped moving.

'We should get some rest,' Maya said, looking around. 'Where's Rakan? Is he taking the first watch?'

She started crawling into her bedroll.

'He is indeed,' Taran confirmed, and then instead of getting into his own, he moved next to Maya. 'Is there room for two in there,' he asked. 'I think the best way to keep warm is to stay close, don't you?'

Maya giggled as Taran squeezed in next to her.

'I'm not sure we'll be able to respond to any threat very quickly pushed together so closely like this,' she said, sighing in contentment as Taran's arms closed around her from behind as she turned her back toward him.

'Oh, I am still so cold,' she murmured, feigning a shiver, and turned a little to reach over her head with her arm, pulling Taran's mouth down to hers. 'If only there was a way to create a little extra heat,' she whispered huskily, eyes full of meaning.

Taran's arms pulled Maya tightly against him, and she sighed, moving her body in encouragement before suddenly pausing, looking about.

Taran smiled.

'Rakan's taken a walk well away from camp, and he's given us the night. He'll keep watch throughout.'

Maya's eyes opened wider in mock affront.

'You two planned this?' she said, pretending to be displeased.

Then, as Taran's lips brushed her face, she closed them.

'Then if he's given us the whole night, let us not waste any of it,' she murmured, and this time as their lips met, they didn't part except to gasp for breath.

***

Jared was in such a good mood that he whistled softly as he sauntered back toward the barracks and his apartment. He'd spent the evening with a noble's daughter who'd sought his eye the previous week.

It was dark, late at night, and the air was freezing, so the hood of his cloak was pulled close around his face. His booted feet left prints in the ankle-deep snow that had fallen over the last week, and he greeted a couple of late-night wanderers but mostly kept to himself.

This joviality wasn't too out of character now, for over the last two and a half weeks he'd been summoned over a dozen times to the palace to meet with Tristan and the leaders of their alliance along with sundry other merchants and nobles.

He knew that, in the eyes of all there, he was now viewed with measured respect.

The merchants and nobles had been the easiest to mix with because Tolgarth was Freeguard born and bred, and thus they wanted to support one of their own. The fact that he was promising to help them reduce their tax burdens further cemented their favour.

Dafne and Ostrom had been harder work to convince, but he'd read them well.

The End of Dreams

Rather than present himself as too sure, he deferred to Ostrom whenever it didn't weaken his position. He took time to compliment his advice in the meetings and often talked of how the desert spears were the epitome of work ethic as they worked ceaselessly to repair the walls.

Jared laughed inwardly to see these efforts, knowing how futile they were. They'd already decided to put everything into one throw of the dice by meeting Daleth's army head-on in the field. So what was the point in repairing the walls as opposed to making fieldworks? However, the nobles and merchants demanded the repairs, thinking that the walls would still keep them safe if the battle was lost. It was laughable.

What amazed him was that they hadn't the foresight to have every one of Ostrom's spearmen train another citizen. By the end of the winter, they'd be able to field a relatively trained, and large, spear levy. Instead, they had only five thousand peasant swordsmen training in the barracks. Utter stupidity.

It surprised him that this Taran, who was held in such high regard, had overlooked or not pushed such a simple way forward. Yet there was a big difference between being a gifted warrior and a master strategist. Likewise, Ostrom had failed to see the obvious, but then again, maybe it was because no Freestates merchant or noble would sully their hands with a blade and thus the idea was beyond comprehension.

Dafne's approval had been much harder to win over. She was as shrewd as she was big and strong.

Jared had initially thought about trying to seduce her, but decided against it. It was quite possible she wouldn't be attracted to him, and it was also too transparent a move. By all accounts, he also had a reputation for targeting far younger, attractive women.

Instead, he'd taken a slower, subtler approach.

Dafne wasn't to be taken in by flattery of her skills or that of her archers. Initially, he was flummoxed, but then, when he'd asked about her home, her eyes had softened. She'd spoken fondly and wistfully, surprised by his interest in her culture, unaware that it was by now mostly a charred ruin.

Tristan was delighted that one of his retinue other than Taran was now looked upon with respect. Frustratingly, he'd not yet deigned to invite Jared to a private audience so Jared could study him even closer, but there was still plenty of time, and it wouldn't take long.

He was tired and close to the small wine house that he often met Galain in. The girl's appetite had left him with a hunger and thirst he rarely felt, so he turned, moving off the main thoroughfare. The huge mansions changed into smaller houses and apartments, still opulent, as he headed toward where he could satiate his other needs.

Jared sighed at the thought of how proud Daleth was of him. To know the love of such a king made life worth living. For a while, his thoughts drifted to how he could better serve Daleth beyond this war and into the next.

Without being aware of the journey, he found himself opening the heavy wooden door into the small establishment.

It was a place where the wealthy could share a discreet and very expensive wine whilst business was conducted. The food was exquisite, and deals were made here that made the rich even richer and the poor even poorer. It was dark, prestigious and expensive, thereby dissuading those not of the highest wealth, influence or position.

It was busy despite the hour, with maybe twenty patrons inside. Smoke hung heavy in the air as many of the Freestates elite enjoyed smoking the various semi-poisonous plants that were traded with the Eyre. They induced a euphoric state whilst supposedly sharpening the mind.

Jared inhaled through his nose. He didn't like the effect breathing this smoke had on him. He made his way to the bar, the hood of his cloak still pulled up, and looked around.

To his surprise, he saw Galain deep in conversation with Rafeen from the barracks. It was so untoward that it gave Jared pause. A mere corporal would never frequent this kind of establishment, and yet here he was, deep in conversation with Galain. Two empty flasks of wine and a third, half-empty, indicated they'd been here some time.

Jared was intrigued.

Galain was a typical opportunist, and yet being seen socialising with someone of such low rank would seriously diminish his reputation. There must be something very interesting afoot to take this risk.

Jared quietly ordered an expensive bottle of wine and carried it over to the table in the corner where they sat deep in conversation.

Without even looking up, Galain waved his hand irritably.

'Leave us be, barkeep,' he said, looking into his goblet morosely.

Jared stood uncertainly for a moment, but then laughed good-naturedly.

'Tell me, my friend,' he asked, 'what can I do for someone so dear to me to make him smile again ... other than take the place of a mere corporal he's socialising with.'

At the sound of his voice, Galain and Rafeen's heads snapped up.

Then, as Jared pushed his hood back, Galain fell back off his stool, surprise and terror etched on his face. Galain's reaction wasn't feigned but was as genuine as any man could feel, and Jared's blood went cold.

For a moment he thought maybe his guise had slipped, but that was nonsense.

'What is it? It's I, Tolgarth, you've no need to fear me!'

'You, you, you're dead!' Galain barely managed to croak, and from the petrified look on Rafeen's face beside him, even if the corporal hadn't said the words, they were exactly what he was thinking too.

Jared sat down, reaching out, pulling a reluctant Galain back onto his stool.

'What's this nonsense? I'm alive here before you,' and he fixed Rafeen with a piercing stare.

'What's this all about, Corporal? What have you filled Galain's head with? Tell me, that's an order!'

Whether it was the tone of Jared's voice, the order he gave or simply that Rafeen had to give voice to his fears, he looked at Jared with eyes so wide that they looked as if they'd fall from his face.

'We found you, dead, a long time dead. The smell, it was so bad from your room.' Rafeen's voice started to climb so that people began to look round. 'We found you there, naked in a chest. You're not here, you can't be here, we buried you!'

Jared's heart started hammering, and thoughts flew through his head as fast as an arrow from a bow.

'Who knows this terrible lie?' he asked, trying to keep calm and vying for time.

'I told the king this evening, and most of the soldiery know. How can it be you're here before us? Are you a spirit? What evil is this?' Galain shouted, standing.

Jared felt the weight of everyone's eyes on him. The loud voice in such a quiet room, the panic it held, and now the words that were said.

Jared stood as well.

'I need to address this immediately,' he said, moving swiftly across the room to the door. Rafeen was shouting his name, demanding to know how he was still alive when he was dead.

Jared got to the door, stopped and reached up, sliding the deadbolts across, locking everyone in. He turned, shrugging off his cloak. He stood there looking around a room that was now so quiet that he could hear the small drip from a spill on the bar as the beer fell to the floor.

'Either die in your chairs like cowards or, if any of you here have weapons,' Jared said, his cold voice carrying across the room, 'you can die like men.'

He drew his long sword and dagger, and without any further pause, started thrusting, cutting, and slashing his way through the room.

Screams that sounded like music to his ears fell silent as his flashing blades delivered killing blows until only Rafeen remained standing with a sword in his hand, Galain cowering behind him.

'Come.' Jared beckoned. 'Fight for your life.'

He stood back, allowing the trembling Rafeen to step forward. The corporal lunged, but Jared contemptuously parried, and his riposte scored a long cut on Rafeen's forearm. Rafeen cried out in pain, and his sword clanged to the wooden floor.

Jared stepped back.

'Pick it up,' he instructed, savouring the moment.

Rafeen bent down, tears streaming from his wide, terror-filled eyes. He took his sword in both hands and leapt forward, swinging an overhand cut, but Jared sidestepped, and as Rafeen overbalanced, moved forward and drove his dagger into Rafeen's belly.

'Please, please, no,' Rafeen sobbed.

In response, Jared drove the blade in deeper, twisting and pulling it upwards, until the life fled from Rafeen's eyes.

The End of Dreams

As the corporal's body fell to the floor, there was only Galain left, who sat, fists clenched against his mouth, whimpering.

'D-don't kill me,' Galain stammered, his voice barely audible.

Jared's smile in response was as cold as ice.

'You will live on,' he said soothingly. 'Look into my eyes and see the truth of what I say.'

He reached out, taking Galain's forearms in an inescapable grip. Galain's wide eyes stretched even further in morbid fascination as Jared shifted before him. The final look in Galain's eyes as Jared thrust his dagger into Galain's heart almost appeared to be one of gratitude.

The killing and the shifting had taken little time, but the situation was a mess. He hadn't been ready to shift. There was so much he didn't know, and now there'd be questions, difficult ones, and people would be suspicious.

He looked around at the hellish scene. He'd been stupid and had killed Galain with a thrust to the heart, bloodying the shirt he needed to wear. Nonetheless, he stripped and quickly exchanged clothes. Fortunately, Galain was close to Tolgarth's build that their clothing fitted each other well enough.

He drew his dagger to disfigure Galain's face, but paused. Instead, he dragged the body to the fireplace and pushed it into the roaring flames. The stench was horrific as the hair caught fire, and the skin started to melt. Above the fireplace was a mirror, and he looked in repulsion at Galain's face reflected back at him. He'd have to get used to it.

Suddenly, there was a loud hammering at the front door.

'Open up in the name of the king,' voices shouted urgently.

It seemed the screams had drawn attention. There was no back door in this establishment, and Jared wondered whether he should fight his way out, but that would mean the end of his mission and Daleth would be so angry.

The crashing intensified, and the door shuddered. They were using something to break it down, and Jared frantically looked around.

He took his discarded sword, and gritting his teeth, cut his chest deeply above his heart, then both arms for good measure, before tossing the sword and dagger by Galain's burning corpse.

The door was almost off its hinges as he curled himself into a ball behind an upended stool in the corner and closed his eyes, trying to still and calm himself, even as blood drenched his trousers. He'd cut himself deeply, perhaps too deeply, but it needed to be realistic.

The door crashed open, and he heard the cries of shock and alarm as the soldiers took in the scene.

'Who the hell do we send for?' a man asked. 'The captain is dead.'

'Send word to the palace. Let them sort it out,' another replied. 'Keep your wits about you, men. Whoever made this mischief might be alive amongst this lot.'

Jared was at the back, and the footfalls came ever slowly closer, punctuated by confirmation of the death of everyone they checked.

Jared felt his shoulder being tugged, and he screamed so loudly that the soldiers jumped back in shock and surprise. He kept on screaming, over and over.

A sergeant stood over him, shaking his shoulders.

'You're safe. Relax man, you're safe.'

But Jared continued to scream, forcing his eyes wide in panic, his fingernails digging into the sergeant's forearms.

'It's Galain, the king's advisor,' another said.

'Dammit, we'll not be able to do anything for him if he doesn't calm down,' the sergeant muttered. 'Sorry, sir,' he said, raising his fist, and the next moment Jared felt the world spin, and everything went black.

***

Chapter XVII

Taran awoke long before sunrise with Maya warm against him, his arms still around her where they'd remained the whole night.

Despite the thin layer of fresh snow blanketing them, they were warm beneath the fleeced leather, and he was loathe to move. He lay there for a while, looking at Maya as he propped himself on one arm. It mattered not the lines around her mouth and eyes, nor the white hair which blended with the snow on the ground. She remained the most beautiful woman he'd ever thought to lay eyes on, let alone lie with.

Slowly, ever so slowly, he tried to wriggle from the confines of the bedroll so as not to wake her, but failed, and her sleepy eyes flickered open.

'Hey,' she murmured, 'don't leave just yet.'

For a moment Taran almost gave up and wriggled back, but Rakan needed rest despite his promise to give them the full night, and even a few hours of proper sleep would do him good.

He knelt, looking into Maya's sleepy eyes, and gently ran his fingers through her hair.

'Go back to sleep for a while, my princess,' he whispered, lips brushing hers ever so softly. In response, Maya sighed, closing her eyes and moments later was asleep again.

Taran smiled. He loved his ability to make her relax, although he was surprised at how quickly he'd done so.

He was about to stand when something caught his eye against the snow, and he bent down, gently brushing the powder to one side, to discover bright green spring grass pushing through.

He looked around, noticing it everywhere, a resurgence of growth in the middle of winter. His heart leapt with joy, for it could only mean one thing.

Maya's gift had returned.

He was tempted to wake her, to share his excitement, but held himself back, knowing her rest was more important. Despite his short sleep, he felt rejuvenated and whole again after being a shadow of himself for so long.

The night air was still, and he walked slowly, the *crump crump* of his soft step loud in the empty quiet of pre-dawn. Snow fell gently in large, wet flakes and visibility was poor. Had he been in the Rangers' boots, he'd have chosen this night to approach the camp, but then again, they might well have walked right past without seeing it, had they been but ten strides away.

Barely visible bootprints guided him to Rakan, who was all but covered in snow, gentle plumes of vapour escaping into the cold night air.

Rakan turned, and his eyes were bright as he smiled at Taran.

'There's plenty of time before dawn. Why not go back and enjoy it?'

Taran was touched by the genuine love and kindness that shone from his father's eyes.

'I'd rather you get some rest,' he replied quietly. 'We've a long day ahead, and we need you strong too, and if I return and wake Maya, we'll both be too tired to run today.'

'In which case,' Rakan patted the snow next to him, 'keep watch beside me while I sleep.'

Rakan closed his eyes and was snoring softly within a few breaths. Years of soldiering had given him the ability to snatch sleep in an instant.

Taran envied him a little. The chill was slowly eating away at the warmth he felt, as even colder air fell from the mountains to the south, washing across the plain. He wondered if they could completely evade the Rangers if the snow got heavier. Sadly, the tracks they'd leave, and the sheer number involved in the hunt meant even if it delayed their death, they couldn't avoid it.

He sat there, eyes looking into the whiteness, wracking his brain to come up with a plan that would give them a chance at staying alive, and not just for an extra day or two. Frustratingly, it didn't matter which way his thoughts turned, nothing useful came to mind, and he cast aside idea after idea as nothing more than desperate dreams.

To the north and east, the groups of Rangers shadowed them, ensuring they headed southwest along the base of the mountain range. Maya was undoubtedly correct. Soon they'd run head-on into a trap from which they'd never escape as they came face to face with the Rangers coming from the southwest.

He shook his head, looking down at his hands. He might be able to kill one or two, maybe more before he died, but it wouldn't be enough, and he couldn't stand the thought of failing Maya. Even giving his life wouldn't save her from the same fate.

He stared up at the sky, wondering to which god he should send a prayer, for surely that was the only thing left to try. Then his frown eased, replaced by a smile.

It was the one direction he hadn't thought of and therein lay their only hope, however small. The sun had still yet to rise, but they should get an early start before visibility improved and they were seen.

He shook Rakan's shoulder.

'We need to wake Maya and get an early start,' Taran offered as Rakan's eyes snapped open.

Rakan searched Taran's face.

'Do I detect some hope in those eyes of yours?' he asked, pushing himself to his feet and shaking the snow from his shoulders. 'Because if that's the case, I'm ready to move out whenever you are.'

They hurried back to the camp, only to see Maya moving around even before they reached it.

'She's already up and ready,' Taran said, turning to Rakan. 'Now let me share my idea with you both.'

Maya's hands were behind her back, and she looked like a small girl who'd been caught stealing a cake. Her head was down, and she giggled in embarrassment. Such was the mischievous look about her that Taran laughed back in surprise.

'What's going on?' he asked, looking down to see she'd laid out some rations for them to eat. 'Have you done something to the food?'

Maya shook her head.

'Sit down and eat,' she bade them both, hands still hidden.

Taran and Rakan settled down, doing as they were told.

'It seems we're all in a good mood this morning,' Rakan observed. 'I should give you two more room every night if this is the outcome.'

With a snort, he leaned forward to grab some food.

'Here,' Maya said, pulling two small bunches of spring flowers from behind her back, and pressed them into the hands of Taran and Rakan. 'My gift is back,' she announced joyously, clapping and dancing around.

Rakan's eyes widened in surprise as he held the small offering delicately in his calloused hands, appearing somewhat embarrassed.

Then she stopped, looking at Taran.

'You brought my gift back to life,' she said, stepping forward and kneeling to wrap her arms around him. 'Now, try. See if I've brought yours back too.'

Taran paused for a moment, but the thought that came to mind seemed to do so of its own volition. Whatever the outcome of his plan in the days to come didn't matter at this moment ... he needed to know.

'Will you marry me?' he thought, projecting his question toward Maya.

She leapt up, hands held to her face, tears filling her eyes, and then knelt again to hold Taran close and kissed him furiously.

'I'll take that as a yes,' Taran gasped breathlessly, as Maya paused, nodding emphatically. 'I want you to know,' he projected, looking into her eyes as he shared his thoughts, 'that I've never been so sure about anything in my whole life. I want it to be you, and always you beside me, as my wife.'

This time Maya's kiss was tender before she whispered softly in his ear.

'I want it to be you, and always you beside me, as my husband.'

'His gift works?' Rakan asked, a little uncomfortable. 'I just want to make sure.'

Maya burst out laughing.

'Yes, Rakan. Yes to that and much more,' then shared the news of Taran's proposal.

Rakan's arms enfolded them both. He didn't say anything, but his eyes were moist when he released them.

'However much I want to savour this moment, we need to leave now,' Taran advised, stuffing food into his pocket, 'and this time we choose a different path.'

As Rakan and Maya turned to him, he tilted his head.

'We go *up*. We have to try and climb the mountains to the south. Instead of going around them to reach the grasslands, we'll go over. It won't be what the Rangers expect, and when they find out, they'll have to come up after us. It might be we'll die up there to the cold, but then we might not, and that's better odds than ending up in a trap.'

Maya and Rakan exchanged hopeful glances as Taran continued.

'I'm not sure what you think, but I'm sure their numbers won't matter as much up there, nor their skills, if we can keep them behind us. If the mountain range here isn't too deep and we survive, we'll also avoid those who were coming to meet us from the southwest.'

Rakan threw Taran's pack at him and then donned his own as Maya hastily readied herself.

Taran and Rakan both looked down at the flowers they held.

'I'll get upset if you throw them away,' Maya chided, and when they looked at each other for help, she couldn't help but laugh. 'Only joking,' she added to their relief, then started to run.

'After you,' Rakan said, bowing to Taran. 'I know you fell in love running behind her.'

Taran nodded in agreement and broke into a jog. She certainly had a behind to fall in love with, he thought.

Rakan took a last look around the campsite, reluctantly dropped the flowers, and followed after.

***

'This is unlike the beginning of any winter I've ever experienced before,' Shinsen observed, his teeth chattering as he spoke to Chochen and Nadlen.

He looked around at the snow that reached halfway up the horses' forelegs and was only getting deeper by the hour.

'Fortunately, with all this fresh snow,' he continued, 'there's a chance it's covered our tracks from the shrine, but we shouldn't take any chances. The enemy infantry will have a hard task of pushing through these drifts, and their light horse won't fare much better either. So, as long as we move every second day, we're unlikely to be caught even if they did find signs of our departure,' he added, trying to spark a conversation to lighten the mood.

Chochen and Nadlen dipped their heads in agreement. The vapour from Chochen's nose had frosted his moustache, and he kept breaking the ice from it with his gloved hands.

Behind them, stretched out into the distance, were men, women, children, and vast herds of horse and cattle, all moving northward, away from the shrine. An exodus which had seen the discipline and obedience of the clan members stretched to the limit. Countless tears had been shed with no fear of shame when they'd left over a week ago, with many a long glance behind.

It hadn't been an easy decision to leave their holy sanctuary, where provisions to last the winter had been stockpiled throughout the year. They'd swiftly fashioned horse-drawn sledges to salvage as much as they could, but, despite the animals' strength, progress was slow.

Shinsen felt sure they had sufficient supplies to last the winter, and beyond. However, with such severe cold weather, he was now worried that exposure might bring them down. That morning, he'd given the order for everyone to remove and stow their plate armour. It was a decision any prudent commander would make in this freezing weather. Nonetheless, it had only added to the grim sense of defeat as everyone recognised they'd not be seeking a fight and were truly running.

Morale was now unsurprisingly low.

'So we spend the whole winter, moving camp every other day, hunting and fishing the frozen land and streams and then what? In spring we come full circle, back to the shrine to see if it stands and to find the enemy still in our lands?' Nadlen asked.

Shinsen shrugged.

'I fear that's the only course left open to us unless we make a more permanent winter camp or return to the shrine earlier. Yet both of those choices increase the risk of us facing a battle we cannot win.'

Chochen spat into the snow.

'You speak true words, but they still make me sick to the stomach and our people as well.'

The End of Dreams

'This is no way to live,' Nadlen complained. 'Winter is a time for drinking, eating till full, praying, making children, and telling tall tales. Now, all we have are half-rations and hardship every day.'

'Yet are we not of the Horselords, my brothers?' Shinsen spoke with a hint of anger in his voice. 'When have we ever baulked at hardship? At least we can still look forward to such things of luxury, unlike our fallen brothers, who lay cold and unburied to be torn apart by the wolves.'

Chochen and Nadlen looked abashed, but Shinsen hadn't finished.

'Let's also not forget that whoever this enemy is, they'll be suffering as we are in this weather. We can pray that they'll return to their homelands for the winter and if the Moon Goddess smiles upon us, they'll not return. They're not an army of occupation, for we've no cities to occupy. Then, in time, we can gather our strength and exact justice on our terms, and on their lands, instead of ours.'

Nadlen clenched his fist.

'Yes! Now that's what we need to tell our people. What better revenge than invading their lands, killing their people as they have ours? This will give our knights something to dream about.'

'Yet we've never gone beyond our borders,' Shinsen cautioned. 'Only in centuries past did our ancestors war across the lands that are now called the Freestates. How will we ever find them? We've no maps of the world beyond, nor memory.'

The three of them were quiet then, trying to solve the riddle.

With an exasperated sigh, Nadlen spoke.

'Shinsen, your words of caution speak the truth of the matter, but we needn't worry. We need to put our faith in the Moon Goddess to show us the way. You may not have faith, Shinsen, but I do. She'll help us find from whence they came, and then we can burn their homes to the ground!'

Shinsen nodded.

'I'm sure the Moon Goddess will help us this time.'

Chochen's eyes narrowed.

'Don't mock our religion,' he scolded. 'Just because you don't believe like the rest of us, doesn't mean you should mock my words.'

Shinsen raised his hands in defence.

'Trust me, I'm more a believer now than ever before. When a man feels his death is close, then who do we turn to? Our wives, our children, but ultimately our goddess.'

With that, he looked around.

'We'll head north until we meet the mountains, then we turn west. For now, let's make camp and give our knights the thoughts of revenge to fire their blood and warm their hearts.'

He turned to Chochen.

'You said a moment ago about the drinking, eating till full, praying, making children, and telling tall tales. Well, let's ensure that tonight at least, we do every one of those.'

'Some of them more than once,' Chochen laughed, winking.

They laughed out loud together, but it was hollow, for inside, there was still little but sorrow.

***

'I have my sincere doubts that any gods would want to live on top of a mountain if it gets so cold up here,' Rakan ventured, shouting to be heard above the wind. However, his voice was whipped away, and he shook his head, kept it down, and followed Taran and Maya upward, ever upward.

The wind had blown away the clouds, and the sky was the brightest azure blue. There was no warmth to the unopposed sun, it simply reflected from the snow so that Rakan had to keep his eyes half-closed the whole time.

He looked behind, and there they still were, dozens of figures, clambering up the mountain below them, relentless. He couldn't help but smile gleefully as he kicked at some loose rocks, sending them tumbling down the mountainside.

They'd done this in earnest earlier in the day, when their pursuers had gotten closer. The Rangers had made the mistake of staying bunched together, following directly below them on the same path.

It hadn't even been something they'd thought of initially.

Maya, who'd led the group, advised of loose rocks as she climbed, not wanting Taran to dislodge them onto Rakan, who as ever was the rearguard.

They'd got to an area that was fairly clear of snow, the wind having whipped it away, and there was lots of loose scree with some fairly large rocks precariously settled upon it. As they'd stood looking at which way to go around, Rakan had pointed back down the mountain at their pursuers getting closer and then they'd all instinctively started kicking away at the scree.

It hadn't taken much effort, and then moments later it starting sliding of its own. They'd jumped to the side onto solid rock as thousands of pieces disappeared over the edge. Even above the roar, they were sure they could hear cries from below. When the dust had settled, and they looked down, it was to see bodies strewn about and the hunters pulling back to create more distance.

So now, every chance he had without slowing his climb, Rakan would send a rock or two flying down, reminding the Rangers that life was a fragile thing on the mountain, whether hunter or hunted.

His arms ached from overexertion, and he kept trying to follow Maya's advice. She was the lightest, and despite being relatively strong, was the weakest amongst them. Yet it was him and Taran who held her back.

Use your legs more, she kept exhorting them, *arms for balance and stability, legs for power.* Rakan shook his head in silent admiration at the range of skills she possessed as she found them ways that were easier to follow.

Sometimes the gradient relaxed enough so they could walk, other times, and these were what Rakan hated, they'd face an almost vertical climb. The only options were to backtrack or go up, and with the Rangers below them, the last thing they wanted to do was go back. If they found it hard, so would the Rangers with the added danger of rocks coming from above.

The day passed slowly, and as they climbed, it got colder and colder, yet at least they were alive. Their morale was high too, for it felt as if instead of running away, they were, in fact, leading a race that could see them escape the trap as long as they kept moving at speed.

The wind, which had swept away the clouds earlier in the day, now drove others over them, the fleeting shadows cast by the sun getting longer and longer as they climbed on.

They came to a very steep rock face, and Rakan barely made it to the top despite trying to use his legs and was thankful when Maya and Taran hauled him up, indicating a deep crevice for their camp, sheltered from the wind and the snow.

'This is the best place I've seen on our ascent so far,' Maya pointed out, 'and it's just about big enough for the three of us. I fear our friends below won't quite have our comforts, and with this rock face below us, I think we're safe enough should they try to come upon us in the night.'

Taran peered inside.

'Not quite as good as a warm tent, but it'll do. Come, Rakan. Let's get some rocks ready just in case we need to dissuade any night-time visitors.'

Together, they began gathering anything larger than a fist and placed them near the edge.

The wind howled, and Maya moved smaller scree to block up some openings at the back of their shelter before unpacking their bedrolls. To make things worse, huge flakes of snow started to fall, whirling around as if stirred by some mad god's hand.

'Come in,' Maya shouted.

Rakan shook his head.

'One of us needs to keep watch,' he called back, but again, she beckoned him in.

'I don't care how skilled those Rangers are,' she retorted. 'If they don't find shelter of some kind, they'll be dead from exposure. That last climb was tough, and in this wind and visibility, there's no way I'd be able to do it, and I doubt they'll be able to either. We're safe for now. If the wind drops, then yes, we take it in turns to watch, but in the meantime, let's try to keep warm and rest!'

Maya pulled Rakan inside the small opening and started moving some rocks to block it, before putting their packs on top, for the most part, sealing the entrance off.

It was such a relief to be out of the wind that Rakan soon stopped grumbling and Taran handed out some food.

Now Rakan did grumble.

'I'm famished,' he said, looking at the meagre portion, but he knew the reason why and didn't say more. How long they'd be on this mountain was anyone's idea, but then he smiled. 'If your gift of healing the land has returned, maybe that spirit travelling thing you do is back as well. You could see how far we have to climb and whether we've got a chance to cross, and if so, maybe scout south to see where the clans are.'

Maya smiled and nodded in agreement.

'I've thought about this the whole climb. I can only try. But, first I need to sleep.'

She leaned close to Taran, whispering, and he nodded as she invited him to share her bedroll. She pushed the other two at Rakan.

'We'll keep each other warm,' she smiled, 'which means you get two. If we get out of this mess, we're going to find someone to keep you warm, that's a promise!'

'I can find someone quite easily, thank you,' Rakan mumbled, with a roll of his eyes.

'Maya's talking about someone who doesn't charge you for the privilege,' Taran laughed, and yelped in pain as Maya prodded him in the ribs.

'Hmmm,' Rakan mused. 'I'd never considered that would be a possibility. Gives me one more reason to survive. I rather liked that Dafne ... you know the Eyre leader. She seemed robust enough.'

Maya's laughter peeled out, tears running down her face.

'Robust? Rakan, we need to talk about what makes a woman a good partner, not to mention educate you on terms of endearment. Whilst robust might suffice for armour or a shield, might I advise you never to use that term around anyone you consider worthy of your affection.'

'Well,' Rakan chuckled, 'it seems I'm learning new things every day. Use my legs more than my arms when climbing, don't tell a woman she's robust. Next, you'll be telling me how to ride my mount!'

The three of them burst out laughing at his ribald joke before lapsing into a comfortable silence.

It should have been pitch dark as Taran held Maya in his arms. Her head was on his chest as he lay, gazing at patterns in the rock above him, for with the return of Maya's gift, she gave off a subtle glow. It gave their otherwise grim camp a somewhat warm feel.

His fingers gently pushed into her scalp, massaging, and he felt her relax, twitching slightly as sleep finally took her, and he smiled, his heart content.

He lay awake for a while, thinking back over the recent past, where every night he went to sleep with dreams full of killing, torture, and revenge. He thought of Tristan and realised that he hated him no longer. He pitied him for his ideals, his way of life, his greed, but knew killing him was not the right thing to do. If somehow they ever managed to return to Freeguard, he'd work to resolve things without bloodshed.

Daleth, well, there could be no forgiveness there.

Even now, he tried to have them killed, to stop them from realising their mission. It was a mission he obviously knew about, and if he knew about it, had he already dealt with the Horselords?

The thought was chilling. Were they putting themselves through all of this for nothing?

Daleth, he thought, if one day I have the chance, I'll have my revenge. I will kill you. With that final image in his mind, he fell asleep too.

Rakan opened one eye, checking the others' breathing, then quietly got out of his bedroll. Carefully, he moved the packs aside and stepped out into the freezing wind, keeping one of the rolls wrapped close around him.

It was cold out here, but he was pretty sure the cold of the grave was even worse. He wouldn't put it past those fanatical Rangers to attempt an attack this night, so he settled himself down on the edge of the fall and stared down into the darkness.

***

Jared sat in Galain's bed, looking around the room, imprinting everything in his mind. He studied even the smallest item, trying to better understand the man he'd become.

He noted the exquisitely carved pieces of woodwork adorning the room and the various tools that showed Galain had a rare skill he'd never be able to emulate, and had been unaware of. There was so much he needed to find out, and quickly.

As he allowed himself to be looked at by a healer who fussed over his injuries, Jared made every attempt to appear nauseated, confused, and weak.

He'd been nowhere near ready to shift to Galain's form. True, he'd got to know him relatively well, but he hadn't even found out the detail of his daily duties, important responsibilities, or dark secrets.

The list of things that he didn't know was long, and he'd expected to spend at least another few weeks, maybe even a month, before making the change.

He'd been sloppy, and that was nigh on unforgivable. Tolgarth's dead body had indeed started to smell, yet he'd bathed it in spirits, thinking that would help delay the decomposition. Stupidly, that had helped so much that people had identified it, not that he could have explained away a corpse is his chambers, whatever the identity.

Anyway, what was done was done, and he now had to try and play for time. He'd got himself out of his immediate predicament and shifted to his intended target, albeit earlier than planned. Now he would use the trauma of this horrible event to cover his loss of memory, as was fairly commonplace when such a thing was witnessed by a fragile mind. Not that it had been horrific in Jared's view. It had proved very entertaining.

He was thinking this all through when the door opened, and Tristan came in with Ostrom, Dafne, Ultric, and a young man he didn't recognise in tow.

He'd put off seeing anyone for a few days, but it was a fine line he was treading. Prove useless for too long and he'd be discarded, for there was no place for incompetents in any court. If this happened, he'd be unable to find a way back to where he now was, the closest confidant to the king. He just had to hold up the ruse for long enough to smooth over any wrinkles in his facade.

Tristan's face was a strange mixture of almost genuine concern and frustration. As advisor to the king, Galain would have been very close and been entrusted with knowledge of intimate secrets and plans, so Tristan wanted him to recover, even if for that reason alone. Tristan didn't care for Galain, just what he knew and how good he was at his job.

Ostrom and Dafne's concern seemed a little more genuine, whilst Ultric stared off vacantly with those blind eyes of his. The young man's face was etched with genuine pain and red around the eyes.

Jared wracked his mind for whom he might be ... possibly a nephew or servant. Whoever he was, he could be ignored whilst others of such rank stood before him.

'My king,' Jared said, bowing his head. 'Please forgive my lapse. Be assured I'll be fit within a day or two at most. Strangely, I've been ill-affected by what happened, and there's such darkness in my mind where I know so many things should be.'

Ultric's usually impassive face turned at the sound of his voice, and it was as if those blank eyes stared right through him.

Tristan looked relieved but worried at the same time. 'We do need you back, Galain, me more than most, but ...'

'Tolgarth?' Ultric said, his face covered in confusion. 'Isn't Tolgarth dead? Aren't we here to visit Galain?'

Tristan, annoyed at being interrupted, glared over his shoulder.

Ostrom laid his hand on Ultric's arm, quietening him.

'Galain, what happened the other night?' Tristan asked, cutting to the point.

'I'm sure that's Tolgarth,' spoke up Ultric, his head cocked to one side. 'What's going on?'

'You're losing your mind,' Tristan snapped angrily. 'Ostrom, will you have your man keep quiet, or perhaps have his tongue removed to match his eyes!'

'I apologise, King Tristan,' Ostrom said and turned to Ultric, speaking softly.

Ultric shuffled slowly out of the room to stand just outside.

Jared's heart had almost stopped in his chest. How, by the gods, could a blind man stumble on to who he'd been with such random luck? He shook his head and refocussed because Tristan's gaze was back upon him.

'My king. There's not much to say beyond what you likely already know. I was drinking with Rafeen, a young corporal of no consequence who'd found Tolgarth's body. The wine house was dark and full, and as we sat drinking, a hooded man came in. We paid him no attention until he turned and bolted the door. And then ...' Jared started to sob slightly for emphasis, '... he just drew his sword and dagger and started cutting everyone down. He came for me, and I thought I was dead, but young

Rafeen, he managed to jump in between us and stab him before he himself was cut down.'

Jared drew a deep breath, as if composing himself.

'I saw the man stumble away and fall into the fire before I passed out. I know it's so very little considering what happened, but I've never seen the man before.'

Tristan reached out, patting Jared's shoulder awkwardly.

'I don't know what I hoped to hear, but indeed it seems either it was a random act of violence or perhaps even someone from within Freeguard who wanted to weaken me by killing you.'

Ostrom coughed, and Tristan moved aside.

'Galain, I'm sorry for what you've endured.' Ostrom said sympathetically. 'But a nobleman's daughter has come forward, distraught, saying she spent that evening with Tolgarth and he was also seen leaving her quarters. Then there's a noble who claims he saw Tolgarth just moments from the wine house before the massacre took place. All of this was hours after his body was found, a body which I've seen and looks to have been dead for weeks.'

Ostrom leaned in close.

'The man who came in wasn't Tolgarth or looked like him, by any chance?'

Jared quailed. He should have foreseen this and kept the story closer to the truth from the beginning, but how could he have known the stupid girl would have said something or the noble.

He kept his face and voice weak, with just a little quaver to hint at confusion.

'I don't believe so, my lord. Yet his hood was up, and he moved so fast. I don't think it was him, but I can't be sure.'

Ostrom went to ask more, but Tristan raised his hand.

'Leave the man be. He's been through enough. Thankfully, the gods favoured him, for he's still alive whereas all the others are dead. Let's just be thankful when such gifts from the gods fall upon us.

'I want you back at tomorrow evening's meeting, Galain,' Tristan commanded, turning away. 'We have much to discuss!'

Tristan walked from the room. Ostrom nodded to Jared as he turned away and Dafne bid him goodnight, leaving the young man behind.

Jared could see the love in the man's eyes, born of genuine concern.

There was an awkward silence during which the young man walked over and sat on the bed.

'How are you feeling? Is there anything I can do for you?' he asked, and as he said this, his hand moved under the sheets, and he leaned forward to kiss Jared on the mouth.

Jared froze for a moment, then thrust the young man away with a strength he hadn't intended to show.

'Touch me like that again, and I'll kill you,' he rasped, before he could stop himself.

The man's face crumpled in shock before tears began streaming down his face.

'Oh, don't think I don't know who you are! You're a liar. You were bedding Tolgarth even as you bedded me! Well, I was a fool to care for you!' He turned and strode from the room, shoulders shaking.

Jared sat there in shock.

Galain had been rather too good at keeping some secrets and Jared had been so unprepared for that one, he'd let his true self show for a moment.

He shook his head. He'd have to make amends somehow, but only so far. He could take any form, but he wouldn't be able to fake that kind of attraction, even though he knew several Rangers who enjoyed the company of other men intimately.

Movement by the open door caught his eye as he caught sight of Ultric turning away.

Damn that man, there was something uncanny about him, and he couldn't have someone casting any kind of doubt in people's minds when he was in such a precarious position.

He'd just have to stay calm, work hard, be better than he'd been before. He'd get closer to Tristan, study him, every move, every laugh, every mannerism. Each day would bring him closer to being able to shift and take Tristan's mantle, the ultimate goal so he could overthrow this pathetic city from the inside.

He'd make a report to Daleth tonight, missing out some of the more delicate details as to why he made such an early shift. Make it seem the timing had been too perfect to pass by, for he didn't want to upset his father, the god he worshipped.

He lay there pretending to sleep as the comely healer came in to check his dressings. He'd been so close to trying to seduce her, and it seemed the gods had somehow smiled on him by delaying his move. It would have appeared to those around him very out of character indeed.

He'd tread carefully. Despite being the master of his craft, from hereon he'd be under constant scrutiny, from the least likely of them all, a blind man. But he'd be flawless, his acting so sublime that none would have cause for doubt, none at all.

Jared closed his eyes, all doubts disappearing as he imagined the praise Daleth would heap upon him.

***

Chapter XVIII

Maya awoke to find Taran's arms still tightly around her, and despite the precariousness of their situation, she'd never felt safer than in that moment, his youthful strength keeping her close.

Yet the positive feeling evaporated as quickly as her feeling of sleepiness when she remembered her spirit journey.

'Wake up,' she said, planting a soft kiss on Taran's lips and then gave in to the moment when he pulled her even closer to turn it into a longer one.

Maya wriggled free to a look of mock hurt on Taran's face and looked around to discover Rakan absent.

'Rakan seems to have decided to take watch after all,' she pointed out. 'We need to get moving as soon as we can. Get some food ready whilst I get him.'

She crawled free of the bedroll, and immediately the cold started to permeate her clothing. Moving the backpacks aside, she stepped out carefully onto the ledge. In some regards, the ferocious wind had helped keep the mountain free of any deep snow, or they'd be in even more serious trouble than they already were.

'Rakan,' she said, as she approached him.

He turned, smiling, then stiffly got to his feet.

'You should have taken some rest,' she scolded.

Rakan scratched his head.

'It's a long sleep when you're dead, and I don't want to try that one just yet. I do actually get some rest when I watch. Call it a gift that I have if you will,' he said, and followed Maya as she turned back to their shelter.

The End of Dreams

'I was able to spirit travel last night,' Maya began, 'and whilst I have news, most of it isn't good. Our small measure of luck is that we're at a narrow point on the range. That said, we still have maybe two more weeks before we start our descent into the grasslands beyond, but I fear that our supplies will run out days before then.'

'As we suspected, more Rangers were coming from the southwest to encircle us, and they've now turned back. I believe they'll try and get around the mountains before we get over, and they might well do so.'

'Then we'll kill them, one group at a time,' Rakan stated hopefully.

'There were over a hundred,' Maya said quietly. 'I think every one of Daleth's finest, without exception, is here to finish this story on their terms.'

Rakan's face turned pale.

'Then we stay on the mountain, journey back east along the ridge, kill them as they come up.'

Taran shook his head.

'As Maya pointed out, we've no real supplies to last. With that many, some would circle, some move ahead. They'd take their time, and we'd die of exposure, hunger, cold, or their blades. You know the truth of this.'

'Our only chance is to move far faster than we have been,' Maya continued, 'get further ahead of them. But even if we do, our main mission is over, for there's more bad news. As I scouted beyond the mountains, I was drawn by scavenging animals to a battlefield with tens of thousands of dead horses and men. Then, further south, Daleth has a vast army encamped, unopposed, around the Horselords' shrine. I didn't come across any survivors. I could have searched longer, but I was afraid of the drain it would put on my body.'

Rakan shook his head in disbelief.

'Then we need to focus on staying alive. We get over fast and lose the Rangers in the winter snow, then just forget about this war and make our escape into new lands. They'll give up chasing us, eventually.'

'They'll not give up,' Maya said sadly. 'You know they'll not give up. If we make our escape, we have to try and make it back to Freeguard.'

Rakan spat out onto the ledge.

'A curse on everyone there, they can all rot. We need to look after ourselves!'

Maya put her hand on Rakan's arm.

'That's the old Rakan speaking. Don't forget there are thousands of good people, people like me and Taran, who need us, people like you, who need you too.'

'Then what are we waiting for?' Rakan snapped, looking outside. 'Lead the way. I'm getting too warm in here.'

They ate quickly, packed up their bedrolls, and then Maya led the way in the dim, early light. She pushed the pace hard, and none of them had any breath to say anything. Often she came back to help Rakan, and he'd grumble but be grateful, nonetheless.

When they stopped for a brief respite, Rakan turned to Taran.

'You know,' he whispered, 'she'd definitely make it if she went ahead on her own. I don't think they'd catch her.'

Taran nodded.

'I've been thinking the same thing.'

He beckoned to Maya.

'What is it,' she asked, hair blowing in the wind like a snowy cloud around her face.

'We've decided that you should go ahead at your own pace. We're slowing you down. This is about survival, and the two of us are lessening your chances and ...' Taran stopped.

The look on Maya's face was so hard, so stern, that it took his words away, and Rakan looked sheepishly at his boots as Maya raised her finger, prodding it hard into Taran's chest.

'Is it the case that men with muscles have no brains? You think by sacrificing yourself you'll save me? Doesn't that sound strangely familiar? I think I tried that once and how did that work out for us? No. We live together, or we die together. In this world and the next, I'll always choose to be by your side. Never forget it!'

'As you wish,' Taran whispered.

'Now, how about you pick up the pace instead, you donkey,' Maya scolded, smacking Rakan, and pushed him toward the slope, then smacked him harder again. 'I said faster!'

Under such harsh judgement, he picked up his pace.

'Do I need to give you the same?' she asked, looking at Taran, then giggled, and shook her hand in pain. 'Damn, his backside is harder than stone, a bit like your head.'

The End of Dreams

The wind picked up, threatening to pull them from the mountainside, but Maya's eye for terrain picked a route which was sheltered by huge boulders jutting from the mountain like spines along the back of a lizard.

It was exhausting, but they pushed themselves hard throughout the morning, with Maya climbing ahead of Rakan and Taran, determined to maintain a swift pace. As the sun approached midday, Maya enjoyed a brief respite on a shallow ledge covered in dead bracken that led, like a path, around the side of the mountain. As Taran pulled himself up, groaning, Maya flashed him a smile and gingerly edged around to investigate.

A huge gust of wind blew, and Maya flattened herself again the sheer rock behind her as it tried to pluck her free. She pushed her weight backwards onto her heels, waiting for the wind to pass, when suddenly the ledge gave way.

She screamed as she fell, twisting as she became airborne, clawing at the mountainside, trying to find something to grasp onto. Taran dived toward her, arms outstretched, and he slid to the edge of the ledge. Hanging half off, he grabbed her outstretched hand at the last possible moment, and she swung to hit the rock face.

Taran groaned with the effort, his other hand grasping some of the brackens. He was too precariously balanced. If he tried to pull her up, they'd break. Rakan was too far behind and yet to make the ledge, and Taran knew it would be too late by the time he did. The bracken's roots that had weakened the ledge were pulling free even as he held on.

'Look at me,' he shouted at Maya above the wind. 'Use your gift, fast, it's the only chance we have.'

Maya, her face white with fear, reached out, touching the rock face with her free hand, trusting in Taran's strength to hold on to her.

Her gift responded immediately, and she shone like a star, lighting up the mountainside, yet this wasn't what Taran was hoping for, but what happened next was. The mountain itself didn't respond, but every bit of old lichen or bracken did, for suddenly within his hand, the bracken firmed and swelled. Its roots pushed into the hard rock, seeking out cracks, working their way in, and becoming strong once more.

As soon as Taran felt this, he heaved, pulling Maya up with one arm, his muscles bunching as she helped, pushing with her feet, finding purchase before climbing past him. They moved away from the edge and held each other close, waiting for the trembling to subside, both of their hearts beating fast.

Rakan finally heaved himself onto the ledge.

'So that's what you two have been up to,' he huffed. 'How about helping an old man climb if you have so much free time on your hands.'

Maya just looked at Taran, raising an eyebrow, and he shook his head as they resumed climbing. This time Maya stayed close, not just because of Rakan's comment, but because her confidence had been shaken at how close death had been to claiming them.

Throughout the day, the black, ant-like figures of the Rangers below followed, relentless in their pursuit. Despite Maya's fast pace, they had hardly increased the distance between themselves and the Rangers, who never had to backtrack or pause to plan a route, simply following the trail Maya had set.

After a relentless afternoon of climbing with no further mishaps, shadows started to lengthen, and Taran called for Maya to stop.

'Don't stop for me,' puffed Rakan as he caught up. 'I've still got some energy left, and this doesn't look like a good place to camp. There's no shelter here, and the damned wind is picking up again!'

Taran shook his head.

'It's getting too dark. If one of us slips and is injured, that's the end,' he said, looking at Maya pointedly.

'No, Rakan's right.' Maya acknowledged, looking at where they stood. 'If the wind keeps up, and the temperature drops, we'll die of exposure. We need to push on. I'll light the way, just stay close.'

Maya resumed her climb and called upon her gift, and the aura that emanated from her was enough to allow them to continue.

She climbed faster and faster, determined to find a suitable shelter for the night, Taran and Rakan struggling desperately to keep up. Yet the spirit travel of the night before and the rigours of the day began to take their toll.

As they reached a shallow cave in the mountainside, Maya turned to Taran.

'This will have to do. Let me just sit down a moment,' and then as she leaned back against the cave wall, her eyes fluttered and then she was asleep in an instant.

'Give her a hug,' Rakan said good-naturedly.

Taran laughed.

'She's asleep, and I can wait. Let's set up camp first.'

'What does she do when she's happy, lad?' Rakan prompted.

Taran thought for a moment, then smiled.

'She shines,' he said, and took Maya in his arms, stroked her hair, then gently massaged her neck as she unconsciously curled into him.

Sure enough, she began to glow softly, lighting their cave as Rakan hastily set up camp, doing his best to use the packs to create a windbreak. It wasn't as good as the night before and together they got Maya into her bedroll before Taran wriggled in beside her with Rakan taking the other two bedrolls for himself.

Rakan yawned before turning tired eyes toward Taran.

'Having pushed as long as we did, I think we've got a good lead on them. I feel safe sleeping tonight.' He closed his eyes and was snoring within moments.

Taran was so exhausted that the noise didn't bother him at all, and he followed suit, Maya warm against him.

***

The palace gardens were blanketed in deep snow, the paths treacherously icy in places. The vibrant colours and heady smells had faded away, although the scene was no less beautiful.

Ultric shuffled carefully over the slippery ground, the sounds of the garden as different to his ears as the view was to Ostrom, whose hand gently held his arm in case of a slip.

'Why do you insist on torturing me like this?' Ultric shivered, hardly recognisable as he was swaddled in so many robes.

Ostrom shook his head.

'This country has little that I enjoy except for the food, and yet I'd never thought to see snow in my lifetime. Now, whilst you may be horrified by the stuff, I have to say I've always secretly wanted to see it and it hasn't disappointed.'

'Well, my king, I was rather hoping that this would show you how cursed this nation is, and give us reason to return home, so if we're to die, it's with dunes not drifts around us. Sadly, I note the majority of our army now shares your strange fascination. They're constantly playing in the horrible stuff with every free moment they have, much to the amusement of the locals.'

Ostrom chuckled.

'I have a feeling we've been insular for too long, my friend. The endless rolling dunes of our homeland might sing a song that my soul longs to hear, but as I look around, I recognise there's other music in this world. In time, it might even sound as beautiful as home. Now I can begin to understand why my Sancen came here on his travels.' He looked up at the canopy of the trees as he spoke. 'I know you've seen these lands in your own way, my friend. Tell me that I'm wrong.'

Ultric was silent for a while, then shrugged.

'I can't deny what you feel inside, we each see and feel things in different ways. Yet if I may be so bold, I think you seek to find beauty here because this is where you feel your days will end.'

Ostrom laughed softly.

'There's no keeping anything hidden from you. Indeed, whilst we shall see in the next year, I doubt I'll see the summer, nor will many, if any, of our men.' He shook his head, clearing it. 'So, tell me, what have you heard that has eluded us mere mortals? I can read you almost as well as you read me. You have something on your mind.'

Ultric turned blank eyes toward his king.

'There's the usual gossip from around the city that's mostly positive, including Maya's pursuit of Taran. It's now common knowledge, and the countryfolk are singing new songs about them, which turned out to be slightly prophetic.'

'How so?' Ostrom asked.

'Well, last night, I was surprised to hear very briefly from Maya. Her gift has returned, and we spirit talked.'

'Go on,' Ostrom prompted.

'She's now not only found Taran and Rakan but also the happiness that brought her gift back from whence it was hidden. Dare I say that in this instance, love has proven very powerful indeed, for she told me Lord Commander Taran's gift has also returned in full.'

The End of Dreams

'At last, some good news,' Ostrom murmured.

'Maybe I'm getting soft as I'm getting older,' Ultric continued. 'But that part of the story warmed my somewhat cold heart even if it's unable to warm my freezing body on this horrendous day.'

Ostrom remained quiet. He had many questions to ask, but he'd learned by now that Ultric would answer them all if he were patient, although the seer's reports meandered frustratingly at times.

'However, they're in immediate peril,' Ultric went on. 'It seems that throughout their journey they've been hunted, first by lancers, and now by scores of Daleth's Rangers. Currently, they're trying to escape over the southern mountains into the grasslands. They're lucky to have evaded death as long as they have. Every day could be their last, and their path gives them the only chance of evading their pursuers, if only temporarily.'

'Then before the Rangers catch them, they'd better find the Horselords,' Ostrom said, frowning.

'Indeed, but that's where the news gets worse. Maya discovered a vast battlefield, and then when she spirit travelled to the Horselords' holy shrine, an army of Daleth's men was encamped there. Either the clans have been annihilated or are running.'

'From all I've heard, they never run, which means they're all dead,' Ostrom sighed. 'Sadly, I fear our intrepid band will soon join them.'

Ultric carefully placed one foot in front of another, his face thoughtful.

'I tend to agree, and yet by all accounts, Taran, Rakan, and Maya have escaped together from perilous situations before. I pray for their safe return, however with the weather, mountains, and Rangers, against them, we should plan for a scenario where they're not coming back, where we fight without the Horselords or Taran as our forces' commander.'

'Could things possibly be any worse?' Ostrom hissed.

Ultric sighed deeply, and Ostrom's heart sank.

'They can, because that's not all.' He clasped his hand in an uncharacteristic gesture of nervousness.

'If you can tell me without hesitation that we're effectively doomed, what is it that gives you pause now?' Ostrom urged. 'Speak freely, for you know I'll not judge harshly, for I trust no one as I do you, old friend.'

Ultric smiled, nodding gratefully. He drew a deep breath.

'There's something strange about Galain. When first I heard his voice, I swear I heard Tolgarth speaking, yet I also heard a hundred, even a thousand other voices.'

Ostrom shrugged, a little relieved.

'It was more than a little embarrassing when you spoke your mind so freely at his bedside before. But, let me assure you, that was Galain. There's no doubt in my mind about it.'

'Have you not noticed how absent-minded he is of late, as if he's unsure who he is? I tell you, his voice doesn't seem to fit him. It's not his own,' Ultric said with conviction.

Ostrom sighed.

'He survived a terrible slaughter, Ultric. He's not a man of war, and many would be left a quivering wreck by such an event, so in this regard, his behaviour is normal.'

Yet Ultric wasn't giving up.

'Then how is it that in a room with several decent swordsmen, everyone died from their wounds and yet Galain survived? All he had were deep cuts, and he was saved by a corporal who is known to have little skill with a blade.'

Ostrom paused for a while, considering.

'I concede the last is very unusual. I think that Galain angered the wrong noble in one of his dealings and is loath to admit it. In this land, it's acceptable to kill someone for greed if you can get away with it and then you're applauded. Look at what Tristan did with the late Lord Duggan.'

'Then what about his association with Tolgarth and that business of the captain's body being found weeks after he died? We've both sat across the table from what was apparently a walking, talking corpse!'

They walked in silence then for a while, each deep in thought.

'This riddle is something everyone has pushed to one side as if being too hard to solve, it's better to forget,' Ultric chattered, shivering.

'Facing the fact that the dead walked amongst us is something I'm happy to avoid as well,' Ostrom muttered, making a sign to ward off evil. 'Yet I believe the answer to this is far simpler than any of us has considered, and indeed it only came to me just now.'

Ultric's blank eyes turned toward him.

The End of Dreams

'Tolgarth was gifted.'

'Gifted,' Ultric echoed. 'In what way?' he asked, intrigued.

Ostrom laughed. 'Just like you, my friend, just like you.'

Then, when Ultric still looked perplexed, he explained.

'He was gifted with an identical twin brother just like you, and no one knew. All these years, they must've kept this a secret until one died or was killed by the other. It's the only explanation that makes sense. Supposedly there were detailed journals in his lodgings, likely so they could keep easier track of what the other did.'

'Perhaps you're right,' Ultric conceded.

As they walked in silence, Ultric couldn't let it go. He wasn't convinced, not at all. He'd study Galain closely, something wasn't right irrespective of Ostrom's assurances. Yet his king could only be pushed so far on a subject once his mind was made up, so he decided to drop it for now.

Ultric exhaled loudly.

'Sometimes the sand is hidden from plain view by the dune. Why didn't I think of that? Sometimes your wisdom surprises me. Now, oh wise king, please find a way to defeat this Daleth and his evil horde.'

Ostrom grimaced.

'I am not so wise. Sadly, my friend, the answer to that is beyond me or anyone I fear.'

Together, they turned back toward the palace, the final sentence chilling them more than the snow ever could.

***

Jared felt like a failure, something he'd never previously experienced, but then he'd never disappointed Daleth before. Now the agony of doing so was eating away at him.

Following Ultric's initial shocking comments that Jared was Tolgarth, Jared knew that the old man continued to study him acutely. Years of assuming identities had honed Jared's perception skills so that he picked up subtle signals from Ultric, a twitch, or change of posture that gave this away whenever Jared spoke.

He'd expressed his concerns to Daleth, that Ultric, despite his blindness, could see right through him.

'You must not risk discovery by shifting to Tristan's form,' Daleth had ordered when they'd communicated the night before. 'It's likely this man has a gift akin to a truth seeker. You've positioned yourself close enough to influence Tristan and to pass on invaluable intelligence. This one man's doubts will simply remain that if you stay as you are. However, if you try and shift to Tristan's form, you'll likely be found out, however hard you study him.'

Jared was devastated, he'd failed to accomplish his main objective. Even now, he couldn't help but study Tristan as he sat opposite him.

He'd stayed awake all night trying to think of a way to make amends. Killing Ultric featured a lot in his thoughts, but it was too high a risk, especially within the palace or grounds where the man rarely ventured beyond now snow had fallen.

He was so deep in thought that he didn't register Tristan clear his throat to gain his attention until the second time, and he looked up and bowed his head in apology.

Two kings disappointed in such a short space of time. He needed to be better!

***

Tristan sighed, restraining himself from voicing his displeasure and gave himself a moment to relax and reflect.

Several days ago, on Galain's first day of return to duty, Tristan had awoken to find no breakfast or clothes readied in his bed-chamber. Then things quickly became worse, as throughout the day, Galain didn't recognise people, forgot recent conversations, and actually seemed lost in what was effectively his own home.

True, he'd suffered a traumatic experience and survived a horrific slaughter, but that only earned him a limited measure of sympathy. Of course, it explained why Galain initially seemed like the village idiot, but there was little room for charity in Tristan's mind, and he'd come close to dismissing Galain several times.

However, to his credit, Galain didn't try to pretend, he simply owned up to having blanks in his memory and asked Tristan to help fill them. Once done, Galain seemed to have no problem retaining the information, and so the constant questions were becoming less frequent.

Obviously, Galain was aware of how close he'd come to losing his position and was doing all he could to keep it. It was a wise move, and Tristan realised with relief that Galain was actually becoming a far better version of his previous self.

Now, having snapped out of his daydream, Galain finished pouring Tristan a goblet of watered wine, adding exactly the right tincture of herbs to it.

Tristan smiled in relief that this was done to perfection and held the warm goblet in his hands. He closed his eyes and breathed in the aroma before placing it aside without drinking it just yet. He preferred to let it cool for a while before he imbibed its sweet taste.

He opened his eyes to find Galain staring at him, and the man blushed a little.

'My apologies, my king,' Galain said. 'Sometimes, I find myself appreciating my position all the more, for I know at times I've come close to losing your faith, so forgive my look of gratitude.'

Tristan laughed.

'You've made sufficient amends and progress, Galain. Let's not let recent failures blight the present or the future. Now, let's talk about our plans.'

Tristan's instruction was met by a blank stare he'd seen all too frequently of late. Whilst this look irked him immensely, he pushed his feelings of irritation aside.

'I'm talking of our plans to vacate this beautiful country and finding sanctuary far to the southeast should our future look bleak. We'd put it on hold whilst our beloved Lord Commander Taran tried to recruit the Horselords, but now I think we should consider preparing. This will be a long winter, and what better way to spend it than ensuring we've a future of wealth, whether here or abroad.'

Jared nodded, smiling inside as an opportunity at redemption presented itself.

'I was worried, my king, for whilst I recalled our initial conversations, I wasn't sure if we'd progressed any. I'm glad to know for once my memory served me correctly. In fact, I've given it some considerable thought since we last spoke.'

Jared paused, seeking approval, and Tristan gestured for him to continue.

'Timing will be crucial. Leaving just before the battle will see the alliance resolve splinter without you to lead them. The desert soldiers will fight, but the Eyre will probably capitulate and the Freestates soldiers too. Daleth will then be able to continue his conquest unchecked with minimal losses, and you'll never be able to stop running as he conquers every land you seek refuge in. Sooner or later you'll run out of money and die destitute. Of course, leave too late, and you'll be swiftly caught by Daleth's lancers and meet whatever grisly end awaits.'

'I know, I know,' Tristan said. 'This is not new, nor is it insightful.'

Yet Jared had been playing for time, trying to come up with something, anything, that would please not just Tristan, but Daleth too.

'I think there's another option to seriously consider,' he said, mind whirring. 'We could leave with your full wealth and all the Freestates soldiers within the next few weeks. We do this while the snow is deep, and Daleth and his men are hibernating through the winter and have no idea of your departure. Head south through the desert and far beyond to carve out a new kingdom of your own.'

Divide and conquer, thought Jared to himself. Split the alliance, then kill Tristan a week into the journey.

Tristan took on a thoughtful look.

'You impress me, Galain, that's an interesting option, although in truth I'm loathe to leave until I know whether or not the Horselords are coming to our aid.'

Jared smiled inside. If only he could share the news of the Horselords destruction that he'd heard from Gregor and Daleth. He paused, thinking.

'What's on your mind?' Tristan prodded.

Jared couldn't believe it. Suddenly, it was as though the solution was shown to him by the gods.

'Forgive me, my king. I'm not sure I've thought it through fully. I've no wish to make more of a fool of myself than I've already done of late.'

'No, no,' Tristan leaned forward, intrigued. 'Tell me.'

Jared frowned, then sighed as if he was reluctant to say anything.

'I'm wondering if we have anything to lose by seeing if Daleth would consider a truce for standing the alliance forces down and offering free passage through our lands. It could well be that if we give him enough incentive, you could retain your position and wealth.'

Tristan laughed mockingly.

'We've already decided the most likely outcome of any battle is for us to lose, and thus we're considering our escape plan. So why, by the gods, would Daleth ever consider just letting us be?'

Jared shook his head.

'It's hard for me to say, my king. Maybe because whilst we'll likely lose, against our alliance, a lot of his men will die. He might have plans for future conquest that would then be put on hold.'

Tristan drummed his fingers on the tabletop.

'We couldn't trust anything Daleth says, that's the problem. I recall when he stood at the gates of the fortress and promised if our champion beat his, he'd turn away. Look how that ended up.'

Jared nodded.

'You're right.' But he smiled inside for he could see Tristan was still thinking about it as he played on the king's greatest weakness. Greed.

Now to gently play him a little more, Jared thought.

'In which case, my king, let's discuss how much gold coin we have in the treasury, and how much we'd have to leave behind. I'll then work out how many horses we'll need. Speed will be important, and a wagon, whilst able to carry so much more, is too slow. Then, we must find some soldiers with skill at riding to protect you first and foremost, but also the small amount of wealth that comes with us.'

Jared noted with satisfaction that Tristan's face turned pale as his choice of words hit home. The thought of leaving behind so much wealth had focussed Tristan's attention fully on his last inspired proposal.

'Let's call upon the royal treasurer and ask him for ourselves.' He offered Tristan the warmed wine, knowing it would now be at his preferred temperature.

Jared watched Tristan's face as the king went through different emotions, and remembered every detail, because maybe, one day soon, he might still become him regardless of Daleth's current order.

He was sure Tristan would follow through with seeking peace, and he laughed to himself, for a greedy man would be willing to believe anything if it kept him wealthy. He'd believe all the way up to the moment his throat was slit because his greed made him blind.

Jared would be patient and let Tristan make up his own mind without pushing further. Soon the king might even think it was his own idea and his self-belief would strengthen his resolve.

Then, and only then, would Jared report back to Daleth and he'd again bask in his master's praise, for he'd have truly redeemed himself.

***

They'd made it to the peak of the first mountain over a week ago, and the view had been breath-taking.

The sky had been clear, a perfect blue without a cloud in sight, and yet despite the sun shining unobstructed, it had been so cold that all three of them had found their teeth chattering constantly. They'd looked back down the mountainside to see the Rangers far below, moving fast, trying to catch up. Nonetheless, despite the urgency, they'd taken a few moments to simply look in awe at the world to the north stretched out below them.

Everything was white, as though the gods had erased every impurity from the landscape to start again upon a blank canvas.

Yet it wasn't just the view that left them breathless, it was because the thin, damp air was so difficult to breathe. Rakan was gasping like a fish out of water, suffering terribly.

Now, eight days later, they hardly had the strength to continue.

Day after day, and night after night, of relentless pursuit and cold drained them. Dwindling rations led to further energy loss and the wind and snow fed their despair, yet when they made camp, they found solace in the others' company.

'Give me your hand,' Taran projected, unable to speak out loud.

Rakan reached out so that Taran could help him to the crest of the next ridge.

'I don't believe it,' Rakan croaked, his face too frozen to reveal any expression.

The End of Dreams

They'd made it to the final ridge. Everything before them was downhill, and far, far below, lay the lands of the Horselords.

'We need to keep moving,' Maya shouted, her voice whipped away by the wind. But the others read her lips, and they stumbled over the crest, leaning heavily on the long branches they'd broken from some ancient, frozen trees several days before.

Rakan looked over his shoulder, and sure enough, closer than ever before, came the Rangers' ghostly shapes. There were less now, around thirty remaining, and Rakan grunted in satisfaction at the demise of so many. Yet there were still more than enough, and then there were more coming around the mountains in an attempt to head them off.

The snow on this side of the range was thick with a crust of ice on top, and it was slow and painful going despite their need for haste.

Taran searched the barren landscape, trying to see if there were any rocks formations they could traverse to quicken their descent. But as far as they could see, only a few large boulders punctuated an otherwise rock-free, snowy blanket almost all the way to the bottom.

'We're moving too slowly,' he shouted. 'If we can't move faster, the Rangers will be on top of us by midday.'

They redoubled their efforts, throwing caution to the wind as they waded forward.

'This isn't going to work,' Maya called after a while. 'We need to think of something.'

She paused, hoping for inspiration, while the others gathered around, thinking desperately. She'd loved the snow in her childhood, yet as she grew older, it had made her job of hunting and foraging much harder. She suddenly smiled, because before she'd been a huntress, there was a time when her father had pulled her around on a wooden board with a rope.

Maya clapped her hands with excitement.

'We're going about this the wrong way,' she said, taking off her pack, unwrapping her bedroll.

Taran rolled his eyes at Rakan.

'I'm pretty tired too,' he said, 'but now's not the time for a rest.'

Yet he followed suit, knowing Maya was up to something.

She lay it out on the snowy slope and turned to the others.

'This is going to be scary, but fun. Use your branch to slow yourself down if you go too fast.'

Without further ado, she wriggled into the bedroll and pulled her pack and equipment in as well.

Shouts sounded from far above them, and they saw the Rangers make the crest, bounding downwards.

'Follow my lead!' Maya cried, as she pulled the fleeced leather up to her chin, pushing her feet hard against the bottom, and started to wriggle. She started to slide, slowly at first, but then faster and faster.

'Come on!' Taran cried, and with Rakan following suit, they copied Maya and within moments were sliding down the mountain.

Taran started going too quickly, and he was bounced into the air before crashing down again, the air knocked from his lungs. He remembered Maya's suggestion, and with a grunt of effort, managed to sit a little and pushed the end of his branch into the snow, slowing himself down.

He could see the others had already done the same, for they were further behind, coming down at a more controlled pace. Yet as he looked higher up the mountain, he saw the Rangers sliding too. From what he could see, they simply lay on the ice and were now in pursuit.

With a warning shout, the others looked behind to see their lead being eroded, so they lifted their branches and everyone sped up.

Had this not been a race to escape death, Taran might have found a way to enjoy the experience. However, they were forced to travel at a speed that battered his already painful body. However, what would have taken two days on foot to descend, only took the rest of the morning.

He slowed just enough as they came closer to the bottom so that the others drew alongside.

'Let's go as fast as we can,' he shouted. 'We need as much lead as we can get!' He lay flat, looking up at the sky as the others did the same.

It was stomach-churning to start, but the gradient started to ease as did his speed, and shortly thereafter, he was stationary.

He pushed the bedroll away and stood, only to sink to his thighs in snow.

Rakan and Maya pushed over.

The End of Dreams

'Leave it,' Rakan said, grabbing Taran by the shoulder as Taran reached for the bedroll. 'Stay in single file, we take it in turns to lead.'

With a quick glance behind them, Rakan starting wading through the snow, Taran following and Maya behind, leaning heavily on her branch as they headed south toward a distant line of trees.

The progress was painfully slow, and behind they saw the Rangers had reached the bottom of the slope and were spreading out in a long line, pursuing.

'They're closing,' Maya shouted, panic creeping into her voice.

Taran pushed past Rakan, taking the lead, breaking through the worst of the snow, giving Rakan some respite from the punishing role.

'If we can reach those woods, we've a small chance,' Rakan called. 'Ditch the packs, just keep the weapons. We need every bit of speed we can muster.'

Everyone tossed the packs to one side, and the race continued.

Maya, who'd unflaggingly led them up and across the mountains, was struggling to keep the pace. She limped and used the long branch to help keep the weight off her right leg, hurt on the descent, and started to fall behind.

'Take the lead,' Taran shouted at Rakan, and dropped back, grabbing Maya's hand. 'Look at me!' Taran beseeched. 'We'll make it. Come on. We can do this.'

Maya looped her arm around Taran's shoulder and he half carried her along, lending her his strength.

Rakan took a moment to catch his breath.

'I do believe they're tiring. They don't seem to be pursuing so fast.'

They pushed on, only to stop in their tracks moments later.

The deep woods were far closer now, and yet rising from the snow, maybe two hundred paces distant, a line of Rangers stood. Snow fell from their heads and shoulders from where they'd lain in ambush.

'By the gods, we're undone,' Rakan breathed. 'That's over a hundred ahead of us, no less. We can't escape this.'

He started wading around in a large circle, packing the snow down, clearing the ground so they could fight.

'Help me,' he gasped.

Taran slowly shook his head and pulled Maya close, looking into her eyes.

'I love you,' he said simply. 'By now, I think you know how much. My only regret is that for a while, I let myself think otherwise. No two people have ever been fated to be together like us, and maybe because our love shines so furiously, we were never meant to enjoy it forever. Surely nothing is intended to burn this bright for so long.'

Maya shook with emotion in his arms, and he held her close. Taran stood back a little before looking over to Rakan and reached out his arm, beckoning.

'I'm still going to fight till my last breath,' Rakan grumbled, stumping over, but he held them both tight and didn't want to let go either. 'There's no need for words,' he said, voice cracking with emotion.

Reluctantly, they let one another go, and while Rakan and Taran stamped the snow down, Maya pulled her bow free from its cover and took the leather cap from her quiver. She inspected her arrows one by one as she pushed them into the frozen ground, leaning on her branch for support.

The Rangers took their time, approaching slowly, knowing their quarry had nowhere to run, no hope of escape. The three of them now stood still, waiting. Taran held Maya's hand, sharing the love he had for her with his mind, knowing that words could never come close to truly expressing what he felt.

The Rangers stopped about thirty paces away and slowly worked their way around, forming a perfect circle with the three of them at the centre.

'Run. Flee, before it's too late!' Taran projected toward the Rangers in front of him, and they staggered for a moment, but then stood firm.

Again Taran tried, throwing emotions of an agonising death, even using his own fear to project at them. For a moment, they took a step backwards, then resumed their positions.

'Amazing,' called one, stepping forward from the rest. 'Truly, had your gift been discovered at birth, you'd be standing with us, not against us. But whatever words or feelings you conjure into our minds, my brothers behind you are not affected. It seems you can only affect those upon whom you focus and even then, not for very long. It will not be enough. The time for talk is over, you've said your farewells. Your story ends here and now.'

The End of Dreams

The Ranger drew his swords, and all around them, the sound of steel scraping from scabbards sounded loud in the quiet.

Taran, Rakan, and Maya faced outward, back to back, and watched death approach.

***

Chapter XIX

'I don't want to do it,' Yana said, shaking with fear, having listened in disbelief as Tristan had outlined his plan.

'What you want to do and what you will do are two completely different things,' Tristan growled. 'I knew I kept you alive for a reason when I had Ferris killed, and I can assure you it has nothing to do with your surprising skill at running the hospital. Until only this morning, I kept questioning why I allowed you your life, and then it became apparent that the gods had stayed my hand. You still have a part to play that will earn you redemption.'

A cruel smile gave Tristan a demonic look as he leant forward.

'So, let me make this extremely clear for you. There are two simple choices before you. Accept the mission, return successful, and you'll be rewarded beyond your wildest dreams. Or in direct contrast, you can choose the same fate as Ferris and Duggan before him.'

Yana's shoulders sagged as she realised the situation she was now in. She faced certain death at Tristan's order, or a few weeks away, death at Daleth's hand, as it was unlikely the Witch-King would receive an envoy. If he did, he'd likely have her killed on sight for aiding Taran, Maya, and Rakan's escape, let alone her father's insurrection. There was only the slimmest of chances the flag of truce would keep her safe or that Daleth wouldn't recognise her.

The only way she could avoid certain immediate death would be to agree to the mission. Then, once on her way, she could circle Freeguard and head southeast toward the desert tribes. This wasn't what her dreams were made of, becoming queen to Taran's king. Yet she'd escape death for a while and live in the scorching sun, likely enslaved, but at least alive until Daleth continued his conquest.

'Of course,' Galain added, standing behind Tristan, 'we'll send you with an escort of twenty men under a flag of truce. A small necessity befitting someone of your rank and privilege to ensure you don't get lost or waylaid on your journey.'

Yana cursed inside, head spinning, as she tried to figure a way out of this mess with something approaching what she wanted, what was supposed to be, yet it defeated her.

'Daleth will probably kill me and the men you send with me, assuming we even get as far as seeing him,' Yana pointed out. 'Why would he even consider a truce when we're in such a desperate situation?'

'Don't seek to concern yourself with the minds of kings,' Tristan snarled. 'I'm responsible for the wellbeing of an entire people, and I'm entrusting you with a mission that has the chance to potentially save them, however small that chance might be. I have to look at every option, even the unpalatable ones.'

Yana could barely look at Tristan's face as he continued.

'Take it as a compliment. I need to send someone of noble rank to show my sincerity, and I've chosen you because you have a shrewd and calculating mind beyond your peers in this city. Just think of the gratitude it would earn you from the citizens, irrespective of their station, if you saved the day.'

Yana stood silently. Tristan's last words made the situation slightly more palatable. She'd go to Daleth, for what other option did she have? If she survived, and the negotiations went well, then she'd indeed be the saviour of the city. That was a currency she'd capitalise on because if she were a renowned heroine, it would make her ascension to the throne so much easier. If things went badly, she could attempt to change sides, and she could be very persuasive, especially if her life depended on it. Her charms were impossible to resist for most, unless their name was Taran.

'My king,' she said, 'I'll do as you order, and when I get the truce, I'll expect my reward to be beyond my wildest dreams.'

A satisfied smile spread across Tristan's face.

'There'll be no word of this to anyone. Galain has everything organised already, for we felt you'd see sense. The journey to Freeguard will take three weeks in this abominable weather and the same to return with Daleth's reply, and thus you'll return before the spring thaw.'

Tristan stood.

'Now I'll leave you with Galain,' he said, and left the audience chamber without a backwards glance.

For whatever reason, Yana thought, as she sat with Galain, he was no longer the bumbling oaf of an engineer she'd first thought him to be. In fact, if she didn't know better, he seemed a changed man, more assured than almost anyone she'd ever met.

I'll be queen one day and Taran my king, she swore to herself, and if this is what it takes, I'm going to damned well do it.

So she sighed and started paying attention to what Galain said. Ultimately, her life depended on playing the game perfectly, and she had every intention of coming out with a stronger hand than when she'd started.

***

Make camp for a day or two at most, hunt the local area for game, then up camp and slowly move to the next. Shinsen now wondered if this was the right tactic, for they had an equal chance to be moving toward danger as opposed to away from it. However, at the very least, this way they supplemented their supplies with fresh meat here and there, and kept everyone busy, giving them less time to ponder on their situation.

Shinsen knew that amongst the knights, be they men or women, there was a growing sense of resentment. Whilst this had yet to manifest itself in any physical way, the longer it built without release, the more dangerous the situation would be when it finally arose.

Things were not helped by some priests and old knights who'd accompanied them on their exodus from the sacred shrine. The priests bemoaned that by forsaking their shrine and ways, the Moon Goddess had deserted them forever. The old knights simply scorned everyone for their cowardice. Now many felt they'd lost not only their honour but the love of their deity.

The End of Dreams

They'd pushed northward for fourteen punishing days, and would soon head west, and yet Shinsen was tempted to backtrack south. The winter was harsh, and the further north, the worse it became.

'What do you think?' he asked Chochen and Nadlen, sharing his thoughts on where to head, and he waited as they considered the choices before them.

Their horses walked carefully amongst the trees of a large wood that gave them a little respite from the wind. Riders cursed as their mounts slipped on hidden roots and their long, heavy lances knocked branches, sending showers of cold snow down on those below.

Shinsen had chosen this route on purpose, to keep minds focussed on the challenging terrain.

'What if we're pursued? The invaders might have found and followed our tracks. We could well find ourselves facing a fight before we're ready,' Nadlen stated. 'What then?'

Shinsen guided his horse around some rocks before answering.

'A good point I'd already considered. They'll not be able to force a battle, and I doubt their lancers will seek to engage. Our chargers are heavier, but in the snow, their lighter horses are less agile, slower, and we'd decimate them. Their infantry would not be able to intervene in time. We'd have to retrace our steps and avoid battle. Yet the way our people are feeling, half would likely seek a fight as opposed to turning away again. Most of our knights consider themselves stripped of honour already and so it might be easier for them to ignore our commands.'

Shinsen sighed.

'You've helped me answer my own question. We continue north for the remainder of the day before turning west.'

They rode on for a while, lost in their own thoughts.

Shinsen looked to the left and right of him at the long line of mounts winding through the trees, and he saw the sagging bodies, no longer sitting tall and proud. His people were bowed and broken of spirit, and his heart beat with a despair he'd managed to push aside until now.

These were the finest knights of the three clans that had come together. Eight hundred knights chosen to be the vanguard of their force, and yet they looked like they were dead men riding.

Oh, goddess of the moon, he thought, help me save my people, help me save your people. He stopped, ashamed that his weakness had led him to true prayer once again when his whole life he'd forsaken the lore and religion of his people.

The sun broke through the clouds as they moved from the tree line into the crisp brightness beyond. The mountains that marked their northern border stood high and mighty above them.

His eyes suddenly widened in shock, and he turned to his horn bearer who always rode close.

'Sound line formation,' he ordered, his throat tight with excitement, for there before them, in a wide-open plain, was a cavalryman's dream.

Maybe a hundred and sixty or so enemy swordsmen stood, weapons drawn surrounding three others, obviously with intent to kill them. It mattered not who the three were, what mattered was that they were all invaders upon this sacred soil. His knights needed to feel pride again, victorious, even if against just shy of two hundred foe. Blood spilt would be a measure of honour regained, the first step of many on a journey of revenge.

They were perhaps four hundred paces distant, and the snow looked to be waist deep for the enemy soldiers, making it impossible for them to run and escape. For the clan chargers, it would barely slow them at all.

He saw the distant figures turn toward the sound of the horn, almost unconcerned.

'Sound the advance,' he called.

The horn sounded again, and the horses started to trot, eating up the distance quickly.

'The canter,' he shouted, and gripped the saddle with his thighs, steadying himself. 'Charge!' he bellowed, and the horn blared again and again. He lowered his heavy lance, tucking the haft under his shoulder.

It mattered not that they weren't wearing their heavy plate armour, for this wouldn't be a fight, rather it would be a slaughter like those inflicted upon his dead brothers.

There would be no survivors.

***

The End of Dreams

'Very impressive. You just don't give up with those tricks of yours, do you?' The Ranger glared, his black eyes boring into Taran's and the circle started to close. 'Don't you realise it's too late? Whatever you try, the most it will give you is maybe one more heartbeat of life. This ends now with all of your blood staining this snow and then, well, it'll be as if you never lived.'

A horn sounded, and Taran's head whipped around to see in the near distance a long line of heavy cavalry, Horselords by the look of them, emerge from the trees.

'Oh, very funny,' the Ranger laughed, slowly wading through the snow, but when the horn sounded again, his mocking look changed to one of confusion, then disbelief.

The Rangers all stared toward the long line of horsemen that were advancing toward them and when the horn sounded a third time, Taran turned to the outspoken Ranger.

'We might die here, but know this,' Taran called, interrupting the Ranger's thoughts. 'Despite all your skill, all your training, the days of the Rangers are over!'

'No, no, no!' the Ranger screamed, the realisation of what was about to happen showing on his face.

The horn sounded a final time, and Taran sheathed his blades, turning to hold Rakan and Maya in his arms.

'Not quite the way I expected to die, but surprisingly, I fear this might be worse,' he said as he watched the enormous wall of men and horses come hurtling toward them. 'They don't care who we are, we'll die along with the Rangers.'

Yet he wasn't going to just give up, fixing those in the middle of the charge with his gaze, Taran projected hard.

Turn!

Yet the packed ranks didn't allow it even if he could see riders trying to drag on their reins in response to his thoughts.

'I can't make them turn,' Taran shouted, gritting his teeth, fighting the urge to run, while continuing to try.

'But maybe I can. Stand behind me,' Maya commanded, thrusting the branch she'd used to support her across the mountains into the snowy ground. She closed her eyes and reached for her gift.

It responded instantly, and as Maya shone, the branch changed from bleached, dead white, to a lustrous, silver sheen and started to take root.

Taran felt the ground shift at his feet as the roots sped through the frozen soil. As he watched, the branch swelled rapidly, becoming an enormous trunk that shot toward the sky.

Maya grabbed both Rakan and Taran and pulled them into the lee of the trunk as it continued to grow. Moments later, the riders swept around it, screaming their war cries.

The Rangers, the elite of Daleth's army, trained by one of the greatest warriors to ever walk the land, found themselves in a situation for which they had no answer.

The deep snow hindered them from running, rolling, or spinning from the tips of the lances, and when they did manage to evade or deflect them, there was no avoiding the hundreds of pounding hooves. To a man, they were thrown off their feet and then churned into a bloody mess when the line simply swept over them as if they weren't even there.

Taran, Maya, and Rakan watched as the horses sped by in a blur. They sheltered behind the tree surrounded by snow that had been churned into a red morass, waiting as the charge slowly came to a halt.

Rakan spat on the ground.

'Those Rangers deserved that and more, but we aren't out of the woods yet. They intended to kill us too, and I'm not sure us hiding behind a tree will change that.'

Taran held Maya as the huge horses approached, using his gift as they, like the Rangers before, formed a large circle around them, the tips of their weapons stained red. He focussed, reading their leader, having recognised him not just from his bearing, but from the looks the riders cast his way as they waited for an order.

Taran glanced at the silvered tree above them, the trunk, the branches, and the leaves that rustled in the wind.

'Take off your hood,' he said softly to Maya in the silence, and then turned to Rakan. 'Follow my lead.'

He knelt.

The End of Dreams

But he didn't kneel toward the clan leader, Shinsen, as he now knew him to be called, but instead toward Maya and he touched his forehead to the frozen ground.

Rakan followed suit in surprise, and as Maya pulled her hood back, her white hair fell across her shoulders, dazzling in the sunlight.

It was as if the world around held its breath, and then the riders slowly dismounted, awe and wonder upon their faces.

'What's happening?' Maya whispered from the corner of her mouth.

'They've just seen their sacred tree grow before their very eyes, and below it is a white-haired vision who is in the image of their goddess. You've come in the time of their greatest need, a need that matches our own.'

Even as Taran spoke the words, the riders all knelt to the ground, touching their foreheads to the bloodied snow in homage.

Maya raised her arms out wide as if embracing them all and let her gift flow, so she shone like the moon. Long grasses and flowers grew around her, pushing through the snow, and soon she stood surrounded by a summer's field in the middle of winter.

***

Daleth downed his fourth goblet of wine. He hadn't eaten and doubted he would, at least tonight. He shook his head in denial. Two weeks of calling out to his Rangers, every night the same result, emptiness, no response, not from a single one.

The final communication had shown them all in position, ready to close an inescapable trap on an unsuspecting prey. Nothing could go wrong, victory had been utterly assured.

Yet since that time. Silence.

Even now, the thought that his elite Rangers, trained to fight and win their whole lives, were no longer on this earthly plane, was almost impossible to fathom. He shook his head, trying to imagine how all of them could be dead, for there was no other explanation for this void.

Dead as they closed in upon three fugitives who'd been responsible for, or connected to the death of, every Ranger so far in this conquest.

Now, he could hardly bring himself to think that the three of them, Taran, Maya, and Rakan, were still alive, mocking him, taunting him as they left his best men dead and frozen somewhere behind them.

Had Maya's gift grown so strong that she could open the earth and have it swallow the very men who walked upon it? If so, what would this mean when the armies finally met if she was alive and with the Freestates forces?

Would his army disappear before his eyes, and what of himself?

He was agonisingly mortal, as his recent brush with death had reminded him. Anybody who could defeat a Ranger was a threat to him, yet anyone who could defeat all of them might well bring about his downfall if he wasn't careful.

Of over two hundred Rangers, only two now remained.

Gregor, who shared his king's disbelief, was now returning to Freemarch to see out the end of the winter, and Jared, who continued to prove himself invaluable.

Jared, who, as Tristan's closest advisor, shared with Daleth every intimate detail of the defenders' preparations and whom in a display of rare genius, was now behind the meeting Daleth was about to find himself in.

Daleth looked at his reflection in a mirror, walking backwards and forwards a final time, and smiled. He still struck an imposing figure, tall and mighty, yet both of his knees were now heavily bound so that his gait looked stiff and ungainly.

His face had also been subtly tainted with powders, a hint of yellow to make his complexion look a touch unhealthy with the faintest of dark rings ghosted about his eyes to hint at a lack of sleep.

He walked into the throne room, looking around. As expected, his bodyguard were alert, attentive, but it wasn't them he was looking at. Instead, there, just behind a curtain, were two long walking sticks, out of sight. Yet a sharp eye would maybe catch a glimpse of them and then beneath the oak table a small leaf of sleep weed, perfect.

He nodded to the door guards, and they heaved on the gold plated rings, and the doors swung inward to reveal the Freestates emissary.

Daleth stood waiting as Yana approached.

The End of Dreams

She'd given her name as The Lady Seren and yet even had Jared not told him of who was coming, he might well have recognised the subtle likeness to her grandfather had he looked hard enough.

She approached, her confident bearing a show, and knelt in respect, a respect born of fear. He offered his hand so that she might kiss it. As she did, he pulled her to her feet, staring hard into her eyes as he released her hand.

Without a word, he moved around the table, sat in a comfortable chair, and stretched his legs out before him, totally at ease.

He motioned to the chair opposite, and Yana sat, her eyes never still as she looked around the chamber.

'This room does draw the eye,' Daleth acknowledged, his deep voice filling the chamber, making Yana jump. 'Yet as I look at the opulence, I wonder how much the people had to pay for their rulers to enjoy such privilege. The people of this land worship the god of greed who rewards those who accrue wealth. Unfortunately, it seems King Tristan was so true to his faith that he didn't spend enough to protect himself or his people.'

Daleth shook his head as if in mock despair.

'So, Yana, daughter of Laska, how can I trust whatever it is you have come to say when you've started with a lie about who you are? Tell me why I shouldn't enjoy your screams for past and present transgressions, for I assure you, I enjoy killing others for less.'

Daleth smiled as he saw Yana's face pale even more and her pulse fluttered in her neck before she composed herself. She bowed her head and to her credit when she raised her eyes, they were filled with a fierce determination that Daleth found admirable.

'I am who and what you say, and yet I'm not here to seek your forgiveness. Rather, I'm here as a mouthpiece for Tristan, King of the Freestates, leader of the three nations' army. I believe he sent me, knowing that as my life would have little worth to you, I'd try all the harder to make this mission succeed.'

Daleth nodded.

'Perhaps true, but maybe you felt if I didn't recognise you when you used your alias, then there'd be a chance of keeping your head on its shoulders were you to change sides?'

Yana grimaced, wondering if her thoughts had been so transparent.

'Not at all. Someone who changed sides so quickly could never be trusted. No, I'm here to speak plainly on behalf of my king, to see if there are any routes we can take other than that leading to the mass slaughter of both our armies.'

Daleth leaned back in his chair, laughing good-naturedly.

'I admit you have some fine troops in your alliance from the intelligence I've obtained. The desert spearmen have a reputation as do the Eyre archers, and indeed we experienced that truth at Tristan's Folly, but the slaughter will be one-sided, I assure you. We have the numbers, we have the leader. So tell me, what do you have to say that I would have any interest in hearing?'

'Tristan offers you a truce.'

Daleth roared with laughter, enjoying the charade.

'For all the aforementioned reasons, there's no need for a truce. I'll win as soon as spring comes.'

Yana nodded.

'We agree, you'll win, but you'll lose as well.'

Daleth hissed in mock frustration, but Yana continued.

'Tristan is prepared to recognise you as his master as long as he retains his kingship. He'll add his men to your army as opposed to them fighting it. He'll organise for your army to be kept supplied as it passes through the Freestates lands and into the desert kingdom beyond. He'll continue to send supplies of men, food and equipment as a vassal king, allowing you to continue your conquest for years to come.'

Yana paused briefly, but Daleth's face betrayed nothing, so she continued.

'It's that option, or we'll bleed your army as much as we can on the field of battle. Yes, we'll lose, but you'll not have enough fighting men to continue your conquest for decades to come. That is what this is all about, surely? The conquest of new lands so you can continue to drain them of life to extend yours.'

Daleth's eyes widened, and Yana pushed her perceived advantage.

'You see, we know of your gift and its cost. Why leave dead lands behind you when a vibrant one that feeds you and feeds your army as you conquer distant countries is far more valuable?'

Daleth raised his hand, secretly bored, stopping Yana from saying any more.

'Guard,' he called, and several marched over, led by Baidan. 'Escort the Lady Yana to her quarters. We shall continue this conversation on the morrow.'

As she was led out, Daleth admired her form, yet he was equally disappointed that she'd been so easily led. She'd said everything he knew she would, that Jared had told him she would.

To destroy the enemy from within, to dismantle it from afar, was a game he enjoyed. However, when the time came, he'd also enjoy smashing the enemy to pieces on the battlefield, and with midwinter already past, it wouldn't be long now, not long at all.

***

'The way back to your holy shrine is no longer dangerous. The army that occupied it is headed directly toward Freemarch, leaving it safe for you to return to, but I warn you, I have bad news.'

Maya looked around at the faces of the clansmen staring back at her, Shinsen, Nadlen, Chochen, and Taysen, a cleric of the Moon Goddess she'd not engaged with before. Despite her warning, the faces that returned her gaze only held reverence and joy with perhaps a hint of exhaustion from the revelry that had gone on long into the previous night.

Taran sat next to her, their knees lightly touching, quietly letting her speak. He'd initially suggested that letting these people believe she was sent by the Moon Goddess was a sure way to have them follow her. Maya had shaken her head immediately, insisting she'd not lie or mislead these people into laying down their lives any more than she had to the countryfolk of the Freestates. If they came to fight, it would be in the full knowledge of why and what they stood to lose.

Rakan had shaken his head in disagreement at her decision.

Taran, after a brief moment, had smiled broadly, wrapping her in his arms.

'You always show me the righteous path,' he'd said. 'The truth it is, even if it puts us in danger, for we'll be simple trespassers on their lands even if as emissaries of the Freestates.'

Yet here they were, still alive the following morning, and despite Maya's protestations to the contrary, they saw her as more divine now as they had when they first laid eyes on her.

'The bad news,' she continued, 'is that before they left, they torched the entire shrine and settlement, burning everything to the ground, including your sacred tree of the goddess. None of the priests who remained was spared. They've desecrated your holy place, the heart of your people, and it grieves me to bear such terrible news.'

Maya sat, waiting in silence, letting the enormity of her words sink in. Pain, sadness, and fury crossed the faces of the four opposite her, yet these emotions slowly cleared away to be replaced by that of a calm acceptance as they digested what she'd said.

Taysen, a youngish man with a gravity that hinted of knowledge beyond his years, spoke after looking at those either side of him.

'As a cleric of our religion, it is my place to respond first. My initial reaction was to cry with sorrow, and yet I realise my brothers have swiftly arrived at the same conclusion I have.'

The other clansmen all nodded in silent agreement.

'Our shrine is where the tree of our goddess grows,' Taysen continued. 'Until yesterday there was but one tree of the moon, yet by divine intervention, where one was destroyed, another has grown. If that's not a sign from our goddess, then I don't know what is. I speak for us all when I say that from this moment, this is where our shrine will be, where our people will gather, children will grow, and tales of our deeds will be told.'

Shinsen then spoke.

'I'm not a man of religion and those here know this, but I swear that at the moment of my deepest despair I prayed to the Moon Goddess, and as the sun shone through the clouds, you were there. I didn't *see* you then, I didn't *know* you, and you were to die alongside those who surrounded you, yet here you sit. You sought shelter beneath the tree of our goddess that you called forth at your will. You gave us the opportunity to kill those who'd desecrated our lands, regaining some honour when it was much needed. You tell the truth instead of trying to hide behind lies, and now ... now I truly believe.'

Maya smiled.

The End of Dreams

'I believe in the truth, and as such, I tell you, had I held a staff of ironwood, then an ironwood tree would be standing in the plain yonder.'

Shinsen smiled back.

'As we are speaking truthfully, had that been the case, then you'd be dead back in that field instead of sitting here. But it wasn't an ironwood tree, it was moonwood.'

Chochen raised his voice.

'Speaking the truth is one of our religion's tenets, even if you don't follow it. We believe our lives are preordained, that we're fated to be whom we are, and these last few weeks saw me question my own faith. Yet at my lowest ebb, like with Shinsen, you appeared. You think you were there randomly? You think that staff you held was chosen by you? I tell you this. You were guided to us at the moment of your greatest need as we were guided to you.'

'Not forgetting,' Nadlen added, 'that on top of all this, you're white-haired. Old yet young, the very way we perceive our goddess to be. Older than the world, yet youthful and a bringer of life, for as we lay beneath her loving gaze, with her blessing, our children are conceived.

Maya laughed, and the mood around the circle was light.

Shinsen leaned forward.

'I know you said much last night, but we were all drunk, and I want to ensure nothing was forgotten or left unsaid. So tell us all again, now we're sitting here together sober, in the cold light of day, everything you can of your journey and quest.'

Maya retold the tale, and as she did, the sun slowly crossed the sky. Fires were built, and food was cooked. Maya recounted everything from the beginning so that all would understand that this wasn't just a fight for their land, it was a fight for the world. She explained about Taran's gift and others, but how this also came with a curse so that balance was achieved. Lastly, she spoke of their desperate mission, to find help where it was least expected, to save their king whose kingship hardly deserved to be saved but whose subjects surely did.

As she spoke, her hands moved, full of expression, almost hypnotic. She held everyone with the passion and power of her voice and the truth it held.

Taran sat beside her, at times his hand unconsciously caressed the back of her neck, and as dusk approached, people who were not privy to the conversation stopped and stared, for a soft glow emanated from her.

Finally, she fell silent, and leaned into Taran, realising how thirsty she was. She gratefully accepted a cup from his hand as silence replaced her musical voice, broken only by the crackle of flames.

Shinsen stood, taking in a deep breath.

'It has been hundreds of years since any clan left our sacred lands, preferring to find honour in fighting without anger or loss amongst ourselves. We preserved our way, worshipping our goddess and our steel, honour and duty-bound at all times. For hundreds of more years, I expected this to remain so. Yet in mere weeks, our way of life has been challenged, our supremacy as we saw it humbled, our honour stripped away, our future as a nation on the edge of a precipice.'

He looked to the sky briefly, as if seeking inspiration, then continued.

'We came together, what remained, as one clan, to find a way to survive, to maybe take back that which was taken, and to redress the balance. Despite this undertaking, I walked lost in the wilderness, for in truth, I could not see how this could ever be achieved outside of my dreams, until yesterday, until now.'

'You came seeking help, and I know I speak for not just those beside me, but for those thousands behind me when I say to you. We will follow you, Lady Maya, for you were sent by our goddess whether you believe it or not, in *our* time of greatest need.'

Shinsen stood and suddenly drew his sword.

'We will follow you to our salvation or our deaths,' he said solemnly, and knelt, offering her its hilt in a sign of fealty and obedience that brought Maya to tears.

As she stood to receive his offering, the others dropped to their knees too. Nadlen, Chochen, Taysen, and then, when those who stood further from the fire saw what was happening, they followed suit. Like a ripple on a pond spreading outward, every knight knelt in homage to the figure who stood shining not just in the glow of the firelight, but in her own power.

Maya took the hilt of Shinsen's sword in her hand.

'I accept your fealty,' she said softly, 'but only while you consider me worthy of it.'

Then Maya knelt to embrace him.

Suddenly, the forest erupted with a roar as the knights surged to their feet, lifting their weapons high in the dying sun, saluting their new leader.

Shinsen stepped over to Taran, gripping his forearm.

'You are indeed gifted,' he said, nodding toward Maya, 'far more than with just the reading of minds.' He smiled. 'We follow her, but I know that means we'll follow you too in battle. So it's time we got to know one another, you and I. My people ...' then he paused, '... *our* people need to enjoy this moment and rest, and from the looks of you three, you need to do the same, and eat, a lot.'

Shinsen turned away, walking over to Rakan.

'So, what gift do you possess, old man?'

Rakan laughed.

'I have these two,' he said, 'but I've always been gifted.'

'How so?' Shinsen asked.

'I'm gifted at killing people.' Rakan smiled grimly.

'Then you're now in good company, my new friend. Now, come meet some of your new brethren, and share your tales with us so that we know you better too.'

Rakan turned to tell Taran and Maya, but they had eyes only for one another. He smiled. They'd survived again, against the odds, and his heart warmed to see them happy and safe for the now.

'I always find telling old tales is better done with a good goblet of wine,' Rakan said with a wink as he turned back to Shinsen.

'I always find listening to old tales is better done with two goblets of wine,' Shinsen responded, and laughing, they moved toward a campfire where Rakan was met as if a long-time brother returning home.

***

Ultric shambled through the snow, insulated by several layers of clothing deep in thought. Most nights, he visited the palace gardens in spirit form and then the following morning, after meeting with Ostrom, he'd walk the treacherous paths. Despite the discomfort, the solitude he found here gave him the silence he needed to reflect.

The gardens were beautiful despite the winter cold and being left to nature's hand now that Taran was no longer tending them. He chuckled to think a man with such skill at war would have a way with gardens, but everyone kept something hidden inside either with or without intent.

Despite Ultric's blindness, he was Ostrom's eyes, but his skill to listen, to hear what was meant to remain unheard, or what was even unsaid, was by far his greatest gift. Now it gave him the greatest cause for concern.

These last few weeks, he'd become completely fixated with Galain, and he couldn't let go.

He'd even taken to spying on him in spirit form. Watching Galain closely as he travelled the city at night, to see who he associated with, following his movements, trying to listen in on his conversations. Yet nothing he said or did was out of place or untoward in any way. But Ultric knew with a fervent belief that something was wrong.

The problem was that he had no idea what that wrong was. There was no evidence, and after all this time, he had no explanation and was now beginning to doubt his own senses, even though throughout his whole life, they'd never let him down.

Every word he heard Galain utter seemed to be in a different voice. Yes, he *sounded* like Galain, but everyone else at the same time. He also lied frequently, for Ultric could sense his heartbeat giving him away just as if Galain screamed an admission of deceit out loud.

Ultric paused, reaching out to find the last stubborn rose left within the garden, and savoured its subtle scent. To his finely tuned sense of smell, it was divine, but had anyone else smelt it, it would have been just another dying bloom with nothing to offer.

The rose scent reminded him of Maya and her love of them. She'd reached out to him earlier in the evening, a whisper in his mind until he'd focussed and found her waiting. He'd listened intently to the news of their arrival in the grasslands, and being saved by the remaining Horselords who'd escaped the earlier massacre.

She'd told him everything, including how Taran was adamant that their mission had been compromised by a traitor from the start. They'd

The End of Dreams

been relentlessly pursued, hunted down by both lancers and Rangers alike.

So who'd passed on the detail of their mission?

Several minor nobles and merchants knew of it thanks to Tristan's insistence that they attend counsel. Any one of them could be responsible, but not one had aroused Ultric's suspicions like Galain.

Galain was a liar, and he was not who he seemed to be.

He couldn't keep coming forward with his suspicions to Ostrom without concrete proof, but he now knew how to determine whether Galain was the traitor. Without question, whosoever was passing on information had to be using spirit speak, for any other way would be too slow, too dangerous and require additional help.

Ostrom had called for a meeting with Tristan, and they'd convene on the morrow. Ultric would formally deliver Maya's news, and he'd ask that the meeting be closed to everyone except the inner circle. He'd know by the afternoon whether Galain was the traitor, but then the hard part would be proving it to the others.

One step at a time, he thought to himself, as he carefully placed his feet on the treacherous path, retracing his steps back to the palace, one step at a time.

***

Chapter XX

Yana had slept fitfully, the feeling of jeopardy that surrounded her mission impossible to escape even in her dreams.

Yet the only terrifying moment had been upon their approach to Freemantle days before, when a contingent of lancers had charged toward them, weapons lowered. Fortunately, the flag of truce had been respected, and her bodyguard had even been allowed to keep their weapons.

Upon arrival, they'd been given a palatial house to stay in, just across from the palace, and whilst guards were positioned all around, they offered no threat. Food was provided, and after her first meeting with Daleth, Yana, whilst not confident in her mission, at least felt her life was less in imminent danger.

Daleth was a hugely imposing figure, but Yana's sharp eyes had detected a couple of things that led her to believe he was suffering and weaker than his frame indicated. His gait had been ungainly, and she'd spotted evidence of sleep weed, a drug she knew only too well.

They'd met twice since. Both meetings had been short. Daleth had listened to her, had even shared his desire for conquest into further uncharted lands, and Yana had been quick to extol the virtues of a truce to allow that to happen unopposed.

She'd allowed herself to feel ever so slightly confident, until now.

'You're to attend my king,' Baidan instructed, his face impassive. 'Pick ten of your men, and come immediately.'

Baidan had never been warm, no one here had been, but there was something about his demeanour, a hint of restrained violence, that made Yana's insides clench.

The End of Dreams

'It's to witness Daleth's decision,' Shalast, the sergeant of her escort assured her, as they pushed through the deep snow.

Yana said nothing. It made sense, but it didn't alleviate her feeling of foreboding.

The short walk left them all chilled as they were finally ushered into the throne room. If they were cold before, then the sight of Daleth's soldiers standing to attention beside every pillar, hatred in their eyes, made the atmosphere anything but friendly.

Daleth was there, pacing up and down, his hand on the hilt of an enormous sword belted at his waist, full of restrained energy.

'I've been considering your proposal these nights,' Daleth said, turning toward them, his voice full of anger, 'and this is my answer!'

The Witch-King drew his sword, striding forward, and Yana's guard quickly drew theirs, pushing her behind them as they formed a defensive circle.

Daleth didn't pause his advance for a heartbeat, and his soldiers attacked in unison. The sound of clashing steel rang loud in the chamber along with horrific screams and cries for mercy as her guard was butchered.

Yana found herself alone, splashed in blood, and bent, picking up two fallen swords. She turned toward Daleth, flinging herself at him, snarling in defiance, her fury taking him by surprise. For a moment he defended, blocking her strikes, but then spun her to the floor with a blow from the back of his hand.

Daleth stood above her, blood running from the tip of his sword as he put in under her chin, lifting her head.

'Look into my eyes,' he growled. 'You can pass this message to your pathetic king. I can destroy him and all he has around him in less than a day, with no more effort than it took to kill every one of your guards. He is worthless, he is nothing. Do you hear me?' he roared.

Yana, shaking like a leaf, nodded.

'Yet there's some small merit in what he begs for, and I'm willing to throw him a crumb as if he were a peasant. When the time comes, and my armies face his at Freeguard, he is to lower his standard and depart the field with the Freestates soldiers. But he must leave behind the desert warriors and the Eyre to meet their doom!'

'Then, and only then, will I let him keep his throne. He will be my vassal and will serve me as such. He will have his forces join mine to replenish my losses as I continue with my campaign, and he'll do everything to keep me supplied as I push deep into the desert and beyond.'

'There is no negotiation, there are no other options unless he chooses to fight and die like those who lie on the floor beside you. He can even hide behind his god of greed, and sell it to himself that he does it for the riches he can accrue, whilst he remains alive, and others die around him.'

Daleth nodded to his men, who lifted Yana to her feet, dragging her through the gore toward the doors.

'Wait,' she cried.

Daleth turned, lifting his finger, and the men stopped as he strode over. He bent down, his face close to hers.

'Would you prefer to end your life here? You have your message. What more do you need?'

'I might ask the same of you,' Yana gasped. 'Do you want a puppet king who'll try and hide every piece of gold he can from you whilst feeding your army as little as possible? Perhaps it would be better if a queen sat on the throne who's not afraid to do what needs to be done, and would stop at nothing to deliver what's required and more.'

Daleth's gaze changed from anger to consideration.

'Deliver my message, and when the time comes, we'll see.'

He waved at his soldiers.

Yana was escorted to the palace steps, then cast to the snow-covered ground, and she watched as it turned red from her blood-soaked clothing.

'Find your own way,' one said, kicking her hard to get her moving. 'You and your men need to be gone from here by sundown, or we'll kill the rest of you.'

Yana pushed herself to her feet and stumbled across the square, stopping twice to vomit before arriving back at the house to be met with looks of horror from the remaining soldiers.

She pushed by them, ignoring their questions until she found a flask of wine, then sank onto a lounge chair. It didn't matter that it became stained with blood, she drank until the flask was half empty, and still, her hands shook.

She looked at the soldiers.

'Daleth's message was painfully clear. Get the horses ready whilst I clean up. We need to leave here before noon.'

She finished the flask, and let it slip from her fingers, hardly hearing the sound of it smashing on the floor. Drops of wine splashed over an expensive rug, and images of the blood-soaked corpses of her guard flashed into her mind.

Now, when she looked at her hands, they were shaking not with fear but excitement. She'd dared ask to be queen in the event of Daleth's victory, and he'd as much as said yes. Now it didn't matter whether Daleth or Tristan won.

She'd positioned herself well, and her dreams could still be realised.

***

Ultric waited for the audience chamber doors to be closed, and the murmur of the departing merchants' and nobles' voices to diminish. Inside his heart, he was sure Galain was the traitor, but first, he had to prove it to himself. Afterwards, if he was correct, he'd have to find acceptable proof beyond just his word to bring to Ostrom and Tristan.

He followed the sound of Ostrom's breathing to find the meeting table, although he knew the number of steps to take without even thinking. His chair was always precisely half a step to Ostrom's right hand, and if it weren't for his glazed eyes, the way he moved confidently to his chair would have convinced anyone he could still see.

Everyone who needed to be present was there, Tristan, Ostrom, Dafne, and lastly, Galain.

Ultric's gift of reading people was honed to perfection. The subtlest inflexion of a voice could give away a lie, even if he couldn't see the face. He could hear softly spoken words made behind a hand at the back of the room and could detect a heart as it beat faster or slower, understanding whether it beat with pain or happiness, sadness or the stress of telling a lie.

He kept silent as he took his seat, noting everyone's breathing, their heart rate, then let them fade to the back of his consciousness, still there, then focussed on Galain as he delivered his report.

'I bring news of the Lady Maya, who, as we surmised, joined Taran and Rakan on their mission to the Horselords,' Ultric announced.

Galain's heart rate spiked a little, matching everyone else's in the back of his mind, then Ultric continued.

'The story of their journey is a long one, so I'll keep my synopsis concise. If more detail is required, I'll expand. There's good news, but also bad. I shall start with the good.'

Galain's heart beat with impatience, which wasn't unusual.

'They've succeeded in their quest to engage the help of the Horselords, and will, in due course, make the return journey, and they'll arrive before spring,' he announced.

Galain's heart rate increased, yet so far this showed nothing, for good news such as this would pique anyone's interest. He paused, just long enough for everyone's impatience to grow a little, but also for Galain's heart to slow again.

'The other news is that from the start of their journey they were hunted by Rangers, which if it's to be believed, were trained by a daemon-possessed warrior who met his end on the walls of Tristan's Folly.'

He smiled inwardly as he said these last two words, knowing that the name attributed to the western border fortress was not welcomed by Tristan. Interestingly, Galain's heart continued beating as if Ultric had said nothing new.

'There were over a hundred and sixty Rangers who pursued them, all that remained of Daleth's finest, and they were slain to a man!'

He omitted to say that it had been the intervention of the Horselords that secured this victory, for if Galain was responsible for passing on this information, then he wanted to put fear into Daleth's heart, wondering how just three had achieved the impossible.

Gasps met his announcement, even Galain reacted in type, yet his heart gave him away, for it beat with the subtlest hint of anger, not amazement or shock.

'The bad news is all that's left,' Ultric's sober tone brought quiet back to the room, 'and it comes in two parts. One is that Daleth's

The End of Dreams

armies had already invaded the grasslands, decimating the clans there, leaving only a few thousand alive, so the number returning is way below what we'd hoped.'

Disappointment reverberated in everyone's heart except Galain, whose beat with interest.

He paused, longer this time.

'By the gods, Ultric, speak up, man. Have you fallen asleep?' Tristan demanded, never known for his patience.

Yet the pause had done its job, for Galain's heart was settled again and whilst Ultric was already sure, he had one more test.

'The other bad news you may have already surmised. Taran and Rakan were pursued just a few days after leaving, so there's no doubt that their mission was betrayed. The fact that every Ranger was engaged in the hunt proves that someone is giving information to the enemy. Amongst us is a traitor!'

Cries of disbelief and denial of his statement had come from everyone around him.

Yet there it was, Galain's heartbeat exhibiting bowel wrenching panic until he managed to calm himself. Ultric felt a small amount of admiration for Galain's discipline in bringing his entire being back under such tight control.

There was no doubt in his mind now, but he needed space and time to prove it. For this, he needed Galain to believe himself above suspicion.

'I'm certain that amongst the nobles and merchants who attend our meetings, there must be one who is selling this information for profit or for promises of safety. Whichever it is, I believe we need to keep any and all meetings closed from hereon.'

He'd expected Galain's heart to beat with relief then, yet it didn't, not entirely. Instead, it beat with a strange cadence, one he didn't quite recognise until even that settled.

Tristan spoke up.

'So it seems that trusting in our Lord Commander Taran to deliver us, was a fool's dream, and I should have known better.'

'That's not a fair judgement,' Dafne said. 'He, Maya, and Rakan have achieved what no one could imagine possible. How is it Taran's fault that Daleth decimated the clans before his arrival? We should be grateful he's returning to us with any help whatsoever. We had no trained cavalry, and now we have some of the finest to offset Daleth's lancers.'

'Not so fine, apparently,' Tristan growled. 'The Freestates have paid them for generations to keep away from our lands when it seems they were no longer a formidable foe. We have no one, no one to save my throne, my lands!'

'No one?' Ostrom growled. 'No one, really? Is that what you consider mine and Dafne's troops, no one? I didn't come here to save your lands or your title. I came here to fight Daleth to avenge the death of my son! Choose your words carefully next time, King Tristan, or you may find yourself alone when Daleth and his horde arrives!'

Tristan's face paled as he realised his mistake.

'I apologise for my hasty words. They were said under duress without thought, and the hurt they caused was without intent!'

Ultric listened carefully to Galain's heart beating with joy as the conflict in the room continued for some time before the meeting was adjourned.

He'd found exactly what he was looking for. Now he had to find a way to prove it to everyone else.

***

They'd stayed longer than they should have, but not as long as he wanted to, Taran mused, as he rode.

He wished there'd been no war, and he, Maya, and Rakan could have lived amongst these folk, adopted their ways and found true happiness while doing so. There was no duplicity in them, no hidden hatreds, no jealousy. Their prized possessions were not unique, just the weapons and armour they wielded and wore, which by tradition were the same as every other knight, not forgetting their enormous chargers upon which they rode into combat.

Serious arguments were settled by jousting, a painful but non-fatal form of contest that left no one in doubt as to the winner. Afterwards, the combatants would toast the other, leaving no bad blood. They were a family who loved one another, for they shared the same values, religion, and ideals, without exception.

They were also a proud people, proud of their ways and culture, and whilst pride could sometime lead to conceit, in their case, it hadn't. They lived a simple, honest, happy existence, and had done for centuries.

Taran's whole body ached as he looked first at Maya and Rakan, then at the long lines of knights spreading into the distance. Their time amongst the Horselords hadn't been spent in idleness, far from it. He smiled as he thought back on how much had been accomplished.

Maya had assured the clan's people that Daleth's army had left their lands. The revelation of her ability to spirit travel only served to increase their awe, for who else could fly the land at night under the stars and moon, but one held dear by the goddess herself?

So, with their original shrine and settlement destroyed, everyone set about building a new one. Trees had been felled and hewn, permanent structures erected, so that when it was time to leave, the youngest and eldest would stay behind to ensure that the Horselords' legacy had a chance to live on if the worst were to happen.

On the second day, Shinsen had introduced him, Maya, and Rakan to their new mounts, insisting that time was spent learning the clan's way of life, including combat. Rakan and Maya's progress was hard-earned, whereas Taran excelled almost immediately.

'Your gift gives you an unfair advantage,' Maya had complained, as she'd ridden alongside, 'you look so natural,' and had leant to kiss him, affectionately put her hand behind his neck, then pulled him tumbling into the deep snow to the merriment of those around.

They'd been happy times. Whether it was helping to build lodges, learning to control their chargers or wield a lance, there was never a dull moment. Taran had never felt so content in his life and wished with all his heart for this simple existence to continue, though he knew it couldn't.

The shrine and settlement to house the clerics, children, and their protectors, the old knights, were eventually finished. With everything that needed to be done attended to, it would soon be time to head north.

Yet before that, with the shrine complete, Taran and Maya had quietly approached Shinsen and Taysen. Three days later, for the first time in the Horselords' history, two souls born beyond its nation's borders were married under the tree of the Moon Goddess.

Maya had been dressed in a traditional white gown, drawn close around her waist with a thick, silver cord. Spring flowers, having been called forth by her gift, had been weaved into her hair. A simple silver circlet representing the halo of the full moon adorned her brow.

Taran had worn a white cloak, trimmed with fur from a silver fox over his burnished plate armour. Silver tassels hung from the hilt of his weapons and wrists.

Led by Taysen, Taran and Maya exchanged the vows of marriage used by the Horselords since time immemorial. Silver rings were exchanged and to complete the ceremony, their hands were bound loosely together with a silvered rope by Shinmata, Shinsen's wife.

The kiss they shared as Taysen announced them husband and wife was met with a roar of approval from the entire Horselords nation who had gathered to celebrate their union.

The celebrations had gone on for three days. Jousting, drinking, and dancing, with laughter, and happiness, finally dispelling any remaining darkness from every soul.

Then it was time to leave.

It was touching and emotional to see so many genuine goodbyes. Maya had mingled with everyone, and yet people still looked at her with a mixture of awe and love. The children's eyes were as round as plates when she took time to hug them all as she said farewell.

Many of the children had lost parents when the other clans were decimated, yet they'd all been adopted, and now not a single one was without a surrogate family. Many were the kisses bestowed by the departing knights on their children, new and old.

Maya had flown the spirit paths most nights as she'd slept, to ensure their safety and to keep an eye on Daleth's army, in case he sent lancers to finish the mission his Rangers had failed to accomplish. Fortunately, his army still remained wintered in Freemantle.

Despite Maya's divine reputation, Shinsen still had riders out scouting. Taran, Maya, and Rakan took their turns too, much to the approval of those around them. They might not have been born of the clans, but they were now part of them and were loved as if they'd never been anything else.

The End of Dreams

Rakan brought his charger alongside Taran's.

'It's hard to believe so many of these fine people lost their lives to Daleth's army,' he sighed. 'Used properly, these knights could devastate any army they fell upon unaware, but that's not how they fight. Had we returned with all of them, we might have had a chance, but with just four thousand, it really won't make a difference.'

'It will have to be enough,' Taran replied, 'and we must remember, had we not found them in such dire circumstances, we might not have left here with our lives. For all our sakes, we need to find a way to out-think Daleth on the battlefield and win with what we have.'

'But how can we do that?' Maya asked, 'and I ask because I've been mulling that question ever since we found how few knights were left. Daleth has more spearmen, more swordsmen, not forgetting his archers and lancers. For every unit we have, he not only has a counter but also has many more to spare.'

'I believe these knights are the key,' Taran said. 'If they can fall upon the rear of the enemy, they could decimate five times their number or more, and that could lead to a rout.'

Rakan nodded.

'In terms of the damage they could do, I agree, but there'll be no rout, not whilst Daleth lives. But, if he's dead, then perhaps, just perhaps, they might run.'

Taran scratched his chin.

'But how to kill Daleth amongst an entire army? He'll stay out of range of the Eyre, and will probably oversee the attack surrounded by his bodyguard.' He looked to Rakan for affirmation.

Rakan grimaced.

'I think so. He's not afraid of combat, but he won't take a risk when victory is at hand. He'll oversee the battle, and react to whatever we do, and therein lies the problem. We might surprise him, even mislead him, but he can afford to make mistakes. He can afford to lose forty-odd thousand men for our forty-odd thousand and still have more than that left over while we stand defeated.'

They were silent for a while until Maya laughed softly.

Taran looked at her, bemused.

'What is it about our predicament that you find funny?'

Maya looked down momentarily before lifting her gaze, eyes confident.

'I just believe in us. How many times have we faced certain death and prevailed? Daleth should be worried, because if all of his Rangers couldn't kill us three, then with an army at our backs, who knows what's achievable!'

Taran guided his charger closer to Maya's and leant over, pulling her in close.

'I think what would worry Daleth most, is seeing how confident and passionate you are, and how that inspires those around you to be better versions of themselves. That's also a gift, not just that of healing the land. Look at Rakan,' he continued, raising his voice. 'He is your crowning glory, your greatest achievement. Once he could only eat with his fingers, and couldn't count past two. Now he knows which way to face when riding a horse and can dress himself in the morning.'

Rakan's laughter joined their own, and everyone close enough to hear smiled at the banter.

'Shinsen believes it'll take four weeks to reach Freeguard based on Maya's description of the route and the snow we're pushing through,' Rakan advised.

'Strangely, I feel in no rush,' Maya admitted. 'It seems I'm always happiest when it's just us three travelling together.'

'Now look who can't count,' Rakan joked. 'I believe that you forgot to add four thousand knights!'

Maya's laughter rang out with such merriment that everyone joined in.

'I love you, my princess,' Taran said softly, so no one else could hear. 'I'll love you in this world and into the next.'

Maya flushed with warmth at his words and repeated them back.

'However, let's stay in this world for as long as we can,' she added. 'Agreed?'

'Agreed,' Taran said, beaming, and they rode on, hand in hand.

***

The End of Dreams

Daleth squinted against the light. For the first time in far too long, the sun's heat could be felt, and he welcomed its warmth. He felt strong, alive, his strength fully returned.

At his feet and all around, the dirty snow was rapidly being churned to slush. The pre-spring melt was in full flow, and men trained everywhere his eye turned.

He walked amongst them as he had for the last few weeks, urging them to practice harder. Soldiers called for him to join them in their endeavours, but today he excused himself. Instead, he encouraged them with words, promises of wealth, and revenge on the king and people responsible for their nation's death.

His horse was led over by Baidan, and Daleth mounted, saluting the troops as he rode east, the clatter of hooves forewarning those ahead to move swiftly aside as their king passed. This was his current favourite pastime. Roaming the countryside with his bodyguard around him, exulting in his strength and youth as his gift fed off this verdant land. Once the snow melted and spring was in full flow, the energy he'd feel would be like a drug.

He contemplated the coming weeks ahead as he rode.

In several days, Gregor, Julius and their forces would return with tales of blood and victory, bringing his army back to full strength. Then, with the land becoming firmer day by day, they'd march east. Within four weeks, they'd be at the very gates of Freeguard itself, not that he expected to have to break them down. Jared assured that the alliance forces would seek to engage on the low hills to best use the desert spearmen, archers, swordsmen, and now cavalry.

It had been a disappointing surprise to find out that Gregor had not killed all the knights of the clans. Fortunately, Jared reported that only a few thousand would be in the field, and whilst still a dangerous force, Daleth had many times that amount of spearmen.

He could engage the whole enemy line, have a rearguard in place, and still have thousands to fall upon the enemy flank and rear, although perhaps the knights would be used to try and deflect that tactic.

It mattered not what they did … he'd crush them. Then, if as anticipated, Tristan retreated from the field, victory would be even easier. Yana would be arriving back at Freeguard almost any day now, and then Jared would report on Tristan's reaction to the demands.

Jared was still insistent he could assume Tristan's guise and break apart the alliance, but after losing all of his other Rangers, it seemed a risk not worth taking. Gregor and Jared would be vital in the years to come. They were spies without parallel, worth more than thousands of his regular soldiers who could always be replaced.

The loss of his beloved Rangers still hit him like a blow whenever it crossed his mind. He just couldn't begin to imagine how every one of them had died when the net had closed on the fugitives. He shook his head. He'd spent too much time thinking of this already, but it was so hard to let go.

Maybe he should get the army out on the plains tomorrow, he thought, as he rode by another unit hard at work, exhorted by a grizzled veteran. They'd trained so hard in honing their weapon skills, yet manoeuvring in large formations required open countryside, and he couldn't wait to get out of this city and put his men to the test.

They were as impatient as he was, he thought, as he looked up at a dozen soldiers who'd been nailed to crosses and left to die. He didn't blame them for fighting, for there were many times he'd felt like spilling blood, he was so desperate for the winter to finish and spring to arrive.

Then, once Freeguard fell, it would still be spring, and he smiled.

Over these last months, the palace at Freemantle had given up many hidden secrets. Yet, the works of art, statues, paintings, spices, rare metals, and gems all paled in comparison to some simple scrolls that had been hidden in plain sight in one of the administrative rooms.

Against gold and gemstones, what value could parchment have?

But they held the trade routes of the Freestates and maps of lands far beyond the desert. To him, they were invaluable, and his dreams now knew exactly where they were taking him.

He laughed out loud, a deep rolling laugh, and holding onto the horse with his thighs, opened his arms to embrace the sky above. The gods might look down on the world, but one day, one day, he would own it.

***

The End of Dreams

Another week and they'd be at Freeguard. For some, it was a journey that they couldn't wait to finish, and for others, they didn't want it to end.

Taran looked around at the knights astride their chargers, sitting tall in their saddles, glorious in the midday sun, resplendent in plate armour that Shinsen had ordered be worn by all.

Taran, Maya, and Rakan were also outfitted in the same fashion, and being surrounded in such armour made one feel impervious. However, Taran knew that feeling had led to the clans' decimation when they'd faced Daleth's spearmen.

Throughout the journey, the knights had talked of the battle to come and what surprised Taran was the certainty they all exuded. They felt they had everything to gain, either victory under Maya's leadership, or a swift journey into the arms of the goddess should they fail. They were as impatient for this journey to end as Taran and Maya were for it to continue forever.

Never before had they enjoyed such uninterrupted intimacy, day after day, night after night, for so long. It was as if they discovered each other anew with the rising sun and the knights now joked that if Maya was the envoy of the Moon Goddess, then Taran was sent by the god of fertility.

Maya had been so embarrassed when she'd first heard this after they broke fast one morning, that she could hardly look anyone in the eye for days. Now she just flashed her smile and laughed along with everyone else, simply happy to enjoy Taran's physical affections that inspired her own tenfold.

Each time they paused for a noon break, Shinsen and his two closest knights, Chochen and Nadlen, would sit down with Taran, Maya, and Rakan, talking through endless scenarios of how the final battle could be fought. Despite Shinsen's conversion back to the religion he'd discarded as a youth, he was not blinded by it, and time and again they played it out, using pieces from a martial board to replicate the fight. A game that seemed to be played across all kingdoms.

Maya had used her gift of spirit travel to help them get a detailed understanding of the terrain around Freeguard, and as everyone ate, they moved the pieces around a quickly fashioned model in the soil.

They threw dice as formation met formation, to see if they could ever come up with a scenario whereby the god of luck might help them win.

They never came close.

Rakan growled as, once again, they laid the pieces out. There was no question as to where the main Freestates forces would start the battle. The hills slightly to the northwest of Freeguard would be where the desert spears would be positioned, forming a line that would curve around the base facing to the south.

They'd discussed the merits of having them further up the hill, but couldn't risk Daleth simply marching into the city if they were too far away. It had been decided that a thousand Eyre archers hidden on the walls of Freeguard would be able to decimate any unsuspecting foe that tried to manoeuvre through the gap between the end of the spear line and the city wall.

The remaining four thousand Eyre would be directly behind the spears on the hillside itself, adding to their range and giving them a direct line of sight on the attacking formations.

Tristan's Freestates soldiers and the countryfolk levy would be held a little further up the hill, protecting the archers, and also ready to defend the flanks as and when the enemy line started to overlap using their strength of numbers.

They all agreed, the knights were pivotal to even come close to success. They alone could decimate many times their number if only they could launch a charge from behind, but this is where they constantly failed. With his vast horde, Daleth would never be foolish enough to leave the rear of his forces unguarded.

'This is pointless,' Rakan complained. 'We won't have fifty attempts to win this battle, and by my calculations, we've already lost more than that without winning so far. We have one chance, and we have to win. Daleth will not make the mistakes that we need.'

Taran nodded.

'I've needed to see this so many times to be sure and also because I needed everyone else to see this too. For us to win, to have even a chance, I've said it before, and I'll say it again, Daleth has to die, and the earlier in the battle, the better. That way, his units will have no central command and will fight independently or perhaps even break.'

Nods came from all around.

The End of Dreams

'Only if the Moon Goddess herself came to lead us, would we have a chance,' Shinsen agreed. 'But if she doesn't come to us, then we'll end up seeing her anyway, just a lot sooner than we'd intended.' He smiled as he joked of their deaths as if it were nothing to be concerned about.

'How will we ever get close to Daleth?' Maya asked. 'Will he ever position himself close to the fight Rakan?'

Rakan shook his head.

'Maybe later, once we rout,' he sighed.

Shinsen snapped his fingers.

'A ruse! We have some of our forces pretend to rout, to get the enemy to break formation in pursuit.'

The noon break lasted longer than usual as they tried this strategy dozens of ways until Shinsen stood.

'We've wasted enough time, this isn't going to work either. Let's ride while the afternoon still gives us light.'

Reluctantly, they all got back into the saddle again.

As they rode, it still went round and round in Taran's head. Daleth had to die, it was the only way, but whoever tried, had to be willing to die too.

Taran looked over at Maya. He loved her so much. A love worth living for, but also a love worth dying for, and if that was the price to keep her alive, he'd gladly pay it.

'What are you thinking of, my love?' Maya asked, leaning in to demand a kiss.

Taran didn't want to lie to Maya, but nor did he want to share his thoughts, so he paused a moment.

'I love you,' he said, warming as the words left his lips, for Maya's face always broke into a smile as he voiced those words, and he held her hand.

He now had an idea of what needed to be done, but didn't want to share it just yet. There was still a week of happiness before them until Freeguard, and sharing his plan before it was fully formed would only serve to worry Maya unduly.

Suddenly, he remembered the young girl from the village who reminded him of Maya, the words she'd spoken, and a chill ran down his spine.

You will only know the briefest happiness again before you die.'
Taran sighed, and Maya looked over quizzically.

He felt embarrassed for a moment. This was no time to let his fears get the better of him, nor worry Maya with a girl's ramblings.

'I intend to love you in this life for a long time to come,' he said with such determination that Maya laughed.

She leant over to kiss him again, and it was so full of love that it banished the chill and filled him with the desire to live, and live he would, for hers was definitely a love worth living for.

***

Chapter XXI

Jared's mood was dark, as dark as his soul if only he still had one.

He should have known happiness, but that only came with Daleth's praise, and whilst that had been lavished upon him of late, he knew he didn't deserve it, and thus his mood was like the blackest of nights.

His plan had worked. Yana had returned and delivered Daleth's message to Tristan, exactly as she'd been told to. There'd been no attempt at manipulation or duplicity on her part.

Tristan had been overjoyed and promised Yana all kinds of rewards in recognition of her diplomatic skills.

Jared thought it would've been better to keep the mission a complete secret by having her killed, just like the other ten soldiers who'd reported straight to him on their return. He'd met them with poisoned wine and watched them die with disbelief in their eyes.

Worst of all, as Tristan had confided to them both that he'd take Daleth's offer, there was no need for Jared to shift to the king's form. If the coward was going to pull his troops back from the battle, then why take the risk?

Daleth had congratulated Jared when he'd relayed the news as soon as he had a quiet moment. In fact, so lavish had been the praise that for a short while it mollified him. But now, as the night bore on, and the more it played on his mind, the more he felt a failure. He wanted, no, needed, to show Daleth how indispensable he could really be.

Daleth suspected Ultric had the gift of truth seeing, and that was likely correct. How else could the old man perceive there was something awry when he was completely blind? With him dissecting Jared's every move and word, any shift to take Tristan's form was too risky. But what if Ultric died unexpectedly? Then what harm would the shift be just before the battle to ensure the plan went flawlessly?

It was against Daleth's explicit order to harm Ultric, for he was far too close to Ostrom and had possibly mentioned his suspicions. But, if Ultric appeared to die of natural causes, then there was little risk, and if suspicions were voiced, he'd just assume Tristan's mantle sooner than later.

Jared sat there in the darkness in his room, idly spinning one of Galain's woodworking tools in his hand. It was an incredibly thin, boring tool, just as deadly as a dagger if used correctly, and Jared felt his willpower wilt as his bloodlust started to overwhelm him.

It was nearing midnight. A few guards were on duty, but as he was in charge of the palace staff, he'd allowed them to relax a little at night, to save their strength, and they'd gratefully taken to doing just that. Most of the guards patrolled the grounds, as any attack would come from the outside.

Jared's head spun. To obey Daleth had been his whole life's purpose, but to further his king's plans, to help him win an easier victory, to help realise Daleth's dreams, surely that warranted him to use his discretion.

His mind suddenly became crystal clear, and he pared some polishing wax off a small block that sat on Galain's desk. He opened the door to his room, just a few steps away from Tristan's. After enjoying himself with a young woman Jared had arranged, the king was sound asleep, evidenced by the loud snoring.

He smiled, nodding at one of the guards who stood outside the king's door.

'Can't sleep,' he mumbled, yawning, and ambled down the corridor, scratching himself. The guard went back to his dream world, for Galain was often out at night.

He turned the corner, heading toward the stairs, beyond which had been Lady Maya's room, but which also held the apartments for Ostrom, Ultric, Dafne and any other dignitary that the king favoured at the time.

He'd walked this way so many times that he knew every floorboard that creaked and every one that didn't. Also, as head of the palace, he'd ensured that all doors were well oiled to ensure no one's sleep was ever interrupted.

He walked as he always walked, slightly slouched, round-shouldered, without haste, yet he trod silently, his eyes and ears ensuring he went unobserved as he made his way to the furthest door where Ultric slept.

He knew of Ultric's ability to spirit travel, for that was how the old man navigated his way so perfectly without any kind of aid despite his absolute blindness. For a moment, Jared wondered if Ultric might be aware of his approach, but there was only one way to find out.

He gently pushed down on the handle, silently opening the door and slipped inside, closing it without a sound behind him.

Ultric slept with the curtains at the windows wide open, as being blind there was no need to close them, and it gave all the light Jared needed to navigate the room to stand beside Ultric's sleeping form.

He knew he should just do the deed, and the tool was in his hand as he sat on Ultric's bedside, but he just couldn't, not yet. He put his hand hard over Ultric's mouth.

'Wake up, old man,' he whispered, and waited.

It wasn't long before Ultric twitched slightly as his spirit form returned to his body. His blank eyes opened, and he struggled against the hand over his mouth, to no avail.

Jared leaned forward, putting his mouth close to Ultric's ear.

'Do you know who this is?' he asked.

Ultric nodded as much as he was able to with Jared's vice-like grip on his head.

Jared smiled.

'Then, before you die, I want you to know,' he said softly, 'that you were right to be suspicious. I was indeed Tolgarth, and I've been a hundred others before him. I can shift to any form I please, but I serve only one, Daleth.'

As he spoke, Ultric struggled frantically, but Jared barely noticed.

'Maybe one day I'll take Ostrom's form, but first I'll take Tristan's and lead this alliance to the doom it deserves.'

Jared looked at Ultric's face and was satisfied at the terror etched upon it. He took the boring tool and pushed it inside of Ultric's ear. He took his time, enjoying the piteous moans of agony until at last, Ultric lay still, the point deep in his brain.

His thirst for blood quenched, Jared moved quickly, taking the wax from his pocket as he waited impatiently for Ultric's heart to stop. Withdrawing the slim tool, he used some cloth to wipe away the blood that came flowing out before taking the wax, and pushed it deep into Ultric's ear and then cleaned carefully again.

He smoothed Ultric's panicked features, closed his eyes, and placed one arm across his chest. Next, he rearranged the bed linen that had been kicked off the bed, then stood back, admiring his handiwork.

He crept to the door and opened it a sliver.

Seeing no one, he slipped out, quietly closing the door behind him and padded to the stairs, before making his way down to the kitchens.

Kitchen staff worked on shifts throughout the day and night, and he stayed a while eating and talking, making sure he'd be remembered if anyone should subsequently ask of his whereabouts. Despite being humble bread and soup, the food tasted delicious, and when he finished, he went back to his room, feeling satisfied.

When he climbed into bed, his mind was at peace, and he closed his eyes, thinking of the day he'd shift to Tristan's form and tear the alliance apart from the inside.

***

Maya looked across at Taran as the knights made camp within some heavy woods on a hill. They'd chosen to end the day's travel early, to take advantage of the shelter it provided for everyone and to make fires to banish the chill from their bones.

Freeguard was now no more than four day's ride away, and while everyone was keen to press on, the landscape was treacherous. The snow was melting rapidly under the onslaught of heavy rain, and the chargers were tired. There was no point risking injury to rider or mount when they knew that time was, for once, on their side.

Maya had spirit travelled every other night, no longer finding it draining like she used to, and had found Daleth's entire army massed at Freemantle. There were no enemy, lancers or otherwise, near the clan's line of march, and nothing would stop them from reaching their destination in good time. It was strange to feel so safe despite the final battle being close.

Maya beckoned Taran over, taking him by the hand, and called over to Rakan.

'We're just going for a walk, maybe a long one.'

Rakan waved in acknowledgement, and they headed deeper into the woods, walking for maybe an hour, the conversation flowing, interspersed with kisses.

'I think we should head back,' Taran said, shivering, looking up at the sky. 'It looks like it might rain again soon.'

'Not yet,' Maya replied, taking his hand and leading him ever further amongst the trees.

She moved with a purpose, leading Taran as she ducked and weaved amongst the foliage without ever seeming to disturb any.

Taran shook his head in wonder. Maya never seemed to leave a footprint, whereas the soil seemed to want to suck his boots from his feet. Her grace was breath-taking, and without question, she was born to be in the wilderness; a creature of the forest, a magical being.

Maya seemed to find what she was searching for because she cocked her head to one side as if listening and nodded in satisfaction.

'Sit here and wait,' she ordered, pointing to a tree whose thick foliage had kept the ground beneath fairly dry. As Taran complied, she added. 'Close your eyes and don't open them till I say so.'

Taran laughed.

'I'm too cold and tired for misbehaviour,' he protested. 'To manage that, I need a hot fire and a warm bedroll with you beside me.'

Maya's laughter peeled out, and Taran laughed too, for it was so infectious.

'Is that all you ever think about?' she asked, leaning in close, kissing him gently on the lips. 'I hope so, because those thoughts often consume me. But, not right now! Now wait here and do as you're told.'

With that, she skipped off, and Taran could hear her humming a vaguely familiar tune.

'I hope your eyes are closed,' he heard Maya call from some distance away, and he smiled, keeping them sealed. Maya could be so mischievous, and he wondered whether he'd be told to open his eyes only to be hit with a mud pie or a snowball, as had happened several times of late.

He heard Maya's footsteps returning, and she took his hand.

'Come with me,' she said again, gently pulling him to his feet, leading him. 'Don't worry, there's no mud around here to make a pie with. I looked.'

'I thought I was the one who read minds,' he chuckled. 'That's exactly what I expected.'

Maya only led him a short way before stopping.

'Open your eyes,' she said.

As Taran did as Maya had asked, her arm snaked around his waist, pulling him close. Maya's almost magical intuition had helped her find a pool in the middle of the woods, and whilst he'd waited, she'd used her gift to turn it into something out of Taran's most vivid dreams.

All around the pool, flowers had burst open amongst vibrant green moss. The trees were blooming months early, and blossom fell along with the rain that managed to find its way through the canopy of healthy green leaves that covered the woods as far as he could see.

Taran felt warm inside.

'It's almost exactly like the pool where we first ...'

'Yes,' Maya interrupted him as she started to pull Taran down toward the water.

'You cannot possibly be serious. It's going to be freezing!' Taran resisted. 'Have you any idea what such cold water can do to a man?'

Maya kept pulling.

'You've never said no to me before,' she said, looking into his eyes as she backed toward the pool. 'Don't think you can refuse me now I'm your wife.'

'At least let me take my boots off,' Taran laughed nervously.

Maya let go and removed hers while Taran did the same.

As Taran stood barefoot, Maya took his hand, stepping back into the water, looking behind her, placing her feet carefully.

'Oh,' she said, 'this isn't cold at all. There must be a hot underground spring pushing up water from below. That's fortunate!'

'Thank the gods,' Taran breathed. 'I was honestly having second thoughts.'

The End of Dreams

Suddenly, Maya pulled him hard, and he tumbled past into the depths and came up spluttering.

'By the gods,' he cried, 'it's f-f-freezing,'

Maya's lips closed over his, cutting off any further protests.

'It is rather cold,' she gasped between chattering teeth as she broke free. 'Whose crazy idea was this? Trust me, we'll get used to it if we keep our shoulders underwater.' She lowered herself down, eyes full of laughter. 'You see, it's not so bad!'

Taran wrinkled his nose, his face pale.

'It isn't that good either.'

Maya moved to the side of the pool.

'I remember once, a young man I barely knew, but who I was starting to fall in love with, asked me to trust him.'

So saying, she pulled some small leaves from a plant by the side of the water and moved back to Taran.

'Turn around,' she instructed, 'and lean back in my arms.'

As Taran did so, she rubbed the leaves in her hand and started to wash his hair.

A sweet, almost citric scent filled the air.

'That smells amazing,' Taran sighed, his shivers dissipating now he was getting used to the cold.

Maya laughed.

'That's likely because we smelled so bad for so long, we'd just got used to it. Now relax.' Her hands kneaded his scalp as she hummed a gentle melody.

Taran felt himself drifting despite the cold.

Once finished, Maya leaned forward, kissing his lips, her damp, cold hair falling across his face.

'Are you awake, my love?' she asked.

Taran nodded, smiling happily.

'Good,' she whispered, 'because we need to rinse your hair.'

With a push, Maya promptly dunked Taran's head under the water, laughing merrily.

Once Taran had stopped coughing and wiping water from his face, he saw a different look in Maya's eyes.

'I remember,' he said, 'I bathed once with a beautiful girl I was falling in love with, and I stole a look at her as she washed naked behind me. At the time, all I wanted to do was pull her to me.'

'To do what?' Maya asked, leaning in close.

'To do this,' he said, and the next moment they were struggling to peel off soaking wet clothes that clung to their bodies, unwilling to let go. But undress they did and found the other unwilling to let go too.

It was starting to get dark as they walked back into camp, dripping, to huddle close to a fire, shivering uncontrollably in their wet clothes.

Rakan, Shinsen, and the others burst out laughing.

'We'll need to build a bigger village at the shrine if you two keep on like this,' Shinsen teased. 'The Moon Goddess has favoured you two with a love that's a shining example to us all. Now, seeing you two has reminded me that my wife and I have been neglecting one another, so if you'll excuse me, I have something to attend to.'

Rakan stumped over, bringing some blankets.

'Get out of those wet clothes,' he growled, 'but this time just to get dry, nothing else. Now, I'll get you some food.'

Yet the growl in his voice was outweighed by the affection in his eyes as he looked at them.

'Come, Chochen, Nadlen, let's give these youngsters some privacy even if they have little shame,' Rakan chuckled as he dragged them away while Taran and Maya started to undress.

'Will you keep me warm tonight?' Maya asked as she leaned against Taran.

'Every night till the end of days, my love,' he replied.

Maya rested her head on Taran's shoulder, her heart singing as she thought of the baby growing inside her.

Shinsen's joke had been uncannily accurate, they'd indeed been blessed by the Moon Goddess, and she knew exactly when. It had been the night which had seen their gifts return. The night when their love and passion had created the most wondrous gift of all. Life.

She'd found out unexpectedly the first time she'd spirit travelled after regaining her gift. On returning to her body to merge, she'd seen a bright pinpoint of light shining within her tummy. Every night it grew and grew, so that now when she looked, she could clearly see the tiny shape of their child glowing brightly from within.

The End of Dreams

Only once this battle was won, would she tell Taran, for he'd need a clear mind in the days ahead. She couldn't wait to see his face when she told him. After getting married, it would surely be the happiest day of her life.

***

As they entered the city, their reception was as if they'd already won the final battle. Taran rode alongside Maya, Rakan, and Shinsen, while the rest of the knights waited outside the southern gate. As the four of them entered the city, they were surrounded by cheering soldiers, merchants, and other folks who'd flocked to welcome them.

Taran and Maya's names were shouted loudly as people surged around them, some coming forward to touch their boots while others held up babies for Maya to bless.

Maya leaned toward Taran, trying to be heard above the roar.

'Why is it that despite this welcome, this couldn't feel less like coming home?'

Taran nodded in agreement, reaching out to hold her hand as she rode beside him.

If the crowd had been loud before, the screams of delight as they publically showed their affection for one another was deafening, and Maya and Taran started to laugh at the joy it gave everyone.

'Let's really give them something to scream about,' Maya shouted, and almost pulled Taran from his horse as she kissed him.

'If you two carry on like that, it'll cause a riot,' Rakan called from close behind.

'Taran, let's see what they do if you kiss your horse,' Shinsen suggested. 'I'll definitely cheer if you do that!'

He and Rakan couldn't stop laughing for a while.

A familiar old woman pushed her way to stand in front of their horses, and they pulled on the reins, giving her time to move.

'Behold, the Lady Maya!' called the woman, her voice strangely strong, rising about the crowd that stopped to listen. 'Tell us all,' she said, fixing Maya with her gaze, 'who this is riding beside you. Tell us all.'

'He is my true love,' Maya proclaimed. 'It's for him that I live, but for him, I would gladly die.' Maya blushed furiously as the woman smiled and disappeared back into the crowd.

'Wow!' Taran exclaimed as the crowd screamed their names again. The chargers they sat astride snorted at the noise from the deafening crowd. Fortunately, the horses were so well trained that even the jostling didn't cause them to flail with their hooves as they slowly made their way toward the palace.

After a while, the crowd became so dense that they were forced to dismount. Taran turned to a burly soldier in the crowd.

'Would you ensure these are taken to the royal stables please, Jorge,' he asked, using his gift to discover the man's name.

Jorge beamed in happiness at being singled out and nodded so hard his helm slipped over his face, and even the laughter of those around him couldn't take his smile away.

It was like wading against the current in a stream, but finally, they reached the city centre and the palace. Many familiar faces were here, common folk who were now soldiers greeted Maya, and she knew their names even without Taran helping her.

The noise was deafening, and Taran communicated with the others through his gift. The first time he'd done this with Shinsen, the man had fallen backwards off the log he was sitting on, but now he was accustomed to Taran's ability.

'I wonder if Tristan will be as happy to see us?' Taran laughed in his mind, and they all gave their version of what they thought he might say.

As they approached the palace gates, Taran almost tripped over a young girl and was about to move past when he recognised her as the one he'd rescued. He swept her up in his arms, holding her close, and Maya smiled as he told her who the girl was … the one who'd started to weaken the amulet's hold by reminding him of her.

He went to put the girl down, but she held on tightly, shaking her head.

'It seems I have competition.' Maya laughed.

'Are you alright?' Taran asked smiling, gently disentangling himself as the girl shook her head furiously. 'Tell me, have you lost your mother?'

The girl shook her head, her arm pointing out straight into the crowd without even looking. Taran followed her finger and saw the mother coming to get her.

Suddenly, the girl looked up at Maya.

'He saved my life,' she said, tears pouring down her face, 'but I can't save his!' and with that, she dropped from Taran's arms and ran to her mother clutching the woman's leg.

Maya's wide eyes shot a questioning look at Taran, but he just smiled reassuringly, and they moved on.

The crowd stayed back now, respectful of the palace guards at the boundary gates where the trio were welcomed with warm smiles by the archers and spearmen on duty. With a final wave to the ecstatic crowd, they were escorted to the palace's main doors, which opened before them.

'Be calm, son,' Rakan said softly.

Taran looked Rakan in the eye.

'Fear not. I'm a better version of my old self, thanks to Maya and you. Tristan has nothing to fear from me as long as he accepts how things now are, and I'll make sure he understands that.'

'Now let's go greet the illustrious king.'

***

Tristan sat in the audience chamber, observing those around him. Ostrom and Dafne sat at the table with him, Galain waiting to one side, ready and attentive.

Ostrom's face was sombre, he hadn't been the same since Ultric's death and his dour demeanour was wearing thin on Tristan's patience. Dafne was talking to Ostrom too softly for Tristan to hear, which irritated him, but she was probably wasting her time trying to ease the man's sorrow with meaningless, distracting talk.

How foolish to let yourself get attached to a servant, but saying that to Ostrom would likely have unfortunate consequences, so Tristan kept these thoughts to himself.

He sighed, an eye twitching, impatience gnawing at his temper, as he waited for Lord Commander Taran to deign to attend.

Early, he'd been woken to be told that thousands of heavy cavalry were in the distance approaching the city. Whilst he'd readied himself with Galain's assistance, messengers advised that Taran and Maya could be seen at the force's head as it drew closer.

He'd ordered Galain to have everyone notified, including twenty of the best swordsmen whose loyalty had been bought beyond question. These men would do everything in their power to detain or kill the lord commander should he make any stupid move. They waited outside the side entrance to the chamber, ready to intervene the moment they were required.

Sunlight shone in through the windows set high on the walls, yet Tristan's feelings were dark. Taran's successful return with the Horselords complicated things.

Tristan frowned thoughtfully.

He'd already decided upon his course of action. The knights' arrival wasn't his fault, and he was sure the Witch-King would keep to his agreement. What were four thousand extra knights for Daleth's horde to kill? He might hardly even notice they were on the field.

Tristan's thoughts were interrupted by the swelling of sound, that tumultuous roar he remembered only too well from the last time Taran had returned. This time it was louder, and he leaned back in his chair, lifting his boots to the table, doing his best to appear nonchalant, while the floor shook ever so slightly as the noise grew and grew.

The doors to the audience chamber were already open, so when the palace doors were flung wide, the noise washed in like the tide. The sound of spear upon shield, arrow on bow, and the heavy stamp of booted feet echoed loudly.

The jostling crowd at the doors parted, and there, like some damned god from above, walked Taran, with Maya, Rakan, and one other beside them.

All were dressed in intricate plate armour that reflected the light pouring in, and to look at them gave Tristan even more of a headache than he already had.

However, he felt slightly pleased with himself when the guards in the corridor stood stiffly to attention at their posts as opposed to fawning over their lord commander. Money really could still buy hearts, just like it always had.

The End of Dreams

The four strode purposefully into the chamber, and the doors were closed behind them.

Tristan noted how different Taran looked. Despite Taran's burned face, he looked as if he'd somehow regained the youth that those injuries had stolen from him. There was now a brightness to his eyes, and where once they were filled with hatred, they now seemed somewhat amused.

Maya glowed beside Taran, and Tristan's anger threatened to boil over before even a word had been said. Perhaps he should call for the guards and simply have Taran arrested immediately for being complicit in Maya running away. Stealing the king's bride to be could see Taran's head justly removed.

Holding his anger in check, Tristan smiled inside.

Yes, he'd let Taran say what he had to say, let him have this moment of glory, then he'd call the guards and have him executed. He no longer needed Taran, and it would definitely stand him in good stead with Daleth. Better still, he'd dispose of Rakan too. He'd have to consider carefully what to do with Maya, for if she'd recovered her gift, she was again invaluable, albeit more dangerous.

His mind clear on his course of action, he stood, opening his arms. It was time to take the initiative and provoke a reaction to make this all so much easier.

'Welcome back, Lord Commander, welcome back, Major. Welcome Knight of the Clans and welcome home, my betrothed. I've missed you all. Sit, all of you, make yourself comfortable. My betrothed, your place is next to me,' Tristan said, indicating the seat next to him, fixing Maya with his stare.

Maya's eyes bored back into his.

'I'm not your betrothed, not now, not ever. I'm now Taran's wife, and you need to understand this!' Her voice was strong, assured, and brooked no disagreement.

'W-what? Taran's wife? You were supposed to be my queen!' Tristan shouted, letting go of his restraint. 'Even if you're an oath breaker, you're still my subject, and I'm your king. You will obey me. Sit next to me!'

This time Taran spoke up, yet there was no anger or malice in his voice. Instead, it was measured but firm, giving no room for misunderstanding.

'Neither Maya, Rakan, or I, are subjects of the Freestates any longer. We renounced our citizenship. We are now of the Horselords and thus not answerable to your demands or orders. Maya is now the leader of the clans, their queen and mine. As such, you'll forthwith treat her with the respect due a leader of her nation, or face the consequences.'

Tristan's face, already a bright red, began to turn purple as he struggled to form the words screaming in his head.

'Am I allowed to kill this man?' Shinsen asked conversationally.

Ostrom, who hadn't smiled in days, suddenly roared with laughter.

'Many times I've wanted to do such, but it would be inconvenient if you did, and somewhat rude considering there's a queue!'

Shinsen smiled sadly.

'Shame, although it looks like he might kill himself,' he said, as Tristan struggled to draw breath.

'As I've said,' Taran continued, looking directly at Ostrom and Dafne, 'I am no longer of the Freestates, so have relinquished my title of lord commander. So I ask you. Do you still wish me to lead your forces?'

Dafne stood, walking around the table to grasp Taran's arm.

'If not you, then it's no one,' she stated flatly.

Ostrom didn't stand, but nodded.

'As she said. If not you, then no one.'

Taran looked at Tristan.

'What about you, King Tristan? Would you have me lead the Freestates forces too?'

Tristan shook his head, anger etched clearly on his face.

'No. I'll lead my own forces,' he snarled.

Taran frowned, his face changing, his eyes turning cold. He turned to Rakan and Shinsen, looking at them, and they nodded.

'Forgive me,' Rakan said. 'I feel Shinsen and I should leave.' Together, they walked off toward the doors.

'I'm sorry, King Tristan,' Taran said, and drawing his sword, leapt over the table.

The End of Dreams

'Guards!' Tristan shrieked, throwing himself back off his chair in a desperate attempt to avoid Taran's blade. He knew he was going to be too slow, the attack had been such a surprise.

Yet Taran's blow wasn't directed at Tristan, it was aimed at Galain, who rolled out of the way in the last moment just as Taran's blade was about to cleave him in half.

As Galain sprang to his feet, his sword and dagger were in hand, and he backed away warily.

'Guards!' Tristan screamed, louder this time, and shouts sounded outside the chamber as Rakan and Shinsen frantically tried to hold the doors shut.

Ostrom and Dafne stood, swords drawn, about to intervene, but Maya stepped forward.

'You're not in danger, nor is Tristan, don't do anything rash.'

'Help me,' Galain pleaded. 'Help me!'

Strangely, there was no panic in his voice as he backed away, and suddenly there was no shambling advisor as his blade whipped from side to side, artfully parrying Taran's blows.

The clash of steel rang loudly within the chamber, and suddenly Rakan was knocked off his feet by the sheer weight of guards pushing against the doors from the other side.

Galain's face twisted in concentration as he parried Taran's blows, becoming ever more desperate as he blocked them later and later.

Rakan scrambled back to his feet, sword extended, trying to give Taran a few more moments without spilling blood himself.

With more guards flooding in, Taran finally saw an opening. He sidestepped another lunge, his blade flashed down, and Galain's sword hand fell to the floor, still gripping the handle. As Galain stared in horrified shock, Taran followed it up with a sweeping blow that was so fast no one realised it had landed until a red line appeared along Galain's neck. Blood sprayed, and Galain's legs buckled, leaving him kneeling on the floor. Slowly, like a toppling tree, he fell to one side, dead.

Blood flowed toward Tristan, who flinched, pulling his knees up to hug them.

'Kill him, kill him!' Tristan ordered, pointing a shaking finger at Taran.

The guards started to advance.

Rakan backed away hastily from so many blades, and Shinsen retreated from the main doors as more soldiers flooded in, swords bared.

'You will be quiet!' Taran bellowed, turning to look at Tristan, and strangely, Tristan felt compelled to stop.

'Guards,' Taran said, staring at the soldiers massing to attack. 'There's no threat to your king, you may return to your posts.'

They hesitated, unsure.

'Go,' Taran ordered, pointing to the door. 'There will be no more bloodshed today.'

The guards saluted and turned away.

'Why, why are you leaving?' Tristan called, his voice high as his men left.

Taran strode forward.

Tristan shrieked, yet Taran simply reached down and pulled him to his feet and, after righting the king's chair, sat him down.

'What in the nine hells is going on?' Dafne cried into the silence that was only broken by some of Tristan's sobs.

'He was a traitor,' Taran said, pointing at Galain's body. 'His thoughts were so loud that I couldn't help but hear them. They were full of killing Tristan, taking his place, and how Daleth would honour him for it. There were flashes of other things too, something about a betrayal, but I needed to act.'

'What's wrong with you?' Tristan cried, looking aghast. 'Take my place? Galain was my trusted advisor! He was no traitor and fought at the fortress. I don't care what you think or pretend to know with that convenient gift of yours, but you just murdered him in front of everyone. You'll hang for this, whether you consider yourself a citizen of mine or not!'

'Guards,' Tristan shouted again, and the doors opened.

'Wait!' Ostrom raised his hand, his voice loud, pointing at Galain's body. 'Look. Just look.'

His voice held such a strange note that everyone turned to follow his pointed finger as Galain's dead body shuddered and twisted.

Slowly, at first, it changed to resemble Tolgarth, then the face and body shifted rapidly between dozens of skin tones, looks and sizes, the skin rippling as if alive with maggots. Then, abruptly, the changes stopped.

'W-what is that thing?' Tristan gasped, stammering in horror, having held his hand over his mouth to stop himself vomiting.

As they looked closer, the face was almost featureless. It was smooth, pale with no hair, and the dead eyes that were wide open were as black as the bowels of hell.

'Ultric knew all along,' Ostrom said softly. 'He came to me with his concerns, and I didn't listen. I thought he was going a little crazy, but he knew. I feel sure he didn't die in his sleep as we first thought. This thing here was aware Ultric knew something was wrong and likely killed him to keep him quiet.'

'Ultric's dead?' Maya gasped in dismay.

Ostrom turned toward her, nodding sadly.

'We found him dead in his bed. He spoke highly of you, Maya. He saw something in you beyond your gift. He liked you, and he really didn't like anyone, not even me most of the time, and I was his king and friend.'

Maya embraced Ostrom.

'I'm sorry,' she said, sympathising with Ostrom's pain. 'I hope wherever his spirit is, he can see that his death has been avenged, but more importantly, that he's missed by his king who loved him.'

Ostrom nodded gratefully, tears in the corner of his eye as he embraced Maya back.

'So as he was a traitor,' Dafne said, 'then we can be sure he's been passing on every detail of our meetings to Daleth. There's no plan we've discussed that Daleth's not aware of. I felt we had little to no hope before, but now I feel like falling upon my own sword.'

Tristan looked at Taran, still shaking hard.

'I thought you were going to kill me,' he accused.

Taran nodded.

'For many months I thought about that every day, and fed upon that thought, for it sustained me. But now, I wish to follow a different path if you'll let me. I've forgiven you, but now I need to know you forgive me too and will accept my marriage to Maya.'

'Have you read my thoughts?' Tristan frowned, fear gripping his stomach.

'No,' Taran said sincerely. 'I gave you my word many moons ago that I never would, and I'm a man of my word. Only you can release me from that vow.'

Tristan's mind whirred. He had no problem lying to Taran, but his immediate concern was what else Taran might have picked from Galain's thoughts. What if Taran worked out that it was him that was planning a betrayal? He couldn't take the risk that Taran didn't know of his plan to leave the battlefield, betray the alliance, and salvage his kingship.

'You're forgiven,' Tristan whispered, 'but now I need to share something with you.'

'Well then, perhaps there's hope for us all after all,' Taran sighed gratefully. 'What is it you wish to share?'

Tristan thought quickly, and his sharp mind came up with the solution almost immediately. What better way to ensure a lie stayed hidden than to tell a dramatic, outrageous half-truth?

'Daleth offered me clemency and a way to keep my throne.'

Stunned silence met this announcement, so Tristan continued.

'It all makes terrible sense now,' he nodded at Galain's corpse. 'Galain sent Yana as an emissary seeking a truce. He suggested Daleth might turn around if we offered Maya's gift as a means to heal his dying kingdom. It seemed a way to end the war without further bloodshed. My concern was Maya's gift had deserted her, and she'd deserted me, but Daleth wouldn't have known that. Instead, Yana returned with a simple ultimatum.

'What was the ultimatum?' prompted Rakan.

'The only way I'd keep my throne was if I fought for it. When it came to the battle, my forces had to attack Ostrom's spearmen from behind as Daleth's forces hit him from the front.'

'WHAT?' Ostrom roared, surging to his feet. 'You didn't think this important enough to share this with us?'

Tristan shook his head.

'I knew what your reaction might be. I also understood how clever Daleth had been. If I accepted, which I never would, he'd win easily. If I declined and I shared this information with you, the distrust it might foster could split the alliance.'

'I have to admit, that makes sense,' Dafne said.

'Daleth used clever words before to try and weaken resolve at Tristan's Folly,' Maya added.

Inside, Tristan held his breath, for Taran was looking thoughtful. Had he seen through this web of lies and found the truth? Yet strangely, it was Taran who came to his rescue.

'This is what I needed,' Taran declared. 'Tristan just gave us something that might bring us victory. Daleth, in all his slyness, has just outwitted himself.'

Tristan breathed a sigh of relief. Taran didn't divulge his plan, saying he had a few more things to work out, but the meeting ended on a jubilant note. As everyone left the audience chamber, and servants came in to clear up the bloody mess of what had once been Galain, or something else, Tristan laughed inside.

He looked to the frescoed ceiling, at the gods dropping gold coins from above. If he closed his eyes, he could almost feel them landing in his lap.

***

Daleth sat across from Julius and Gregor. They'd joined him to break fast, and had again discussed the coming battle based on Jared's intelligence.

Despite assurances from Jared that the enemy forces would seek to hold the hill northwest of the city, they went over every possible alternative in detail. Plan for everything and be surprised by nothing, was a sound strategy, and Julius and Gregor could only applaud their king's thoroughness.

Daleth knew the alliance had very few strategies they could employ. They were outnumbered, out-skilled, and would be outmanoeuvred. Once Tristan and his swordsmen retreated from the battle, they'd have even fewer options, yet even this he didn't take for granted.

There wasn't a single scenario that they discussed that didn't lead to complete and utter victory. The only variable was the number of troops they'd lose, and in almost all cases, the losses would be acceptable and not impact his further plans for conquest.

The last week had been spent undertaking exercises in the surrounding countryside. His men had changed formations seamlessly, eager to impress their king and show that no further delay was needed. Indeed, none was, and thus they'd march the following day.

The sun shone brightly, its rays warm, reflecting off the brickwork of the palace balcony upon which they sat. All the residual snow and ice had melted away. It didn't matter that his troops would find the soft ground tiring for the first two weeks of the march. By the time they reached Freeguard, it would be as hard and unforgiving as his men.

They were all slightly drunk, despite it only just approaching noon. Daleth had allowed everyone this day to relax, to enjoy themselves, to eat, drink, and even fight within reason. Now, throughout the city and beyond, alcohol was being consumed with wild abandon.

Julius, despite being naturally dour, was turning out to be rather amusing having drunk like a fish. Daleth made a mental note to encourage him to drink more often, so his company was easier to cope with.

Gregor had already made a dozen toasts, part of a drinking game that Daleth couldn't quite follow, when Gregor raised his goblet.

'My king,' Gregor started to say, but his eyes opened wide in horror as the goblet fell to the table, splashing wine everywhere. But the look of horror wasn't at spilling his wine, it was because his hand was still holding the goblet, having been severed cleanly at the wrist.

'Brother!' he screamed, standing, but that was the last word that ever left his lips, for suddenly blood sprayed from his neck as his remaining hand came up, fruitlessly trying to stem the spurting blood.

'By all the gods,' Daleth cried as he flung himself back from the table covered in crimson.

Julius did the same, looking on as Gregor's life fled him.

Then Gregor started to change in front of their eyes.

Having recovered from his initial shock, Daleth watched in fascination as he recognised his own features in Gregor's changing form before it shifted to a myriad of others before his eyes. Daleth knelt over Gregor's body as it slowed its movements to see dead, black eyes set in a pale, smooth face, staring back at him. Shaking his head in wonder, Daleth was astounded by how this Ranger he'd known for so many years, truly looked like.

'Th that thing was Gregor?' Julius asked, moving forward to look closer at the body. 'I never knew a gift like that existed. I always wondered what his was ... other than being a hard bastard. Now though, I can see why he needed to change form. Imagine looking like that.'

Daleth laughed, although inside he felt chilled.

His final two most valuable Rangers were now dead, and it was no coincidence that Jared had earlier reported Taran's approach to Freeguard. If Taran was caught alive, he'd make sure his death was agonising.

The only man he'd ever feared had been that damned Kalas, and now this young man, a deserter, was proving to be equally deadly. Was he someone to be feared?

'No!' Daleth roared, surging to his feet, making Julius stand back in shock. There was no challenge he couldn't overcome, no man who could stand against him. The gods were making sure his climb to be by their side was like no other to ensure he was worthy.

He wouldn't fail.

'This matters not at all,' he said contemptuously, flicking his hand toward his bodyguard, who stood looking on. 'Clear this up.'

Victory will soon be mine, he thought, for only the gods could stop him, and the gods were already on his side.

'Tomorrow we march!' he bellowed, lifting his sword to the sky to salute them. 'Tomorrow, we march!'

***

Chapter XXII

Yana sat in the dark, feeling utterly alone for the first time in her life.

She'd left her father and old life behind in pursuit of a dream, and for a while, it had seemed so close to becoming a reality. Now, however, the dream had turned into a nightmare.

Inside, she knew the risk had been worth the potential reward. Taran was the stuff her dreams were made of, and leaving behind her dull existence to follow him to Tristan's Folly hadn't been so difficult. Yet as she looked around, surrounded by wealth beyond her wildest dreams, it offered no succour.

She'd watched Taran from a window, trying to catch his attention as he was mobbed by thousands of adoring people. Yet Taran had eyes only for one and Yana had felt like being physically sick at the realisation she'd lost the opportunity to own his heart forever.

Maya had done what she herself should have done; thrown everything to one side to pursue what mattered most to her, irrespective of the cost or risk.

She'd thought she'd done enough, but no, she could have done more. She should have travelled with him, but instead, Maya had seized the moment and was now back victorious with Taran as her husband.

Now Yana's heart swung between loving Taran in one moment, and hating him in the next. Yet despite her pain, she could still see how irrational her feelings were.

She drank straight from a flask of wine, not bothering with a goblet, and chewed on a hunk of meat she'd found downstairs in her kitchen. Her servants were still all downstairs too, but they couldn't help her anymore. They all lay cold and dead, having drunk from a flask of water laced with dark weed.

It was their own fault. All they'd been talking about was *Taran this,* and *Lady Maya that,* as if it was some kind of fairy tale. She'd have to expend some considerable amount of wealth to have the bodies disappear, but it had been worth it to shut them up.

Even now there was revelry in the streets, but for what reason? The alliance would still lose the war in one foul sweep of Daleth's hand. What then Taran's love for Maya, what then for this city?

Yana had briefly walked the streets to buy the wine she now drank, and people were talking of Taran unearthing and killing a deadly traitor hidden in the palace within moments of his return. Soldiers were notoriously loose-lipped when drunk, and her heart had turned cold when she'd learned it had been Galain. Galain, who'd sent her on her mission, the man closest to the king.

She shook her head. Would she be happy if she were to become queen when it seemed her happiness only lay in Taran's blue eyes? She thought so, and maybe in enough time, it would actually become so. She needed to be resolute, for Daleth only admired strength. If she showed even a hint of weakness, she'd die alongside the thousands who'd perish, instead of rising up to rule over the survivors.

She raised herself to her feet, a little unsteady but determined and resolute. She needed to pull herself together, so she headed toward an open window to get some fresh air and clear her thoughts.

As she looked out, a unit of soldiers was marching across the thoroughfare from the palace. She was about to turn away, but when she looked back, they were heading unerringly toward her abode. Her heart began to hammer in her chest. Perhaps Tristan was summoning her for advice now that Galain was dead? But then she noted they held a short but heavy wooden item between them with handles affixed.

What was it for? Then she realised it was to break down her door, which, being night-time, was barred from the inside. It was a battering ram of some kind.

Her mind started to whir. This couldn't be about the dead servants. But if it wasn't, it soon could be if anyone looked in the kitchens. No, she was now the only one alive who knew of Tristan's intent to betray the allied forces, to save his life and wealth. He'd undoubtedly decided that given Galain's death, she was now a loose end that needed to be cut off permanently.

Thankfully, she was still dressed, and she grabbed a pouch of coins, the meat and flask, then stuffed them in a satchel. Even as she was doing so, there was an almighty crash against the front door.

She ran upstairs to the roof terrace, her heart pounding, but fortunately, the blood-rush was swiftly clearing her head. She knew Maya had made her exit from the city across the rooftops, and intended to follow her lead. But she needed to get a horse before she escaped through the gates, for she didn't have Maya's skills in the wilderness.

Thankfully, a pouch of gold spoke louder than anything else, and until people knew a warrant was out for her arrest, she was well thought of. She had to get to the stables, use the gold to purchase a horse, and then use Tristan's name to get the western gate open. The fact she'd passed through it late at night on her recent mission would smooth this part of her escape.

Travelling west would take her toward Daleth and his advancing armies, but that was where she'd go, to warn him of the death of his spy and the Horselords' arrival. That kind of information might buy her life and secure her future if the gods of luck smiled on her.

She laughed with an edge of hysteria as she ran gingerly across the rooftops. Killing the servants had been fortuitous indeed, for when the bodies were found, they'd distract the soldiers, and every heartbeat mattered.

She needed to be long gone from the city by midnight, or she'd never see the light of day again.

***

Tristan smashed his fist into the table.

'She wasn't there?' he snarled, and the new Captain of the guard, Huron, blanched, nodding apologetically in dismay. Tristan felt some small satisfaction that his anger still scared those soldiers around him, even if not those he wished to scare the most.

'Her door was barred from the inside, and her servants were all dead, my king. She wasn't known to have any suitors that she entertained, despite lots of interest. She was seen entering the property earlier this evening, so it seems she was either abducted or escaped over the rooftops,' Huron offered in explanation.

Tristan knew it was the latter, and they'd soon hear that she'd left the city once the gate guards were questioned. She was as slippery as she was sharp.

'You're dismissed.' Tristan waved his hand. 'Make sure you keep this to yourself,' he said with a dark, warning look. 'For if your failure becomes public, I'll have to ensure you and your men are punished, so that others carry out their duties more efficiently.'

The captain hurried away, thankful that Tristan's wrath hadn't found a more physical outlet.

Tristan stayed up late, his mind working quickly to establish the best path forward. Even if Yana wasn't dead, she was gone, so no one would ever find out how his tale had deviated ever so slightly from the truth. His intention to lead the regular Freestates swordsmen away from the final battle still stood firm. He'd ordered the city treasurer to double their pay, and tomorrow he'd tell them the good news in person, so they knew without a doubt who their benefactor was. Money could still buy loyalty over love and honour if there was enough of it.

That way, when he led his troops on the day of battle, they'd follow his orders without question, not wishing to bite the hand that fed them so lavishly. The peasant swordsmen levy he was less sure of. It was unlikely they'd have the stomach to fight once he left the field and would probably follow him anyway, but there was no way he'd double their pay.

The contingent of knights that Taran had enlisted wasn't large enough to matter. The alliance was still vastly outnumbered, and Daleth would sweep them aside. Fortunately, he'd be well out of the way when it happened.

A twisted smile spread across his face. Finally, he'd have his revenge for Taran's endless insolence, the latest of which was the casual dismissal of his claim over Maya. Taran would die in this battle, but it was imperative that Maya survived.

The death of tens of thousands would be forgiven by the surviving people sooner if they were well fed with the lands flourishing under her gift. With Taran and the Horselords dead, he felt sure Maya could still be coerced into becoming his queen with nowhere else left to go. He could even make the outcome of the war look like a victory.

But how to keep Maya close and safe when she didn't want to be near him was something he'd have to think on. Fortunately, there was time, and in the interim, he'd be gracious and agreeable.

Taran said he'd shortly explain his plan to everyone, although he'd kept it to himself until now. Tristan felt it was either because he feared another traitor or, more likely, that he didn't have a plan with any chance of victory. Tristan snorted contemptuously. No plan could win this war, any fool could see that. Daleth had taken away any last hope when he'd decimated the Horselords.

Ostrom and Dafne, along with all their troops, would soon be dead and, in time, forgotten, but it didn't matter as long as he remained king. Every one of his ancestors would applaud his decision, as would the gods of greed, as putting oneself first was what they expected from any of their servants.

Tristan smiled, feeling more at ease than he had in a long time. He was on the winning side, and no one knew it.

***

'I don't like it.' Maya looked at Taran, her eyes fierce and determined as she propped her head up on one arm. 'You need to think of another way.' She dropped her head back onto his chest, and feeling his arms wrap around her again, wriggled in closer.

'There's no other way,' Taran soothed, his fingers gently massaging the muscles on Maya's back that went taut again as she propped herself back up.

'Then it doesn't have to be you. Choose someone else.'

Taran sighed.

'Please, we've been over this again and again, and we're going around in circles. We have two, maybe three more nights together before, well, before Daleth arrives.'

Taran could see Maya's pulse thumping hard in her neck.

'Let me share your thoughts?'

Maya shook her head.

'I don't understand,' Taran said, a frown creasing his brow. 'What is it that you don't want me to know?'

Maya looked at him, aching to tell him everything. Tell him of their baby, of her fears of losing him, of not being by his side. But sharing such with him would cloud his thinking, cause him to worry, distracting him when he needed to be at his most focussed.

Maya smiled and told him half the truth.

'My worries consume me, and you've enough of your own without adding mine to yours.' She raised her forefinger to stop his denial. 'Yet I promise you this. When we win this battle, when we stand together afterwards, then I'll never ask you not to look into my mind again. Does that ease your concerns?' she asked, her hand moving over his chest, her lips brushing his neck.

'Hmmm, don't try to get around me that way,' Taran purred.

'What way?' Maya asked, her look and voice so full of innocence that Taran couldn't help but laugh and the mood lifted.

'It's true,' Taran admitted. 'I have my doubts, and then there's that girl and the things she's said.'

Maya shook her head.

'She's just a girl, and we control our own fate, our own destiny. Anyway, I still want you to come up with another plan in the next two days,' and she sighed as Taran's fingers traced her spine, drawing circles.

'It's amazing,' she murmured. 'I never knew true happiness until I met you, or what being truly in love was all about as, before you, I'd only ever loved my parents. I also never dreamed how making love could be so special.' Her leg slid up over Taran's thigh beneath the blankets as she pulled him close.

'When we're together like this,' she continued, eyes roving around the small cottage, the flames from the fire filling the room with a cosy glow, 'I sometimes wish my life could be this moment forever. I'd be happy to my last breath, in your arms, enjoying your touch, knowing this is enough, where I belong, where I was always meant to be.'

Taran held Maya close, kissing her head.

'You have such a way with words and they touch my heart. I cherish every moment with you too, and I so want to get to know you better, with our whole lives ahead of us.'

Maya felt Taran's strong heartbeat through her fingertips.

'If that's what you want, then we shall make it happen,' she said, determination in her voice. 'First, though, you have to do something for me.'

'What's that?' Taran asked, intrigued.

Maya moved above him, her white hair falling over his face like a waterfall, and she kissed him for what seemed an eternity.

'Make love to me like this is the first time, the last time, and the only time,' she said softly, holding his gaze.

There was no need for further words, and the room shone brightly as Maya glowed in Taran's arms.

***

'It's almost exactly as we anticipated, my king,' Julius said, shading his eyes as they looked to the hills northwest of Freeguard, while the sun crested the city to the east.

Daleth nodded.

'Indeed, brother. In some ways, I'm disappointed, yet they've no viable alternatives. Holding that hill strengthens their defence. My only surprise is the knights are absent and aren't going to use the slope to add momentum to their charge. However, in some ways, it's also a shrewd move. It forced me to split our spearmen to provide a rearguard, meaning the desert spearmen won't be overwhelmed as quickly on the hill. It only delays the inevitable, but now we can expect the Horselords to appear from the south, you'll see.'

Daleth took in a long breath, enjoying the fresh air. Spring had come early to this part of the land, for the grass was already unseasonably deep on the hill where he stood. His position gave a perfect field of view over the small plain between him and the enemy forces stationed on the hillside to the north.

It had taken four weeks of marching, which, despite the initial soft and muddy terrain, had been thoroughly enjoyable. Every night the men had laughed in anticipation of the slaughter to come as Daleth spent time around various campfires. He'd even left his horse behind at Freemantle so that all could see he shared every muddy step.

A true king who led by example.

The End of Dreams

The entire army was brimming with bloodlust, and Daleth felt it running through his veins too. The desire to lead from the front was almost overwhelming, but the Eyre archers' skills were legendary. Many a fine warrior would die today as death unfairly found them from above. He'd not take the risk and would orchestrate the battle from here.

He looked about, nodding in satisfaction.

Around the southern base of his hill, and extending northeast, close to the walls of Freeguard were twenty thousand spearmen, insurance against the absent knights. The spearmen were not best pleased to be the rearguard, for they'd expected to whet their spearpoints at the start of this battle. However, guarding their king was an honour and the backs of their comrades a necessity. These were the experienced spearmen who'd decimated the Horselords before and they'd finish the job with relish if the remaining knights showed up as anticipated.

Two thousand lancers waited slightly to the north of his hill, bloodied but unbowed. For the last week, they'd suffered ambush after ambush as they scouted ahead of the main army, suffering over four hundred dead. Now they were impatient to wreak their revenge on the Eyre archers who'd been the main perpetrators. Once the battle was joined, they'd charge through the gap between the enemy line and the city walls and take their revenge on the Eyre.

Slightly further north, were his main attack force, thirty-five thousand spearmen, supported by two thousand archers, ready to advance directly on the twenty-five thousand desert warriors.

He'd have bet a cart of gold that those spearmen would have been enough to win the battle alone had it not been for the Eyre stationed slightly higher up the hill. However, in anticipation of this, at the centre of his line of spearmen, was a surprise for the enemy, five thousand heavily armoured assault troops.

His original assault troops had suffered catastrophic losses taking the walls of Tristan's Folly. Yet, the armour and weapons of those who'd died had been salvaged, and during the winter, replacements had been trained in using the double thickness plate and maces. A spear formation's defensive strength was formidable, but his assault troops could literally push right through them.

Slightly to the rear, and spread equally between the east and west flank, were twenty thousand medium infantry. Once the spearmen of both sides fully engaged, they'd flank both ends of the line, enveloping it from the side as the assault troops broke the middle.

He glanced over his shoulder to see Yana flanked by guards, and studied her briefly, wondering what to do with her.

She was cunning, a survivor, and beautiful beyond reason. In some ways, he respected her more for not trying to seduce him to gain his favour. Had she tried, she'd already be dead, for he was not a man to be manipulated.

'Do you think Tristan and his men will still withdraw from the fight?' Julius asked, his question interrupting Daleth's thoughts.

'Our newest recruit seems to think so,' Daleth said, nodding at Yana.

It mattered not whether her intelligence on Tristan was right or wrong, for things could change by the hour, let alone in the weeks that had gone by since Taran's return with the Horselords and her approaching his camp.

As Daleth looked across to the distant hill, he could see the Freestates swordsmen positioned behind the Eyre in two large formations. Half were well trained, but half were a peasant levy. If there'd been a change of heart and the King of Greed had found the stones to lead his men into battle, then ten thousand of Julius' Nightstalkers were prepared to punish him for his stupidity.

Every contingency had been planned for, and he carefully studied the positions of his formations again, ensuring every one was in place.

He noticed Baidan standing close by, accompanied by fifty bodyguards. Baidan's gaze roved everywhere, looking for threats, as his men did the same.

It was time.

'Signal the advance,' he commanded, and his horn-blower sent out the command into the still morning air as the flag bearer confirmed the order.

Everything was how it was supposed to be, but the thought still nagged at him ever so slightly.

Where were those damned knights?

***

The End of Dreams

Maya sat astride her horse, heart in her mouth as an enemy horn sounded, and the deep line of enemy spearmen began to advance. Her hunter's eyesight was so acute that she could make out the towering figure of Daleth quite clearly, surrounded by around fifty of his bodyguard. Taking a brief moment, she sent a silent prayer to the Moon Goddess, having started to worship the deity as she'd become immersed in the Horselords' culture.

Tristan was mounted alongside, and she cursed having to be near him. But, in a rare moment of honesty and humility, Tristan had admitted he wasn't the figurehead his troops really needed. Therefore, Maya was helping to lead the ten thousand swordsmen, which even Taran agreed was a good idea.

Taran's plan, the only one which everyone believed had a chance of success, was bold to the point of suicidal, and she wanted to be next to him. However, if the plan was to succeed, it required the Freestates swordsmen to do their part too. Maya would have to keep faith that Taran would survive, or she wouldn't be able to function this day.

The enemy formations were steadily advancing. The long lines of spearmen were flanked by swordsmen, and as they drew closer, she could discern the familiar shapes of heavily armoured assault troops with her keen eye.

She galloped her horse a short way down the hill to the Eyre and their commander.

'Target the middle of the line,' she called.

Dafne waved in acknowledgement as Maya drew close.

'I'd already seen them. I'm glad we had these forged,' she said, holding a heavy, tipped arrow. 'I thought we wouldn't be using them, but it seems old Rakan was right. He's as smart as he is handsome. Make sure you tell him for me if we live through this!'

'Rakan, really?' Maya smiled, then heeled her horse around, coming back up to Tristan as the Eyre bows sang behind her, sending volley after volley into the sky.

The enemy lancers started to move forward from the distant hill, and she nodded in grim satisfaction as they headed toward the gap between the city and Ostrom's spearmen. They'd pay a heavy price to the hidden archers stationed on the city walls.

It was now or never.

'It's time to advance down the hill,' Maya stated, fixing Tristan with her gaze. 'Let's put on a show to ensure Daleth's attention is on us. He'll definitely want to see us hit the back of Ostrom's spears. Unfortunately for him, his swordsmen will be too late to react before we turn and hit his spear line from the flank. Remember, lead your men further down the hill to delay their swordsmen while we roll up the end of the line. We'll then come and join you.'

Tristan hesitated, looking around nervously.

'Shall I order them, or shall you?' Maya shouted.

She felt a surge of hope. The battle was unfolding precisely as Taran had foretold. Daleth even stood on top of the hill directing the battle, exactly where they predicted he would.

Tristan shook his head nervously and stood in his saddle.

'We advance,' he said weakly, his voice breaking. He grabbed a water flask from his saddle and drank some water before trying again. 'We advance,' he shouted louder, and the banners at the head of the Freestates swordsmen were raised high.

In good order, the massed ranks marched down the hill, passing the Eyre toward the rear of Ostrom's men.

'It will all go to plan,' Maya reassured as Tristan looked around wide-eyed. 'Get ready to order the charge! Even now, Daleth's attention will be on us. He'll not want to miss seeing you betray the alliance.'

Suddenly, the lines of spearmen clashed together like thunder. Battle cries and screams filled the air.

Maya looked back at Dafne and waved her sword in the air.

Dafne nodded, and three of her archers loosed green fire arrows high into the sky, not only to catch Daleth's attention but to signal Rakan, Shinsen, and Taran.

Maya dismounted, slapping the hindquarters of her horse, which galloped away.

She turned to see Tristan still on his horse, standing high in the stirrups, looking back at the troops. He raised his sword high, and for a moment she was relieved, he was going to lead the charge himself, but then he shouted a command and Maya couldn't believe her ears.

'Withdraw,' he bellowed, his voice strong and commanding. 'Lower the banners and withdraw up the hill. Withdraw, withdraw!' he shouted, and the command was taken up by hundreds of voices chanting the same command.

'Stop!' Maya shouted. 'What are you doing?'

But even as she moved toward Tristan, several Freestates swordsmen ran forward and grabbed her arms, pulling her back.

'Let go of me,' she screamed, 'let go!' Her foot lashed out, kicking one hard. For a moment, he relaxed his grip, and she swung her fist, landing a solid blow, but it wasn't hard enough. He hit back, catching Maya square on the chin, and still being partially restrained, she couldn't protect herself. Two, then three more blows, and her head spun, her legs giving way.

She heard shouts and screams, but they faded as she lost the fight to stay conscious.

They needed to attack, they needed to distract Daleth ... but then everything went black.

***

Taran saw the fire arrows arc into the sky through the thick grass and felt something akin to relief. It was almost time, and it wouldn't be soon enough. He was suffering terrible cramps, his heart raced, and the longer they waited, the more likely the chance of their discovery.

Yet there was a little more time, so he thought over the plan, calming himself with the knowledge that there was no other way.

Its success hinged on a desperate gambit, that if successful, would not only see Daleth killed early in the battle, but his army decimated.

Two days before, having identified that this was the only likely vantage point Daleth could choose to command the battle from, they'd dug twenty-five pits in a small semicircle around the hilltop.

The likelihood of the fifty knights within the pits making it out alive from this phase of the plan to slay Daleth was slim. More pits and knights might have increased the chance of success, but the risk of booted feet pushing through the thin turf into a hole and being discovered was already too high.

So much depended on Daleth and his bodyguard being distracted enough to help this part of the plan succeed and the further deception play out.

When he'd laid out his plan in detail to the others, and described his own role in killing the Witch-King, Rakan had demanded to come along, knowing what was at stake.

Taran had refused.

'You have another task with equal risk, and the only person I trust to do it is you. Your role is perhaps more important than mine, for should I fail and you succeed, then the Witch-King's death might still follow.'

Rakan had remained defiant.

'In which case I'll go in that damned hole, while you sit astride a horse.'

But Taran hadn't allowed his resolve to weaken.

'We've gone over this already. When our journey first started, your skills in dealing death far surpassed mine, but now the roles are reversed. My gift will give me a huge advantage if I get close enough to Daleth. It has to be me on the hill.'

Rakan had eventually conceded the argument, so, when Maya warned that daybreak would see Daleth's armies at the gates, the chosen knights had squeezed inside the pits, armed and armoured, with only a small flask of water to slake their thirst.

Taran and Chochen had been the last to jump in, and Maya had knelt by the side of the hole.

She'd kissed Taran.

'Remember, whilst I might love you in this world and the next, you'd better stay with me in this one! Come back to me, my prince. I'll make sure Daleth's entire attention is on us. Believe in me as I believe in you.'

'That's why I have you there, and Rakan, where he is. I trust no one else with my life and our happiness. Now, work your magic!'

Taran had then hunkered down as Maya carefully placed a thin wooden lattice over the pit and replaced the turf.

For the following hour, she'd walked around the hill, calling upon her gift, and the land had answered. Spring grass grew forth, flowers blossomed, and all traces of the excavations were covered by the waving stems that reached to a man's waist.

Now, having barely slept at all throughout the night, the wait was nearly over.

'It's almost time,' Taran whispered softly to Chochen.

The End of Dreams

He could hear Daleth's voice; the Witch-King was close.

'Our lancers look to have taken heavy casualties. It seems there were Eyre archers placed in the city to cover the gap.' Taran heard a man say. 'Those damned Eyre are a thorn in our side.'

'You're right,' Daleth growled. 'All that planning, and we fell for the obvious lure. Still, it'll make no real difference. They were never going to play the pivotal part in this battle, and it seems maybe a third made it through.'

'Look, my king, signal arrows. What do you think they're for?' another voice exclaimed.

'I don't believe it,' Taran heard yet another of Daleth's men say. 'Tristan's leading his men to attack!'

There was disbelief in the voice, and Taran smiled grimly to Chochen next to him.

'If I didn't see it myself, Julius, I'd have never thought it possible,' boomed Daleth. 'Yet fight or not, he's dead anyway, but this is something I didn't expect. I thought he'd take my offer to withdraw and live, even if I didn't mean it.'

Taran looked at Chochen.

'Withdraw?' he mouthed silently, a frown crossing his brow.

'My king,' said the man Taran now understood to be Julius. 'It seems Tristan's taking your offer after all. His troops are now withdrawing back up the hill. Yes, his banners are lowered. He's pulling back from the fight!'

'Do you see that, Yana?' Daleth shouted. 'Tristan has shown his cowardice for all to see. He's taken my offer and flees the field!'

Taran's eyes opened wide in surprise. Yana was here, and it seemed the agreement between Daleth and Tristan was nothing like what had been described. Taran's plan was now beginning to unravel, thanks to Tristan's treachery.

Daleth's laugh boomed out.

'Divide and conquer, Julius. Divide and conquer! This shall go as well as we hoped, if not better, for who knows what the other troops will do when they see him run.

'Look over there,' Taran heard Daleth say. 'The knights of the clans are finally showing themselves to the south of us, chasing a few hundred of our lancers. They aren't fast enough to catch them, so it looks like our lancers will live to fight another day.'

'Do you think they'll charge our spear line knowing what happened to their brothers back in the grasslands?' Julius laughed. 'I'll make a wager they do!'

Taran only wished he could see Daleth, to be able to read his thoughts, but that just wasn't possible. Worryingly, Daleth's focus was no longer on the main battle now that Tristan's swordsmen were withdrawing instead of launching what should have been a surprise attack. He briefly wondered what had happened to Maya, that she'd been unable to stop this taking place.

'What are those lancers doing to the south of us?' Taran heard Daleth ask curiously. 'Didn't they all head north?'

There was curiosity mixed with doubt in the Witch-King's voice, and Taran, with a sinking feeling in his heart, knew their plan was about to be exposed.

He turned to Chochen.

'It has to be now,' he said simply.

Chochen nodded, and raised a small horn to his lips, the horn of the clans. He drew breath and blew a note so loud in the enclosed space that Taran thought his ears would burst. A heartbeat later, Taran and Chochen exploded from their pit, the turf-covered lattice flying into the air, swords and armour shedding dirt as all around the other knights did the same, answering the call.

Shouts of alarm sounded as if spewed from the land, and like the undead rising from their graves, the knights arose, then attacked.

The numbers were about even, and the element of surprise gave the knights an initial advantage. A dozen of Daleth's bodyguard were quickly overwhelmed before they could form a cohesive defence, and victory looked like it might come swiftly as Taran downed a man in front of him.

Taran fixed on Daleth, but the Witch-King and his bodyguard were now over the initial shock and fought back.

As they converged on the bodyguard, Taran shouted Daleth's name and those pale eyes turned to look at him, and a smirk spread over the Witch-King's lips.

'Not enough,' Daleth shouted. 'Not enough.'

The End of Dreams

The momentum of the fight began to turn.

The knight's heavy armour that had allowed them to shrug off many initial blows from the surprised bodyguard started to slow them. Normally they'd have been sat astride a charger, so, as they tired, the bodyguard's superior swordplay tipped the balance.

Taran fought furiously, Chochen at his side, yet he was blind to everything but Daleth ahead of him, and every bodyguard he killed saw him a step closer.

He heard a cry of pain and Chochen fell, mortally wounded, even as Taran despatched his killer. Then suddenly Taran became aware that no other knights were standing, Chochen had been the last.

'Stand back. Leave him alive,' Daleth boomed, and the bodyguard in front of Taran withdrew.

Taran's lungs were heaving, and he looked around quickly. They'd come so close. Only ten of Daleth's bodyguard remained. Taran was near exhausted himself. Yet he'd fight to his last breath, and if the gods smiled on him, he might prevail.

He glanced down the hill during this brief respite, seeing the lancers who'd escaped the knights filter through the ranks of spearmen. The four thousand knights who'd chased them had halted a mere two hundred paces from the rearguard, facing down an enemy they couldn't conquer.

The spearmen from around the hill and toward the city were quickly coming together to face this familiar threat, creating a large formation, two thousand wide by ten deep. They were shouting, taunting the knights to charge, knowing that the knights' code forced them to attack an enemy head-on at its strongest point.

'We meet again, Taran, although last time I saw you, you were almost a corpse,' Daleth said, drawing Taran's attention back to the Witch-King. 'Then again, you were at least going to be a handsome-looking corpse. What on earth happened to you? Did you fall face first in a fire?'

Taran didn't answer, just playing for time, keeping his sword raised. He moved toward one of Daleth's bodyguards, but the man moved away, refusing to engage. Others circled him should he commit to the attack, but they were respectful of his superior skills and Daleth's order.

Daleth shook his head in admiration.

'I have to salute you. I don't doubt this is your plan, and you even decided to put yourself in this position. Honestly, I thought nothing could unsettle me this day, but when you and your men jumped out of the ground, I almost browned my breeches.'

He laughed at his own joke.

'Sadly for you, you didn't bring enough men. Now, you want to kill me, the Witch-King, and win the battle. They're two entirely different things and let me tell you this, neither is going to happen this day.'

Taran glanced down the hill.

Daleth followed his look.

'I'm tempted to let you live long enough to see them all die as well, but I've run out of goodwill. After all, I want to savour watching my men slaughter yours, now you've failed.'

'Stand aside,' Daleth ordered his men.

Taran was shocked. Daleth was going to face him singlehandedly, and his hopes soared. He could still win.

'I'll kill you,' he said. 'For all that's good, I'll kill you.'

Daleth's bodyguard reluctantly stood aside as their king strode forward. Taran hadn't appreciated just how huge Daleth was. The Witch-King's sword was as long as Taran was tall, yet Taran smiled at his approach. He'd beaten bigger, even if not taller, and with his bare hands.

They circled slowly.

Taran read Daleth's mind and was already moving to block the king's sweeping blow in the next instant. The impact of Daleth's heavy weapon jarred his arms, almost causing him to drop his sword. He backed away hastily, and mostly evaded the next blows rather than pit his strength against a physically stronger foe.

There'd be no quick end to this fight, for Daleth was skilful, and his reach devastatingly long.

Blow after blow Taran dodged or deflected, conserving his strength, as he watched Daleth for signs of tiring, but the Witch-King seemed inexhaustible.

Despite this, Taran's confidence grew, and he soon started to make small attacks of his own. Not over-committing, not going for a killing

The End of Dreams

strike, and shortly Daleth's forearms were bleeding from a myriad of small cuts. Every time Taran landed one, Daleth just smiled.

'You're truly skilled,' Daleth said approvingly. 'Not one of my men here has ever drawn blood from me. It would seem your gift gives you quite an unfair advantage.'

Daleth attacked again, his blows coming faster than before. Taran, despite reading the moves, found it harder and harder to block them and he back-stepped lightly before feeling a heavy blow to his side.

Daleth paused his attack, watching intently, as Taran's vision dimmed with pain. Taran was sure he'd blocked every one of Daleth's strikes, but as he looked down, he saw, to his surprise, the feathered flight of an arrow jutting from his side where it had punctured his cuirass.

'You can read my mind,' Daleth observed, 'but not everyone's.'

Taran's leg gave way as another arrow took him in the thigh.

Daleth moved forward.

'Life isn't fair, war isn't fair. The good, whatever that means, don't always win, and today neither you nor your friends will be victorious.'

Taran coughed, a bloody spray coming from his mouth, and he fell to his knees in shock.

Daleth drew back his sword, and Taran didn't have the strength to raise his own through the pain.

'Don't kill him, don't kill him!' Yana screamed, and she rushed forward, hurling herself at Daleth.

The Witch-King turned and casually flicked his sword out, catching Yana in the chest. She fell forward to the floor beside Taran, blood pumping furiously from the gaping wound.

She tried to say something, tried to reach out with her hand, but she died before Taran's eyes.

Daleth shook his head in amazement at her fruitless sacrifice, then tossed his sword, spinning into the air, and as he caught it, drove it straight through Taran's armour.

Taran couldn't help but cry in agony. The pain was beyond belief, the sword had torn through his stomach and out his back.

Revelling in Taran's agony, Daleth withdrew the blade slowly, then raised it, dripping blood above his head.

'Wait, wait,' Taran begged, 'I need to tell you something first, please.' He watched through hazy eyes as Daleth lowered the sword, using its tip to knock Taran's blade out of reach as the king squatted before him.

Taran looked at the sky. Seeing the beauty of the clouds despite the encroaching darkness, and remembered the little girl's premonition.

You will only know the briefest happiness again before you die.

'What words do you have for me boy, that I shall remember you by?' Daleth demanded, and knelt close, gripping Taran's shoulders.

Taran turned his head slightly to nod down the hill.

'See the lead knight?' he said through gritted teeth, barely loud enough for Daleth to hear. 'Do you see him? Kalas is coming!'

Daleth's head whipped around and sure enough, at the centre of the knights' line was a man in shining silver armour, Kalas' armour, and under the helm was flowing blond hair as the knights started at a trot toward the rearguard.

For a moment, panic gripped Daleth's stomach before it subsided. 'I don't believe that's him, but even if it is,' he snarled, 'they'll not break the line. Watch them die against my spearmen, as did the rest of their kind. Witness the end of your dreams if you can stay alive long enough!'

Taran laughed, blood bubbling over his lips.

'They aren't the one's who'll break your line,' he said, his vision dim as Daleth suddenly looked on in horror.

The three hundred lancers who'd filtered through the spearmen had moved halfway up the hill and split into three centuries whilst Daleth and his bodyguard were distracted. Even as Daleth watched, they broke into a charge down the hill toward the back of his unsuspecting spearmen.

'NO!' Daleth shouted, casting Taran to one side, a sharp pain causing him to draw breath as the knights began their charge, lances lowered.

Daleth surged upright on legs that suddenly seemed strangely unsteady, watching in horror as the three hundred lancers crashed into the back of the line, breaking it asunder. The lancers turned left and right, and they tore through the shocked rearguard, flinging armoured men aside like straw dolls.

The End of Dreams

Moments later, into the disintegrating mass at the centre of the line, the knights' charge also hit home, and Daleth's men disappeared under the wave of horses. Like the lancers before them, the knights' charge split, and as if brushed aside by a god's hand, the spearmen scattered before them. With their defensive line broken, Daleth's men cast down their long spears, screaming in panic as they turned to flee while the slaughter began.

Daleth dropped to his knees, rubbing his eyes, barely able to hold himself up.

'What's wrong with me?' he asked bewildered, as his remaining bodyguard surged forward.

Taran held up a tiny dagger with the last of his strength.

'Salamander poison. I told you, I'd kill you,' he whispered, and laughed weakly as Daleth collapsed next to him.

As the remaining bodyguards ran forward, swords swinging down, Taran looked north to the ongoing battle.

'Daleth is dead!' he projected with all his fading might. 'The Witch-King is dead!'

Then, while the swords hacked and pierced his body, darkness descended, and he projected one final word.

'Maya.'

***

Chapter XXIII

Maya.

She heard her name called in the blackness, and it brought her back to the light to find herself surrounded by worried faces. A kneeling soldier applied a wet cloth to her forehead while others spoke around her. She couldn't understand their words through the ringing in her ears, while all around were twisted bodies, broken and dead.

She stood unsteadily, gently pushing aside the soldier's helping hand, only interested in what was happening on the far hill. She focussed, her keen eyes spying the bodies strewn about. Of the few that still stood, not one wore the shining armour of a knight. But she could see, even from this far, the huge form of Daleth lying still on the ground.

Tears came to her eyes. Taran had called her name at the end, she knew that's what had woken her, and her heart broke into a thousand pieces.

Blurred by the distance, she saw the knights of the clans charging down thousands upon thousands of fleeing enemy spearmen, and she knew Taran's audacious plan had been successful. Rakan had done the impossible, leading three hundred knights, dressed as lancers, and broken the rearguard.

But the fight was still tipped heavily in the enemy's favour. Below, Ostrom's spearmen had been flanked to the east by thousands of swordsmen, and the end of the line was splintering, folding in on itself.

She didn't have the will left to fight, she just wanted to curl up in a ball, close her eyes and never wake up.

The End of Dreams

But where was Tristan, and why weren't the Freestates swordsmen attacking?

Then she remembered, and her despair changed, began to darken, and turned to a rage that fuelled her flagging strength. She screamed, fingernails digging into her palms, and the voices that had begun to filter through her anguish fell silent. Then just as suddenly she composed herself, a coldness replacing all other emotions.

'What happened here?' she demanded, gesturing to the several hundred bodies, pale and still in the grass.

The soldier who'd tended her answered.

'King Tristan's men set upon you and tried to carry you away. We follow you, not him, and it was wrong, so we fought to stop them. We succeeded, but this was the cost,' he said, gesturing.

Maya put her hand on his arm.

'Thank you,' she whispered.

She looked around and realised only the countryfolk levy were still on the hill.

The soldier, anticipating her question, offered the answer.

'King Tristan left for the city already, my lady, and the five thousand regular swordsmen followed after him. They told us we'd be safe as long as we didn't enter the fray, because the king had reached an agreement with Daleth for us to be left unharmed.'

Maya shook her head, and the screams of the battle below washed over her. She wanted to find Tristan, to make him pay, but the battle was not over, and would soon be lost.

'Bring my weapons,' she called, and another soldier ran forward to drop them near her feet, and she donned them swiftly.

The others gathered closer, nearly five thousand strong. They stood, unsure, the sound of battle high on the air, awaiting her lead.

Maya drew a deep breath.

'I will give you a choice,' she called, her voice clear, then paused, so those soldiers in the front rows could relay it to the ranks behind. 'All of you know me, and that I speak nothing but the truth. No lies, no deceit.'

She waited a moment, even though she knew that with every heartbeat, hundreds were dying.

'My heart is broken in my chest. My Taran,' and she paused, pointing behind her, 'is dead atop that hill somewhere close to Daleth's corpse. He went knowingly to his death to save not just me, but all of us and all of this,' she said, sweeping her arm around.

'You say Daleth gave Tristan his word you'd be left alive, but I tell you this. Daleth lied. That is what he does. He's dead, you might say. Well, his army fights on and do you think they'll stop when the desert spears below us are crushed. No, they'll come up here and slaughter you before heading to the city where they'll butcher your wives, mothers, fathers, and children in their bloodlust.'

'Whether you live or die today as soldiers is your choice, but the only chance of living freely is to be willing to die. I won't ask this of you whilst I stand aside and watch you bleed. No. I simply ask you to stand beside me, and if die you must, it will be by my side.'

'Will you follow me?' she cried, and five thousand throats roared back in approval.

'Is there a signaller here?' Maya looked about, and a man ran to her side. 'Form ranks,' she ordered, and after the man sounded the command, she waited impatiently, but to lead a disorganised mob into battle would see them slaughtered.

Fortunately, it didn't take long.

'Sound the advance at the double,' she cried, and drew her sword and raised it above her head.

They hurried down the hill, toward the Eyre, who having depleted their arrows, were casting aside their now useless bows and drawing their short swords.

'Help the east flank,' Maya cried out to Dafne as she passed, then fixed her gaze toward the seething mass of black-clad swordsmen who were decimating the end of the desert spearmen's line.

Shouts of warning from those who saw them approaching gave the Nightstalkers time to prepare to face this new attack and Maya could see her force was terribly outnumbered.

'Halt,' she cried when still around fifty paces from the enemy.

The signaller blew his horn, bringing the Freestates forces to a ragged, nervous standstill.

Maya stepped forward. There was a terrible pressure within her head and body, and it felt as if she'd split asunder. Her vision dimmed, and she dropped to her knees.

Her face was wet with her tears, her heart was broken, and she cried with anguish toward the Nightstalkers. Then, as if released by such sorrow, her gift poured forth like never before, but this time, tinged with darkness.

It flowed into the soil at her feet along with her tears, and the next moment, thin, blackened saplings thrust from the ground like spears. Up they shot, in the blink of an eye, impaling hundreds of soldiers in an instant. Vines followed, not green and lush, but red like bloated veins. They twisted and writhed, snaring feet, trapping legs, pulling men to the floor as thorns tore and ripped open flesh.

Then, as Maya rose to her feet, dark light shining from her eyes, the enemy cohesion disintegrated in bowel-wrenching fear.

'Charge!' Maya cried, her voice strangely distorted, and ran down the hill. The thousands at her back followed with a roar. The Nightstalkers' skill with swords far outstripped hers and the Freestates soldiers, but most of Daleth's surviving elite were already stumbling backwards, frantically hacking at the vines rooted in their flesh or looking in disbelief at their impaled comrades.

As the forces met with a mighty crash, the last vestiges of discipline fled from the enemy swordsmen, and they scattered, fleeing down the hill, only to be cut down in their hundreds from behind.

Maya paused, taking a moment to assess the battle. She grabbed the signaller standing alongside her.

'Sound the reform!'

The horn sounded several times before men began to return and form up. Maya looked around at the soldiers, all dripping with blood and gazing down at herself, saw the same. It was as if they'd stepped from the nine hells.

'We help the desert spears,' she shouted, pointing at the rear of the enemy line above them, idly wondering if the pain she felt would diminish if she killed enough of the enemy.

Somehow, she doubted it.

***

Rakan sat propped against the dead horse behind him, watching the battle with interest.

'It's gonna be close,' he said through gritted teeth, 'but I think we've got the edge on you bastards now.' He coughed, blood running down his chin.

He turned to look at Julius, who sat next to him. They'd been watching the fight together for a while, but the conversation was now over. Julius' dead eyes stared across the battlefield, Rakan's sword still trapped in his belly. Julius had always been a hard bastard. You didn't get to lead the Nightstalkers by being soft. Yet when he'd faced his former commander, it seemed Julius wasn't as skilled as Rakan remembered. Yet as he looked down at the dagger hilt flush against the right side of his chest, Rakan had to concede Julius had been skilled enough.

He wished he could have found Taran, to hold him in his arms so he could cross to the next world with his son. But he couldn't move his legs, and keeping his eyes open was proving difficult. He strained with his force of will to hold back the blackness so he could watch the battle play out. It was too close to call, and he needed to know.

Rakan looked at the knights in the distance. To a man, they'd killed the rearguard that had fled before them. Now the three thousand knights that remained were engaging the enemy archers and some formations of swordsmen that had turned to face them.

Rakan sighed. He might still have been sitting pretty on his horse had he not decided that finding Taran was worth dying for. Nadlen had joined him along with three others, but they now all lay cold around him, surrounded by the bodies of Daleth's remaining bodyguard, who'd fought to keep them from the hilltop and the Witch-King's corpse.

He smiled as he saw a glow on the field amongst the Freeguard swordsmen. He wondered why they'd taken so long to join the battle, but it didn't matter. He was just glad that Maya was alive, although he knew the devastation she'd suffer knowing of Taran's death.

Rakan yawned. He needed to sleep. But the battle was at the most crucial point. If the knights could charge the rear of the enemy spear line before the desert troops broke, then the day might go to the alliance. If they were too late, then things would not end well. It was too exciting to miss.

His eyes closed.

Damn.

He'd open them again soon, see how the battle had ended, and then, then he'd go and find Taran's body as he'd have a bit more strength.

Good idea, he thought, as a tear ran down his face.

He still remembered the first time Taran had called him father, it had been the happiest day of his ...

***

Shinsen sat astride his charger. He didn't know who was more exhausted, him or his mount, but he could feel the beating of its mighty heart beneath him and knew if he asked any more of the great beast, it would die.

He looked about, feeling immensely proud. His knights had fully regained the honour that had been stripped from his people, the blood moon visited righteously upon their enemy. However, only around fifteen hundred knights were all that remained, and with the battle still raging, he prayed to the Moon Goddess they'd be enough.

A gauntleted hand grasped his, and he turned to look into the eyes of Shinmata. His wife's blond hair was splashed with blood where it hung from beneath what had been Kalas' silver helm, but she'd never looked more beautiful.

Tears formed in his eyes, for he hadn't seen her since the initial charge and had feared her killed. Her steady gaze, full of love and belief, said more than words, and for a moment, he drew strength from her presence. His lance had broken long before, but his heavy sword felt light in his hand once again as he reluctantly turned away.

'Line formation,' he ordered hoarsely to the knight on his other side.

The man raised the horn to his lips, trying to blow the two notes.

'Here,' Shinsen offered, pulling out a leather flask. 'Whet your throat, man, and try again.'

The knight gratefully accepted the flask with shaking hands and drank deeply before passing it back.

This time, the horn sounded, and the knights slowly moved into formation. They were just above the base of the hill, and above them, the majority of the enemy spear line was still alive. As his tired eyes flickered over the battle, he saw about eight thousand enemy swordsmen to the east flank being held back by the rapidly thinning ranks of the Eyre.

To the west flank, Maya led her swordsmen into the rear of the enemy spear line and was causing havoc, but it wouldn't be enough. Overall, the enemy was winning; the Eyre wouldn't last long, nor the desert spears, and then what resistance remained after they disintegrated could be crushed piecemeal.

'Sound the trot,' he ordered, and the horn blew again. He leaned close to his horse's ear. 'I am sorry, my brother, that I'm asking this of you, for I know you've already given me everything. But give me one more charge, just one more and we can both rest, maybe forever. But be happy, for we'll both rest in the arms of the Moon Goddess.'

He raised his head, looking around to see many of his brother and sister knights doing the same. He loved them all. He turned to Shinmata.

'To live and die by your side is the greatest honour I've ever known!' he shouted, and she raised her bloodied sword to her lips in salute and acknowledgement.

'The canter,' he ordered.

The horn blew, and the chargers strained up the gradient, the heavy armour and knights they bore, a weight they could now barely carry.

He looked up the hill and was grateful to find that the screams, the clash of weapons, and no doubt the pounding of hearts, had covered the sound of the horn and his knights' advance.

He held off the order for the charge until they were but a mere thirty paces away. In the last rank, some of the spearmen heard their approaching doom, and frantically pulled those alongside to turn and defend, but it was too late.

The chargers leapt forward, throwing themselves into the rear of the enemy line that fell like wheat before a scythe. Shinsen was sure he felt the last mighty beat of his horse's heart before it died beneath him and he fell, rolling into the midst of the enemy as the charge continued, horses' hooves flailing indiscriminately by his face.

The End of Dreams

He reached out for a fallen long-shield, to pull over his body because there was no way he could rise, but a hoof caught the side of his helm, and he knew nothing more.

***

Tristan was furious, barely keeping his anger in check. He'd ridden ahead to the city, leaving orders for Maya to be brought by his following soldiers, only for them to return bloodied and empty-handed. The peasant levy, he'd been told, had fought to secure her release, and whilst they'd died in their hundreds in doing so, they'd succeeded. Part of him understood why his swordsmen hadn't wanted to continue the slaughter of their own countrymen, but another part didn't care.

'My king,' Captain Huron said, interrupting Tristan's thoughts. 'We should return to the field. The battle is on a knife-edge, and we could tip the balance!'

Tristan stood undecided and horrified at the thought of stepping from the transient safety of the city back into the nightmare that played out before him. He'd recently watched from the battlements as the Eyre archers within the city had dropped their bows and run from the west gate. Now, as he followed their progress, he saw them join their brothers and sisters, who were getting slaughtered on the lower slopes.

'My king. This can be your victory,' Huron repeated. 'We can hit the enemy swords from the rear whilst they attack the Eyre. If we do this, we'll decimate them, and then the enemy spearmen will break when we fall upon their flank afterwards, but we have to hurry.'

Tristan thought for a moment, looking at the devastation laid out before the walls of his city. As far as he could see, dead bodies lay strewn around, and from how few were left standing, he surmised at least a hundred thousand had fallen, never to rise again.

Daleth was dead.

Like everyone else, he'd heard Taran's final cry. The problem was, with the Witch-king dead, the bargain he'd struck would be worthless. If the enemy won, he might escape with his life but would lose his city, crown, and wealth.

Ostrom's spears were down to the last few thousand; Dafne and her archers the same. The knights ... it was hard to tell. The peasant swordsmen were fighting, and from the shining light at that end of the field, they were led by Maya.

Against them, an exhausted enemy that still outnumbered the remaining alliance forces by nearly two to one. Yet they'd be vulnerable, their morale fragile from suffering such horrendous losses and the death of their leader.

He had to protect his wealth. He could do this.

Tristan straightened his shoulders.

'I do believe the day can be ours, Huron. The battle has unfolded exactly as I foresaw. Order the gates to reopen. We move at speed to engage the rear of the enemy's east flank.'

Tristan ran down the steps, his legs weak from nervousness, but also now from excitement. His swordsmen were fresh, eager, and now the largest individual alliance force. When victory was his, he could afford to be magnanimous and offer any healthy alliance survivors the chance of staying to help rebuild his kingdom without fear of them taking it from him.

A few years from now and this war would be but a distant memory.

He leapt astride his horse, drawing his sword.

'Follow me, at the double!' he shouted, and as sergeants relayed his order, the Freestates swordsmen ran at pace through the gates.

Thousands of citizens lined the walls, and whereas before they'd watched in horror and despair at the slaughter, many of the nobles and merchants now shouted in hopeful salute as Tristan rode out.

Tristan's back straightened as he felt them recognise his impeccable strategic timing. It didn't matter that thousands of peasants also screamed abuse at him. The voices of the poor carried no weight and were only ever used for complaining.

It seemed to take forever for the swordsmen to clear the gates and form up. Tristan felt his heart waiver, but fortunately, Captain Huron's excitement at his side helped keep his courage intact.

In contrast, reaching the battlefield seemed to take hardly any time whatsoever. As they neared the fighting, enemy soldiers stumbled toward them, blinded or maimed with horrific injuries. One held out

The End of Dreams

his hands in supplication, reaching to grab Tristan's boots, and he struck instinctively in revulsion, cutting the man down.

Taking their king's lead, the Freestates swordsmen butchered everyone in their path.

As they pushed forward, Tristan looked along the line of battle to see almost no one on horseback. Instead, the knights and spearmen of both sides simply stood knee-deep in the dead and hacked and thrust at one another whilst they still had the energy to do so.

There were less than a thousand of the original five thousand Eyre archers remaining as Tristan's men finally came to their aid. They fell upon the rear of the enemy swordsmen, who, being so close to victory, were horrified to find themselves beset front and rear. The Eyre archers, realising this was their last chance, surged forward with newfound, desperate energy.

Tristan swiftly pulled back, not wishing to put himself in danger as the fighting raged, ready to withdraw to the safety of the city walls should the need arise, but his troops were doing well. True, many of them fell to the enemy swords, but whilst out skilled, they hadn't fought for hours already, and their freshness gave them a huge advantage.

Eventually, the last enemy swordsmen fell, and Captain Huron led the Freestates swords and let them loose upon the enemy spearmen to help the dismounted knights.

Tristan was ecstatic.

The battle had teetered on a knife's edge, and they hadn't just tipped the balance, their appearance had thrown the outcome of the battle decisively in the alliance's favour.

Tristan found the courage to cut down some disorientated stragglers again, feeling the heady rush of taking a man's life. As he looked down at himself, splashed in blood, he felt he cut a heroic figure to those on the walls and to his men around him.

Some two hundred enemy lancers suddenly appeared from the woods above the Eyre, bloodied, many with arrow wounds, a testament to the skills of Dafne's people. Tristan panicked and turned his horse, ready to gallop back to the city, and yet there was no charge, the lancers simply dismounted, and left their horses behind.

They walked down the hill, throwing sabres and other weapons aside to sit near Tristan and he realised they were surrendering. As he looked about in wonder, he saw the fighting becoming less widespread. There were stubborn pockets here and there, and he watched in wonder as twenty knights charged their lathered horses into a stubborn pocket of enemy swordsmen. Almost all the horses fell shortly after breaking through the front ranks, not to enemy weapons, but from exhaustion. Swords rose and fell, blood sprayed, and the screams continued.

A little beyond, there seemed to be hundreds of injured writhing in mud on the floor, but he realised in horror, that they were soldiers of both sides who were too tired to stand, yet who still stabbed and hacked at each other as they wrestled amongst the blood, entrails, and vomit that soaked the hillside.

Gradually, the fighting became more localised. Huron and his men moved from one pocket of fighting to another, and whilst their numbers dwindled rapidly, they helped turn the tide of each fight they came across.

Tristan didn't know for how long he sat astride his horse, watching every small battle play out, but eventually, Huron returned.

Tristan heeled his horse toward the captain, who leant on his sword, catching his breath.

'The day is ours, my king,' Huron gasped.

'We won,' Tristan whispered, realisation slowly sinking in. 'I won,' he said more strongly.

'What are your orders, sire?' Huron asked.

Tristan breathed in a huge lungful of air, considering his next move.

'Round up the enemy who've surrendered, and bring them here,' he said, indicating the lancers. 'Then, find out who of importance lives and report back to me.'

He leant back in the saddle, easing the ache in the small of his back, and at the same time felt an invisible weight lift from his shoulders.

He was surprised to note the sun was still high, having barely passed its zenith. So many lives had been lost in such a short space of time, it was hard to contemplate. But all that mattered was that he'd survived, and he was still king.

The End of Dreams

By the time the enemy survivors were all rounded up, it was late-afternoon. Huron and the remaining Freestates soldiers Tristan had led from the city did the work, for everyone else had simply fallen to the floor in exhaustion and were unable or unwilling to assist.

Even this delay did nothing to dampen Tristan's buoyant mood.

Fortunately, his horse had a wineskin in a satchel, so he passed the time drinking, and it had never tasted so good.

Huron came to report again.

'The Lady Maya still lives over yonder,' he nodded to the west. 'She and those with her can barely move. King Ostrom lies dead somewhere along with most all of his men. Dafne lives, though I could get no sense from her. She's crying over there a way. Shinsen's been found alive, although it's hard to say whether he'll survive. Just over three thousand of the enemy surrendered, although many others fled the battlefield throughout the morning. What shall we do with the captives?'

Tristan looked to the sky, picturing the gods of greed judging his decision. To keep the captives alive would mean imprisoning and feeding them, and that would cost him gold.

'We give them what they'd have given us,' Tristan said, turning to look Huron in the eye. 'No mercy. Kill them all.'

Huron blinked in shock.

'My king, are you sure?'

Tristan glowered at him.

'You've done well this morning, but never make me repeat myself again.'

A short while later, the slaughter began.

As screams filled the air once again, Tristan felt the thrill of a blood-rush fill his veins, for he now understood why war held such an allure.

The winner could take absolutely everything.

***

Maya barely had the strength or heart to move, but knew she had to. There was no decision to make, there was no other choice.

She stumbled toward the city along the lines of thousands upon thousands of dead. The survivors sat, stood, or lay amongst them, almost as broken and twisted as the corpses themselves. The looks on the faces of those who lived were dazed. There was no glory felt, no appreciation of life, not yet, maybe not ever.

She knew she could stop to help, point the way to the city, and encourage those who still lived to act as the living. She could tell them to rise and return to their families, to show their loved ones that they were alive in body even if no longer in heart or mind.

But she didn't have the strength.

With her heart and soul so torn, she would have cried the whole way had she the tears left to cry. Then, there he was. Tristan. The King of Greed, sat astride a horse, smiling broadly as he surveyed the field of battle.

He was the only one who looked happy, and for a moment, Maya felt like dragging him from the saddle, taking her dagger, and plunging it into his chest again and again. If anyone deserved to be dead, it was him.

No, she chided herself, today had seen enough death already. She could never be a murderer, however much she wanted to cut his rotting heart out.

As she approached, he turned and stared without recognising her. From head to toe, she was splashed in gore, and a helm sat askew her head with armour so battered and broken that she could have been anyone.

He nodded, hardly disguising his disgust at her horrific figure, and turned away to talk to a nearby captain.

'I need your horse,' she said gruffly.

'What was that?' Tristan turned toward her again. 'Whatever it is you said, you need to always add, *my king*,' he growled. 'Just because we've fought this battle together, doesn't give you the right to address the king of this land as you please!'

'Get off your horse and give it to me now, or I swear by the gods I'll kill you in a heartbeat!' Maya shouted, and her eyes shone with such a dark fury that Tristan's horse reared, and he was almost thrown.

'Lady Maya,' he said nodding, eyes wide. 'Forgive me. You need to return to the city and require my horse. We've so much to talk about, you and I.'

He dismounted, passing her the reins with shaking hands.

The End of Dreams

'Trust me,' Maya spat, 'I'll never return to that city while you rule, and there's nothing else we'll ever say to one another.'

She slowly and painfully swung herself into the saddle and flicked the reins, urging the horse away from Tristan.

'Never say never,' called Tristan after her. 'You'll be back.'

Maya ignored him, her gaze set upon the hill to the south. She wanted to gallop all the way there. The horse had the energy, but she didn't have the strength, and the battlefield was too treacherous. So she let it walk slowly, past the mounds of corpses of horses and men whose eyes stared accusingly at her as if offended she was still alive whilst they lay dead.

Finally, her horse reached the hill and began its ascent. It snorted, tossing its head, and she leaned forward, gently stroking its neck, more to comfort herself than to actually calm the horse.

Near the hilltop, bodies lay everywhere, and as her eyes took in the grisly sight, she drew in a sharp breath.

'Oh no,' Maya moaned, reining in her horse and dismounting, almost falling as she did so, for there was Rakan.

She hurried to his side and knelt. An ugly dagger protruded from his chest, and he just sat there, eyes closed, as if he'd simply fallen asleep watching the battle unfold before him like a play.

She stroked his hair back, and his eyes opened slightly. The smallest of smiles creased his lips and tears formed at the corner of his eyes.

'You live,' Rakan sighed with relief.

Tears streamed down Maya's face as she gazed upon him.

'Our Taran didn't make it,' he continued, choked by pain and sorrow. 'But I'm going to join him soon, especially now I know you're safe. It's time for me to go.'

Maya shook her head, tears falling across Rakan's face.

'No,' she said, 'not everyone I love needs to die, and there are still things you need to do, for you and for me.'

'You mustn't,' Rakan whispered. 'I forbid it. The price is too high, and there's nothing left to live for.'

'It's not your choice to make.'

Maya smiled sadly, then leant forward, and spoke quickly in Rakan's ear. She grasped the dagger, yanking it free, and put her hands on his face, letting her gift flow, healing his wounds, and the colour returned to his pallid cheeks.

Dizziness washed over her, sleep fought to claim her, but despite the exhaustion, and the price of using her gift in this way, Maya somehow held herself awake. Her hair, where it wasn't covered in blood, was now grey, and as she withdrew her hands from Rakan's face, the backs of them were veined and wrinkled. Not that it mattered, not anymore.

She brought the horse to Rakan's body, and being well trained, when she tapped it on the fore shoulder, it lay beside his fallen body. It wasn't easy, but she strained and pulled Rakan onto the saddle, and the horse regained its feet. Maya secured Rakan, tying his hands to the pommel and his feet in the stirrups, then stepped forward to whisper in the horse's ear.

'Time to go home, boy,' and with a gentle slap to its hindquarters, the horse dutifully set off down the hillside toward the city.

With almost no strength left, Maya stumbled to the crest of the hill, moving amongst the bodies of dead knights and Daleth's bodyguard until she found Taran.

Despite knowing what to expect, her heart almost stopped beating as she gazed down at him, laying bloodied and broken next to Daleth. Nearby was Drizt's small dagger, and from Daleth's green-hued pallor, she realised how the Witch-King had met his end.

'Oh, my prince,' she sobbed, dropping to her knees next to Taran's corpse. He was so cold, so broken and bloodied, so unlike the youthful young man she'd fallen for, but then she was so different from the youthful woman he'd fallen for too.

She unbuckled his armour, barely finding the strength to do so.

There were dozens of gaping sword wounds all over his body that had been inflicted before and after death. The shafts of two broken arrows jutted out, and with a considerable effort, she pulled them free.

'I love you in this world, and the next,' she sobbed, tears splashing over his body. 'The problem is, I cannot live in this world without you.' She touched her stomach. 'I should say, we cannot live in this world without you, especially now I'm so old.'

The tiny baby inside of her kicked hard, as if in response to her words.

The End of Dreams

For a moment, her resolve wavered as her thoughts went to the unborn child she was carrying, then it firmed once more.

'You can't go to the next world looking like this,' she said, pushing the hair back from Taran's scarred face, her fingers gently tracing the ripples of the terrible burn and the gaping wounds in his neck and torso. 'We can't have you waiting for us, not like this. Please forgive me when you see me.'

She looked up at the sky. The sun was soon to set and yet for her, for over a hundred thousand others, there'd be no tomorrow. Leaning forward, she lay her hands upon Taran's forehead and reached for her gift. It seemed so far away, almost out of reach, whereas earlier it had come so easily. Yet she didn't give up and tried again, and this time it answered.

She kept her eyes open, letting her gift flow, watching as Taran's wounds healed, as the terrible burn on his face faded, watching as her hands shrivelled and age spots appeared and despite his body now being whole, she didn't stop.

Where before her gift had seemed reluctant, now it was a willing, limitless force. Brighter and brighter, she shone, channelling the power to flow through her and Taran's corpse unchecked. The light was blinding, and it was difficult to see, and still, she called for more.

The baby in her stomach kicked and kicked again, and her sorrow reached new heights even as everything started to fade away.

'Goodbye, my love,' she whispered. 'I hope you're waiting for us on the other side.'

Then all went dark as her eyes closed and the sun set on them both.

***

Chapter XXIV

The survivors shuffled their painful way toward the city gates, leaning on one another for support. Many carried injured between them on makeshift stretchers fashioned from spearshafts and tunics.

There was nothing to celebrate, not yet. They'd survived the battle, although many wondered for how long, as they cradled arms less a hand, or hobbled with a stump where once a foot had been. Barely a single one was without injury, unlike the Freestates swordsmen who'd joined the fight near the end. Earlier, they'd escorted Tristan in triumph back to the city, carrying him on their shoulders.

Dafne limped between two of her archers, a leg heavily bandaged.

Tears streaked her face not only from the pain of her wound but at the horrendous price her people had paid in the battle. The feeling of loss of so many friends from the swamps of her homeland was acute. Thoughts darker than the coming night coursed through her mind, when her attention was caught by a glow.

The sun was setting, slipping below the horizon, yet this light grew stronger and stronger. The walking wounded all came to a halt as they gazed, their shadows cast long on the ground behind them. Suddenly, the light flared so brightly that everyone had to look away, shielding their eyes. Then, just as quickly, along with the sun, it was gone, leaving everyone bewildered. Now, only the guttering torches on the nearby city walls provided the light to guide them to safety.

As the wounded eventually shuffled through the open city gates, they talked in hushed wonder of what they'd witnessed, distracted for a while from their pain.

The End of Dreams

They were greeted by thousands of countryfolk who waited hopefully to see if husbands or sons had survived, and many were the cries of despair mixed in with those of relief. Yet irrespective, none turned away to lose themselves in their own happiness or loss, rather they comforted the grieving who had lost friends or family and helped those poor souls who'd fought and suffered terribly whether they knew them or not.

The new hospital grounds, rooms, and beds were soon full to overflowing, so the wounded went to the barracks at the west gate as well. Soon even that was full, and the wounded kept coming.

Shinsen, who'd recovered enough to walk despite one side of his face being completely still, turned to some of his less injured knights.

'Requisition the mansions on either side of the hospital until everyone who is injured is housed. If the owners refuse, then throw them from their homes, and tell them to come find me and my sword!'

As they left, he continued his search for Shinmata, asking everyone who'd listened if they'd seen his wife, as he'd been unable to find her on the battlefield.

The healers worked throughout the night, often just taking away the pain from the wounded, for there was frequently nothing else they could do. Thousands of countryfolk volunteered to help, and not a single survivor was alone, whether it was to pass into the next world, or to see the next day.

Most of the injured were so exhausted they fell asleep as soon as they lay their heads down, be it on a bed or on the stone floor, making it easier for their wounds to be treated.

Dafne was one such, forgoing a bed so that others more seriously hurt could find some small comfort.

When she awoke the next day, she was warm, and her head rested on something soft. She opened her eyes to see herself looking up at Rakan on whose thigh her head rested.

'Am I dead in the hall of the All-Mother?' she asked, as he looked down on her.

Rakan smiled, but the sadness in his eyes took away from the gesture.

'No. I fear we're still alive at the gates to the nine hells.'

Dafne nodded, tears coming to her eyes as reality came flooding back in painful waves. She sat, pushing away the blanket that lay across her body.

'My people believe that unless we're laid to rest in the soil from which all life grows within a day of perishing, then our spirits will wander, struggling to find the embrace of our ancestors. I must rouse my people, at least those who can still walk, for we must find and bury our dead, or at least as many as we can.'

The sky to the east was brightening as she spoke, and already many were awake. Moans of suffering hung on the air, softened by the murmured reassurances from those who looked after them.

'Then let me help you,' Rakan offered, 'but we must find the strength to give the same honour to all who died, or this city will fall to a plague as it would have to Daleth.'

He pushed himself to his feet, pulling Dafne after him.

Rakan tried to gain assistance from the Freestates garrison soldiers who'd returned with Tristan, but they refused, telling him they took no orders from a knight of the clans. Rakan just nodded and walked away to their mocking laughter. Up until yesterday, their blood would have stained the ground, but he could stomach no more at present.

He and Dafne gathered as many volunteers as possible. Knights, Eyre, the countryfolk levy, along with wives, fathers, and mothers who were strong enough to help. They gathered whatever tools they could lay hands on, anything that could help break the soil to start burying the dead.

They moved slowly and as quietly as possible together, around three thousand of them, to the western gate. Rakan ordered it opened, and they walked hesitantly through, reluctant to see the horror until they all came to a halt, blinking in wonder.

As the sun rose and light spread across the land, many of the volunteers fell to their knees, the despair in their souls lessened. Not lifted, for that would have been impossible, but lessened, for before them lay a miracle.

Nearly one hundred and thirty thousand souls had perished on the plains and hills outside of the city. The land had been stained red, the soil churned to a bloody mire by boots, hooves, and the fingers of those who fought, clawed, and died upon it.

The End of Dreams

It had been a grisly, haunting scene a thousand times worse than the most terrible nightmare, but no longer.

As Rakan stood next to Dafne, they gazed around speechless. Rakan had witnessed Maya's gift many times, and the growth of the tower oak still stuck in his mind as the most incredible display of her power he'd ever seen, but it paled in comparison to her dying swansong.

The open plains, the hills, in fact, the land as far as the eye could see, had been transformed.

Not a single, broken body could be seen, having been drawn into the ground as if by the All-Mother herself. Trees grew everywhere where none had previously been, creating beautiful copses dotted around the landscape. Bright grasses waved in between the trunks wafted by the early morning breeze, with wildflowers of every colour catching the eye in all directions, right up to the city walls. Butterflies flew with wild abandon in their tens of thousands, and the scent of new life filled the air.

It was as if the gods themselves had come down during the night to erase the terrible stain left upon the land, renewing it afresh.

Rakan wiped tears from his eyes as he gazed southwest toward the hill upon which Taran, and then Maya had met their fate. He was strangely relieved that he hadn't seen them in death, and would now remember them together as they'd been in life, beautifully in love.

Dafne's hand closed around his in support, understanding the source of his pain, and he nodded his appreciation.

'Now that I know our fallen have been looked after, I must return to help the living,' Dafne said, softly in the hushed silence.

Rakan nodded.

'The land may be healed, but there are many who'll need our help in the days and weeks to come.'

Dafne looked up at him.

'Whilst Maya healed your body, don't think you don't need help too, for your heart is broken. Maybe in time, I can help you mend that,' she said, unusually hesitant.

Rakan sighed.

'Maybe in time. I have something I need to do before I can even think of moving forward because there's something behind me holding me back.'

'Then do what you must,' Dafne advised, 'and become whole again, for we,' then she shook her head, smiling shyly, '*I* need your strength to help me through the days to come.'

***

Tristan was drunk, happily drunk, and enjoying himself immensely. It had been five days since the battle, and the palace was now a throng of laughter and happiness, with the elite of the city revelling in their new lease of life.

He'd never felt so alive, so complete as at this moment. Not only had he survived, but he'd killed with his own hands, disposed of any number of inconvenient loose ends and was now the toast of the attendant nobility and merchants alike. His bloodied sword hung above a newly made throne, a sign of his strength, and was the object of much discussion.

It didn't matter that everyone here just pretended to like him, that was, after all, the Freestates way. Behind their hands, they talked with jealousy and resentment at the unchallengeable position he was now in. Yet despite this, they also admired him, even though it hurt to admit it.

He'd managed to retain his position as king and had the armies of other nations do the majority of the killing and dying for him. He'd stolen an unbelievable victory, and whilst there were whispers of some kind of treachery, only he knew how far and deep that went.

Even his greatest loss, the much-discussed death of Maya, had not been without its benefits. The talk of the party was the power of Maya's gift, which had healed a land broken asunder by the battle. She'd saved the city from disease and, more importantly, the expenditure of money in having the battlefield cleaned up.

Without doubt, he'd lost a valuable asset, but the two attractive daughters of a merchant who was trying to get first rights on the old lands of the Witch-King, would go a long way to helping him forget about her later tonight.

He looked around, noting Huron looking happy with himself.

The captain was proving to be valuable, adept, and loyal, and on the morrow would lead the garrison soldiers out to start restoring order to the city. Now the war was behind them, the merchants and nobles were insisting their homes be vacated by the injured and dying, who'd had the temerity to squat there after the battle.

Tristan could sympathise, and Huron would start putting things to rights. Able-bodied survivors could either work the fields that needed farmers or return to their homes in whichever lands they may be. This city was not, and never would be, a place for those of low status unless they were the servants of the elite within its walls.

In fact, he suddenly realised, the newly trained peasants needed to be dismissed from the garrison ranks. It would be prudent to remove their weapons and take them off the city payroll now they were no longer needed.

So much to do, so much to think about, yet the wealth waiting to be accumulated was breath-taking. The lands to the west were now his to claim, and they'd need to be renamed. The power of the Horselords was broken, so the Freestates no longer needed to pay a tithe. The Eyre would come begging for help before long too.

He downed another goblet of wine, smiling graciously as another merchant presented him with gifts.

Yes, the peasants and their families had to go as soon as possible, especially as they'd had the temerity to shout abusive comments when he'd toured the city these last few days.

It seemed that Maya and Taran's names were still some kind of prayer to which they clung, hoping to invoke some kind of further salvation from their problems. How foolish. Salvation was costly, and could only be bought with gold, not prayer.

The night wore on, and eventually, people began returning to their homes. Tristan yawned and found to his annoyance that the merchant's daughters had disappeared along with their father. He'd drunk too much wine anyway, and there were plenty more days, and especially nights, to enjoy now.

He graciously nodded to the few remaining guests who were making the most of the rich food he'd provided for them. He laughed to himself, for their taxes would soon be raised to pay for the very delicacies they were eating. Music was still playing, and he thought to tell the musicians to return home, but doubted a star falling from the heavens would keep him awake once his head hit the pillow, so he let them be. They'd only been paid to midnight anyhow.

He made his way unsteadily toward his room, clutching the bannister for support as he reached the top of the gilded stairs. He sang loudly, uninhibited from the wine, knowing the guest apartments were vacant. That insufferable Ostrom and Ultric were both dead, and Dafne seemed to want to slum it in the streets with her people, more fool her.

He stumbled into his room, making his way carefully to the bedside table, drank deeply from a goblet of water, and lay down on the bed fully clothed. It was gloomy, with only moonlight coming through the open windows. He made a mental note to appoint someone on the morrow to take Galain's place so that his room was prepared every night.

Sighing in contentment, he closed his eyes, only to feel a breeze on his face, and wondered who'd opened his window if he had no personal assistant.

Suddenly a hand clamped over his mouth, a hand so strong and hard that even though Tristan tried to scream, it remained trapped in his throat. It held his jaw shut with such force he felt his head pushed deep into the pillow.

He opened his eyes, and in the dim light, recognised Rakan above him.

'You should know,' Rakan hissed, looking down, his face mostly in shadow, 'that before Maya died, she told me briefly of your actions; that your men attacked her while you fled the field, and more besides.'

He paused, ensuring his words hit home.

'The one chance my son had,' he continued, 'was you adhering to the plan, distracting Daleth long enough while the knights and I broke his rearguard. In the unfolding chaos, Taran would've had a chance to kill Daleth and survive. We'll never know if that might have happened, for you took away that possibility.'

Tristan moaned, trying to say something, but Rakan continued.

'Taran's strategy worked perfectly. Perfectly except for you. Your betrayal led to him dying, even though his plan and sacrifice saved everyone's lives, including your own.'

The End of Dreams

'Not only did your action lead to my son's death and thousands of others, but Maya couldn't live without him either, and thus you're directly responsible for hers.'

Rakan looked into Tristan's terrified eyes, brimming with tears.

'You seem to regret your actions now I'm here,' he said conversationally.

'Do you know what Maya's last words to me were? She asked that I forgive you, that I let you live, so that the bloodshed would end. Can you actually believe it? I never have, nor ever will, meet someone with such a pure spirit as hers. She asked me to spare your life despite knowing hers would soon end. She wanted me to have a chance at love having lost her own. She even blessed this land as she passed.'

Rakan shook his head, slowly removing his hand from Tristan's mouth, allowing the king to breathe, and Tristan warily sat.

'We should all follow her example,' Rakan continued, not even looking at Tristan. 'To choose forgiveness over revenge, generosity over greed, love over hate.'

'Yes, yes,' Tristan sobbed, his hands together, eyes as wide as plates. 'Forgive me!'

Rakan smiled.

'Maya did, and one day, I hope I can be like Maya. I promise I will be, but not yet, not today.'

As the meaning of the words registered on Tristan's face, Rakan grabbed his hair, pulling it back, and even as Tristan started to scream plunged a dagger into the king's throat, cutting it off before it began.

Tristan clutched frantically at the horrible wound, blood spurting from between his fingers.

Rakan stood from the bed, contempt on his face as he gazed dispassionately while Tristan's legs kicked feebly.

'You'll be the last king of greed, and no one will remember your name. As for Maya and Taran, they'll be remembered forever.

Rakan wiped the blood from his blade disdainfully across the sheets, then walked calmly to the open window and climbed onto the ledge.

Maybe now, he thought, as he clambered down the trellis. Maybe now my heart can start to mend.

***

The days that followed were difficult ones for the wealthy merchants and nobles of Freeguard. First, they found their king had been assassinated, and then shortly after, whilst a successor was being debated, the peasantry staged city-wide protests.

Food and medicine prices had been raised to drive the poor from the city, and injured soldiers were roughly evicted from occupied mansions by the regular Freestates garrison troops. This led to even more vociferous gatherings.

Then, one day, the Freeguard captain, Huron, ordered his men to use force to remove protestors from around the palace, and twelve innocent people died.

A shocked, fragile peace briefly returned to the city.

Then, one week later, the remains of the peasant army rose up, armed and armoured. Supported by the remaining knights, Eyre archers, and desert spearmen, they marched upon the palace.

The fight was short, bloody, and brutal, and after centuries of being under the rule of a king of greed, Freeguard finally became free of tyranny.

The tables were turned completely, and the deposed merchants, nobles, and defeated garrison soldiers were offered the chance to work the fields or starve, and finally, peace descended three weeks after the war actually finished.

A farmer's son, who'd fought bravely in the final battle, was elected by popular vote to be the new caretaker king, with his young wife as queen. They accepted on the condition that it would only be until such time as Taran and Maya returned from the arms of the All-Mother, as everyone knew they owed their lives to the two star-crossed lovers.

Thousands demanded a statue or shrine be built on the southern hill to remember them by. Eventually, it was decided that the hill would remain untouched until the end of days, for nothing was more beautiful a reminder of the Lady Maya, than the wonder she'd created.

Over the next year, as the injured fully recovered, most of the remaining men from the desert decided to stay, having found the same peace amongst the long grasses as they once had amongst the sand dunes of their birth. By contrast, all of the Eyre returned home as they recovered.

The End of Dreams

Dafne proved the exception, as she stayed to help oversee the running of the city. It was rumoured that she and Rakan had been the key instigators behind the uprising. Therefore, it was unsurprising that when she left, it was to accompany Rakan south with Shinsen, Shinmata, and three hundred knights to the grasslands, the home of the Horselords.

Within Freeguard, sorrow was slowly replaced with wary happiness, broken hearts were mended, and new life sprang forth to replace that which had been taken so abruptly.

Yet those who lived through these times would never forget the darkness that had almost overwhelmed them, and ensured their children wouldn't either.

Tales of Maya, Taran and everyone else who'd died to save the land, were told over meals, drinks, or at bedtime, so their story would eventually grow to become a legend.

***

Chapter XXV-Epilogue

'I'm sorry, Mother,' the girl cried, 'I didn't mean to. I really didn't.'

'Your father will go hungry because of you!' The woman laughed, sweeping the girl into her arms, holding her close. 'Best we don't tell him.'

The flap to the large tent opened, and a tall man walked in.

'What was that? Why will I go hungry?' he demanded in mock anger. 'Oh no, please don't tell me ...' Then he laughed aloud as a rabbit hopped around the tent, seeking a way out, before bolting past his feet to freedom.

'That gift of yours will be the death of us, one day.' He smiled, opening his arms, taking the girl from her mother. 'You cannot bring everything back to life, my little one, especially when your mother caught it for our dinner. More importantly, we've yet to understand the price you'll pay for using it.'

The girl kissed him on the cheek, smiling cheekily.

'Now, go pick some vegetables from the garden,' he laughed, putting her down and guiding her gently to the tent flap. 'Then go fetch some water from the stream. I have something to say to your mother.'

He watched her fondly as she skipped away.

'Oh, and what does my husband have to say to me in private?'

'It's just that I love you, and always will, in this world and the next.' The man closed his eyes, resting his forehead against hers.

'Let's enjoy this world for a lot longer first,' she said, pulling him closer still, her mouth going to his ear. 'I have something to say to you too,' she breathed, gently biting his lobe. 'We're going to have a boy, and he'll be gifted too, I can tell already.'

The End of Dreams

Taran's eyes opened wide in happiness, and he picked up Maya, swinging her around, planting kiss after kiss on her willing lips as her arms encircled his neck.

The tent flap opened, and Rakan walked in with Dafne and Shinsen close behind.

'When will you two ever stop?' Shinsen laughed, turning away. 'Come on, Rakan, Dafne, let's leave them be. It seems they're in the mood for love. We can come back later.'

Maya turned to Taran as they left, pushing him gently down onto the bed, her black hair falling across his face as she leaned forward.

'We have more than just love you and I,' she whispered. 'We have something much more.'

'And what is it that we have?' Taran teased, his hands brushing back her hair, tracing his fingers over her glowing, youthful features.

Maya's dark eyes bored into his.

'What we have is brighter than the sun, sought after more than immortality, rarer than a falling star, and worth both living and dying for.'

'What we have is true love.'

THE END OF BOOK THREE

If you enjoyed this book, be sure to read the sequel;

The Circle of Fate

Dear fellow fantasy lover.

PLEASE TAKE A MOMENT TO RATE THIS BOOK
on Amazon. It would mean SO much to me.

On another note.
If you have any comments or questions regarding any of my works,
please don't hesitate to contact me through my website.

Thank you
Marcus Lee

BOOKS BY MARCUS LEE

THE CHOSEN

Prepare for an original and bold epic fantasy that spans worlds and is filled with magic, creatures of legend, immense battles, unforgettable quests, and an incredible prophecy that might just save the human race.

Within the depths of the Mountain of Souls, orphans are raised to be remorseless assassins. Abandoned by a society ravaged by endless war and greed, hundreds die during selection so that a determined few, honed by training and enchantment, can ascend to join The Chosen.

Malina is one of those orphans.

Cursed with yellow eyes and deathly pale skin, she is neither popular nor strong and is certain to die on her first day, broken and forgotten like so many before her.

Fate, however, has other, far more reaching plans for Malina than a quick death. The return of The Once and Future King is imminent, The Chosen are pivotal to his ascension, and no two destinies have ever been more intricately entwined.

Yet what happens if the path laid out before her is not the one she decides to take?

Book 1 - THE MOUNTAIN OF SOULS

Book 2 - THE LAST HOPE

Book 3 - THE RIVER OF TEARS

***

BOOKS BY MARCUS LEE

THE BLOOD OF KINGS & QUEENS

'Old legends die hard.'

Prepare yourself for action, magic, love, betrayal, wolves ... and goats!

Garet ... once a rebel general, a blight reaver, a warrior, a hunter, and a love-struck man.

Now, eight years after the rebellion was won, he has lost ... everything.

A bitter recluse, he counts out his remaining days in the mountains, far from the rule of the latest despotic king to sit on the throne and the blight that afflicts the realm.

Yet destiny hasn't finished with Garet, and nor, it seems, is an old prophecy that hangs over his head, forgotten.

Someone from his past, someone he'd rather was dead, comes seeking his help, and for better or worse, his life will never be the same again.

Love can be to live or die for, but revenge, that's always to kill for!

***

BOOKS BY MARCUS LEE

POEMS INSPIRED BY TRUE LOVE

'The perfect gift for yourself or the one you love.'

Poems Inspired by True Love welcomes the reader into true love's warm embrace, taking them through a soul-gripping journey of laughter, lust, and undeniably romantic moments.

Through emotive storytelling and sultry lines, poet Marcus Lee lovingly awakens one's psyche to the innermost amorous stirrings of the heart. In equal measure, these poetic outpourings serve as a vital reminder that one is not alone in their ocean of feelings.

Above all, this poignant collection of over 100 poems invites you to "behold a radiance that burns and sustains you", a radiance that goes by the name of True Love.

***

Printed in Great Britain
by Amazon